SILENT
LIES

SILENT LIES

LIES

A NOVEL

M.L. MALCOLM

LONGSTREET PRESS
Athens, Georgia

LONGSTREET
PRESS

Published by
LONGSTREET PRESS, INC.
325 Milledge Avenue
Athens, Georgia 30601
www.longstreetpress.net

Copyright © 2005 by M. L. Malcolm

1st printing, 2005
ISBN: 1-56352-750-2

Printed in the United States of America

Jacket and book design by Burtch Hunter Design LLC

For John, my counselor in perplexity and the love of my life

ACKNOWLEDGMENTS

Seeing *Silent Lies* in print is a dream come true, and there are many people who helped turn my dream into reality:

Scott Bard and all the folks at Longstreet Press: Bryn, Claire, Chris and Burtch, who transformed my manuscript from a lonely computer file into a beautiful book;

Andrea Pass at Maximum Exposure P.R., who held my hand and made me take deep breaths while she worked her magic;

Erika, Vida, Sarah, Wendy, Karen, and especially Laura, each of whom read my work-in-progress and told me what I needed to hear;

Diane, Carol, Ted and Mary, for not pulling any punches during the year it took to whip the final version into shape;

Susan B. (you can be my personal shopper any time);

The members of the S.O.F.A. Babes book club, for their support, inspiration, and for always laughing at my jokes;

My wonderful in-laws, Daniel and Marian Malcolm, who graciously shared the stories that became the genesis for *Silent Lies*, and to whom I will eternally and joyfully owe a enormous, unpayable debt of gratitude;

My fabulous children, Andy and Amanda, for putting up with an often-distracted mother, and growing up into wonderful young people nonetheless;

My sister, Tara, for always being there when I needed her;

My mother, Lea Wolfe, who always told me that I could accomplish anything I wanted to;

And most of all, my husband John, who made me believe it.

Heartfelt thanks to all of you.

SILENT LIES

The rain was falling even harder now. No chance he'd be able to flag down a cab. Not that he really needed one. He didn't have anywhere to go.

He pulled his hat down low onto his forehead and started walking in the direction from which he'd come. Damn that woman. What was it she'd thrown at him? "You can't outrun your pain, Mr. Leo Hoffman. So just stop running."

Just stop running. But he hadn't been running. To run, you needed a heart and lungs. Hot blood and willpower. No reason to run if you've nothing to fear. And you don't fear what you can't feel.

Then as if to prove her point the pain hit him, slamming into his chest like a frozen fist. He reached for a lamppost to try and steady himself as he fought for air, and struggled against the vivid images relentlessly flooding his brain.

He saw again his daughter's eyes, so like Martha's, staring at him with an unforgivable mixture of hope and fear. So different from the little girl who'd sat at her piano, full of sunshine and music, swinging her feet as she played because her legs were still too short to reach the pedals. He heard his wife's laughter, and felt her warm breath on his neck as she moved underneath him, warm and welcoming.

There were too many memories. Too many plans gone so horribly wrong.

When at last his tears came they carried no sound, only the soul-shattering silence of his remorse, muffled by the rhythm of the rain.

CHAPTER 1

THE PRODIGY

ⱺᴖᴧᴖⱺ

HUNGARY, 1910

Leo studied the oncoming rider. From his perch in the ancient oak tree at the edge of the river he could see that the man's face looked strained. Sweat covered the flanks of his horse. *Perhaps he would stop*, thought Leo. Here the banks of the River Tisza were low and broad. It was a good place to let a tired horse drink, and both the horse and its rider looked like they could use a rest. Leo wanted a chance to watch them for a moment longer.

When they reached the point on the road nearest the tree, they halted. Leo could see the man eyeing the generous shade of the old oak. He then stared down the road, as if trying to estimate how much farther the day's travel would take him.

Smelling the water, the horse whinnied, and stamped an impatient hoof. The man patted the horse's neck and said something soothing. He spoke in a language that Leo did not understand. It was a vaguely familiar language, but not the one spoken in Leo's village. It was not the language of the people who called themselves the Magyar.

To Leo's delight, the man dismounted. Grasping the reins, he led his horse down to the water. They were just below the tree now. Leo thought the horse was the most beautiful animal he had ever seen. The Baron had some fine horses, and occasionally a soldier or a visiting nobleman would come into his father's smithy on a handsome mount. But this horse was a breathtaking blood bay gelding, with a black mane, wide chest and graceful legs. Perhaps he came from Mazohegyes. Leo's father told him that the best runners were bred there.

And the rider matched the magnificence of his horse. Despite the layer of dust covering his clothes, Leo could see that the buttons on the man's vest were made of silver. His riding coat fell from shoulder to hip with the supple ease of fine wool. His leather gloves covered his hands like a second skin. All this, Leo knew, meant that he was a man of wealth. Yet he did not display the ornamentation of a nobleman. He wore no fur, no elaborate embroidery, not even a family crest upon his saddle pad. Nor did he wear a soldier's uniform. *How odd. He's clean-shaven, and looks no older than twenty or so. He's rich, but he's not a nobleman, and not a soldier. Where could such a man have come from?*

Now the man was speaking to his horse again, in that other language. Leo concentrated on the sounds. He'd heard that language before, spoken by soldiers, and once by a group of noblemen on their way to see the Baron. The Austrian nobles. That was it! German. The man was speaking German.

A cool breeze swayed the branches of the old oak. The rustling leaves caused the man to lift his eyes. Leo froze, wanting to remain undiscovered. The man glanced up. Then, seeing nothing, he turned back to his horse.

Leo exhaled silently and steadied his grip on the huge limb that held him up a good thirty feet in the air. He enjoyed this vantage point, that of seeing without being seen, and he did not want to be caught.

The man was now sifting through one of his saddlebags. The horse was heavily loaded. Could this man be a peddler? No. Peddlers drove carts pulled by old workhorses. Or they had no horse at all, and carried their wares in baskets, or in bags slung across bent backs. No, this man must be taking a long journey. But where? Across the farmlands? As far as the mountains? Or even further?

Leo looked away from the river. The late September sun lit the nearby fields of ripened barley with a golden aura. Beyond the fields, a line of fir trees marked the beginning of the forest where the Baron hunted. The mass of green extended all the way to the horizon. On the clearest of days, a gray halo capped the far edge of the forest, a sight that could easily be mistaken for the shadow of distant clouds. But Leo knew that those shadows were cast by the foothills of the Carpathian Mountains.

Leo knew that everything he could see from his tree belonged to the Baron. He also knew that everyone in the village paid the Baron rent; paying one's rent was a major topic of conversation among the men of the village, especially now, near harvest time. He knew all this because he was very good at listening. He paid attention not only to the words a man used, but also to the motion of his hands. The posture of his body. The way he held his eyes. He listened to everything the men had to say as they passed through the village, stopping to rest their mounts and refill their bellies, before traveling on to places with names like Szeged, or Miskolc, or the capital, Budapest.

Most of what Leo heard he remembered. He learned from listening to the conversations of the visitors to his father's stable that an emperor, Franz Joseph, ruled the countries of Austria and Hungary, and that even the Baron had to obey the Emperor. He learned that many farm people were moving from the countryside into the cities to find work. He'd even heard that in Budapest there existed something called electricity, a substance that could produce a light without a fire, though he found this rather hard to believe.

Leo also remembered names, faces, and odd words. Words that were new to his ears stuck in his brain like sharp thorns, that he picked at and picked at until he could make sense of them. And he never forgot the name of a horse that visited his father's stable. Never. He remembered the ones who'd come in lame, and the ones who carried the jaundiced eye of a creature mistreated by its master. He remembered the ones who came in prancing, showing off the elaborate finery of a nobleman, and the sway-backed, sturdy-legged workhorses of well-to-do peasants.

"Lee—ooo."

The familiar voice interrupted Leo's musing. The stranger turned in the direction of the sound, a look of mild curiosity on his face.

Leo winced. He was trapped. If he did not answer, Klari would come straight to the tree. She knew where to look for him.

"Here!" he answered, and began to climb down. The game was

spoiled now. Either this man punished him for spying, or his mother punished him for being late. And Klari would be frightened. And probably punished for not finding him sooner. Leo did not wish to bring his mother's temper down upon his sister's head.

Underneath him, the horse started, and the man jumped. It took him just a fraction of a second to locate Leo making his way down the tree.

"What have we here?" he asked in perfect Hungarian, a look of amusement on his face. "I didn't know that squirrels grew so large in this part of the country!"

Leo laughed, relieved that the traveler did not seem annoyed. When he reached the ground he clicked his heels together and bowed quickly, just as he had once seen a junior officer do when greeting his captain. Leo's father never forgot that the captain did not pay him for the shoes he'd put on the man's horse. Leo never forgot the elegance of the lieutenant's manners.

The man seemed impressed by Leo's elaborate bow.

"And such well-mannered rodents! Still, you should have let me know that you were up there. It's not polite to spy."

Leo blushed and looked down at his feet. His boots suddenly looked unusually shabby.

"You are what, ten? Eleven?"

"Ten," Leo confirmed in a muffled tone.

"A ten-year-old boy should know better than to spy on people. Spying is a dangerous business. Suppose I had been a Cossack deserting my regiment, or a royal messenger, on a secret mission from the Emperor. I might have shot you."

Leo swallowed hard. Getting his ears boxed was one thing. Getting shot was something he had not considered.

The lecture was interrupted by the arrival of his sister. Leo could see the hesitancy in her eyes as she approached.

"Good day sir," she said, attempting a clumsy curtsy.

"Good day, miss," the man answered politely, treating her with more dignity than her ragged dress deserved. "I take it you have come to collect this young man?"

Klari's chin wiggled up and down slightly.

"Do you live nearby?"

The chin wiggled again. Leo loved Klari dearly, but often found her shyness frustrating. He jumped into the conversation.

"My name is Leo Hoffman. This is my sister, Klari. She's fifteen. We live in the village just beyond the bend in the river. Our father, Laszlo Hoffman, is the blacksmith there, and we have a stable as well. Perhaps...perhaps you would like to come and rest your horse?"

Klari's shocked expression conveyed her opinion of Leo's boldness. But the stranger did not seem insulted; he seemed pleased.

"Why thank you, Leo Hoffman. In fact, your village is my destination. I'm glad to know that I'm almost there. I would offer you a ride, but as you can see, my horse is carrying quite a load already. My name is József Derkovits, and, if the Baron will give his permission, I will be your schoolteacher."

Leo furrowed his brow. Schoolteacher? What could he mean, exactly? The only school he knew about was the Yeshiva, somewhere in the North, where a boy could study the Torah and learn to become a rabbi. It was obvious that this man was no rabbi. Why would he be teaching in a school?

His perplexed look caused the stranger to chuckle with amusement. "Don't worry, Leo Hoffman. You will get an explanation soon enough. Now go with your sister—Klari, is it? We will meet again, I am sure. And no more spying," he added, with a shake of his forefinger.

Klari grabbed Leo's hand and ran, leaving him no time to say anything more.

Once the river was behind them, Leo pulled her roughly to a stop. "What are you doing, running away like that?" he burst out angrily. "He meant us no harm. I wanted to talk to him. I wanted to show him the stable. I wanted—"

Klari rolled her eyes. "Oh, Leo, you want to talk to *everyone*." She might be shy around others, but she always spoke her mind when she was alone with Leo.

"Please, can't you see how rich he is? What if you were to upset him? Besides, Mama is waiting for you to go home and build the fires, and she'll be angry if you're late again."

"She's always angry," Leo muttered.

Klari sighed. It was true. Their mother was always angry. Especially at Leo. "Well, at least you're not in trouble at the moment. I'm the one who gets the brunt of it lately, for refusing to marry the Goat." She put her fingers to either side of her head, pretending to have horns, and made a face.

Her antics did not have the desired effect on her brother. "They'll make you, you know. Eventually you'll be married to him, like it or not."

"They'll have to tell him no soon, Leo. He's too old to wait. Why, he must be close to fifty. They could beat me again, but that won't change anything, and the Goat won't be happy with a black-and-blue bride. Plus I swore I'd make him miserable if they forced me to marry him. I'll put too much pepper in his food, and too much lye in his clothes! I know he *said* he'd wait, but they'll give up. Or throw me out." Klari finished her sentence with a shrug, giving the impression that either possibility suited her just as well.

Leo had to smile. Klari might be shy, but she was stubborn as a mule when she put her mind to something. And she wasn't afraid of a beating. She'd taken enough of them for his sake. When he tried to argue with her about it, she'd just scold him, telling him it did no good for both of them to be punished. Leo didn't know what he would do without Klari. She was the only real friend he had.

But in a way Leo felt sorry for old Mr. Schwartz. The Goat wasn't mean, just old. Old and lonely. His wife had been dead for years. Everyone in the village assumed that the childless old widower would be content to live out his days alone. Then Klari's heart-shaped face caught his eye. Klari Hoffman, with her freckled complexion and her quiet ways, inspired Ky Schwartz to want to marry again.

Greta and Laszlo Hoffman were thrilled when he first approached Laszlo about marrying Klari, just a month ago. A successful man! A wool trader! They never dreamed that their only daughter could make such a fine match.

Klari was horrified. The proposal triggered a battle in the Hoffman household every day, but the prospective bride would not yield. Thinking of all this, Leo regretted his outburst. Klari didn't really do anything wrong by dragging him away. If the stranger had told the truth, he'd soon see the mysterious man again. A school. A wave of excitement surged through him. "Race you," he cried out impulsively to his sister, and scampered off in the direction of the village.

Klari paused before darting after him. She looked back in the direction of the handsome stranger they'd just met. *He remembered my name*, she thought, blushing again, and then took off after Leo, her own limbs energized by an unfamiliar sense of exhilaration.

⊙⊦⊙

An hour later the rider and his splendid horse arrived in the center of the village. József Derkovits looked around carefully, soaking in the details of the place that was to be his home for the next two years. A dirt path served as a street. Narrow, rectangular houses, constructed by calloused hands out of rough clay bricks, sat side-by-side in careful rows. The walls were tinted white with a chalky, opaque wash, each building topped by a heavy thatch roof. The pungent aroma of paprika, the one spice essential to Hungarian cooking, wafted heavily from the drying pods that hung from the eaves of every home.

Incredible, he thought, as he surveyed the place, feeling the heat of the occupant's furtive stares. *This is 1910. Budapest is leaping into the twentieth century, and the rest of the country is no better off than it was three hundred years ago.*

He shuddered when he thought of the accommodations the local *fogado*, or public guesthouse, would offer. Ah, well. He was here to make a difference, he reminded himself, not to enjoy a vacation. He would give some of the young peasant boys an education. A chance at redemption. Of course that would necessitate some hardship on his part. Now, if he could just get the Baron to cooperate.

Early the next morning József Derkovits found himself perched on a stiff chair in the Baron's ornate front parlor, waiting for the old aristocrat to make his appearance. He knew that the Baron would let him sit for some time. The letter he'd brought with him from the Emperor required that the Baron receive him, but it could not force the arrogant old bear to be polite.

At length the Baron entered the room. He was dressed in fur-trimmed hunting garb, for he was hosting a grouse-shooting expedition that morning. The delay caused by József Derkovits' sudden arrival put the Baron in an even fouler mood than usual.

"Seat yourself," he growled, as József stood upon the man's entry into the room. József complied.

"So, you want to start a school, is that it?"

József politely ignored the Baron's snide tone. "Not I, personally, sir. The Parliament, and the Emperor. The government has passed the Homestead Schools Act, in order to educate the illiterate peasantry, to bring Hungary forward, and help us regain international prominence in the twentieth century."

"Spare me your speeches. I read all the pretty descriptions in the Emperor's letter. Tell me, how is it that *you* have been chosen for this great honor?"

"I felt it was my duty, your Grace. I volunteered, as did many other students from the University in Budapest—"

The Baron cut him off with a snort. "Mr. Derkovits, my ancestors were among the first warriors to lay their weapons and their honor at the feet of Saint Stephen when he founded the Magyar kingdom, over a thousand years ago. My family has fought for king and country for generations. We have withstood invasion by the Mongols, the Turks, the Russians, and the Romanians. But this…I worry that this latest invasion will be the end of us."

"Invasion, sir?"

"Don't be coy with me. You and your 'chosen' people. Invading every nook and cranny of the Empire. Jews in banking. Jews in industry. Jews in commerce. Jews in *Parliament*, for God's sake. Comes from letting them into the trades a hundred years ago—now they're even marrying Magyars and buying themselves titles! And young Jews like yourself, living off your father's wealth, bloated by this fashionable, philanthropic fervor. Wanting to teach everyone Hungarian, so they can all be citizens. As if speaking the right language could alter one's blood! You won't find a true Magyar selling textiles to the French. The Emperor's

army and the civil service are the only two decent careers for a gentleman. And none of this traipsing all over the countryside to teach a
bunch of rock-headed peasants how to read."

József waited patiently until the Baron had run out of wind. His sur-
name pronounced him a Jew. Although, as a nation, Hungary had been
kinder to its Jewish population than many of its neighbors, he harbored
no illusions about the degree of acceptance that wealthy Jewish bourgeois families, such as his own, would ever achieve among the old
Magyar families. Unlike the areas closer to Hungary's border with
Poland, most of the villages targeted to benefit from the Homestead
Schools project boasted no more than a handful of Jewish families, who
were employed in the various trades necessary to run the vast landed
estates still controlled by the Magyar aristocracy. He'd volunteered to
become a teacher to help his nation, not his religion. Old bigots like the
Baron would die out, eventually. Their opinions no longer mattered. He
kept his response gracious.

"I understand that your Grace does not wish to be inconvenienced.
The local diocese has given permission to hold classes three times a week
in one of the church's meeting rooms. Only boys ages six through twelve
will be allowed to attend, so as to minimize disruption of your operations.
All we need is your permission to announce the program to the villagers."

"The Emperor's letter doesn't give me a great deal of choice in that
regard, does it? Very well, Derkovits. Go start your school. Teach a few
peasants to read. But don't let it interfere with the work on my estate."

"Thank you, your Grace," József responded, aiming his acknowledgment at the Baron's retreating back. Step one was accomplished.
Now came the real work.

∽✿∾

The next morning József posted a notice in the village center announc-
ing the opening of the school. He'd written it in both Hungarian and
Hebrew, as the innkeeper had confirmed that a dozen or so Jewish families lived in the village. He doubted that any of the peasants could read
Hungarian. It was likely, however, that someone among the Jewish pop-

ulation could make out enough Hebrew to translate for anyone interested. He wanted to make clear that the school was available for all boys younger than thirteen, no matter what their background. The Hungarian nation was a huge melting pot of different cultures, all brought by conquest, commerce, or compromise into the Austrian-Hungarian Empire. Education was the only way, József believed, to bring opportunity to his country's many diverse peoples.

The notice soon attracted at least two dozen curious villagers. From a small distance József watched them gather, as he pretended to busy himself with his knapsack. After a few minutes a young boy, no older than seven or eight, shot away from the group, obviously obeying a command. The remaining people broke up into small groups, talking quietly and glancing suspiciously over at József from time to time.

In a few moments the child reappeared, followed by an elderly priest. The man's heavy beard was gray and unkempt. From the look of his garments, the flock he tended was neither wealthy nor generous. *The Baron does not seem any more generous to his church than to his tenants,* thought József, as he watched the old man study the newly posted announcement. Even from this distance, he could see the priest's lips moving as he read.

As he expected, the priest soon made his way over to him, followed by a few of the brave and curious.

"You're the man who put up the announcement about a school?" asked the priest, making it more of a statement than a question.

"Yes, Father. I believe your bishop gave permission for classes to be held at the church."

"But it's a school for the Jews?" The priest's tone conveyed a mixture of incredulity and accusation.

"It's a school for everyone, Father. That's why I wrote the sign in Hungarian and Hebrew."

"You will teach religion?"

József shook his head. "No. I will teach reading and writing in Hungarian, mathematics, and science."

The priest opened his mouth to say something, and then shut it again. He turned to face the cluster of people waiting behind him, and raised his hands, as if offering a benediction. "The Emperor has decreed it. The Bishop has approved it. There is to be a school. For all boys in the village under the age of thirteen."

He turned his attention back to József. The expectant chorus of faces behind him did the same.

József cleared his throat and tried to think of an appropriate response. "I am honored to be here as a teacher," he uttered at last. "I hope that you will all allow your children to get an education. It is the key to their future. To the future of our nation."

He was greeted by reactions ranging from amazement to skepticism. József could only hope the simple people he'd come to serve understood the true importance of what he'd said.

෴

József Derkovits' school opened the following week. Fifteen boys attended the first class. One of them was Leo Hoffman.

From the very first day, Leo lived to be at school. He accomplished his many chores with incredible dispatch, eager to free up his time to examine, over and over again, the mysterious pages that Mr. Derkovits handed out to his pupils. Soon, the lines and circles that initially had no meaning started to make sense as words. Words exploded in his mind, and began to paint pictures. Then the pictures began to tell stories: stories of people, and places, and scientific facts, all of which forced Leo to stretch the limits of his formerly unchallenged mind. And the more he learned, the more he felt that he was becoming a part of that other world—the world beyond the village.

Leo had never liked working in his father's smithy. He hated the noise, the heat, and the acrid smells. He preferred to work in the stable with the horses, where he could practice using any new words he'd heard on his quiet but cordial four-legged charges. But now he began to resent the work that always left his hands dirty, causing his fingers to leave smudges on the pages he prized so highly. He made a habit of carefully washing his hands before working on his studies, cleaning every last bit of tack oil, soot and dirt out from under his fingernails before he dared to touch the precious pages.

And Leo always paid attention. He listened. He noticed things.

He noticed that Mr. Derkovits' fingernails were never dirty. He never smelled of sweat or horse manure, and his shoes always gleamed with polish. Mr. Derkovits' physical movements were smooth and authoritative, like a thoroughbred's. His curly brown hair was always neatly brushed into obedience. His voice was deep, and he measured his words more carefully than Leo's mother measured spices into her *goulash*. When Mr. Derkovits stirred his coffee, he made sure the spoon never touched the side of the cup. And he always spoke gently to his horse.

❦

Ten months after the arrival of the schoolmaster, the son of the innkeeper arrived at the smithy to give Leo's father a message. The plump and pimply teenager found the blacksmith hard at work at his anvil, his heavy shoulders covered in sweat.

"Laszlo Hoffman, Mr. József Derkovits would like to see you today at five o'clock," the boy announced, his chubby chest puffed up with self-importance. "He requests that you meet him at the inn."

The smith picked up his massive bellows and reanimated the fire's hot coals with gigantic puffs of air as he talked. "Of course. I imagine he wants to see me about new shoes for his horse. An animal like that should be reshod before the shoe is well worn, not after he has worked hard enough to put his mark on it. Tell him I will be there."

Later that day, Laszlo left his two older sons in charge of the smithy and went home. When he reached his house, one of the larger ones located near the center of the village, he flung the door open and called to his wife.

"Greta! Do we have some hot water? I'll need to clean up today. I have an important meeting."

As the house consisted of just two rooms, he was not surprised to see his wife and daughter standing in what served as the kitchen, dining room and parlor. To the rear was the bedroom for the entire family, although the two oldest boys, Tibor and Franz, often slept in the stable to give everyone more room, and to keep on eye on the horses boarding there.

"The teacher, Mr. Derkovits, wants to see me. I must have a bath," Laszlo continued.

His statement was punctuated by a loud clang. He looked over at Klari, who'd just dropped the large cooking pot she'd been carrying onto the hard-packed dirt floor. She knelt to the ground immediately, her face scarlet, and started to lift the heavy iron caldron up.

Greta Hoffman wasted no time in telling her daughter what she thought of such clumsiness. "You stupid girl! Who would want you for a wife?" she carped, turning around to cuff Klari soundly on the back of the head as she tried to stand. "It's lucky for you that was still empty!"

Laszlo had already started peeling off his clothes. "Greta, I need my white shirt, my vest—the embroidered one, not the wool. And the new red wool trousers."

"I'm saving those for Tibor's wedding," responded his wife, now petulant.

"And as we have no bride on the horizon as yet, I will wear them today," Laszlo responded, a touch of annoyance creeping into his voice. "This young man has been received by the Baron. I must show some respect. I'm to meet him at the inn."

"And what for?" Greta's dark brown eyes narrowed as her calculating brain attempted to consider all the reasons for such a meeting.

"I'm a blacksmith. He owns a horse. I imagine that's reason enough," Laszlo responded. "Klari, bring me some hot water."

"Yes, Papa." Klari hastened over the fireplace where another iron pot sat, warm among the ashes. She took a metal pitcher off a hook above the hearth and dipped it into the hot water that filled the large vessel.

"You must charge him more," Greta chided Laszlo's retreating figure. "A man who dresses like that can afford to pay more."

"Since when do I base my price on the size of my customer's wallet?"

"He doesn't pray. Not even on the Sabbath," she shouted into the next room.

"When a man prays and doesn't pray is a business for him and God to settle, not a reason to charge him more for shoeing his horse," Laszlo shouted back. "I'll see how difficult a job it is. But he has a fine mount, no mistake about that. Now FIND THOSE TROUSERS!"

⊙✛⊙

At precisely five o'clock Laszlo entered the inn's public dining room and saw the schoolmaster sitting at a table in the far corner, drinking a cup of Turkish coffee. He suddenly realized that he had no idea what the etiquette of the moment required, and wished that the schoolmaster had come to his stable instead of sending for him this way. In the stable, Laszlo would have been much more comfortable; the Hungarian love of horses was a national passion, one that reached deep into men's souls and sliced through the strict lines of social distinction that would otherwise forbid any kind of interaction.

Fearful of giving offense, Laszlo stood near the door and silently waited for the younger man to notice him. To his relief Derkovits looked up, and, seeing the smith hovering in the doorway, gestured for Laszlo to come in and take a seat across the table.

As Laszlo sat down, the schoolteacher reached into his vest pocket and pulled out two cigarettes. He offered one to Laszlo, who declined with a puzzled shake of his head. Although he enjoyed tobacco, Laszlo did not understand why men from the city preferred thin stubs of paper to the peaceful smoking of a long pipe. A pipe was a luxury, to be enjoyed after dinner among friends. Not at all like a cigarette, which city folks seemed to indulge in with the casualness of scratching an itch.

József studied the man sitting across from him for a moment, unaware that his scrutiny was causing Laszlo to feel even more ill at ease. It struck him that Leo did not look at all like anyone else in his family. Laszlo was a great bear of a man. He had the broad features of a peasant; everything about him was brown—olive brown skin, brown hair, brown eyes, brown beard. The two older Hoffman boys were also brown-haired and sturdily built. Both Klari and her mother were petit and dark—even darker than the men in their family.

Leo, on the other hand, was strong but slim, with lighter skin, black hair and blue eyes. Rather startling, deep blue eyes. Indigo eyes. József would never forget the first time he had seen those eyes light up at having understood a point of grammar. In his ten months of teaching, he'd received few such satisfactions.

A cloud of smoke surrounded József's even features as he began to speak.

"Leo is a very intelligent boy," he said to Laszlo, as if he were complimenting a fine horse. "He has a sharp mind and he applies himself well. Struggles a bit with mathematics, but enjoys reading. In fact, his verbal skills are tremendous. It's a pleasure to deal with at least one student who seems to have a genuine interest in learning."

Confused, Laszlo nodded. Wasn't the man going to talk about his horse? He decided to be bold and broach the subject himself.

"You are happy with the treatment your horse is getting at my poor stable?"

A slight frown rippled across Derkovits' brow as he paused to consider this nonsequitur. "My horse? I've seen nothing wrong with my horse. He seems to be superbly well treated. Have you noticed something wrong?"

"Well, you could be thinking about getting the animal some new shoes."

"New shoes? If I wanted new shoes on my horse, I would drop in at the livery to tell you, or send a message home with Leo. I asked you here to discuss your son's education."

"My son's education?" repeated Laszlo, now totally lost.

József gazed up at the giant beams criss-crossing the ceiling while he considered his next remark. His older brother and his friends had all warned him that teaching in the countryside would prove frustrating, but he had not come prepared for the near-feudal existence to which he'd been exposed. Not only did their days progress like they were still living in the eighteenth century, the peasants' expectations were trapped there as well.

József knew that Laszlo, like his neighbors, rented the land for his stable, his shop, and his home from the Baron. Most paid their rents out of the paltry wages paid to them by the Baron for farming his crops. They could be thrown off the land at any moment. There was no security, and surely no future, in such a life. After ten months of living among the peasants, József no longer saw the countryside as peaceful and quaint. Instead he saw the unfairness of the system that allowed a tiny group of aristocrats to control the country's landed wealth.

If he could only save one soul, give one talented boy a chance at a real life, his decision to spend two years in this backwater would be rendered worthwhile. He wanted to convince Leo's parents to send Leo to a special school in Budapest. His own pride was at stake; he must bring home to his friends and the smug, skeptical friends of his older brother the story of at least one success.

"Let me back up a bit," József said, exhaling another stream of smoke with a long, patient sigh. "Leo stayed after his classes yesterday, and we had a little conversation in German. By the way, where did your son learn to speak German?"

Laszlo's head jerked, moving on his stocky neck in the manner of a startled tortoise. "Excuse me, sir, but we speak only Hungarian in our house and have spoken no other language since my grandfather was a baby in his own mother's lap. We are Hungarians!"

József resisted the temptation to roll his eyes at Laszlo's patriotic outburst. "Yes, yes," he responded reassuringly. "No one doubts your loyalty to the Hungarian nation. I am only surprised to find a boy who speaks German so well. After all, the Hungarian language has no relationship to German whatsoever, or to any other European language, for that matter."

Laszlo eyed him as if he suspected a trap. "It's true, Leo speaks well. Too well. He could speak before he could walk, and his busy mouth often earns him a beating. But he speaks no German," he stubbornly insisted, "Leo speaks only Hungarian. And the Hebrew necessary for our prayers."

József shook his head, stubbing out his cigarette with exasperation. "I'm telling you, in addition to an endearing expertise in his native tongue, the boy speaks German. His grammar is uneven, but his accent is flawless."

Laszlo did not look convinced. "How do you know it is German and not some clever trick he is playing on you?"

József paused before answering. He'd expected the reaction of a proud father, a parent pleased and grateful to learn that his son was talented, not a response that challenged his own credibility.

"My mother was German," he answered, his voice rising with impatience. "I was raised speaking German. I also speak some Russian, and French, and a little English. And I'm *telling* you, the child speaks German as well as you speak Hungarian!"

"Perhaps he has learned it from you, then?"

"German? From me?"

"Do you not teach German in the classroom?"

"No, I do not. No." József looked slightly chagrined. "Oh, this may sound ridiculous, but, well, I only speak German to my horse."

"To your horse?"

"Yes, well, you know, one does talk to one's horse!" *Why on earth am I telling this fool all this? The German's beside the point, anyway.* He lit another cigarette, and continued in a calmer tone.

"I take it by your reaction that this news of Leo's ability is something of a revelation. Well, it's not really of any importance where he learned German. The point is Leo is an exceptionally talented student. He deserves a chance at a real education."

Laszlo considered this. "Why not Tibor, then, my eldest? Surely the oldest son should have the right to this, not the youngest."

József tried to fashion a response that would not prove insulting, for he knew Tibor was rather slow-witted. "The time for Tibor to have such an education is passed. He's eighteen. Soon he'll have a wife, and you will be a grandfather."

Laszlo did not argue. "Franz, then?"

"He's already seventeen. To profit from an education, one must begin young. Already, at eleven, Leo is rather old to start. But if I spend a year tutoring him, and if he is as talented as I believe him to be, he may be able to catch up sufficiently to enroll in an academy in Budapest, later, when he is twelve."

"And where would the money come from for such an education?"

József had anticipated this. He blew out another puff of fragrant smoke. "I will donate my services as a tutor. Then I believe we can get the boy a scholarship. A trust or a philanthropic committee will pay for his education as a charitable act. And he can live with my brother and his wife, in Budapest. I have already obtained their permission." He paused, hoping that this lengthy explanation had helped Leo's father change his mind.

But Laszlo shook his head, and let out a deep, melancholy sigh. "The boy has had the mark of the evil eye on him since the day he was born. If I had not been present at his birth, I would have sworn that my own son was stolen by the gypsies, and Leo left in his place.

"He was born on the first day of the new century—probably he's already told you this, though he's been beaten often enough for drawing attention to himself in such a way. And the labor of my wife to bring him into this world! Leo practically tore my poor Greta in half in his haste to leave her womb. Now you say he has some kind of gift. Well, if he does, it's the work of the devil. No, good sir. No. Leo is of no use to the family in Budapest. Here he can work with his brothers. Let him earn a living in the stable."

József stared at Laszlo. He bit his bottom lip, but otherwise held his frustration in check. It was obvious that this man was not only blind to his son's talents, he actually held them against the boy. But he was not going to give up that easily. "Well, there is no hurry. You may think about it, and change your mind. Thank you for your time, Mr. Hoffman."

Later, back in his small room, József turned all of the possibilities over in his mind. There must be some way to break down Laszlo Hoffman's resistance. He knew that education was not completely unimportant to the family. Although there was no synagogue within a day's ride, the traveling rabbi did stop at the Hoffman household to give Hebrew lessons when he made his rounds through the village. But to suggest Tibor! József had once come across Leo doing a very funny but rather shocking imitation of the rabbi trying to teach Tibor how to read Hebrew. Why would Laszlo deny the one son with true academic talent the opportunity to develop it?

What about the sister? Klari. It was obvious to József that Leo was the apple of his sister's eye. She waited for him every day after school, and once Leo had guiltily confessed that Klari now insisted on doing many of his chores for him, in order to give him more time for his studies. Perhaps Klari could help. It was worth a try.

⚮

The next day József located Klari at the village well. He watched as she strained to turn the heavy winch that pulled the large wooden dipper up from the depths. Her small frame did not seem capable of such heavy work. As she poured water into her own bucket, she wore the same expression he saw on so many of the faces in the village. An expression of weary patience, which revealed no expectations. An expression that only changed when Klari looked at her younger brother, Leo.

Klari jumped as József approached her, causing water to slosh over the rim of her bucket and onto the dust in front of her feet. She looked down at the puddle, apprehension plastered across her face, as if she expected a reprimand.

"I'm sorry," József said cordially. "I startled you. Please forgive me."

Klari looked up at him. Her eyes widened. Then, suddenly, she smiled. József had never seen anyone's countenance so completely changed by a smile. *Good God. When she smiles, she's actually pretty, if one could look beyond the dirt.* Encouraged, he smiled back.

Klari stood, frozen with delight, unable to believe that Mr. Derkovits, *the beautiful man,* was actually talking to her. He stood less than three feet away. The sun brought out the ginger undertones in his hair. The silver of his vest buttons flashed like trout slipping away in a stream. Klari did not want to move. She did not want him to move.

József coughed, hoping to break what was becoming a rather awkward silence. Still Klari did not speak or move; she just looked at him, in an oddly expectant way. He glanced down at the bucket she carried.

"May I carry that for you?" he asked, reaching out to take the bucket.

"Oh, no sir!" Klari blurted out, twisting away and spilling a bit more water on the worn fabric of her skirt.

József dropped his hand. "Very well, then. May I walk with you?"

Klari looked around for the other person to whom he must be speaking. Seeing no one nearby, she dropped her voice to a whisper.

"Walk to where?"

József tried to hide his impatience. "Just—wherever you happen to be going with that water. I would like to talk to you about something."

Klari looked around again. She saw a neighbor standing at the corner of her house, leaning on her broomstick, staring at them. Catching her glance, the old woman turned away and resumed her sweeping.

Klari thought hard. Nothing went unnoticed in the village. Still, what harm would a walk do? It might be the only chance she ever had to spend a moment alone with *him.*

"I'm going home," she replied, bravely taking one step forward.

"Very well then." He waited for her to start walking, then fell in beside her, keeping a respectful distance.

"Klari, I would like to speak to you about Leo."

"Oh, yes, of course." She kept her eyes on her feet as she walked.

"Leo is very special. I'm sure you know that. I would like to tutor him privately. Then, if he's ready, I will take him back to Budapest with me when I leave next summer."

She stopped walking. Another smile transformed her face.

"Take Leo with you? To Budapest? To be your valet? Really?"

Here was the enthusiasm he'd been hoping for! "No, Klari, no—that is, I don't want Leo to be my valet. I want him to go to school. To a real school. To get a real education."

He paused. The confused look on Klari's face triggered a more elaborate explanation.

"You see, Klari, Leo is gifted. He is what you call a prodigy—a child who has abilities far beyond his years. I know this little village is an odd place for God to put a prodigy, but I was lucky enough to find him, and I want to take him to Budapest, where he can develop his talents." He paused again, scrutinizing her face, hoping his words made sense to her.

But Klari knew what Mr. Derkovits was saying. Leo was different. And Mr. Derkovits recognized his differences as a gift. A gift from God. He understood that Leo was special. And now he wanted to take Leo to Budapest. It was the best news she'd ever heard.

Grateful joy radiated from her face. József smiled back, happy that Klari seemed so receptive to his plan. Now for the difficult part.

"I've spoken about this with your father, but he doesn't seem very keen on the idea."

The mere mention of her father drained the animation from Klari's face. "No," she said somberly. "No, he wouldn't understand. He's never understood about Leo. Leo is different. He's not one of us."

"Not one of you? What do you mean? You don't mean—your mother—?"

Klari blushed and shook her head, embarrassed by the misunderstanding. "No, not that way. He—he is my father's son."

"What is it, then? What is it that your father does not understand?"

Klari's eyes pleaded with him, asking him to take the message from her mouth without requiring her to speak. József waited.

"Leo comes from ancient blood," she said at last.

"Ancient blood? What does that mean?"

She did not respond. Joseph lowered his voice. "Don't worry, Klari. Whatever you have to tell me will not change my opinion of Leo."

Still, Klari hesitated. But—didn't he already suspect? Just by acknowledging Leo's gifts, didn't Mr. Derkovits already know? And he was going to help Leo. It was better for her to tell him now. Better that he know the truth.

Klari looked beyond József, beyond the rows of whitewashed houses, to the flat edge of the horizon. When she spoke her voice was distant.

"For five generations we've lived on the Baron's land, Mr. Derkovits. My great, great grandfather came, my grandmother told me, from a place called Galacia, ruled by the King of Poland, who was cruel to the Jews. But in Hungary, it was said, Jews were allowed to work. So the family came across the mountains. To escape the killing. To try to live and work in peace.

"This place has been good to us, my father says, and to many other Jews like us. There has always been peace, here, on the plains, in my lifetime. But I've been told that it was not always that way. My people have many stories. And the gypsies tell even more. Wars come. The Romanians fight the Magyar. The Russians fight the Emperor. Or sometimes the Magyar themselves, they find a reason to kill us. Even though we eat Hungarian food, take Hungarian names, speak the Hungarian language, and work on the Sabbath—still, they find reasons to trouble us."

She shrugged, looking up just long enough to cast an embarrassed glance at his face. Then she looked again to her feet.

"What are you trying to tell me, Klari?" József asked, hard-pressed to temper his growing impatience. He hadn't asked for a family history. To his relief she began to speak again, even more softly this time.

"This has always been a land of war, Mr. Derkovits, and always, the men—the men do violence to women."

She paused, hoping that József would comprehend the rest without any further explanation. But he just looked at her, the question in his eyes encouraging her to go on.

Klari put down the bucket she'd been carrying all this time. "It was during the trouble—the trouble many years ago, when the Magyar tried to free themselves from the Emperor of Austria. So much blood was spilled. I don't know what they say in Budapest, but here it's said that people swam in rivers of blood. And, during that time, my great-grand-mother was—given a child against her will. The child of a Magyar soldier. That child was my grandfather.

"The few people in our family who knew of this attack said that the baby should be killed at birth, but my great-grandfather would not permit it. They had no children of their own. 'A child is a gift from God,' he said. 'It is not the child's fault.' And then, my grandfather looked just like his mother's brother. No one asked any questions. Then my father, too, was born with the face of his mother. So their shame was hidden. But Leo—"

"Leo is different," József said for her, understanding, now, the child's black hair. His blue eyes. The talent that seemed to spring from nowhere.

"Leo is different," Klari repeated in her quiet voice. "My mother has never forgiven him…for being born. My father hates him, for he is a living reminder of his family's shame. And they never…they never…understood. Really, no one in the village understands. Leo is not just different. Ever since he was a baby, I knew. He is…*special*."

József let out a long sigh. Klari's story explained so much. And the love this girl had for her younger brother was touching. It was obvious that she had been his protector.

"Thank you for telling me this, Klari. Does Leo know?"

She shook her head. "No. I know only because my grandmother told me, to unburden herself before she died, five years ago. I think she must have told my father, when Leo was born, so that he would not…suspect…my mother. And I believe my father hated Leo from that moment." She looked briefly into his eyes again, and József caught her silent plea for his confidence.

"I will honor your secret. No one needs to know. It's not as if Leo were the result of some adventure on your mother's part. He can't help the blood that runs in his veins. But you can help him. Perhaps, if you were to speak to your parents, to try to convince them to let Leo come to Budapest—"

"You said that you've already spoken to my father?"

"Yes. He doesn't seem interested in giving Leo an opportunity."

"But Leo would live with you?"

"With my brother, Miksa, and my sister-in-law, Erzsebet. They have no children of their own and are in a better position to take care of him than a bachelor like myself."

"I see."

"Do you think if you spoke to your parents—do you think that you could help?"

She shook her head. "It's not my place to speak to my father about such things. It would only make him angry. I could ask my mother, but that would serve little purpose…"

Her voiced trailed into silence. She pursed her lips, closed her eyes, and shuddered. Then she straightened her shoulders and looked József full in the face.

"I think I can do something that will help," she said firmly.

József was startled by the sudden change in her demeanor. He was on the verge of asking her to elaborate, but then decided not to. He did not want to risk diminishing the shy girl's resolve by asking her too many questions.

"Good. That would be excellent. Thank you. Thank you, Klari."

She smiled at him one last time, her face as full of longing as music played on a gypsy's violin in the moonlight.

But Klari's emotions were lost on József Derkovits, who doffed his hat and sauntered away, completely pleased with himself.

One week later, Klari Hoffman was betrothed to the old widower, Ky Schwartz. In exchange, her father, delighted at her change of heart and the new wealth it would bring to the family, agreed that Leo could study for a year with Mr. Derkovits, and, if he still showed promise, go with him to Budapest.

On Klari's wedding night, her husband treated her kindly. His calloused hands moved tenderly over her white breasts. He touched her hair, and he called her sweet names.

When the old man climbed on top of her, Klari closed her eyes, and filled her mind with thoughts of József Derkovits.

CHAPTER 2

THE STUDENT

❦

BUDAPEST, 1914

Leo jingled the loose change in his jacket pocket as he strolled down the broad pedestrian street known as the Corso. *Just enough for a pastry or two,* he thought, and his mouth began to water. He quickened his pace, using his long legs and engaging smile to help him maneuver through the crowd.

Even on a day that threatened rain, the residents of Budapest packed the sidewalks of the tree-lined promenade along the Danube, determined not to let the weather interfere with their afternoon of pleasure. They took coffee at one of the cafés, or stopped into one of the grand hotels for a newly fashionable English tea. They shopped. They gossiped. Both men and women gave long, sideways glances at their own reflections as they meandered by the plate glass windows of the many elegant stores, critiquing and admiring. And they watched each other watching.

Perhaps he should bring a pastry home for Madame Erzsebet as well. That would mean stopping at Gerbeaud's. It was not necessarily his favorite, but after living with Erzsebet Derkovits and her husband, Miksa, for two years, Leo knew that to Madame Erzsebet, the writing on the box would mean as much as the taste of the pastry inside it.

What was it that Madame liked best at Gerbeaud's? Oh, yes, the

"Rigo Jancsi" torte, named for a gypsy violin player who'd stolen the heart of a French princess – a *married* French princess, no less! Leo was convinced Madame Erzsebet liked the torte less than she enjoyed the story behind it. *How ridiculously romantic women could be!* Well, if he was going to make a trip to Gerbeaud's, then he would get the house specialty, a "Gerbeaud" torte, for himself. He felt his stomach rumble as he imagined himself biting into layers of walnut apricot filling topped with a thick chocolate glaze. Off to Gerbeaud's then.

A short ten-minute walk brought Leo to the door of Budapest's most famous bakery, located in Gizella Square, a few blocks from the Corso and the gray waters of the Danube. It was several minutes before he emerged again, carrying a small gold-embossed box in one hand, and a half-devoured tort in the other. Another ten strides and the last morsel of the rich, buttery treat disappeared down his ravenous teenage throat.

Licking his fingers, Leo strolled back across the square. By now he took the beauty of the city for granted, and no longer stopped to gawk at the striking edifices surrounding him. Not the neoclassical Houses of Parliament, nor the Royal Palace, with its ornamental pilasters, columns and turrets, or even the ornate spire of Matthias Church caused him to stop and stare as he made his way around Budapest. He was no longer terrified by riding the subway, nor startled by the loud noises of a city constantly under construction, as the Hungarians worked to turn their capital into a place that would rival the other gems of Europe. Leo was no longer awestruck by Budapest, "the Queen of the Danube," and "the Paris of the East." He was at home there.

Two years previously the proud schoolmaster, József Derkovits, had brought the astounded boy to the Derkovits family's grand Italianate villa, located on the city's most flamboyant residential boulevard, Andrassy Street. Then, confident that his sister-in-law could help Leo obtain the necessary social graces, and tired of his role as noble mentor, József left on a long-delayed trip to Paris, to catch up on two years of creative relaxation before settling down to assist in expanding the family fortune.

Of course, it helped that Madame Erzsebet had been just as thrilled as Leo about his arrival. The only child of wealthy bourgeois parents, Erzsebet was pretty, plump, sweet natured, socially self-conscious, and exceedingly spoiled. Her round brown eyes communicated a gentle gullibility. She spoke in an animated and childlike fashion, gesturing frequently with smooth, manicured hands that had never suffered the ill effects of any manual labor more strenuous than arranging flowers.

The one real sorrow in Erzsebet's privileged, pampered life was that she and her husband, Miksa, an attentive man who loved humoring her many demands for beautiful things, remained childless. Although it was not, medically speaking, too late for her to have a child, at thirty-one Erzsebet had stopped hoping for pregnancy and started praying for a miracle. When József first approached them about Leo, she decided that this waif from the country was as close to a miracle as she was ever likely to receive.

In Erzsebet's opinion, taking Leo to raise was a marvelously quaint and romantic endeavor. "Why, it's just like that play we saw in Vienna. What was it called?" she asked her husband, after three hours at Budapest's finest tailor fitting Leo for his first dress suit.

"Pygmalion," was Miksa's typically brief reply.

"Oh, yes," Erzsebet responded, and instantly forgot again. "I suppose we'll suffer a few awkward moments. One cannot expect too much from a boy raised in a stable." *But it would be so entertaining to help him adapt to his new life,* Erzsebet thought, filling her uncluttered mind with idyllic images of motherhood. She would teach him and dress him and cultivate him into a fine young man, and become the beloved mother she had always dreamed of being.

Upon his arrival in the Derkovits home Leo spoke infrequently, but when he did so he was unfailingly polite. His most difficult adjustment seemed to be letting the household servants see to his needs. For the first few weeks, every domestic in her employ came to Erzsebet to complain about Leo showing up where he did not belong: in the kitchen searching for a snack, in the laundry asking for an iron for his shirt, or in the cellar collecting logs for the fires.

When Erzsebet corrected Leo, she mistook his silence for shyness. What his foster parents did not know was that Leo limited his conversation not because he felt shy, but because he was totally focused, with every fiber of his being, on assimilation. He could not bear to embarrass

József, or disappoint Klari. So, during every waking moment, he studied the people around him. He scrutinized how they dressed. He analyzed their conversations. How they held their forks and glasses. How they walked, and sat, and greeted each other. He was captivated by the smallest nuance of expression. He noticed everything.

And when he finally did speak with something other than polite responses to predictable questions, he did so in a manner so at ease with his environment that those acquaintances unaware of his origin would have been staggered to learn that he had not been born into the well-to-do society in which he now lived.

For Leo had discovered long ago that people feel most comfortable when they are around others more or less like themselves. He therefore worked to become just like everyone around him. The gift of mimicry that formed the foundation of Leo's fluency with languages extended to more than his speaking ability. So subtle were his methods of imitation—a stance, a gesture, a slight inflection of speech—that no one suspected his whole demeanor was a form of camouflage. He might look in the mirror and still see the poor boy raised in a stable, but the people around him did not. They felt comfortable around him. They did not realize that their comfort was grounded in the seductive power of familiarity.

Erzsebet and Miksa were extremely pleased with how smoothly Leo adapted to life in Budapest. Indeed, Erzsebet was so happy with Leo's progress that she soon decided to take a bit more credit for him. She stopped introducing him as a foster child, and instead explained that he was a distant cousin from the country. Vague references to lost land and financial hard times, a credible refrain after the agricultural crisis of the late 1800s, provided a sufficient explanation for his presence in the household.

Leo enjoyed Erzsebet's attentions, although he was a bit dubious about the clothes Madame Erzsebet assured him were truly fashionable. Her favorite outfit for him, a double-breasted sack suit with matching vest, cuffed trousers and two-tone spats, seemed a little excessive. Much to his relief, Miksa Derkovits intervened just before school opened, insisting that Erzsebet get some "normal clothes for the boy." When he showed up at the schoolyard in September, dressed in a nubby gray Norfolk jacket, with suitably nonchalant tweed trousers and a billed cap, Leo looked the part that he was ready to play.

The administrators at the school he attended had the good sense not to identify him as a scholarship student. The rugged existence of his former life had given him an athletic physique, and Leo soon earned the respect of his classmates by excelling at lacrosse, soccer, and, most important of all, equestrian sports. Although Leo was very intelligent, no amount of talent could make up for his deficient academic background. Except for his outstanding performance in his language studies, his marks were rarely better than average, so he did not inspire a tremendous amount of jealousy among his peers. For the first time in his life, he was accepted.

But excited as he was by his new life, Leo missed Klari. And, he had to admit, he missed Ky Schwartz as well. Klari had never explained to Leo why she changed her mind about marrying old man Schwartz, but after being married for three months she'd cajoled her husband into allowing Leo to come and live with them.

Once Leo became a part of their household, he thought he understood why Klari had given in. The man was old, but he was clearly in love with his young bride. And while he was far from rich, he had more money than the Hoffmans were used to. Ky Schwartz was generous with his wife and his wife's family; Leo and Klari were out from under the hostile eyes of their parents. Moreover, Klari's husband could read Hungarian as well as Hebrew, and he seemed to understand the importance of Leo's studies. The first year of the marriage was a happy time for all three of them.

By the time Leo left for the capital, Klari's stomach was round with the presence of a child, due to be born in November. "I'll have a nephew for you to spoil when you come home to visit," she'd called to Leo gaily, as he and József Derkovits headed out of the village in a hired carriage. "Write to us! Ky will read me your letters!"

Leo wrote faithfully, once a week. He told Klari and Ky about the wonders of Budapest: the underground train, the huge buildings, the music, the food and the fine clothes. He told her about Miksa and Erzsebet and his school. He told her about how different it was to live in a household where there were no prayers—no Hebrew or Yiddish spoken—no acknowledgement at all that they were all Jewish. How strange it was that most wealthy Hungarians spoke French to each other, rather than their native tongue. How odd it was to live in a place where one's wealth and the wealth of one's friends was openly discussed, but God was never a topic of conversation.

Then, two months into his first school term, Leo received a letter from the rabbi who regularly visited his village. And for the first time in his life, he wished that he'd never learned how to read.

Klari's baby refused to be born. She died trying to deliver it. Blaming himself, Ky Schwartz drowned himself in the river within hours of Klari's death. He left a note giving all of his possessions to Laszlo, and, begging his father-in-law's forgiveness, pleaded to be buried with his wife and their unborn child.

Even now, despite the rabbi's words, Leo did not feel as if Klari were dead. He somehow felt that she was still at home with Ky, waiting for Leo to return. He could see himself, dressed in his dazzling clothes, climbing out of a motorcar with his arms full of wonderful presents for the new baby. He could see Klari, running up to greet him, warming his heart with the smile that had for so long been the only bright spot in his life.

So clear was this picture in his heart that Leo could not bring himself to go back to the village and find Klari gone. He had no desire to see his parents or his brothers. Klari was the only one who shared his dreams. Klari was the only one who loved him. He told himself that all the people who cared about him now were in Budapest. He saw no reason to go home.

To Leo's relief, Miksa and Madame Erzsebet seemed delighted when he cautiously asked to stay with them during his school holidays. Miksa saw it as an opportunity to broaden his education. Erzsebet was relieved, for she secretly worried that Leo might go home and never return. For his first winter vacation, Erzsebet dazzled Leo by bringing him to Vienna. He felt his whole body vibrate with awe while watching the spectacle of the Emperor's coach and escort making their way down the broad avenues of the intimate, formal old city. They spent the summer in St. Moritz, on the lake, where Leo learned to swim and to like caviar. The next year they visited Prague and Salzburg and Berlin.

Erzsebet always found an excuse for Leo to stay with them, and neither Miksa, nor Leo, ever argued with her about it.

Already, it's June 28th, thought Leo as he joined the crowd heading down the subway stairs. *I take my last exam day after tomorrow!* Madame Erzsebet had suggested they go to Salzburg again, and Leo, as usual, had responded enthusiastically. He understood that his duty, in exchange for the special treatment he received, was to show just the appropriate amount of gratitude. He assessed the reaction that Erzsebet wanted and supplied it. It was not premeditated or false. It was simply how he behaved. It was the fundamental essence of his charm.

At the moment Miksa was out of town, accomplishing his biannual inspection of the distant factories that had been the genesis of his family's fortune. The house was often empty in the afternoon, because Madame Erzsebet took advantage of her husband's absence to spend a few extra hours at Budapest's famous café, The New York.

It was not, she often insisted to Leo (as though he asked her to justify herself!) that she spent her time at The New York idly drinking coffee. Why, *tout le monde* could be found at the café. It was the only way to stay *au courant.* It was said that in Vienna one could spend hours in a coffee house and no one would notice; in Budapest, you could live there and no one would notice. The coffee houses were the central nervous system of the city. And even a boy Leo's age knew, unequivocally, that the brain center of all the artistic, social, and political activity of Budapest, was The New York.

Located in the ground floor of a splendid Beaux-Arts building erected by an American insurance company in the heart of the city, the café presented a study in excess. With its twisted, gilded columns, crystal chandeliers, marble tables, neoclassical frescoes, flashing mirrors and flawlessly poised waiters, it was the perfect venue for conversation, inspiration, meditation and infatuation. Businessmen stopped in during the early hours of the morning for a leisurely coffee and a calm moment to examine the morning papers. Deals were struck, the markets dissected, and trips to the office became an afterthought.

Next came the artistic crowd, for whom the lunch hour meant breakfast. Arguments and accents rolled through the room, thicker than the heavy cigarette smoke, as journalists and writers found their regular tables. Manuscripts took shape; sonatas were born. Current events, artistic techniques, politics, popular fashions and contemporary philosophies were all rigorously critiqued. Conversations begun at noon merged and mutated through the late afternoon, then blended with the witty or winsome contributions of a new set of *habitués,* as the crowd shifted once again, with the exodus of the affluent for the theaters and cabarets, and the influx of patrons for whom the coffee house was the evening's entertainment. Near eleven o'clock, everyone who could afford it returned for a late supper, and a hearty serving of entertaining gossip. Oh, it was true, insisted Erzsebet, there were many, many, coffee houses in Budapest, but the most glamorous, the most scandalous, the most sublime, was, unquestionably, The New York.

So when Leo arrived at the villa, he was not at all surprised to find that Madame Erzsebet was not there. He deduced as much from the silence that greeted his entry. If Madame were home, he would hear her heavily accented voice chirping *"Salut, cheri!"* from the parlor, or drifting down the grand circular staircase, as he came in the door at his normal hour of four o'clock. His detour to the bakery on the way home from school had not set him behind by more than half an hour. If the gossip at The New York was exceptionally intriguing today, she might not make it home until six o'clock, missing tea time altogether.

"Just enough time for a nap," thought Leo, as he dropped his package on the marble foyer table whose pedestal, in the shape of a fierce, gilded lion, hailed each visitor with a noiseless but toothy roar.

Leo headed straight to the library. He'd discovered that the couch there, overstuffed and covered with a thick, red velvet brocade, was the perfect place for a nap. He would never dare shed his shoes and flop down for a rest if Miksa or Madame Erzsebet were home, or even stood a fair chance of coming home, but today he had the house to himself. Why, it was even the maid's day off, and the chauffeur would be parked outside The New York, probably playing a game of dice with some of the other drivers. The two housekeepers would have finished their work at four, and the cook was off tonight because Leo and Madame Erzsebet were going out for supper, later, after the theater. The house was empty.

Or so he thought. When he opened the library door Leo was startled to find that someone had stolen his idea. Lying on the couch, yards of mauve chiffon spread around her, was Madame Erzsebet's best friend, or, at least, her best friend on the days they were speaking to each other.

She spoke first, without rising from her reclining position. "*Bonjour, Leo. Es-tu étonné de me voir?*"

"*Mais, oui,*" he replied, without embellishment. Leo was, indeed, surprised to see her, and saw no reason to hide it. He would never have expected to find Countess Julia Katiana Nadasy Podmaniczky away from her roost at The New York at this time of day. He tried to remember whether she and Madame Erzsebet were on the ins or outs at the moment, but he couldn't recall. In fact, Leo was rather annoyed that he would now be required to socialize when he had been looking forward to a comfortable snooze. In an uncharacteristically undiplomatic manner, he stalked across the room and flopped down into a leather chair by the fireplace.

The Countess, for her part, was both vexed at being interrupted and pleased that someone had come home. She'd been alone for more than an hour, after one of the housekeepers, who knew her as a friend of the family, showed her into the library to await Erzsebet's return. The Countess' sole purpose for stopping by this afternoon was to establish an alibi. She was to meet her newest lover at five o'clock, and had hoped to use tea with Erzsebet as an excuse for being away from her husband. She'd not counted on Erzsebet's absence from the villa, for her friend was always among the first to leave The New York in order to get home and change for an early evening meal with Leo and Miksa.

Well, at least now the Countess could say, if questioned by her husband, that a visit to the Derkovits' home had comprised a good portion of her afternoon.

The Countess sat up languidly, in no hurry to make conversation. The child seemed in a pout about something, anyway. Julia's rapacious brown eyes narrowed as she looked at Leo, now slouching in the chair, his long athletic legs stretched out in front of him. Of course, he was no longer a child, really. He must be close to six feet tall. She studied his profile as he sat there, contemplating the solid lines of his cheekbones, the succulence of his lower lip. A thick forelock of black curls had escaped its pomade prison and reclaimed its rightful place on his forehead. He reminded her of a jaguar. A young, black jaguar, lean and strong, with tremendous potential coiled beneath its quiet exterior.

In her mind, Julia was always comparing people to animals, because she was so much like an animal herself. Her hair was the color of a falcon's wing, and she wore it in an avant-guard bob. Her deep-set brown eyes flickered incessantly around the room, in sharp contrast to the calmness of her body movements, giving one the impression of a predator about to make an unexpected strike. Her arched eyebrows provided the only softness on her angular face, where a straight, insignificant nose positioned itself over a slash-of-crimson mouth and a slightly pointed chin. The whole effect was striking, and dramatically sensual, if not particularly feminine.

Erzsebet and the Countess were friends because Erzsebet was flattered to have a friend with a title, and pleased at the access her friendship with the Countess gave her to at least a few members of Hungary's old nobility. The Countess liked having a friend who was as endearingly naive as Erzsebet, because she enjoyed shocking her. Their shallow attachment to each other was based on the shared notion that life's overriding goal should be the pursuit of pleasure. However, Erzsebet never dreamed of the extremes to which her dear friend Julia went to make sure she sampled every pleasure life had to offer.

For the Countess was a woman who capitulated to physical desires in a spontaneous, bestial manner. She looked upon the conventions imposed by society the way a tigress might regard a small fence erected to keep it from feasting on a new lamb: vaguely amusing, somewhat irritating, but in reality only a small obstacle to overcome when she decided to pounce.

And pounce she did. She took lovers often, but did not keep them long, for affection bored her. Her voracious sexual appetite seldom caused a problem for her among her peers, for she was also bored by gentlemen. This helped her remain reasonably discreet, for she did not wish for news of her trysts to reach her aging, doting husband.

Instead of creating needless jealousy and potentially troubling gossip, Julia plucked partners from those segments of society where genuine cruelty was never more than a hair's breath away. Sometimes she adopted a disguise, refusing to disclose her identity. Twice she had pretended to be a prostitute, and allowed herself to be taken to a cheap hotel room. She did not enjoy serious pain, but she found nothing more exciting than the threat of physical brutality. The man she was to meet today was a Hussar, a soldier trained to be a merciless killing machine. The thought of being touched by hands that had actually killed and tortured another human being made her shiver with anticipation. Other than scenarios involving bodily harm to herself, there was no fantasy too outlandish, and no sexual deviation too outrageous for Julia to try. If she was in the mood.

And she was beginning to be in the mood right now. Luckily she'd heard Leo's footsteps falling on the marble floor in time to slip her fingers out from under her silk lingerie before he actually opened the door. She was now both aroused and frustrated. Leo looked scrumptious.

Darling Leo. Just fourteen. Surely he was a virgin. She smiled a small, self-mocking smile. That was one experience she'd never had – to be a young man's first lover. The image of herself mounted on him flashed through her mind. Why not? She knew Erzsebet well enough to know about Leo's true background. He would never risk exposing her, risk being disbelieved, risk being sent back to some stinking stable. And surely he would not say no. *Pourquoi pas?*

Unaware of the Countess' lascivious thoughts, Leo spoke, resigned to the fact that he could not be rude to a friend of Madame Erzsebet's.

"Not in the mood for the café, today, Madame?" he inquired.

The Countess stood up. She moved over to the chair where Leo was sitting. With one lissome motion she positioned herself on the floor in front of him.

"No," she replied, her voice already growing husky with desire, "I am not in the mood for the café today. I am in the mood for something entirely different."

She placed one hand on each of Leo's knees and leaned towards him. She knew that at this angle the soft drape of her neckline would reveal a tantalizing view of her small, firm breasts. She inched her body closer to his, spread his legs open, and moved her hands up his thighs until her breasts pressed tightly against his knees and her fingers rested inches away from his groin.

Leo's breath came in short, quick bursts as sexual lightning struck his adolescent body. His body told him, violently, how he should react to this stimulation, but his mind splintered in a thousand different directions. This was impossible! Why was she doing this? What would happen if Madame Erzsebet found out? What would happen next? What if she stopped? What if she didn't? What if someone came home?

The Countess' voice broke through his mental chaos, her words dripping with wanton invitation. "Are you a virgin, Leo?"

From the deep recess of his rational mind, Leo's antennae went up. Something about her tone of voice was significant. Something in the tenor of her voice suggested to him that there was a right and a wrong answer to this question. The truth was yes, he was a virgin. But as he realized that his virginity mattered to her, he seized upon a solution to his confusion. She had a script ready for him to follow. All he needed to do was respond to the right cues. And that was his talent.

Nodding his head and feigning a shyness he did not feel, Leo replied in a low voice, "Yes, Countess."

Of course, of course she'd been right! Oh, how luscious!

She looked up at Leo's flushed face. "You must know how beautiful you are."

"No, Countess." Leo blushed.

He blushed! How adorable! The Countess had searched for sexual satisfaction grounded in suspense, mutual domination, and near-terror for so long that she had forgotten the sweet taste of seduction.

"But you are, you know," she said, stroking Leo's cheek. She moved her fingers down to his mouth, traced the outline of his lips, then parted them, and touched the tip of his tongue with her forefinger, invading and conquering. Her own hands were beginning to tremble with lust.

"Would you like for me to show you how beautiful you are?"

"You will have to show me." He managed to convey both a request and a command.

The Countess let her hand drop to Leo's burning crotch. With excruciating indolence she undid his belt, unbuttoned his pants, and unleashed his quivering organ. She pressed it against her cheek, rubbed it along her neck, and nuzzled it like a kitten, then used her tongue to trace the outline of one blood-swollen vein. Then he was in her mouth.

By now Leo's grip on the arms of the chair was strong enough to leave permanent marks on the leather. He leaned back and closed his eyes. He heard himself groan, as if from a great distance, and knew he could play the role of the passive recipient no longer. Grasping the Countess's head, he shoved himself down her throat, not caring if she suffocated, not caring if he died. The ferocious spasms of his orgasm seized every muscle in his body, and for a moment his mind vanished.

When his body relaxed, Julia released him from her mouth, and sat back on her hands. They regarded each other warily.

He saw a mischievous smile form on Julia's lips. This game was not over. Taking the lead once again, she stood up and lifted her skirt.

"Take off my underwear," she commanded.

Leo did as he was told, smoothly slipping the lace-edged knickers off her small hips. He could not help staring at the mound of dark curly hair which appeared from underneath the silk, its pink center swollen and glistening.

"Touch me," she ordered, and waited to see how he would respond.

This time Leo did not feign timidity. He could tell now that she was the captain, and he her soldier. He slipped out of the chair and knelt on the floor in front of her. Then he thrust three fingers of his right hand deep inside her.

He did not expect the heat he felt there. Her muscles pulsed. His own blood pounded in his ears again, and with four sharp jerks he became fully erect.

"My, my," said Julia, gazing down through half-closed eyes, "the strength of youth." Her eyes hovered for a moment on Leo's erection.

"Lie down," she ordered abruptly.

There was no warmth, no tenderness. Leo removed his hand and lay on his back on the floor. Julia unceremoniously tugged Leo's pants down below his knees, then, lifting her skirt, settled her sea of chiffon around his taut limbs. Leo slid into her without resistance. Arms straight, pressing her hands hard into his chest, she strained to push him deeper, deeper, *through* her.

"Grab my ass," she whispered hoarsely. Leo clumsily fumbled through her dress to find the round mounds of flesh. He could not believe their softness.

Julia began to move, slowly at first, grinding herself against the hardness of his pelvic bone. Then she moved faster, and faster, slamming her body into his with frenetic abandon. Leo tried to judge when to intervene. He decided by the quickness of her breathing that something was about to happen. Seizing her hips with both hands, he rammed himself up into her, and was rewarded with a cry that sounded as if he'd twisted it out of her spine. Her body tensed and twitched, and he rammed her again, arching his back and pulling her harshly down onto his throbbing cock.

As the full strength of her orgasm rampaged through her body, Julia bent down and bit deeply into Leo's shoulder. It was all he could take. Leo came as well, heaving and thrusting his way into blindness.

It could have been minutes before they moved, or it could have been hours. At some point she sat up and gazed at him as if she were scrutinizing the pieces of a jigsaw puzzle. She did not speak. Leo took this as a good sign, for in the two years he had known her, the Countess was seldom at a loss for words. All traces of mockery had vanished from her face. He fought the urge to reach up and touch her. Somehow he knew that a gesture of intimacy would break the spell between them. At that moment he was not a boy becoming a man, and she was not a woman approaching the end of her youth. They were simply a male and a female. Their silence communicated all that was necessary. They both knew that this would happen again.

The bang of a door, a flurry of activity in the foyer, the sound of shouting in the street, and the rapid pace of Erzsebet's footsteps in the hallway jolted them into action. Julia bounced off Leo and smoothed her skirt. He jumped off the floor, yanked up his trousers, hitched his belt, and shoved a hand across the top of his head, desperately trying to undue any damage. Glancing down, he saw Julia's panties on the rug, snatched them up, and shoved them into his pocket before Julia could retrieve them. He then flung himself into the chair by the fireplace just as Erzsebet burst through the door, tears streaming down her face.

She saw Leo calmly sitting in the chair by the fireplace. Julia stood at the window, looking out into the street below, as if trying to discern the cause of the general commotion. A light rain had started to fall.

"Dear God, help us! What will happen now?" cried Erzsebet hysterically, crushing a crumpled lace handkerchief against her tearstained cheek.

"Madame! Erzsebet! What has happened?! What's wrong?! What is it?!" cried Julia and Leo, tripping over each other in their attempt to comfort the distraught woman.

"Haven't you heard?" gasped Erzsebet in astonishment, "What have you two been doing all afternoon? My God, do you not know? Archduke Francis Ferdinand has been shot! Assassinated in Sarajevo! They shot the heir to the throne! Everyone at The New York says there's going to be a war!"

CHAPTER 3

THE LOVER

The politics of Europe in 1914 resembled a balancing act in a very large circus. Each actor executed carefully rehearsed maneuvers in order to reach and maintain his place in the wobbly pyramid forming in the center ring, all the while dependant upon the expertise and loyalty of his fellow performers to prevent a lethal tumble. When Franz Joseph declared war on Serbia, a month after the assassination of the Archduke, the entire spectacle crashed to the ground, with many players unsure of why, or how, they had fallen. Within a month the entire continent was at war.

In Budapest, the Emperor's subjects cheered the departing troops with robust enthusiasm, for the Hungarian thirst for vengeance passed from generation to generation as undiluted as their passion for music or wine. Sure of a quick victory, no one expected blockades and food shortages and rationing. No one expected to spend months in vermin-infested trenches, where dysentery posed a larger threat to life than enemy gunfire. No one expected to be suffocated or maimed by poison gas, to be torn to shreds by barbed wire, or to be picked off in the night by omnipresent snipers. No one expected half a generation to die, and no one anticipated defeat.

The capture of Brussels, the first major success of the Austrian-German alliance, was a special victory for the Hungarians, falling as it did on August 20th, the festival of St. Stephen. News of the victory added to the special gaiety of the day set aside to honor the canonized founder of their country.

In Budapest, flags flew from the windows of every home. Bottles of Tokay, the golden Hungarian wine reputed to be "silk on the tongue and fire in the blood," were lovingly opened and sampled. Hungry celebrants readied feasts in every kitchen, preparing to savor quail soup, stuffed eggs, chicken and apple casserole, aspic of suckling pig, duck pâté, goose-breast pudding, paprika stews of every description, homemade sausages, croissants, honey bread, and mouth-watering tortes. Hungarians lived to eat, and the quality of the food eaten in Budapest on the festival of St. Stephen was rivaled only by the dinners prepared in Paris on Christmas Eve.

The afternoon of St. Stephen's Day found the Derkovits and Leo, along with hundreds of their compatriots, heading for Margit Island, a verdant sanctuary in the middle of the Danube. The island was connected to both sides of the city by a spectacular "Y"-shaped bridge built by the famous French engineer, Eiffel. A public park, the sanctuary's acres of pasture-like lawn made it the perfect spot for a picnic.

Drowsy after a hearty lunch consisting of cold roast paprika chicken, goose-liver pâté, crusty French bread, fresh fruit, and long, thin crepes stuffed with jam, all artistically arranged by Erzsebet on a tablecloth of white linen, Leo decided to stretch out in the shade of a nearby oak tree. Resting with his hands underneath his head, gazing into the branches of the majestic tree, he relived the details of his encounter with the Countess, just seven weeks ago.

The event was never far from his thoughts. He'd seen her several times since then, always in a crowd of people, cool and slightly disdainful, in keeping with her normal attitude towards him. He knew better than to feel hurt. The whole episode seemed unreal. But he had, in fact, kept her knickers, stored away in the closet of his room, so he knew the experience had not been a dream. He wondered what she would think if she knew how often those shimmering undergarments had already been used to inspire his own lustful, but sadly, solo, sexual releases. She would probably be amused. Damn! He was getting hard just thinking about her. He would have to flip over onto his stomach for a nap.

Leo was shaken from his reverie by the sound of Madame Erzsebet's voice, exploding into a series of mild but colorful French and Hungarian expletives, none of which he had ever heard her use before. He sprang up, fearing the cause of such an angry reaction, for he lived in terror of the idea that Erzsebet and Miksa would find out about his illicit episode in the library.

To his amazement, Erzsebet did not look angry, despite the hateful words spilling out of her mouth. In fact, she was now beginning to cry. Huge, forlorn tears filled her eyes, then splashed onto the remains of her lunch. Miksa was patting her back, an uncomfortable and somewhat impatient look on his face.

"Oh, how could you! Idiot! Selfish bastard!" Erzsebet sobbed. Sure that he did not want to interfere in an argument, Leo was about to creep away for a walk when Erzsebet turned and beckoned, summoning him with a rapid flutter of her hand.

"Leo! Leo! Come here, *mon cheri*, to console me. For you shall soon be the man of the house if Miksa has his way."

Dreading what would happen next, Leo stood up and walked the few paces separating him from Miksa and Erzsebet. They did not fight very often. This was the first time that Erzsebet had tried to drag Leo into an argument, and he did not like the look of things.

"Can you believe this?" Erzsebet shrieked as he drew closer. "My husband has decided that he must enlist in the army. To be an officer, no less. The Emperor doesn't need middle-aged men to help him beat those stupid English pigs!"

"And the French," Leo interjected, at a loss for something more comforting to say. He fought the indelicate urge to compliment Miksa on his decision. Like most young men of fourteen, Leo thought that military service was a heroic path to glory. Of course Erzsebet would be upset, but that could not be helped. There was, after all, a war to be won.

With more tears flowing, Erzsebet leaned over to search in the picnic basket for a clean napkin to dry her face. Leo took advantage of her bent posture to give Miksa a warm but silent smile of congratulations.

Miksa smiled back, then raised his eyebrows and lifted one shoulder slightly to communicate his resignation at Erzsebet's emotional reaction. Now the two men were allies.

Seizing a napkin, Erzsebet continued to chastise her husband. "It's bad enough," she said, her voice cracking into a high-pitched whine, "that your brother, József, had to go straight from Paris to Vienna without even coming home for a visit. War shouldn't happen so quickly. People should be given the chance to get their affairs in order first. But he can handle hardship more easily. He is still young, only twenty-five. You are thirty-seven. Surely they cannot use *you* on the battlefield. Or you could have waited until you were asked."

"Erzsebet, *cherie, s'il te plait,* thirty seven is not old, and certainly not too old to be a soldier. This country has given us so much. Do you not think that I ought to give something in return?"

"But not your life!" cried Erzsebet wildly, looking into his eyes with a desperation verging on panic. "Oh, Miksa, I'm not that brave, I'm not *at all* brave, I'm not brave enough to lose you." She collapsed into his arms, her shoulders heaving with sobs. By now the melodramatic scene had attracted the attention of several curious onlookers.

In truth, Miksa did not completely understand the strength of her reaction. In his mind their marriage was based on a light-hearted affection, infinitely pleasing, but not exactly the stuff of which great love affairs are made. He did not think that either one of them was the sort to succumb to a grand passion. Maybe he had misjudged her. Still, he did not approve of this, well, sniveling. After all, there was a war on. And it was unnerving for her to act as if he were as good as dead.

But Leo, watching as Erzsebet's sobs gradually quieted, understood. He understood because he noticed the subtle messages people generated. He understood that Erzsebet loved Miksa, but that her love for him did not inspire her terror of losing him. She was petrified of being alone. She had gone from a home where she was humored and spoiled, to a marriage where her rich husband catered to her every whim. She had no idea how to manage her own life. If Miksa were killed, who would take care of her? Who would pet her, and pamper her? Who would admire her plump loveliness, and her gracious ability to make life pretty? Leo saw her weakness, and tried not to judge her for it. But despite his empathy, he, too, found her reaction distasteful.

It was several minutes before Erzsebet pulled her tear-drenched face away from Miksa's shoulder. She turned around and looked at Leo, then stretched out her smooth hand towards him.

"Leo, *mon petit prince*, at least you will stay with me, will you not? You and I will be brave together."

"Of course, Madame," replied Leo, in his most chivalrous tone of voice. "I will take care of you."

As he took the hand offered to him, Leo felt an ominous pit open in the bottom of his stomach. He looked away at the river, shimmering vibrantly in the late afternoon sun. He looked back at Erzsebet's face, coyly pleased with his promise.

Leo knew that this was no longer a question of putting on a good performance, of discreetly becoming whatever Erzsebet and Miksa wanted him to be. Fulfilling those sorts of expectations did not seem to really touch him, inside. Erzsebet's plea asked for more. Leo had never been asked to take responsibility for someone else. He was not sure how to do that. For the first time he wondered whether he might not want to, one day, escape the expectations placed upon him as the price of Erzsebet's generosity.

"That a boy, Leo!" cried a much-relieved Miksa, giving Leo a solid punch on the upper arm. "Now we will pull through this together! With honor! Like Hungarians!"

"Like Hungarians!" echoed Leo enthusiastically. The thought filled up the hollow place that had been building inside him. Although, at times, he was no longer sure who he was, he knew, at least, that he was Hungarian.

ॐ

Despite Erzsebet's initial hysterics, Miksa's departure proved uneventful. Erzsebet spent more time shopping, and some time doing volunteer work for the Red Cross. She also managed to spend much more time at The New York. When not keeping Erzsebet company there, Leo spent his hours wandering the fascinating streets of Budapest, where the daily drama of human existence provided endless hours of entertainment. There was always something of interest to capture his attention. Perhaps a drawing at the National Hungarian Lottery, where two freshly scrubbed girls from the state orphanage, decked out in full native dress, would pull the winning numbers from large glass drums, the crowd hushed by nervous expectation. Perhaps a gypsy band would be playing in the lobby of the Hotel Hungaria, seducing tips from the passing throng with eternally wistful melodies. Perhaps a peddler would be selling sausages and oranges from a cart in the middle of a busy street, hawking his wares with hyperbole worthy of a politician. At any given moment he could look around him and notice something he had never seen before. He was not always busy, but he was almost never bored.

When the school term started, many of the young professors were no longer there; they were now soldiers. The talk during breaks was generally confined to three subjects: sports, female body parts, and the latest military campaign.

But Leo was still a student, and not always a good one. The afternoon of a crisp October day found him staying late at school, poring over the answers to a failed geometry exam. While his mind could leap effortlessly through the written and spoken word, it plowed laboriously through the murky world of advanced numbers. Still, he had to learn enough to pass the university entrance exam.

When he felt that he had made some progress towards the correct answers he turned his papers in to his teacher, a graying, pudgy poodle of a man, and then left, muttering a few less mathematical observations of his own.

Leo emerged from the school at four o'clock, and was about to dash across the street when the sight of something out of the ordinary stopped him. There was a car parked against the curb, just to the right of the school gate. Automobiles were not all that unusual in Budapest, but they were not so common that the sight of sleek machine went unnoticed, especially by a teenager. He stepped closer to inspect the vehicle, then stopped in his tracks.

It was the Countess' car, it had to be! Hers was the only Rolls Royce Silver Ghost in Budapest. He remembered hearing Madame Erzsebet say that it had taken over a year for the car to arrive from England.

Resolving any doubt, the man Leo recognized as the Countess' driver stepped out of the driver's side of the vehicle, and walked around to where Leo was standing. He was a short, rather ugly, round-faced Bulgarian, with a particularly toothy grin. "*Kerem*," he muttered, in badly accented Hungarian, "Please." He opened the rear door.

Leo's heart leapt madly. He knew that he would not be missed at home until six o'clock. For an instant he was tempted to ignore the proffered seat, to shake his head and leave, to execute a power play of his own. Wouldn't the Countess be insulted! Wouldn't that be a step towards freedom! But his whole young body, from the blood pounding in his temples, to his already stiffening penis, to the very cells of his fingertips, screamed out for sexual gratification. He squelched the notion of a principled retreat. With a nod to the chauffeur, he entered the car.

Leo had never been to the Countess' Budapest mansion, for he was still too young to attend formal social functions late in the evening, and the Countess rarely received visitors during the day. Not in the city, at any rate. Picnics and hunting parties were held at one of the Count's country estates, where dozens of acquaintances ate and drank and flirted their way through entire fortnights devoted to the pursuit of pleasure. The Countess, herself, did not hunt. Not during the day.

Upon entering the soaring foyer Leo immediately noticed the difference between this house and the interiors of the homes he frequented on his visits with Erzsebet. Most of the homes in their social circle displayed a fondness for flamboyant luxury, and often revealed their owners' inability to resist temptation.

The home of Count Sandor Nicholas Podmaniczky was luxurious but mirthless. The interior spoke of wealth: old, immense wealth, far removed from its origin or the merit of its masters. Portraits of noble ancestors with fathomless eyes stared down at Leo from the entrance hall. Absent were the cheerful Rubens, Delacroix and Fragonards favored by the self-indulgent, newly rich bourgeoisie. Instead Leo found himself facing a haunting Bellini Madonna, and a solemn Friedrich landscape, its dark colors full of foreboding. A table from Louis XIV's Versailles held an Egyptian statue brought back from the eastern campaigns by one of Napoleon's officers. A Bohemian crystal chandelier hung from the foyer's coffered ceiling. The house was imposing. It was cold. It was not, thought Leo, at all like Julia.

He cautiously made his way to the living room. After showing him in, the driver had disappeared. The house seemed deserted. Of course, it would have to be. It would have to be, if—

Where could she be? A peek into the front drawing room produced no clues. His pride flared again. What was he supposed to do, sit and wait? No. He would go find her. If she were here. If she were waiting for him. He spun on his heel and marched back to the front stairs, his aggravated pace muffled by the priceless Persian carpets underneath his feet. Where would her bedroom be? Facing the gardens, of course. He paused on the stairs and drew an imaginary picture of the house inside his head. The corner of the house would be too cold at night, the top floor too hot in the summer. The center rear. Her bedroom would be in the center rear of the house.

He reached the top of the stairs and made a quick right turn. Down the hall. To the left. A short walk down a corridor covered with Venetian glass mirrors of varying sizes. Two double doors. He whipped them open. The wood cracked loudly against the plastered walls.

He entered a woman's boudoir, soft and gold. He could see two French doors to the right.

By now his hands were shaking with impatience and rage, an anger that preempted embarrassment, should she reject him. He took a deep breath, and slowly opened the door to the interior bedchamber.

She was there, stretched out on the huge bed like a lazy lioness reigning over a kingdom of satin and velvet. She looked over at Leo and gave him a smile full of dissolute expectation. And she was naked. Gloriously, beautifully naked. Leo froze, transfixed by the delicacy of her breasts, the pink firmness of her nipples, the supple slimness of her thighs, the palpable curve of her waist. She rolled over languorously, purposefully revealing to him the sensuous flesh of her shoulders, and the smooth cheeks of her buttocks.

"*Bonjour*," she began, the smile never leaving her face. "*Es-tu étonné de me voir?*"

For the next three years, while the war in the trenches smoldered and then roared, Leo and Julia roared and smoldered in bed. Trained by a true hedonist, there was nothing about the delights of physical inter-action between male and female that Leo did not experience by the time that he was seventeen. Nothing, except for the experience of making love to a woman with whom he was in love. He was bewitched by Julia's sensuality, and thoroughly enthralled by her recklessness; but by the time he recovered from his initial well-hidden infatuation, he knew enough to understand that he was not in love.

In fact, at times, he was not even sure that he *liked* Julia. And even if he had cared for her in a truly romantic way, there were too many strictly defined borders governing their relationship for any genuine intimacy to develop, not the least of which was the ludicrous gap in their age. Moreover, other than their salacious knowledge of each other's desires, they knew little about each other's lives. Their meetings did not make room for casual conversation. Their moments together seemed to exist in a separate place, a physical place on a different plane of reality, so removed from their normal lives that at times Leo felt he led a dual existence. There was school, and sports, and his increasingly busy social life. And then, there was Julia.

Julia was used to leading a double life. To her Leo was just one more interesting facet of her secret world. An unusually durable one, it was true; but that was only because he never showed the poor taste, the bad judg-ment, of hinting that he was in love with her. Love was so boring. It ren-dered passion so predictable. She preferred the thrill of pure carnal lust.

Julia also kept Leo in her stable of lovers because he never disappoint-ed her. He was her pet, her little soldier, her hungry jaguar. She discov-ered a certain perverted maternal joy in watching him mature: physically, as his body filled out and took the final shape of the man he was to be, and sexually, where her dark ruthlessness provided lessons most men would never have the opportunity to learn. Sometimes they saw each other as often as once a week, sometimes not more than once a month. Normally she sent her car for him at school. After a few such episodes she instructed her driver to park down the block. Discretion above all.

Once Leo had taken her in a public place, in the dark recesses of

her private box at the opera, during intermission, after Erzsebet and
the Countess' other guests had excused themselves to the lobby. The
sequins of her gown grated her back as he roughly pushed her up
against the red brocade wall, knowing she could not struggle (much)
and would not scream.

He had to wait a long time after that encounter before she sent for
him again. She had enjoyed it—God yes!—but she had to maintain
control, after all. Of course, he'd never apologized. She would have had
nothing more to do with him if he had. She just made him wait.

The end of their affair came after a particularly ferocious afternoon
in April. Julia started her post-coital conversation by telling him that his
penis was massive and marvelous. Then, with malicious humor, she
described in detail other organs she'd seen that were even more impressive, and when she'd last had the occasion to compare.

At the time Leo showed no reaction. But while Leo had, for three
years, silently assumed he was just one stallion in Julia's stable, his pride
could not tolerate confirmation of that fact. The next time he saw her
car parked a few blocks away from the school, he nodded to the driver
and kept walking.

When the Countess discovered that her car had returned without
Leo, she understood immediately why he had not come to her. Feeling
deeply chagrined, she took out her vexation on a priceless Ming vase,
which shattered into thousands of satisfying porcelain fragments when
it hit the mantle of the fireplace in her bedroom.

Yet Julia also felt relieved. It was unlike her to see someone, even
intermittently, for such an extended period of time. Their continued
liaison had become dangerous, dangerous because of the possibility of
discovery, and, she forced herself to admit, because she might conceivably get—annoyed—as his love life inevitably began to include women
other than herself. Could she be jealous? Impossible! Julia thrived on
inspiring jealousy in others, but, she assured herself, gazing into her
bedside mirror at her perfect skin, she never cared deeply enough about
anyone to feel jealous herself. Her vanity forbade it. Now, after the
unthinkable—who did he think he was, to reject *her*?—the choice was
easy. She never sent her car and driver to summon Leo again. Their

affair ended just as impulsively as it had begun.

In part, Leo was able to walk away from Julia because, at seventeen, he was starting to get other interesting invitations. His opportunities were often unwittingly engineered by Erzsebet, who became ever more dependant upon him, as both he and the war grew older. She relied on him, not only for companionship, but to help protect her from life's little unpleasantries, and he willingly obliged. He handled the inevitable confrontations with merchants and the household staff, and told the indispensable white lies that lubricate social relationships. Their relationship grew into a muted, mutually dependant love: a complex but comfortable blend of mother and son, brother and sister, mentor and protégé.

At some point he stopped addressing her as "Madame Erzsebet" and started calling her by her first name. She never objected. The informal address seemed more appropriate, especially when he began escorting her to social events where there were now infuriatingly few males present. Gone were the grand theatrical presentations, the cabarets, the concerts, and the operas. Of course, there was always The New York, but even café society had been badly affected by the dual shortages of men and money. Most people now entertained in their homes, amassing as many black market goodies as they could in order to achieve a level of style that could be considered patriotically chic.

Leo's charming presence was a welcome addition to these intimate gatherings. The fact that he seemed so much older than he was helped smooth over the social delicacies of the situation. His sexual sophistication, to which Erzsebet was blithely oblivious, added an enticing level of intrigue to his interaction with the lonely women left behind. For the most part he practiced nothing more serious than the gallant art of flirtation. However, a reasonable number of more satisfying opportunities enabled him to resist the temptation to return to Julia.

And so Leo became the tender favorite of wartime Budapest as the stagnant conflict between nations dragged on. After three years, neither side was sure of victory. When the Americans joined forces with the British in the spring of 1917, the German military leaders opted to embark on a massive offensive campaign, in order to win the war before America could deploy enough troops to make a significant difference.

The reinvigorated campaign meant that the war-weary populations of Germany and Austria-Hungary were to be drained again. It meant more money, more men, more sacrifice, and the destruction of more lives.

It meant that Leo, three weeks before he was to sit for his university entrance exams, went, instead, to the Italian front.

CHAPTER 4

THE CONCIERGE

ᴏᴖᴧᴖᴏ

BUDAPEST, 1918

The soldiers who stumbled home to Hungary in November of 1918 were numb. They were numb with hunger, numb with fatigue, and numb with cold, but those deprivations did not compare with the numbness of disillusionment. Honor and country had called them to the battlefields of Europe and then abandoned them there, where a weary grayness drifted into their eyes, settled into their hearts, and wrapped around their souls, souls that had been slit open and sucked dry by the beast of the Great War.

For there had been few clear victories in this war; no tremendous conquests, no glorious triumphs. For most it was a war of grinding attrition, without room for uplifting heroics. Soldiers engaged in a meaningless contest of mystifying maneuvers through blood-soaked mud, designed to capture tiny bits of territory that none of them ever wanted to see again. In truth, it had been a war without a reason, that Austria, Hungary, Germany and their allies lost.

The chaos gripping the exhausted nation at the end of the war affected every aspect of life in Hungary. The Emperor abdicated his throne. Riots broke out in towns and villages across the countryside. Factories shut down. Commerce ground to a halt. Trains stopped running. Even before they were officially released from service, thousands of soldiers simply began walking home. Leo was among them.

He walked for weeks. The nights were the worst. Thinking about his empty stomach and his frozen feet at least helped keep worse images at bay. But at night the dreams came, bringing with them the smells, the sights, and the screams. Better to stay awake as long as he could, better to listen to the nightmare cries of other men as they slept, than to let the war back into his own brain. Leo slept as little as possible.

But the nightmares were there. He'd seen a starving Italian whore sell herself in front of her ten-year-old daughter to men whose lust was their only defense against the constant fear of death. The child would sell them cigarettes when they were finished—cigarettes she'd plucked from the pockets of the bloated corpses hung up in the miles of barbed wire around her village. Leo saw the girl, or what was left of her, hanging from the wires one night. The snipers shot anything that moved.

He'd seen men scuttle like rats among the dead bodies of their own comrades-at-arms, risking execution on the chance that they might find something of value, something they could use to obtain cigarettes or extra rations from the venal scum who operated the black market. He'd seen the real rats, fat and defiant, waiting for men to die, or brazenly feasting on men not yet dead, no longer afraid of their screams.

He'd tried to slip into the role of a soldier, tried to distance himself, to keep a piece of who he had been separate from the bloody anarchy surrounding him. But he could not distance himself from the look of hatred in the eyes of a man he did not know, but had to kill, to keep from being killed himself.

Of the men whose names he'd learned, not one had survived. He had seen hell, and it left him with no illusions about the nature of life. Nothing was sacred. In the end, to most people, the only thing that mattered was staying alive. And you could not count on anyone to help you.

It was the middle of December by the time Leo reached the grand villa on Andrassy Avenue. The gate showed spots of rust. A stone had come up in the front walkway and had not been replaced. The garden in the front courtyard had not been tended before winter's arrival, and overgrown plants lay dead in the scattered snow. Lifelessness clung to the mansion like a bad odor. Leo was too cold, too hungry and too tired to be dismayed. He knocked on the door. No answer. He knocked again, with more force. Then he heard the unmistakable patter of Erzsebet's footsteps.

"Who is it?" her timorous voice called out from behind the door.

Leo tried to respond, but his voice would not. Unexpected tears filled his eyes. It had been just a year and a half since they'd last seen each other. It could have been a century.

He forced his words past the lump in his throat. "It's Leo." A key turned in the lock. A bolt slipped back, a bolt that had not been there when he left. The door opened a crack, and Erzsebet peered through.

He looked down at the sliver of her sweet, round face. Through the two-inch opening she stared up at him, hope barely crowding out the fear he saw in her eyes.

For a moment neither of them spoke. He pushed the door open as she took a step backwards, her eyes still fixed upon his unshaven face.

"It *is* you," she whispered.

"Yes, Erzsebet, it's me." From somewhere deep inside himself he retrieved his most beguiling smile. His eyes lit up for her. "It's me, and I'm cold and hungry, and I hope that I made it home in time for some coffee before dinner."

"Oh, my God! Oh, thank God! Oh MY GOD! LEO IT'S YOU!" Erzsebet flew at him. Leo half-carried her, hanging from his neck, through the foyer. They collapsed together on the stairs, a tearful, laughing, heap of mutual delight.

"But you're all right. You're not hurt somewhere?" she fretted as they both sat up, lifting and checking his arms and legs for some hidden injury.

"No—I mean, Yes, I'm fine! I made it through just fine. My luck held out." That was all she needed to know. There was no reason to tell her more. He paused, wanting to talk about something small and meaningless, hating to pose the question he knew he had to ask.

"And Miksa?"

Erzsebet's face hardened. He saw the glow fade from her eyes. He knew before she answered.

"Dead."

"When? Where?"

"Does it matter?" She spoke with a bitterness that was more disturbing than tears.

"I'm sorry, Erzsebet," Leo said faintly. He was haunted by nightmares, but all of her nightmares had come true.

"Oh, Leo, at least *you're* back now." He could sense from the tremulous sound of her voice that she was about to crumble, but she continued to talk.

"You're the only person I have left. Miksa is dead, and József was taken prisoner by the Russians —I've had no word from him. I only know from the Red Cross reports that he was captured. He is probably dead in some Siberian camp. My family is dead, your family is dead, and the whole world has gone crazy."

"My family is dead?" Leo sat up straight. Somehow the village of his birth seemed like such an unimportant, distant little world. It did not seem possible that the war had touched it, too. Leo felt no real grief for his family, only a sharp pang of yearning. The war had stripped away his past as effectively as it had destroyed the present.

Erzsebet's hand flew to her lips. "Oh, stupid mouth! What a monstrous way to tell you! The rabbi sent me a letter—I'll find it for you. Your brothers were both killed in Slovakia. Your mother died of—forgive me, darling, I can't remember, I'll find the letter! Your father moved with some cousins, to somewhere in Transylvania. There was no one left to work the land, you see. There is no one left, you see, just you and me. There's no one left." Both of her hands fluttered uselessly in the air. Sobs shook her shoulders. Erzsebet had not come equipped for adversity. Life had now asked too much of her.

Leo put his arms around Erzsebet and rocked her, crooning to her with meaningless, comforting noises. Their roles were now irretrievably reversed. He was to take care of her, as he had once promised. For they each had no one else.

❦

Erzsebet eventually calmed down and focused on the menial task of getting dinner ready. Leo relished the simple meal of roast pork, potatoes and cabbage, then relinquished himself to the sleep his body demanded. He did not wake until morning, when the sounds of the city unfolding caused him to leap in terror from his bed. It took him a moment to orient himself. *No more bombs. No more gas. I'm home.*

Home. What was left of it? He must learn the state of the family's finances. With Miksa dead and József missing, he would have to oversee, as well as he could, the running of the various businesses that funded the Derkovits' fortune. He supposed that Erzsebet had been relying on the family's attorney. He would see him today. There was no telling what would happen in the next few weeks, as world leaders decided Hungary's fate. He needed to get down to business as soon as possible.

Leo went to the wardrobe in his dressing room and pulled out a pair of woolen pants. To his consternation, they were now too short and too big in the waist. He glanced at his body in the mirror. He had not realized that he had grown, in fact, finished growing during his tenure as a soldier. He needed some clothes that fit. Well, that would be the second thing he did that day. Shopping! What a luxury.

He found Erzsebet in the breakfast room, setting out china place settings for the two of them. She looked embarrassed as he walked in, and he realized that, but for the cook, whose busy preparations he could overhear in the kitchen, there were no servants in the house to perform any domestic tasks. That did not bode well.

"Good morning!" said Erzsebet brightly. Too brightly. "We're in luck today! Our intrepid cook has found fresh milk for the coffee. I imagine it came from the last poor cow near Budapest. Soon she will be beefsteak, I imagine. What a boring business this is, all these shortages."

"Believe me," said Leo, matching her cheerful tone, "Warm bread and fresh milk tastes a lot better than what I've had to eat lately. Don't be upset! Look how I've grown despite the Emperor's menu." He gestured to his too-short pants. The sight of his stockings sticking out from the cuffs of his slacks sent Erzsebet into a spasm of giggles. He smiled, too, as the cook came in with a tray of hot rolls, fresh black-market coffee, and the treasured milk in a small silver pitcher. There was no butter or jam, or sugar for the coffee, but the warm, yeasty taste of the

bread and the strong aroma of the coffee provided a tremendously satisfying breakfast.

Erzsebet seemed happy to have a small, manageable problem that
she could set herself to solving. "About your clothes. We'll have to see
about having your pants altered. There is a talented lady who has
opened a shop out of her home on Vaci Street; she does good work and
is discreet about her clientele. One needn't advertise that one is having
one's clothes redone, after all."

"Oh? Is it not possible to buy something new?"

Erzsebet winced, her dislike at being the bearer of bad news regis-
tering plainly on her face. "I'm afraid that we, well, Leo, I suppose I
have to tell you…. We seem to be having some financial difficulties. Of
course, everyone is, with the war having taken so much of a toll, but,
well, I think you ought to speak with our attorney, Mr. Rosen. He will
explain things better than I can. It has something to do with our factories being located in enemy territory. And Miksa apparently made a
large war loan to the government before he left, which tied up a lot of
our liquid assets." She spoke as if she were reading from a script, obviously doing her best to repeat what had been explained to her.

"Oh, don't worry, Erzsebet. I will make an appointment with Mr.
Rosen this afternoon. In the meantime, if you would please bring some
of my winter pants to the talented lady on Vaci Street. I would very
much appreciate it." Leo's manner was calm but his mind was racing.
How bad was the situation? Where were those factories, and what did
they make, anyway? Now that the dual monarchy had collapsed, would
the war debts be repaid? For the first time in his life he wished that he
had been born with a head for business rather than a gift for languages.

By the end of the afternoon, he knew the grim truth. An aging Mr.
Rosen graciously showed him into his office, after glancing at a brief note
from Erzsebet giving the attorney permission to discuss the family
finances with an outsider. Yes, the manufacturing capacity of the family's
companies was located primarily in war-torn Rumania and Slovakia.
There were several facilities dedicated to the manufacture of farming
equipment and others for textiles. The territories where they were located
were still part of Hungary, but it was anyone's guess what would happen

now that Hungary had lost the war. At any rate, most of the physical plant had been destroyed during the last year. The insurance covering the factories did not, of course, compensate for damage due to acts of war. The war debt might be repaid, but without a functioning government it was impossible to say if, or when, that might happen. The only remaining assets were the house on Andrassy Avenue, and an investment account that provided a small income for Erzsebet. It was, of course, most unfortunate. Most unfortunate.

After a polite farewell Leo stood outside the door to the lawyer's office, twirling his hat in his hands, trying to absorb the magnitude of what old Mr. Rosen had told him. He knew that just by continuing to live in the majestic villa on Andrassy Avenue they were living beyond their means. Still, now was no time to sell it. And, he could not do that to Erzsebet; he could not suggest that she let go of her home, the one connection she had left to the carefree, comfortable life she'd always known.

Until this moment he had not realized the extent to which he'd taken the Derkovits' wealth for granted. So that was one more joke life was to play on him! He survived the war, but it was back to being poor. One by one he descended the four marble stairs leading from the office of *Ira Rosen, Attorney at Law,* to the sidewalk. With each step down, he let go of a dream. There would be no university. There would be no apprenticeship. There was no fortune waiting for him to claim. There would be no triumphant return to the village of his youth. It was time for Leopold Hoffman to get a job.

But how? Leo placed his felt homburg back on his head and started down the street. There were hundreds, no thousands of men returning from war. There were thousands of Hungarian refugees flooding into Budapest from the outskirts of the empire. The country was in a shambles. *It is not,* Leo thought ruefully, *the best time to be looking for employment.*

And what, exactly, was he qualified to do? He had no work experience of any kind, other than limited exposure to his father's trade as a blacksmith. In a few months he'd be twenty. He was now fluent in French, German and Russian, and also spoke English decently, in addition to his native Hungarian. Nonetheless, his education was incomplete. He shuddered at the thought of toiling away his life as a clerk in a dark office somewhere. There might be no other choice. Surely some of Erzsebet's friends could help him find such a position.

As he pondered his future he found himself wandering in the direction of the Corso. Soon he was walking down the grand boulevard itself. It was, he realized, slightly shabbier than it had been when he left, but largely unchanged. Men and women still strolled along the street, stopping for a chat, a drink, or a glance in the windows of the few shops that had managed to remain open.

A small commotion caused him to shift his attention to the entrance of the Bristol Hotel, where the driver of an expensive roadster, ignoring the fact that the street was closed to vehicular traffic, had driven onto the pavement and was ushering what seemed to be an international delegation of sorts into the lobby. There was some confusion, as the outraged doorman began to argue with the driver. Evidently the driver did not speak Hungarian. In a few steps Leo was beside them. He immediately discerned that the driver was speaking French.

"Peux-je vous aider?" he asked, delicately offering his assistance. The aggravated gentlemen turned their attention to Leo.

"The fool insists on leaving his car here!" the doorman shouted, shaking with rage at this affront.

"Could you please tell me where I may park this car? It's ridiculous that my passengers should be expected to use the back door!" demanded the equally irritated driver.

Leo calmly explained how to reach the motor entrance of the hotel, assuring the driver that it was in no way considered a "back door." Somewhat mollified, the driver retreated to his car, and, with much honking and waving to dismiss the small crowd that had now gathered to watch the scene, he drove off.

"Koszonom szepen," the doorman said to Leo, his smile thanking him as sincerely as his words.

"Szivesen," responded Leo automatically. An idea was brewing in his head. He gazed at the grand hotels of the Corso: the Bristol, the Carlton, the Hungaria. This was it! If there was anywhere in Budapest where skill with foreign languages was an absolute necessity, it would be here, where the richest, the most famous, the most influential foreign visitors to

Budapest stayed when visiting the capital. He was tempted to dash in now to explore the possibility of a position. No. What was he thinking? He must look the part. He could not appear in pants that were too short, in shoes that were not polished, wearing a coat that was well worn. He could not, he thought, show up looking like he needed a job.

Leo was back the next day, hair neatly trimmed and brushed straight back, shoes sparkling, well turned-out in a nearly-new suit of clothes that had been hastily altered to fit his tall frame. Only his overcoat showed signs of wear, and that, given the textile shortages brought about by war, was forgivable. His vibrant blue eyes were calm, his manner poised. He could have been twenty or thirty. Nodding in a dignified manner to the doorman, he was pleased to discern no sign of recognition in the man's face. Leo was a different person from the helpful young man who had been there yesterday. Now he was a professional.

Leo sent his personal card into the manager, knowing that the Andrassy Avenue address would get immediate attention. Within a few moments the hotel manager appeared in the small reception area outside his office, hand outstretched. His gray hair and aging features helped Leo put his age at something approaching sixty. The man moved with dignity, breeding, and a touch of self-importance.

"Mr. Hoffman. How may I help you?"

"No, Mr. Orgovany," responded Leo as he shook the proffered hand, "The question is, how may I help you?"

Puzzled, the older man gestured to a chair. Leo sat down, his body movements full of easy grace, and continued to speak, watching closely for a reaction to his words as Orgovany took a chair across from him.

"Mr. Orgovany, I assume the hotel has one or more qualified people to serve in the position of concierge?"

"Of course."

"How many languages do they speak?"

"I beg your pardon?"

"Collectively, how many languages are represented by the concierge staff?"

"Let me see. Four. Hungarian, of course, then French, German, and English. May I ask where this is leading?"

"Sir, my service to the Emperor has interrupted my education. I speak five languages; those you have mentioned, as well as Russian. Given the, shall we say, current state of disruption in our country, it may be some time before I am able to return to my studies. In the meantime, I believe that I can be of valuable assistance to you and this establishment as a member of your concierge staff, a position which would give me the opportunity to keep my language skills from becoming rusty. I know that I can provide a level of personal service that is exemplary, because it is a level of service I am used to receiving. I would like to propose a two-week trial period, during which I will work as a junior concierge, without pay. If, at the end of that time, you feel we have a mutually satisfactory arrangement, then we shall discuss salary." Leo paused, his features composed into an expression that was part request, part dare, part *fait accompli*.

"Let me see," began Orgovany, "You come in here with no references—"

"Oh!" Leo interrupted smoothly, "If it is a question of references, I should be happy to provide them, beginning with Count Podmaniczky." Leo quickly added a short list of a few of Miksa's friends to the Count's name, hoping that Orgovany would recognize at least some of them. Surely the man would know the Count by name and title. Inwardly he noted the amusing irony of using Julia's husband as an employment reference.

"Just a minute!" Orgovany reclaimed the conversation, but Leo could tell he was more intrigued than annoyed. "I am not in the habit of hiring school boys who would like to come here and play between semesters. I would need a commitment that, if your probation is successful, you will stay for a minimum of two years."

"Sir, I am not a dilettante. I assure you that I would approach this commitment with the utmost seriousness." Now he smiled his most captivating smile. "You run the most impressive establishment in the city. It is the one place in which I would like to perform, yes, perform, for all good service is truly a question of fine performance."

Orgovany remained quiet for a moment. Never in his life had he met a young man with such polish, such poise. Why, it was like meeting a younger, and, he had to admit, better looking version of himself. If he was what he claimed to be, this young man's services would be very helpful indeed. In fact, they could use another concierge. The skeleton staff they'd been forced to use during the war would not be sufficient in the weeks and months ahead. For, even though they had been on the losing side of the war, and, in part, because of that fact, there would soon be many international visitors to Budapest. Many of them would be staying in his hotel. Its owners were British, and he prided himself on maintaining impeccably British standards of service, but the Bristol on the Corso was a Hungarian institution, and it was, he felt, a reflection of his own, personal standards of excellence as well. This young gentlemen would fit in nicely.

Two days later Leo took up his position as junior concierge at the Bristol. Erzsebet's embarrassment at having him work in so public a place, in a service capacity, was mitigated to a degree by the same story he'd told his new employer; it was a wonderful way to stay current with his languages. Leo knew the practical realities of the situation. He would never return to school.

He did not feel demeaned by his new position because he had spoken the truth to Mr. Orgovany; he considered his job to be a performance. He was not serving; he was, in a sense, pretending to serve. And he did it superbly. He arranged excursions, reserved train tickets, hired cars and drivers, organized card games, found ways for shoes to be repaired, found tables at the few restaurants that were still functioning, discovered ways to provide small black market treats to clients unused to deprivation, reserved times for long distance telephone use, helped awkward husbands buy gifts for demanding wives, and helped demanding wives find what they wanted to buy for themselves.

These latter purchases often involved private showings in the client's hotel suite, for the merchandise came not from showrooms, most of which were closed, but from the personal collections of the large numbers of Hungarian nobles and wealthy bourgeoisie now facing poverty. Leo's commissions on these transactions often doubled his monthly salary.

Leo's earnings made it possible for Erzsebet and him to stay at the villa. They were also able to keep one servant, who served as both cook

and maid, and to periodically hire a handy man to perform small main-
tenance tasks. Leo convinced Erzsebet to see her new responsibilities as
a kind of adventure. She helped with small chores around the villa, and
she did the shopping, which involved long waits in long lines at small
stores where rumors indicated that small quantities of food at hugely
inflated prices might be available. She was not alone; most of the *nouveau riche* were now newly poor. And for those who managed to maintain some of their personal wealth, there was often nothing to buy.

At length, in March of 1919, the allies demanded that Hungary sur-
render huge portions of its territory to help create the new independent
nations of Rumania, Yugoslavia and Czechoslovakia. The members of
the provisional government of the new Hungarian Republic resigned in
protest; no one wanted to sign such a treaty.

The person who rushed into the void to seize the reins of power was
a former Hungarian foot soldier, by the name of Bela Kun. Sent to a
prison camp after his capture by Russian troops during the early days of
the war, Bela Kun quickly became an enthusiastic Bolshevik. At the war's
end he was sent back to Hungary, by Lenin himself, with a mission – to
plant the seeds for a Hungarian communist revolution.

The collapse of the provisional government in March of 1919 gave
Kun the chance he needed. To assist his efforts he requested the release of
several other Russian prisoners of war. They were fellow Hungarian nationals whom Kun had befriended while in prison camp. They were men
whose experience in the Great War had left them angry, disillusioned, and
susceptible to brainwashing. Their exposure to Bolshevik propaganda had
convinced them that capitalism was the root of all society's evil.

One of the men freed at Kun's request, who made his way back to
Budapest to help Kun form a new, communist, Hungarian People's
Republic, was József Derkovits.

❧

He arrived in early April, and went first to his home on Andrassy
Avenue, where a tearful, grateful Erzsebet poured out the dismal tale of
the family's experiences. She also told him how to find Leo, and József

lost no time in making his way to the Bristol to greet his former student.

At first József did not recognize the polished young man sitting at the concierge's desk. But in a moment Leo caught sight of him, and when that brilliant smile burst through his vivid blue eyes, József recognized the boy inside the man.

Leo leapt across his desk, momentarily forgetting the decorum that governed all his movements as concierge. He gripped József in an enthusiastic hug.

"My God! It's amazing! How did you get here? Have you seen Erzsebet? Are you feeling well? Come, have some coffee!" Leo steered his former teacher into the lobby café. "Wait here," he said quickly, "I have to get someone to cover the desk for me." In less than a minute he returned, exuberance animating every gesture.

"So how? When? What happened? Thank God you made it through!" Leo continued after ordering coffee for them both, the broad welcoming smile never leaving his face. József hardly knew where to begin. He touched lightly on the details of his capture, brushed over his internment, then related the story of how he had befriended Bela Kun in prison camp.

"So now that Kun is maneuvering to take control of the Hungarian government, he was able to arrange for my release. I may well be a government minister within a few weeks," József finished proudly.

Leo lifted his eyebrows. "But Kun is a communist. Surely you do not intend to play a role in *that* sort of government."

József shrugged. "Compromise is the essence of politics. The next few weeks will decide which way the country is headed. But enough about me! Here you are, sitting behind a desk at the best hotel in Budapest. Not exactly the future we had planned for you, but certainly easier than the life you were born to."

Leo picked up an undertone of cynicism in his voice. So József, too, had changed. Well, they all had. "It's not exactly as exciting as politics, but I enjoy it," he replied. "The challenges all involve keeping people satisfied. Come to think of it, that's not too different from politics."

József only smiled. People did not always know what they needed. It would soon be his job to show them.

"Well, I have to get back to work," said Leo, finishing his coffee. "We'll talk more tonight. Erzsebet must be ecstatic." He felt a lump in his throat and looked away. "We didn't think that we would ever see you again."

József, too, was moved by the sight of his home, his country, and the remnants of his family. He grasped Leo's forearm across the table. "Thank you for all you have done for Erzsebet. Thank you. Now, she is my responsibility." Leo smiled, unable to speak. This, too, was a joke that life had played on him. At first he had resented having to be responsible for flighty, fragile Erzsebet, and now keeping his foster mother happy and safe meant more to him than he was willing to admit.

◈

The reunited household enjoyed only a few weeks of peace before their lives changed once again. Bela Kun did create a communist government. József served in his cabinet as first assistant to the commissar of agriculture, a post for which he was hopelessly unqualified. Erzsebet, delighted to have the opportunity to become a hostess once again, threw herself behind her brother-in-law's efforts.

Leo, whose position at the hotel often made him privy to the latest political gossip, tried to warn them that now was not the time to get involved in politics, especially not Bela Kun's politics. The whole posture of the country was too treacherous. Neither József nor Erzsebet listened. They were too caught up in their dreams.

Determined to crush the threat of communism, England, France and the United States allowed the Rumanians and Czechs to attack Hungary in full force. Kun reacted with wholesale brutality, forcing whole industries to nationalize, and slaughtering those who resisted. The country plunged into a period of complete economic disaster, exacerbated by an economic blockade adhered to by all of Hungary's trading partners, for the fear of communism was universal. The virus must be purged.

Aiding in the battle against the communists was a foul but effective propaganda tool that played upon the prejudices of a thousand years. Kun was a Jew. Over half of his commissars were Jews. This was all that the hate machine needed to create a universal scapegoat. It was the fault of the Jews. The Jews had sabotaged the war effort. The Jews were behind the communist revolution. Only the Jews stood to gain from the suffering of the people. The hate machine ignored the fact that Jewish industrialists would lose the most under a communist regime, that thousands of Jews had fought and died for Hungary in the war, that wealthy Jewish families had loaned the government millions of crowns to finance the war effort, and that many of the people slaughtered by the communist regime were themselves Jewish. Anti-Semitism was too seductive a rallying cry for truth to intervene.

By August the harsh communist experiment was over. Soviet Russia did not come to Kun's aid. Rumanian troops marched into Budapest. Kun and his closest cronies fled to Vienna. József and others like him, who had played a role in the communist regime but were sincere in their determination to save their country, stayed, hoping there might be a place for them in whatever successor government took shape.

⊙⥿⊚

On an evening in early September, in the midst of the Rumanian occupation, Leo finished an exhausting shift and exited the hotel onto the Corso, where he heard a familiar voice call his name.

She was there, behind him, her petite frame wrapped in a handsome sable coat, soft symbol of an era that no longer existed. At first glance she seemed no older than thirty. A closer look revealed the tiny lines around her eyes and the shadows under her neck, silently betraying her loveliness.

"*Bonjour, Leo,*" she said, the forever-familiar, mocking smile rising to her lips, "*Es-tu etonné de me voir?*"

He took her hand and bowed over it, pressing his lips to her slim fingers. "No, Countess, not surprised. Enchanted."

Her smile was replaced by one of genuine pleasure, then, just as swiftly, by a look of fear and concern. "Leo, we must find a place to talk. Immediately."

Warned by the look in her eyes, Leo nodded his assent, fighting off the fatigue he felt creeping over him. Escorting the Countess by the arm, Leo reentered the hotel. He then led her across the lobby to

Orgovany's outer office, which he knew would be vacant at this time of the evening.

Julia was acutely conscious of his hand on her arm; she felt the warmth of it through her coat. God, he had become a magnificent man. He was worth saving. If only she could get him to listen to her.

She waited until they were both seated before she began to speak, knowing that he would react violently to what she had come to tell him. There was no delicate way to break the news. She leaned towards him.

"Leo, you may not, you *must* not go back to the villa tonight. Something horrendous has happened, beyond our control, and it is too late to do anything except save yourself." She willed herself to stay calm as she struggled for some way to communicate the hideous news.

Leo had only to look at Julia's face to see that something truly terrible was behind her visit. The bottom fell out of his stomach. "What is it?" he cried, starting out of his chair. "What has happened to Erzsebet?"

"She and József have been—shot."

"What!" He was standing now, towering over her, his blazing eyes requiring a retraction. It took all the courage she possessed to stay where she was.

"Leo, I wish I could say that it were not true—" Julia's voice rose in astonishment as he literally lifted her by her shoulders, out of the chair and off the ground.

"Where? When? Is she alive?" he demanded, interrogating her in mid-air.

"Put me down," Julia hissed. If someone heard them and came in, if he created a scene now, they could both be lost.

He looked at her as if he did not even realize that he held her dangling in the air. Then he lowered her back down and took a deep breath, trying to regain his composure.

"Is she alive?" he repeated, his voice a toneless staccato.

Julia shook her head.

"Who did it?"

"Counterrevolutionary forces," Julia spat out, her voice now bitter with sarcasm. "The Nationalists. Our 'secret' police. The men we have allegedly *protecting* us from the Rumanians." Then, looking at his face, her tone softened.

"Leo, I'm sorry. I came as soon as I found out. My husband—has connections. Sometimes we find out about these things more quickly than...than others might. I had to be the one to tell you because..." she faltered, then reached up to his tormented face and stroked his cheek. "I want to protect you, if I can, from the same fate."

He shoved her hand away. "Protect me? *Protect me*? Why didn't you protect Erzsebet?"

"Damn it! Because I couldn't! Don't you see? Your brilliant József was a communist. He was in Kun's cabinet, for God's sake. These men are insane with revenge. They blame the communists—and the Jews—for loss of the whole damn Empire. Erzsebet was a collaborator, whether she realized it or not. She was so excited at having a role in government, she didn't care what politics it involved. All she cared about was playing hostess to members of parliament! She didn't know that her dinner parties were her death warrant. I couldn't be seen with her publicly after Kun took over, but I did warn her. I'm sure you did, too. But Erzsebet was always too willing to believe what she wanted to believe. And she believed in József."

Leo looked away. Julia was right. He had not gotten involved in the communist government, in fact, had deliberately absented himself from the house whenever meetings took place there. He was not a political person. But he had repeatedly tried to warn both Erzsebet and József that if the People's Republic failed, they would all be in jeopardy. Erzsebet should have fled in August when Kun's government collapsed—he should have made her leave!

József persuaded her to stay. "Only cowards flee," he'd said. And then, they'd all been lulled into a false sense of security by the relative calm, that prevailed in Budapest after the Rumanians captured the city. So József and Erzsebet stayed in Budapest. And now, they'd paid the price.

Leo pictured Erzsebet as she had looked this morning, sitting happily at her desk as she made her shopping list for the day. His rage ebbed away. His heart felt like an anvil in his chest. He would never see her again. First Klari. Now Erzsebet. He was alone.

Julia sensed that his anger was dissipating. "Leo, the house is being watched. In a few days it will be confiscated as government property, the forfeited property of traitors. If you go back you will be implicated. There is nothing you can do now. Nothing, that is, except save yourself."

He looked at her dully, not wanting to think about self-preservation, not wanting to accept his loss. She went on.

"If you need money—"

"No. Thank you. I'm entitled to rooms at the hotel. I can stay here. Where are they—what have they done with the bodies?"

"I don't know," Julia lied coolly. She would not let him risk his life for the sake of visiting a corpse. Now, there was one more thing she had to say.

"Leo, does anyone here at the hotel know that you are Jewish? Hoffman is not necessarily a Jewish name."

He seemed surprised by the question. "Jewish? I don't really know. I don't suppose so. I've never had any reason to mention it. Why? What does it matter now?"

"I hope you will understand why I am telling you this. You must not, under any circumstances, tell anyone that you are Jewish."

The anger returned to his eyes. "Why? What are you saying?"

"You don't understand the extent to which these men are motivated by jealousy, by bigotry, by hatred. József and Erzsebet were not killed just because they were communists. They were killed because they were Jews. With all the chaos at the moment, there's a chance no one important will make a connection between you and the Derkovits family."

"So I am to hide my heritage to stay alive, is that it?"

"Is it so wrong to try and stay alive when you're being persecuted without a reason?"

"What about honor?"

"Honor? Honor won't warm your gravestone, Leo. I know how much Erzsebet loved you. You owe it to her to stay alive."

"I owed it to her to keep her from dying."

There was nothing more that Julia could say. He would heed her advice, or not. She could not utter what she most wanted Leo to hear. *You must stay alive because I care so much about you.* She had only recently admitted it to herself. Maybe he already knew.

After a silent moment she made a move to leave, pausing only to murmur, "Leo, darling, if you need anything—"

She watched as a range of emotions flickered across his handsome face: grief, outrage, and, perhaps, a touch of gratitude. Then he was once again all business, holding his hand out to her as if she were a departing hotel guest. "Thank you for having the courage to tell me this. Thank you for the warning." The words were appropriate, but his tone was flat.

Ignoring his proffered handshake, Julia moved a step closer to him and closed her hand around Leo's forearm. "You won't go back to the villa?"

He shook his head. She breathed a sigh of relief and let go of his arm. That, at least, was something.

Pulling her sable tightly around her shoulders, she left the office without another word. She knew that she could not risk seeing him again. She also knew that a part of her would always belong to him.

Leo took up quarters in the hotel, and went about his work, performing his duties as if he'd been turned into a machine. Only once, late at night, did he walk by the house on Andrassy Avenue. A brass plate on the door declared it the future offices of the Ministry of the Treasury. Even then, he did not break down.

Stories reached him at the hotel, stories of the massacres of communists and suspected communists, stories of angry mobs murdering Jews. None of it seemed real to him. Nothing mattered. In November, the Rumanians looted and then left Budapest. Another counterrevolutionary government was put in place. Seven months later, the successor to that government signed the Treaty of Trianon, officially ceding seventy percent of Hungary's territory and sixty percent of its population to Rumania, Czechoslovakia, Yugoslavia and Austria. The humiliation and demoralization of the Magyar nation was now complete. Life in postwar Hungary had begun.

CHAPTER 5

THE TRANSLATOR

BUDAPEST, 1925

"Excuse me. Would you be interested in a game of bridge?"

Leo looked up from the train schedule he was examining to see a plump, white-haired gentleman looking down at him. It took a split second for Leo to register that the man had spoken to him in English. When Leo first started at the Bristol, English had not been his best language. Now he was head concierge, and six years of contact with a constant influx of well-to-do British visitors, none of who seemed willing to venture out of their native tongue, had greatly improved his fluency.

He responded in an easy manner, his accent unaffected by any trace of Hungarian.

"I'm not sure that's possible, sir. But I shall be happy to arrange a more suitable partner for you. When and where would you like to play?"

"Well, that's just it," the old gentleman rumbled beneath his white mustache. "We'd like to play right now. One of our the group suggested that you would make an excellent fourth."

The man's accent was American, not British. Of course, a Brit would never stoop to playing bridge with the concierge.

"I'm flattered, sir, but my duties do not include the privilege of playing cards with our guests."

"Well, that doesn't concern us. This is to be a wagering game, you understand. You come recommended as good company, a cool-headed partner. A man whose discretion can be trusted. Can you play? That is, can you excuse yourself and come join us?"

"Might I ask who has given me such a glowing recommendation?"

"Janos Bacso. President of the Commerce Bank. Said you beat him regularly when you stop in to play at The New York."

"Oh! Janos Bacso! Has he invited you? Perhaps I had better play, then, to protect you from his devious tricks," Leo said with a smile, then glanced at the clock on his desk. It was a few minutes before ten o'clock. He could rely on his assistant to take over. And it wouldn't be the first time he'd played cards with a bored guest. A little extra money always came in handy, although he had to be careful not to win too much when playing in his "professional" capacity.

"You must already know that I am Leo Hoffman. And you sir?"

"James Mitchell. Glad to make your acquaintance. So you will join us, then?"

"I have one or two things to wind up here, then I shall be delighted to join you. What suite?"

"You'll find us in 305."

"Very good. I shall be there in ten minutes."

He took note of the room number. One of the larger suites. After handing a few minor matters over to his assistant, he placed a call to room service and ordered a bottle of Moet Chandon champagne and a tray of finger sandwiches to be sent to the room, compliments of the house. *Might as well set the stage.*

He'd met Janos Bacso while courting the man's daughter, Maya, two years earlier. Although Bacso knew virtually nothing about Leo's background, he recognized him as a young man of talent and charm. Given the chaotic state of post-war society, a self-made man like Bacso put more stock in future promise than in pedigree when evaluating a potential son-in-law. Impressed by Leo, Janos had pushed the match.

However, Leo ultimately stopped short of proposing to Maya, even though it would have meant a change of career from concierge to bank officer. He did not love Maya; he was merely entertained by her. A door had closed inside him that she could not open. Although he was tempted, he ultimately decided that he would not dishonor her, or any other woman, by entering into a marriage based primarily on ambition.

Six months later, when he heard that Maya was engaged to a young bank officer, Leo reintroduced himself to her father at a regular, late-night card game at The New York. Although aloof at first, Bacso was friendly enough after he'd won a significant amount of money, and Leo was pleased to have retained his friendship.

When he knocked on the door of suite 305, Bacso opened the door. Behind him, already seated at the table in the parlor, Leo saw James Mitchell, and another man whom he did not recognize.

"Good Evening! Glad to see you! Delighted you could join us!" cried Bacso with enthusiasm. "I was hoping you could get free. You have already met James Mitchell. Our other player is Lajos Graetz."

Graetz stood up as he was introduced. A thin, balding man, whose strict posture made him appear taller than his true height, he wore wire-rimmed glasses on his pointed nose, and looked at the world through gray, almost colorless eyes. Leo was struck by the firmness of his grip, and his crisp, military bearing. A former soldier, no doubt.

Another knock at the door announced the arrival of the champagne. They toasted each other's health, wealth, and fortune. Bacso offered each of them a cigar. Only Mitchell accepted.

Graetz and Bacso did not speak English well, but it seemed that they all spoke passable German, so they settled on that as the language of the evening. As he shuffled the cards, Leo started to make conversation.

"So, Mr. Mitchell, where are you from in America?"

"Shanghai."

"I beg your pardon. Shanghai is in China, is it not?"

"You're right about that! I'm from the American Concession, now known as part of the International Settlement, in the marvelous metropolis of Shanghai."

"You were born there?"

"No, I was born in Baltimore, Maryland."

"And what brought you to Shanghai?"

"Aha!" Mitchell sat back in his chair, obviously embarking on a favorite topic of conversation. "You see, if you knew anything about Shanghai, you would not have asked that question, for no one goes to Shanghai if he has anywhere else to go. You would ask, instead, how I managed to leave."

"Would you care to explain?" Leo inquired, as he dealt the cards.

"Shanghai, Mr. Hoffman, is a great port city. It is also the last port of call for all decent people, and the first destination of robber barons, financial schemers, adventurers, pirates, opium dealers, arms traders and ne'er do wells. It is the only place in the world one can enter without a visa or a passport, with no questions asked, set up shop, and start making a living."

"Surely there are some legitimate business enterprises there as well?"

"Well, yes. Mainly for the Brits. Lots of money to be made in the China trade. They import goods to the teeming millions and export Chinese goods to greedy Europeans. But the law-abiding Brits have lost out now on the most lucrative import, that being the opium that comes from India. It's been declared illegal to bring it into China. Which makes it all the more profitable, of course."

"I see. And in which category do you place yourself? Robber baron? Opium dealer? Adventurer?"

Mitchell put his head back and poured a glass of champagne down his throat. "Capitalist, Mr. Hoffman, venture capitalist. I venture where there is money to be made. I made plenty in Shanghai. I hope to have a few years left to make a little more in Hungary."

"And I hope to make a little here for us tonight," Leo responded, raising his glass to his partner. The cold December wind howled against the window. The play began.

They were at least an hour into the game, with Leo and Mitchell well ahead, when Graetz finally spoke.

"So, Mr. Hoffman, Janos tells me that you have a special talent for languages."

"He is too kind."

"Oh, come now, there is no need for that sort of false modesty. Five languages fluently. Is that correct?"

"Why, yes."

"Do you translate?"

"Do you mean written, or simultaneous verbal translation?"

"Either."

"I'm afraid my verbal skills exceed my ability to reproduce the languages on paper."

"Meaning?"

"I am proficient at verbal translation, slower at written transcription."

"So it is the ear you were born with."

"Yes, as you put it, the ear is what I was born with." Leo had the awkward sensation that he was being put through his paces. He looked at Bacso, whose face revealed nothing. He was concentrating on his cards.

Graetz did not stop. "There are a good many opportunities for men of your ability."

"There weren't when I started here."

"But things are changing now, improving. It's 1925. We're back in the League of Nations. The currency has stabilized. You are wasting your talent here at the hotel."

"I'm happy here. It is an interesting job. I'll have the opportunity to move into upper level management eventually. After all, I'm only 25."

"Come, come Mr. Hoffman. Is that all the ambition you have? To be manager of a hotel?"

Still Bacso was silent. No one had played a card in several minutes. Leo was beginning to feel like a mouse caught in a trap, when Bacso spoke.

"Leo, you are here on my recommendation. I know you to be an intelligent young man, an honest man, and a loyal Hungarian. We have an opportunity we would like to present to you. Now, our country is weak, but there are things that we can do to make it strong again."

"Are we discussing patriotism or capitalism?"

"Both!" answered Mitchell, chortling. Janos Bacso shot him a curt look before continuing.

"You are familiar, I am sure, with the terms of the Treaty of Trianon, which brought an end to the war."

"No more so than the average person."

"You probably know that our country's armed forces are limited to thirty-five thousand men."

"That much I did know."

Now Graetz spoke. "You realize, of course, that this leaves us unable to defend ourselves in the event we face another threat from Rumania or Yugoslavia."

"But do we face such a threat?" Leo's question, innocently posed, set off a chain reaction around the table.

"Always!"

"The French will not rest until they see us under Serbian rule!"

"The Rumanians are salivating over the agricultural capacity of our heartland!"

"Austria would love another piece of Transdanubia!"

"The point is this," Bacso explained. "If we are able to defend ourselves, it will only be because we are able to obtain the best weapons available. Readiness is the best deterrence. The resources we need are new, automatic weapons being developed in the United States and Soviet Russia. There are, of course, strict controls on the shipments of such armaments. But there is the possibility—I can tell you no more— the *possibility* that our soldiers could obtain a supply of these advanced weapons through, shall we say, *unofficial* channels."

Leo looked back at him, puzzled. "What does this have to do with me? Shouldn't this be done through the government? Or the military?"

"That's just the problem," responded Graetz, his thin face quivering with agitation. "The government, the military, is powerless to act. We must rely on the private individuals to accomplish what our hamstrung government cannot."

"I have no interest in becoming an arms dealer," Leo stated emphatically, rising from the table. Bacso reached out and grasped his arm, preventing further movement.

"What have you done lately of which you have been proud, Leo?" the older man asked. "Truly proud? Arranging a picnic? Hiring a driver? Do you not think that the gift God gave you should be used for a nobler purpose? Does the future of your country mean nothing to you?"

The words stung. Leo sat back down.

"What would you expect me to do?"

The other men exchanged glances. Graetz answered. "Simply this. We'll have a meeting, very soon, of the people who could, in theory, supply the weapons, those who could, conceivably, transport them, and the men who are willing to pay for them. They come from different countries, including Switzerland, Soviet Russia, Germany, and America. Having you at that meeting will enable us to communicate effectively. Of course, you will be sworn to secrecy."

"So you need me to translate? That's all? Surely there is someone else who can do this."

"No one else whose presence would not arouse suspicion. No one else we could trust. Otherwise, we would have to have several interpreters present. The more people who know about this, the more danger we are all in."

"But couldn't you merely agree to speak the same language, as we are doing now?"

Again, the men exchanged glances. This time it was Janos Bacso who answered.

"You see, Leo, we need you to do more than just be at the meeting. We need for you to eavesdrop, telephonically, on the other participants, after the actual meeting, to make sure that we are not being betrayed."

"Telephonically? Is that really possible?"

Graetz nodded. "The technology exists."

"And," Mitchell interjected, "You will be very, very well compensated for your services. In fact, if you perform well in this capacity, it could lead to great things for you, yes indeed, *great* things."

Leo thought for a moment. Was it such a terrible crime to disobey laws that had been forced down Hungarian throats? If they were caught, they would go to jail. But wasn't his current life a prison of sorts, anyway? He had substituted mastery of the details of a small life for the riskier challenge of pursuing a great one. Perhaps it was time to take a chance on something. He felt a flash of excitement, a feeling he'd not had in a long time. It felt good. And, in truth, Bacso's words had touched his pride. He knew he could do this well.

"Where is the meeting to be held?"

Bacso smiled. "Ah, there, you are in luck. We are to meet in four days, in Paris. Our affairs should take no more than three or four days. You can take a long holiday and stay in Paris for Christmas."

⚬⟡⚬

The Orient Express to Paris arrived precisely on schedule, early in the morning of December 18, 1925. Leo had enjoyed every moment of the trip. It had been ten years since he'd traveled in such luxury, and he'd missed it. He missed being the object of another's solicitous attentions, of eating a meal cooked to perfection, of having his bed linens readied by a careful hand. The train's whistle signaled their arrival. Paris! To be able to spend a few days in Paris was worth risking a little time in jail.

To maintain the maximum amount of secrecy, none of the other Hungarian participants in the negotiations were traveling on the same train as Leo. He knew only that they were to meet tomorrow morning, in a suite at the Ritz, located in the Place Vendôme. Bacso and the people with whom they would be negotiating were all staying at the Ritz. Leo checked into a small but perfectly acceptable hotel down on the Rue de Rivoli, near the Louvre. They were all to register under assumed names, except for Bacso. The banker explained that, although he had never before stayed at the Ritz, he was so frequently in Paris on business that an alias would be ineffective; indeed, rather than protect him, use of a false name could prove needlessly embarrassing if he were to run into one of his banking colleagues.

After a leisurely lunch in a café bordering the Jardin des Tuileries, Leo walked up Rue Castiglione in search of the Ritz. He wanted to make sure he knew exactly how to get there the next day. The shops along the way displayed luxuries of every conceivable description, from furs worthy of a Czarina, to jewels capable of tempting the crowned heads of Europe, to antiques worth more than most men would make in a lifetime.

At the Place Vendôme he confirmed the location of the Ritz and then headed north again, where the street name changed to Rue de la Paix. Destination: the Paris opera. With typical Hungarian hubris Leo wanted to compare this building with the elaborate opera house on

Andrassy Avenue.

He found the Paris house impressive, but dull by Hungarian standards. Too few flourishes, not enough gilt.

Leaving the Place de l'Opera behind him Leo once again headed west, determined to get at least a glimpse of the famous restaurant, Maxim's. Many of his well-traveled clientele at the Bristol maintained that people-watching at Maxim's provided better entertainment than a performance hall. On his way towards Rue Royal, he passed by the Olympia music hall, world-renowned for its spectacular entertainment. The sight of it made him think of Erzsebet, telling him in her endearingly silly way about a show she and Miksa had seen there during their honeymoon. She always got the name of the performer wrong. The memory brought a lump to his throat. He walked quickly past the theater.

The street broke into another wide-open space, and Leo stopped short. He was gazing at an enormous Greek temple. A bronze plaque informed him that it was in fact the Church of Mary Magdalene. The classic refinement of the building created an oasis of perfect harmony amidst the bedlam of cosmopolitan Paris.

At the edge of the square, across from the church itself, Leo noticed a lively café, and went to investigate. The place looked promising. He resolved to return again, if he could, to savor the view of the church that the small café afforded.

By midnight he was lying in his bed, soaking in the sights, the sounds, the smells and textures of the city. Paris was the city Budapest should be, the city Budapest could have become, if they had not lost the war.

The war came back to him that night.

He awoke bathed in sweat despite the cold December air. Gradually, the cacophonous symphony of an urban morning replaced the roar of mortar fire and the screams of dying men. He blinked. He was lost. Then he remembered. He was in Paris.

At eleven o'clock he entered the modest front door of the grandest hotel in Paris. He could not remember the last time he'd felt so energetic, so full of purpose. He knew he had to downplay his enthusiasm. This was business, after all. He would follow Janos' lead.

Leo was not the first to arrive. Janos Bacso was already engaged in conversation with a man whom Leo did not recognize.

The newcomer was short. His face was round, his mouth thin, and his eyes slightly almond-shaped. He had black hair and an olive complexion. He wore a badly cut suit made from a fabric with a loud stripe that might have looked decent on someone taller, but was rendered comical on the squat man who sat with casual arrogance in an armchair made for a finer class of person. At first Leo thought he was of gypsy blood, but he immediately disregarded that possibility. Janos Bacso would never do business with a gypsy.

Janos quickly made the introductions. "Allow me to introduce Imre Károly, the chief of police of Budapest. He will be a party to our meeting tomorrow evening." Károly rose from his seat, and Leo automatically extended his arm to shake the small man's hand. His handshake was firm but damp. Leo resisted the urge to wipe his hand on his jacket.

He'd never seen Károly, but he'd certainly heard of him. Few people in Budapest had not. He was one of Gyula Gombos' chief henchmen. Gombos was the head of Hungary's small but noisy fascist party. Although the fascists had not garnered much popular support among the Hungarian voters, through sheer ruthlessness and the maximization of their few political connections, they managed to place some people, like Károly, in positions of power. Leo wondered why Bacso was involved with this man.

Of course, it was not the first time that Leo had been forced to be gracious to an avowed anti-Semite. His post as concierge required that he be, to a certain extent, politically color blind. But this was testing the limit. There was now no tactful way to excuse himself, short of feigning a sudden illness. He could not back out just because he did not like the company. There may be valid security reasons for including the chief of police. He would have to wait and see how the game played itself out.

Soon five men were in the room: Leo, Bacso, Graetz, Mitchell, and Károly. To Leo's consternation, no one brought up the purpose of their trip. Despite his burning curiosity about how to accomplish his electronic surveillance, he did not feel comfortable broaching the issue when everyone else seemed content to make small talk. Graetz and Károly debated the relative merits of two types of machine guns. Mitchell told several bawdy tales about what services one could buy from a Chinese whore in a seedy quarter of Shanghai known as Hongkew. After forty-five minutes Bacso dismissed the group, reminding them that the time and place for tomorrow's all-important negotiations would be communicated via a message delivered to their hotel. He asked Leo and Károly to stay behind for a few moments, to discuss "logistics."

"Leo," Bacso began, "Each of us is going to spend the day preparing for certain aspects of tomorrow's meeting. Imre is here as our electronics expert. He has valuable experience in this area, and will assist you in learning how to use the telephone wiretaps we will be utilizing. I will leave you two alone to get acquainted."

So that's it, thought Leo. *He's the espionage expert. Must come in handy in his business.*

"So how about some lunch before we get to work?" offered Károly, proceeding to pinch his bottom lip between his thumb and forefinger in an absent-minded gesture Leo found particularly repugnant. This was going to be a long day.

They decided to eat in a restaurant overlooking the Place de la Concorde. After relieving them of their overcoats, a disenchanted waiter led them to a beautiful mahogany table. Károly sat down and immediately ordered cocktails for them both. Some of the hostility Leo was feeling must have spilled out from under his composed demeanor, for Károly gave Leo a suspicious look.

"Do you have something on your mind?" he asked, and Leo realized that he had to create an excuse for his unexplained glower. Although he would have loved to insult this offensive little man, he did not wish to jeopardize his own position by creating an atmosphere of animosity. His survival instincts took over. Leo responded to the question at Károly's degenerate level.

"Damn French. Here is the waiter looking like he hasn't taken a shit in three days, a special face I'm sure he reserves for his old war buddies. Like they could have beaten the Kaiser and the Emperor without the Americans to haul their constipated little asses out of trouble." He threw another dirty look in the direction of the perfectly innocuous waiter, who, somewhat startled at the depth of animosity he saw in Leo's face, immediately approached the maitre d'hotel about assigning Leo and his poorly dressed companion to another server.

Placated by this response, Károly glanced around to confirm that no one was within hearing distance. He leaned forward in an obviously conspiratorial manner, which made Leo shudder inwardly at the thought of what he was about to hear.

"Listen, Leo," he said, looking around once more. "That brings me to something I wanted to discuss with you. I have a bit of personal business to attend to while I'm here in Paris." The man then literally licked his lips, like a large animal about to enjoy a defenseless dinner.

"I would like to buy a present for a lady friend," he continued. "A lady friend, you understand, not my wife." He waited for Leo's response, and it was gratifying, as Leo raised his eyebrows and gave him a look that silently rang out both envy and approval.

Imre Károly continued, a big, carnivorous grin replacing the scheming look he'd worn a moment before. "Oh, she is a sweet one. The most fantastic piece of ass you could possibly imagine." He rolled his eyes and made a gesture with his hands as if he were holding two ripe melons. "I'd tell you who she is, but, well, she belongs to someone who would take my nuts home in a little glass jar and feed them to his cat if he found out I knew what his girlfriend's tits looked like. So, until I can arrange to have him eliminated from the competition, I need to be, shall we say, uncharacteristically discreet."

He grinned again. Leo shrugged his shoulders and gave a slight nod of his head to communicate total empathy with this delicate situation. He then quickly signaled the waiter to replenish their drinks. He would need more fortification to make it through this lunch.

"The problem is," Károly, continued, reverting to his conspiratorial tone, "I want to get her a present. Something truly amazing, to knock her right off her cute little high-class ass. In fact, she requested that I buy her something really special for Christmas. You might say she feels she deserves a reward."

"So, are you looking for suggestions?" Leo interjected, hoping to avoid a lengthy description of exactly what services this man expected to get in exchange for his token of affection.

"Christ, no! I know what I want. I saw it yesterday. Trouble is these Goddamn French bastards. I could tell from the moment I walked into the store that no one was taking me seriously. At the time I thought, 'They'll listen to the sound of my money!' But then I said to myself, to hell with it. Why should I give them the satisfaction of knowing I would spend my money there after they pissed on me, so to speak? Besides, the more I thought about it, the better it is if I don't buy the thing myself. Even though we are in Paris, I do have a certain," he grinned again, "notoriety. And, the money is not coming out of," another quick, ugly grin, "my regular salary. Plus," he allowed for an exaggerated pause and leaned back, a look of pure egotism greasing his features, "I *am* a married man, and the present is not going to end up around the neck of the current Mrs. Károly."

"Are you saying that you want me to buy a certain necklace for you?" Leo asked, relieved to be at what seemed like the end of a long and distasteful tale.

"Exactly! I like that in a man. Get right to the point. Look, Bacso tells me you speak French as well as a damn French poodle. You have the look, the carriage, whatever the hell you want to call it. I've seen you in action at the Bristol. You will have those little French pricks kissing your ass the moment you walk in the door. Hell, no one will even know you're not a Frenchman, and a rich one at that, so you might not even get overcharged."

Leo was too disgusted to be flattered. He thought for a moment. The story did actually make some sense. He was not beyond a touch of vanity; he realized that he cut a rather dashing figure at the hotel. He did not own many suits, but the few he had, such as the one he wore today, were custom made for him from the finest fabric available in Budapest. It was possible that Károly had seen him at work; Leo was often too busy to notice everyone who might be in the lobby or the café. Bacso, of course, would have filled Károly in on Leo's language abilities. Perhaps—

"Where is the thing?"

"Cartier."

It took a supreme amount of self-control for Leo not to sputter out his drink. Cartier! What kind of money did this man make? And for what? Extortion? Murder for hire? No wonder he felt out of place walking into one of the most prestigious jewelry houses on the whole continent! Károly must have looked like a pig in church. Leo stifled a laugh as he imagined the faces of the Cartier salespeople when the police chief sauntered in, people to whom snobbery was more than an acquired trait. It was a genetic obsession.

"Why Cartier?" he asked with a smile, hoping the real subject of his mirth remained unclear.

"Because this," replied Károly, with a stab of his finger into the air near Leo's face, "is a Cartier quality cunt." He smiled again, if his barbaric flash of teeth could be called a smile. "Do this favor for me. You won't regret it. We'll have plenty of time to play with the telephonic toys this afternoon, or tomorrow, even."

"Look," said Leo, looking for a way out, "I am not sure that we should be taking care of personal business at a time like this. Maybe it would—" He stopped. He could tell by the cold stare he was receiving that Károly did not appreciate his hesitancy. *That's all I need, to offend the chief of police. Merde! What could it hurt?* Tucking his doubts into a dark, quiet corner of his conscience, Leo agreed to make the purchase after lunch.

It was a short walk back to the Place Vendôme and the Cartier showroom. A block before they reached it, Károly pulled Leo aside and handed him a long rectangular wallet, cut from a type of leather Leo had seen only once in his life. The raised speckles on the skin meant ostrich hide. The wallet itself must have cost a fortune.

"Listen, there should be enough cash in here to pay for the thing. It's a sort of a diamond collar. You can't miss it—it's in the center display case, straight ahead of you as you walk in the door. I'll just meet you back at your hotel at three o'clock. You're at the Hotel Du Louvre, right?"

Leo paused. "Wouldn't you rather just wait here? I could just hand it to you."

Károly shook his head. "I want to inventory the equipment we'll be using. Besides, I trust you." He grinned. "You'd never get out of Paris alive with the money or the necklace if you tried anything stupid."

What a way to win friends. Leo tucked the fat wallet into the breast pocket of his suit and the two men parted. Well, now he was in it—may as well finish the nasty business. As concierge at the Bristol he had brokered many purchases for wealthy guests, some of which, he knew, were not destined for lawful spouses. But he'd met few people as distasteful as Imre Károly.

He walked the short distance to the twin marble columns that adorned the entrance to Cartier's, then rang the buzzer that signaled a request to enter. An answering buzzer advised him that the door was now unlocked. He entered the oak-paneled splendor of the showroom and removed his hat. A guard to the inside right of the doorway gave him a stoic greeting.

The center case, Károly had said—Leo walked straight to the velvet-lined display case in the center of the room. The young, attractive sales associate standing behind it saluted him with a glance that was certainly *not* emotionless.

"Good afternoon, sir. May we show you something special this afternoon?"

"You already have," Leo replied in flawless French. He smiled into her eyes. The woman blushed.

Leo looked down into the display case. There it was. A truly spectacular piece of jewelry, fashioned out of emerald-cut diamonds, each one at least four carats in size. Three rows of them were set end-to-end, side-by-side, in barely visible bezels of pure platinum. The flawless stones claimed and liquefied the light, glimmering with unspeakable brilliance.

The necklace was displayed on a small, truncated sculpture of white marble, resembling a woman's neck and shoulders. He immediately understood why Imre Károly would be so taken with this piece of jewelry. It formed a tight collar, reaching high around the neck. The necklace created an erotic sensation; it conjured up the image of a woman captured by diamonds. The wearer would possess, and yet be possessed by them. Men, seeing that necklace around the neck of a beautiful woman, would instantly wish to see her wearing just the diamonds, and nothing else.

With a slight nod of his head, Leo gestured casually toward the necklace. "This also interests me."

The salesgirl gave him a knowing smile and arched her eyebrows slightly. The erotic implications of that necklace were not lost on anyone. "Of course, sir," she responded in a business-like manner. "One moment, please."

In a few moments a middle-aged gentleman emerged from the doorway that led to the private office where important clients were invited to examine prospective purchases at their leisure. He gave Leo a look of unadulterated Gallic appraisal. Henri Guillaume Xavier, a Cartier employee for fifteen years and Louis Cartier's most trusted sales associate, judged people as quickly and mercilessly as he judged diamonds. Evaluating Leo, he saw in the young man's bearing, dress and countenance the hallmarks of a quality human being, and a wealthy one, at that.

"Bonjour, Monsieur," he greeted Leo, in a crisp but amiable manner. "Henri Xavier at your service. And whom do I have the pleasure of addressing?"

"Jean Pierre Printemps," responded Leo, using the French equivalent of "John Smith." He saw no reason to use his real name. Xavier, who took the name for what it was, a request for privacy, nodded his acknowledgment. "Marie-Therese informs me that you are interested in examining one of our latest pieces, the diamond collar. A most extraordinary piece, as you can see, made of flawless, five-carat emerald-cut stones. It signals a complete break from the Art Nouveau style, reflecting Monsieur Cartier's expanding interest in geometric forms. Unfortunately, Monsieur Cartier is in London at the moment, but I shall be happy to retrieve it for you." With a few deft moves he unlocked the display case and removed the necklace, then placed it carefully in a box lined with black velvet.

With a slight bow Xavier invited his client to his private office, where Leo removed his overcoat and settled comfortably into a low-backed chair. Xavier displayed the necklace in front of him. Like most jewelers, Cartier used special lighting designed to show off the brilliance of the stones. The diamonds sparkled like liquid fire.

"Some champagne sir?"

"No, thank you. A loupe, if you please."

Xavier removed a jeweler's loupe from his pocket and handed it to

Leo. "They are all colorless, and perfect."

Leo gave him a look of polite dismissal. He had only a general idea of what to look for *in* a diamond, but he knew precisely how one should look when looking *at* a diamond. After a few moments of seemingly careful study, he handed the loupe back to Xavier. Both he and Xavier seemed satisfied.

"Beautiful. And the price?"

"Fifty thousand francs."

Leo steeled himself against any reaction. Good God! Was he carrying that kind of money?

"I'll take it."

"Ah, an excellent choice, monsieur. Will you carry it with you, or shall I have it sent?"

"I will take it with me."

"And, the financial arrangements?"

Leo reached into his breast pocket and pulled out the large wallet Károly had given him. He opened it. It contained a stunning quantity of crisp 1,000 franc notes. He began to count them. He reached fifty. To his amazement, there were still several 1,000 franc notes left. Leo nonchalantly redeposited them into the wallet and tucked it back into his breast pocket.

"Merci, monsieur," said Louis Xavier as he handed Leo a velvet box containing the necklace. "I hope that it gives the wearer enormous pleasure."

Leo could not resist. "So do I," he said in a totally deadpan manner as he collected his hat and coat. "It's for my mother." He allowed himself a small smile at the startled look on Xavier's face.

Back on the street, he tried to decide what to do. It was now just past two-thirty. He never would have agreed to be the guardian of the necklace had he known its value, not when the owner was someone like Imre Károly. Once again he wondered how the chief of police could come by such a huge sum. And why would Károly trust him with such a thing? Well, he supposed that Bacso had vouched for him as part of this enterprise. And, of course, he had to be eminently trustworthy to work as head concierge at the Bristol. Still, one could go a long way on fifty thousand francs. Now he understood the significance of Károly's warning: "You'd never get out of Paris alive with the money or the necklace."

Warily, seeing a pickpocket or thief on every corner, Leo nervously made his way back to the hotel. He was a bit concerned that Károly was not waiting in the lobby. After waiting a few moments he approached the young man behind the front desk.

"Good afternoon. Are there any messages for room 415?"

"Just a moment, please, I will check your box." He returned with two envelopes, one embossed with the crest of the Ritz, and the other plain, white and inexpensive.

Leo stepped away from the desk and opened the plain one first. Scrawled in a sloppy hand was a message from Károly. He read the short note:

Leo,
Hope it went well. Seems we have some extra time on our hands. Put my present in the hotel safe. I'll come by tomorrow morning at nine.
Imre Károly

Damn! What was going on? He tore open the second envelope. It was an equally cryptic message from Bacso:

Dear Leo,
Some complications have arisen. Our meeting is to be postponed by one day. Wait for contact from Károly.
Janos

Now what? Leo was getting increasingly suspicious. Something had gone awry, and he was not a party to the details. Well, he was just a peon, albeit a valuable one. Still, the whole situation smelled sour, and Imre Károly's stench was the foulest smell of all.

Leo realized that he did not know how to get in touch with anyone other than Janos Bacso at the Ritz. Surely Janos would enlighten him. No, his note clearly said to wait to be contacted by Károly. *Merde!* Well, at least he would get rid of the damn necklace.

He took a step towards the desk then stopped himself. How could he hand over an item of such tremendous value to the desk clerk at a second rate hotel? He knew how easily a small bribe could open the safe of an unscrupulous establishment. Well, what of it? It was the man's own request. Served him right if the thing were stolen. But no, what was he thinking? If the hotel clerk couldn't come up with that necklace tomorrow, he, Leo, would be a dead man, no matter what the story of its disappearance. Damn! Janos could at least tell him how to find Károly. God, he was going to feel foolish trying to explain this mess to Janos.

Wait! Another idea sprang into his head. He could put the necklace in the house safe at the Ritz. The concierge there would be willing to give him a receipt, for the Ritz was a hotel used to safekeeping important jewelry. Then he could just walk over with Károly tomorrow and get it. He might be angry at first, but he would calm down once the necklace was safely in his hands.

Leo congratulated himself on his plan. With the necklace safely stored at the Ritz, he could enjoy his evening in Paris. Then tomorrow he would see what was going on with the rest of this intrigue, and decline to participate if he found anything not to his liking.

An hour later he was once again headed away from the Place Vendôme, with the Ritz, and the necklace, behind him. Tucked into his shoe, to frustrate the notorious Parisian pickpockets, was a receipt for one diamond necklace, valued at fifty thousand francs. He had pretended to be Janos, and given his room number, plus a generous tip, to the junior concierge. The concierge assured him that, as a guest of the hotel, no one but he would be able to collect the necklace, and that he himself must present the receipt to do so. Of course, the concierge might somehow discover that Leo was not who he claimed to be, but that would not be sufficient reason not to turn over the necklace once he had allowed it into the safe.

Feeling confident that he'd put his troubles of the moment behind him, Leo sauntered back up the Rue de la Paix, towards the opera. It was too late to tackle the Louvre today, but he could walk up the Champs Elyseé and sightsee for a while.

As he passed the grand facade of the Madeleine, he remembered the café that had caught his eye the previous day. There it was: Angeline's. He decided that a hot drink would suit him, and headed over to it.

Upon entering, Leo was struck by how similar the interior of this café was to that of The New York, in far-away Budapest. Tall gilt-edged mirrors covered the walls. Angels and nymphs created a Belle Époque pageant along the edge of the ceiling, the center of which was covered with a mural, depicting an idyllic day in a rural Roman paradise. Ornate wrought iron chairs partnered dainty marble-topped tables. At the front of the shop was a small counter, where the delicacies of the day were displayed, to help the indecisive make up their minds, or allow hurried patrons to pick up a treat to take along with them.

Leo chose a seat near the huge front window and ordered a hot chocolate. At four-thirty the winter sun was already fading. Matrons passed by, with long, crusty baguettes tucked under their arms, scarves or berets covering their heads, as they made their way home to prepare the evening meal. Businessmen, their long black coats flapping behind them, walked in pairs, buried deep in conversation concerning currency trades and the price of sugar beets. Children pranced along in cheerful clusters, full of plans for Christmas, the plaid fabric of their school uniforms peeking out from under their short winter coats. After just two days, Leo could tell that he liked Paris. He liked the fervent, free rhythm of the city. He could see himself living here.

A young woman approached the window. Leo sat up straight. He caught her eye briefly, but she immediately, modestly, looked away.

Leo was used to seeing beautiful women, and he was used to having beautiful women look back at him. But the sight of this particular young woman sent little pulses of pleasurable excitement radiating through his whole body.

Like a good tourist, she was reading the menu posted outside before coming in. Leo was fumbling for pocket change, to pay his bill quickly in case he had to follow her down the street in order to meet her, when she passed through the café's double glass door. She moved with unconscious grace over to the front counter, and studied the temptations spread out under the glass.

Leo left his table and walked towards the counter, until he stood just behind her. Her head barely cleared his chin. He could tell that she was petite by the way her simply-cut camel hair coat draped the curves of her body, without clinging to it anywhere. Amber-gold hair peeked out from under her cloche hat, and curled against the base of her neck. He fought an impulse to kiss her right where the escaped ringlets rested.

The young woman sensed someone close behind her. Without turning she pointed to a plate of small, golden, rectangular tea cakes, which Leo had already learned were named in honor of the church that adorned the square in front of the café.

"What are these?" she asked politely. The words were French, but the accent was distinctly German. As she finished her sentence, she looked back over her left shoulder to catch Leo's response, and jumped slightly when she saw he was not a waiter.

"Those are called madeleines. Very tasty," Leo answered in French with a hint of amusement. "Would you care for one? Just come this way."

She smiled. It was a smile that began gradually, like the morning sun peeking over the horizon. By the time its full brilliance hit Leo, he was mesmerized. Her smile transformed her face from beautiful to radiant.

He could not help but smile back. Grasping her small gloved hand as if he were escorting her to the dance floor, he led her back to his table.

"Oh, but you've already finished your chocolate," she said with dismay, as Leo pulled out a chair for her to sit down.

"Oh, no, I have not finished—anything. In fact, I would say, I've just begun. We have just begun. Won't you please join me?"

She hesitated. Leo sensed her unease, and came around to stand behind her, placing a hand on each of her delicate shoulders. He bent down and whispered to her, his mouth nearly touching her ear, each word full of tremulous emotion.

"Please, won't you join me?"

She sat down.

Leo took the seat across from her, trying not to stare as she removed her arms from her coat, and anchored it over the back of her chair. God, she was beautiful. Her face was truly, splendidly heart-shaped. Her emerald green eyes, greener than spring, were punctuated with flecks of gold. Her amber hair glowed.

He extended his hand across the small table. "Leo Hoffman."

"Martha—Martha Levy," she responded, touching his hand for no more than a fraction of a second. There was something achingly familiar in how she moved, something haunting about her smile, yet Leo knew he had never seen her before. *In what dream have we met?*

He noticed the green guidebook she put down on the table as she removed her gloves.

"So, you are visiting Paris for the first time?" he asked politely, still speaking in French.

"Yes." Her German accent once again betrayed her origins.

"What do you like best so far?"

"The people."

Leo laughed. "That's unusual. The French do not have a reputation for making visitors feel welcome."

"Aren't you French?"

"No. No. I'm Hungarian."

"Hungarian! But you speak with no accent!"

"No, I speak French with a French accent, as opposed to a Hungarian one. And you are German, correct?"

Martha blushed. "You can take the girl out of Bavaria..."

"Bavaria? Is that where you come from?"

"Yes. I live in Munich. I'm here for a two-week vacation. I've been going to the University in Munich, but next semester I want to take some time off from school, to work for a while. I thought I should come to see Paris now, before I find a job, because otherwise it might be some time before I can travel.... I'm sorry, I really am prattling on."

Leo shook his head. "No, it's alright. I want to know. In fact, I want to know—everything about you. Do you have any brothers and sisters? How many pairs of shoes do you own? Do you take sugar in your coffee? What's your favorite color?"

Now it was Martha's turn to laugh. "Do you always interrogate your new acquaintances this way?" she asked, randomly flipping through the guidebook to give her fingers something to do. She heard herself talking, but it was like listening to someone else, someone far away, whose voice did not matter. She knew that her cheeks must be flushed, and her eyes must seem too bright, for there was a bonfire raging inside her.

How could this happen? What was there about this man, about meeting this man, that instantly reduced the eighteen years of her life to a meaningless period of waiting, of waiting for this moment, the moment when she came alive? She knew he had awakened her somehow with his smile – that incredible, disarming smile. That smile that was an invitation. She fought not to reach across the table and touch him, to touch his arm, to stroke his forehead, to trace the shape of his delicious mouth. She knew that touching him would be her undoing.

"Oh, look!" she cried, impulsively, attempting to steer the conversation to safe ground, "Here is a description of the beautiful church across from here—the Madeleine. Why, that's the same—"

"Name as the little tea cakes. I assure you it's not a coincidence. Shall we order some?"

"If you wish," she answered, glancing up at him. Then she put her nose back in the book and began to read aloud.

"'A magnificent example of neoclassical architecture, the Church of Mary Magdalene was begun in 1812 by the Emperor Napoleon, as a monument to the victories of his Grand Army. After Napoleon was overthrown, the building was consecrated as a church.'"

She looked up. "Ironic, isn't it, how war and arrogance can give birth to such beauty?"

For the first time in his life, Leo gazed into the face of an attractive woman, and did not see a reflection of how she saw him, or a suggestion of what she wanted him to be. He saw only Martha, exuding a blend of confidence and innocence that struck him as the perfect expression of femininity. He suddenly remembered the silly story of the Rigo Jancsi torte, about a princess who had run off with a gypsy. Now it made sense. The *coup de foudre*. The lightning bolt. Something more than love at first sight. More than being swept off your feet. It was this: the total, inescapable seizure of your heart and soul by another person. Surely she felt it, too. She had to. The flush on her cheeks. The way she looked at him, while trying not to look at him. She was his. She was his already. He knew it.

He tried to soak in what she was saying, as he asked her question after question. She was staying with an old school friend of her father's, and his wife, in their apartment on the Rue de Babylon. She had an older sister, who went to graduate school in Graz, in Austria, and would remain at school over the winter break, to study for her comprehensive exams. Her father was a professor. She planned to be back in Munich in time for Christmas.

"Perhaps we should go?" he proposed, as she finished her last sip of coffee.

"Of course," she stammered, deliberately misunderstanding him, "I should go."

Wordlessly Leo stood up, came around the small table, and pulled Martha's chair out for her. She rose quickly, accepting his help with her coat, but preparing to bolt. She knew that she had to leave, now. She had to flee, to run back out into the street, to escape this tall, handsome man, with his astonishing blue eyes and hypnotic smile.

"Well, it was a pleasure meeting you," she said lightly. "Thank you for the coffee. If you're ever in Munich—"

But she could not finish. He was looking at her with those eyes. She was going to drown in those eyes. She instructed her feet to back away, but her body would not listen. Then his hands were touching her face, cupping both her checks, tilting her face upwards as he brought his lips closer to hers.

Leo wanted to devour her, all of her, then and there, but they were surrounded by far too many amused French eyes pretending not to watch them. All he could do was touch her lips with his own. It was a painfully brief kiss, a consummation and a genesis, and it left them both aching with the taste of unquenched passion. They gazed at each other, the power of their attraction enveloping them like a shared baptism.

"Don't you understand," he said with quiet intensity, his face still only millimeters away from hers, "don't you understand that I will never, never let you go?"

Martha nodded, her chin barely moving.

"Say yes," he insisted gently. "I need to hear you say it."

"Yes," she answered faintly. "Yes."

"Then come with me." Like the earth pulling itself away from the gravitational force of the sun, Leo forced himself to pull away from Martha's face. They gathered up their things and left the café.

It was not quite dark by the time they emerged. Leo put his arm through Martha's, protectively, and thought about where they should go next. His hotel room was out of the question. He did not want to risk running into any of the men he was with. Where could they go? This was Paris! He thought of the thousand franc notes still in his pocket. The price of the necklace had just gone up by one thousand francs. After all, he had rendered the man a service. He was entitled to a commission. If that cretin questioned him, Leo would explain that the extra thousand was a special luxury tax. Leo could not think of consequences beyond tonight, beyond this moment, beyond his tremendous need to be with Martha, *now*.

He stopped and turned to look at her.

"Listen," he said earnestly. "Martha, if you did not make it home tonight, would you be missed?"

"No," she lied. She knew why he was asking, and lied because she had to be with him. She could not bear to be separated from him, not for one moment, until he had become hers, truly and completely hers. She had a key. There was always the chance that her hosts would not wait up for her. If they did, well, she would face the consequences tomorrow.

He explained briefly that there were people he knew staying at his hotel, and that he did not want to compromise her reputation by taking her there. They needed privacy. He'd seen a place near Notre Dame...it was not far away....

A welcoming fire flickered in the fireplace of the small, handsome lobby, where Leo signed them in under a false name as Mr. and Mrs., swearing to himself that he would make the title genuine as quickly as possible. The well-dressed matron working the desk listened sympathetically to Leo's sincere tale of luggage lost by an idiotic porter who stupidly reloaded their bags back onto a connecting train.

"Oh, and on your honeymoon, too," she clucked, making change for the large note Leo had given her and handing him a key.

"How did you know it was our honeymoon?" Leo asked, taken aback.

"*Cheri*, if it is not, it should be. In all my years behind this desk, I have learned to recognize love. You are positively glowing with it."

Hours later they lay lightly sleeping, their bodies intertwined. Leo awoke before Martha, and marveled again at the exquisite curves of her body. He studied her full breasts, with their golden, upturned nipples, the generous curve of her tiny waist, and the shapely form of her athletic legs. The memory of her passionate eagerness, even given the pain she felt initially, made him want to rouse her again. The question of her virginity had been irrelevant. They had stripped and clawed at each other like tigers, unwilling, no, unable to wait, before consuming each other.

Leo ran his fingers lightly down Martha's back to waken her. The stunning green eyes opened, and she smiled.

"Hello, Mrs. Hoffman."

"Mrs. Hoffman! Not yet, I'm not."

"Well, if you aren't, you soon will be. Besides, I feel like you already are."

"Is that a proposal?"

Leo laughed, a warm, rippling sound full of contentment.

"My darling, I adore you. Anything I do not know about you does not matter. Will you marry me?"

"Leo, you're speaking German."

"Do you have an objection to being proposed to in your native language?"

"Darling, you could propose to me in Swahili and I would still say yes."

"Do you speak Swahili?"

She giggled. "Wouldn't you be amazed if I said yes? But, sadly, no. I am limited to the more practical, European tongues, of German, French, and a little English."

"Ah! Well, that is convenient. I speak German and English, too."

"And French. And Hungarian. Or did you leave your native country before you learned to talk?"

"Enough! Foolish woman. Are you hungry?"

Martha extricated her limbs from Leo's body with exaggerated slowness, then sat up on her knees and looked at him defiantly. "I am not foolish," she said huffily, arranging their bedraggled bed sheets around her primly. "I am, however, very hungry, and will permit you to escort me to dinner."

"With pleasure, my treasure. Luckily we are near the Latin Quarter and ten o'clock is still a perfectly acceptable time to go searching for a meal."

They dressed like playful children, snatching each other's clothes and chasing each other around the room. Leo had trouble getting Martha to stifle her laughter long enough to make a calm exit from the hotel under the knowing eye of the patroness behind the desk.

They crossed the bridge that connected the island with the Left Bank. The Seine ran dark underneath them, glistening in the night like liquid silk. Hand in hand they strolled along the narrow streets of the Rive Gauche, tempted by the jazz in this restaurant, the smell of potatoes frying in that one, finally settling on a small café that offered "rabbits stewed until midnight."

"What if the rabbit can't stay awake that long?" Martha asked innocently.

Leo grinned. "Oh, tender-hearted one, worry a little less about *le pauvre lapin* and a little more about what wine you would like to drink," he suggested, tapping her lightly on the hand with the wine list.

"Oh, no violence, if you please, honorable sir, or I shall reconsider my response to your proposal."

He turned serious. "Martha, please don't say that. Don't even tease me. I could not bear the thought of losing you, of not spending my life with you."

The expression on Leo's face made Martha regret her flippant comment. She picked up his right hand, brought it to her lips, tenderly kissed his palm, then nestled his palm against her cheek. After a moment he withdrew his hand and lightly brushed a strand of hair away from her face.

"When can we get married?"

"Well, I suppose you have to meet my father."

"Suppose I come home with you?"

"Now?"

"In a few days."

"Now that's what I call a special souvenir from Paris."

"If you like, I'll tattoo a tiny Eiffel tower on my chest. Just a small one, though."

"Don't you have a job to get back to?"

"I do have a job. You are speaking, Madame, to the head concierge of the Bristol Hotel in Budapest. But I don't have to be back until the day after Christmas."

"Delighted to make your acquaintance. Shall we live in Budapest when we get married?"

"We can live wherever you like. Have dictionary, will travel."

"That's rather daring."

"Yes, it is. But I am feeling rather daring right now. Ah! Here comes the rabbit stew. Bon Appetit!"

They ate in silence for a few moments, each contemplating the enormity of the change that had swept through their lives.

"All because I went to investigate a plate of madeleines," murmured Martha, awed by what had happened to her in the past few hours.

"I have news for you, my dear. I was prepared to chase you down the street if necessary. I could tell through the window that you were the one for me."

"Seriously?"

"Uh-huh. Must have had something to do with the way you wrinkled up your nose when you were reading the menu. Much like what you're doing right now."

"Hmmm. Now it's the cheese tray I'm considering."

"Oh, yes, the glorious cheeses of France. I tell you, we Hungarians eat well, very well, but I believe the French have superior cheese."

"And wine."

Leo adopted a wounded look. "Obviously spoken by someone who does not know Hungarian wine. We can rectify that. Why, with the exception of champagne—"

"Wait! Isn't that then the exception that swallows the rule?"

"Now that you mention it, that is the one thing this evening is lacking. Waiter! Champagne. The best you have."

Glasses filled, Leo raised his to Martha. "My darling, this is the best

I can give you now, but I promise better things in the future. No! Don't interrupt. Listen. I promise to love, honor, and cherish you, and to create the life for you of which you are worthy. Just believe in me."

She tapped her glass against his. "I do believe in you."

Leo watched two, thin parallel lines of bubbles dance from the bottom of his glass to the top. He had so much to tell Martha, so much to share with her, so many things he wanted to do for her. He would need a lifetime.

⊛

Seven hours later the morning burst upon them, cold and clear, for in their haste to get back to bed they had forgotten to close the heavy interior curtains in their room. They made love one more time before rising, with the slow, synchronized rhythm of lovers willing to explore each other without reservation.

This time they dressed wordlessly, communing in the shared privacy of their last moments together before they faced the outside world again.

"Can I bring you back to where you are staying?" he asked as they left the hotel.

She shook her head and smiled. "No, I think not. But when will I see you again?"

Leo pondered this for a moment. He did not know what his day would be like, or how much time his activities would take. The actual negotiations would not take place until tomorrow.

"Martha, I am desperately sorry to say that I have a business meeting. It concerns a new career opportunity for me. I'm sure, though, that I can get free by tonight. Shall we say five o'clock at Angeline's?"

Martha tried not to pout. Five o'clock seemed like several lifetimes away.

They walked to the taxi stand in the square across from the Notre Dame cathedral, where he kissed her, and kissed her again, and kissed her again, unable to make himself let go. Laughing, she pushed him away and jumped into a taxi, blowing him kisses as the driver sped away.

He watched until the cab lost itself in the teeming hive of the early morning traffic, then he started back to his own hotel. Damn! He had forgotten to ask her for her phone number. No matter. Nothing could keep him from being at Angeline's this afternoon.

He was passing a kiosk on the corner of Rue de Rivoli and Rue de St. Martin when a headline caught his eye. *Wait, what does that say?* He fished in his pocket for a franc and tossed the coin to the man at the newsstand, snatching up a copy of *Le Monde* and folding it under his arm without waiting for his change. He stumbled into the closest café where he unthinkingly ordered an espresso and opened the paper. In bold letters he saw spread across the front page:

FRAUD AT THE HAGUE!
HUNGARIAN OFFICER CAUGHT PASSING FALSE FRANCS!

With a heavy feeling in the pit of his stomach, Leo read the article:

A Hungarian army officer, Ion Kovacs, was arrested yesterday after attempting to cash a counterfeit 1,000 franc note at the central bank of the Hague. The clerk who accepted it noticed subtle differences between the counterfeit note and the other, genuine notes in his currency stack. The astute clerk notified the guards immediately, who were able to intercept Kovacs before he left the building.

The quality of the forgery has given rise to fears that this counterfeit scheme may be perpetrated on an international scale. Police in Belgium, France, England, Liechtenstein and Switzerland are already cooperating in an intensive investigation. Merchants and money changers accepting French francs are warned to verify the authenticity of all large bills before accepting them. Any discrepancy should be immediately reported to the police.

Leo dropped the paper onto the café table as if it had burned him. How could he have been so stupid? Now he knew where Károly had obtained his money: from a printing press.

He glanced at the clock on the wall of the café. It was not quite eight o'clock. Cartier would not open for another two hours, but they might already know they'd been duped. Were the police looking for him already?

Panic rose like bile in his throat. He could give the necklace back. He could explain. He would turn Károly in.

No, the French distrusted the entire Hungarian nation. They would thank him for his information, call him a liar and a coward, and he would still go to jail. For a very long time.

His disoriented brain tried to think of other alternatives. He could try to negotiate a deal with Károly. He would give the bastard the necklace in exchange for his own freedom. He would disappear. For now his life mattered. His continued existence was no longer a cosmic joke. He had found Martha.

Martha! He had no way of getting in touch with her. He would have to find somewhere to hide until five o'clock. No, first he must meet with Károly. He needed a plan. Good God, were Janos and the others in on this scheme, too? Had he been the patsy from the outset?

He threw some change on the table to pay for his untouched coffee and went back into the street, pulling his hat low over his forehead. He would probably be safe at the hotel until Károly showed up at nine, for he had paid for his room himself. There was no reason for anyone at the hotel to connect him with Jean Pierre Printemps. Unless, of course, a physical description of him was already being circulated to the public. Probably not. Even if Cartier's had already discovered the counterfeit notes, the management would probably insist on a minimum of publicity. He would have to risk that much.

Within a few minutes he was back at the hotel, relieved to see that Károly was not already waiting for him in the lobby, for he needed time to collect his thoughts, to come up with a plan. He ignored the elevator and sprinted up the four flights of stairs to his room, his adrenaline pumping full force.

Leo burst into the room and sat down on the small single bed, head in his hands. *Now think! Think about how to save yourself!*

Károly's voice interrupted the silence. "Well, you little Jewish bastard, where have you been all night?"

Leo stood and turned to face Károly, who was stepping out from behind the door to the room, the door that Leo had not even bothered to close. Károly did so, and locked it. It was then that Leo noticed the gun in his hand.

Károly came closer, until he was standing just on the opposite side of the bed from Leo. His face wore the sneer of a coward in complete possession of unearned power.

"So, tried my lovely necklace on the neck of a little French whore, did you?" Leo did not respond.

"You had better answer me, pretty little Jew boy. The necklace isn't in the hotel safe. Where is it?"

"You set me up."

Károly chortled, an ugly, rasping sound. "So you've heard the news! Well, we managed to change thousands of francs before Kovacs let himself get caught. *Of course* I set you up, you cocksucking fool. You executed the biggest single trade we accomplished." Visibly gloating, he shared the full extent of his triumph with his victim.

"Imagine Janos Bacso's surprise when I showed up yesterday in Paris and told him that his brilliant interpreter, the man who was nearly his son-in-law, is in reality a vile, untrustworthy Jew. You can see how embarrassing it was for him, to have recruited *your* assistance in the purchase of arms for our organization. Luckily I brought a suitable replacement."

He chortled again, and then continued, his voice filling with grandiose self-importance. "Janos was only too pleased to allow me to persuade you to help us in other ways. The cash we are raising, the guns we are buying, they're not going to aid the spineless military who allowed the dogs of Europe to rape our country. We are fortifying the future rulers of Hungary, the men who have the strength of will to reclaim the Empire!"

Gombos. It all made sense now. Appalling sense. Gombos and his fascist terrorists were behind the entire operation.

Károly grinned, the barbaric, heinous grin that was to haunt Leo for the rest of his life. Then the grin disappeared.

"Where's the necklace?"

Leo felt the receipt for the necklace burning a hole into his foot. "It's not here."

"You expect me to believe that? Take off your coat and throw it to me." Leo did as he was told.

"Now your jacket." Leo complied.

"Now turn your pockets inside out." Without pointing the gun away from Leo's chest, Károly spread Leo's clothes on the bed and searched them with one hand. He found nothing but the wallet he had given to Leo, Leo's wallet, and Leo's passport. He angrily tossed them onto the floor.

It was obvious that the man was losing control. *Good,* Leo thought. *Get angry. An angry man does not think clearly.* He must goad Károly into making a mistake.

"You can't just shoot me here in broad daylight."

"Oh really? It takes time for bystanders to react. By the time anyone realizes a shot has been fired, I'll be gone. In fact, I'll enjoy shooting you. I'll get nearly as much pleasure out of shooting you as I did out of shooting your communist pig friends in their villa on Andrassy."

The villa. It was now the property of the Ministry of the Treasury. Counterfeiting. Of course. He was looking at the man who'd assassinated József and Erzsebet. A horrifying numbness overcame Leo as the full implication of Károly's words hit him.

Then the reaction set in.

Black rage poured out from behind the closed door in his soul, filling his muscles with violent power. Hatred replaced the blood in his veins. Nothing existed beyond his need to avenge their deaths. Leo stood, motionless, poised to kill. He knew how to kill a man with his bare hands. The war had taught him that much.

Károly was still talking. "Alright, you stinking Jew, this is your last chance. Tell me where the necklace is, or I will start breaking pieces of you off until I find it, starting with your well-used testicles."

"It's in a safe place," Leo said through clenched teeth. As he spoke he shifted his gaze a fraction, almost imperceptibly, down towards the bed and then back to Károly's eyes. *Look away, bastard. Look away for just one second.*

Erzsebet's killer stepped into the trap. Keeping the gun pointed at

Leo, he leaned over slightly and awkwardly tried to pull up the side of the mattress with one hand.

Using the bed as a springboard Leo came at him, lunging across the small bed with the speed and strength of a creature from hell. His raised forearm caught Károly full in the throat, pinning him to the wall. The man had no time to cry out, for the force of Leo's blow crushed his larynx. His stunned reflexes were unable to fire a shot. Leo went for the gun, snapping two of Károly's fingers as he twisted the weapon out of the murderer's hand.

Leo saw the pain and terror in the small man's eyes, and he exulted in it. With one push he shoved Károly face first onto the bed, then, lifting the gun high in the air, smashed the metal butt into his skull. Again. And again, until the sight of blood oozing from the back of the dead man's head brought him to his senses.

He became aware, first, of the heavy quickness of his own breath, as if he'd just awakened from a nightmare. Looking at Károly's lifeless body, Leo felt no fear, and no remorse, only a vague sense of having finished an exhausting task. As the power of his malice drained away from his body, Leo started to tremble uncontrollably. He leaned against the wall to steady himself. He looked down. His pants and shirt were spattered with blood. Quickly he removed his shoes, took out the receipt from the Ritz, then stripped off the rest of his clothes. He then used a corner of his shirt sleeve to wipe his fingerprints from the gun. He left the gun, and the wallet with the counterfeit notes, on the bed beside the corpse.

A knock! He reeled towards the door. The chamber maid's worried voice floated in from the hallway.

"Sir? Are you alright? Is everything alright?"

Leo snatched a towel from the wash basin and wrapped it around his waist. He composed his features and unlocked the door, opening it a fraction wider than was decent given his nakedness, using his body to block the woman's view into the room.

"Yes?" He gave her a devastating smile, designed to make her think that the sight of her at his door brought a special joy to his day. The homely girl blushed.

"I thought—there was a noise—you're in no trouble?" she stammered, still flushed.

"Oh, I am so sorry! This is so embarrassing. I fell out of bed. Can you imagine?" His smile invited her to use her imagination for other things as well. "I guess I'm just too big for a small bed. I hope the noise of my hitting the floor did not disturb you."

"Ah, no, sir, it is the man in the room downstairs."

"Oh, please give him my most sincere apology, will you? I'll be checking out today so it certainly will not happen again." Another smile, this one requesting her assistance, telling her she was the only one in the world who could help him with so important a matter.

"Of course, sir. I will explain, sir."

"Thank you." He smiled once more. She melted. He closed the door.

How much time did he have? He could not leave the hotel in a way that would arouse any suspicion. He whipped a razor across his beard, put on a fresh suit of clothes, threw the remainder of his things in his suitcase. After pausing a moment he wrapped his blood-stained clothes in a towel and tossed that in, too. He would have to get rid of them later. He took a few more seconds to wipe the wash basin, the desk, the doorknobs, anything else he had probably touched during the one night he had stayed there.

Before leaving he took an extra blanket from the small closet and covered Károly's body, tossing two pillows over his head, so that anyone glancing in might not be tempted to investigate the rumpled bed linen immediately. He retrieved his coat, wallet, and passport from the floor, put the Ritz receipt in his wallet, and left the room, pulling on his gloves and then carefully locking the door behind him. Now, at least, the police would have to rely on descriptions of him. Thank God he had registered under an alias.

The hopelessness of his situation struck him as he made his way downstairs. Fighting panic, he casually turned in his key and left the hotel, blinking in the bright winter sunlight. Where could he go? What could he do? At any moment the police could be after him, for counterfeiting and for murder. He took out his wallet and examined its contents. He had enough money to get out of Paris, for he still had the better part of a thousand francs from the note he had changed yesterday, at the hotel where he had stayed with Martha. Martha! He could not think of her now. It would break him.

But where could he go? Not back to Budapest. Leo was sure Károly had boasted about his plans. Gombos' men would kill him as soon as he returned to Hungary. Within hours, within minutes, he would be a hunted criminal throughout Europe. How could his life go from blissful to desperate in a few moments? Where could he go, without proper papers, that would be far enough away from all that had happened in the past two days, for him to start over somehow, to create a future that could still include Martha?

And then, the solution came to him. But it meant retrieving the necklace.

Moving as if in a trance, willing himself to walk forward, he made it to the Ritz. If word was out, if the concierge at the Ritz had connected his necklace with the one purchased with counterfeit notes at Cartier, the police would already be there waiting for him. It was a chance he had to take.

Taking a deep breath, he strolled into the Ritz lobby, displaying a calmness he did not feel. He could not believe it was just now nine o'clock. Luckily, the same concierge who had helped him yesterday was on duty this morning.

"Ah, good morning Monsieur Bacso," said the young man affably, gesturing to Leo's luggage. "Checking out, I see?"

Leo nodded. He handed the receipt to the concierge, who politely excused himself. An eternity passed. The young man returned. He handed the velvet case back to Leo.

"It's an exquisite piece. Even around here, one is not privileged to see jewelry of such loveliness very often." Leo nodded again. Speech was beyond him. He left the hotel.

❦

At three o'clock that afternoon, a junior detective from the French Ministry of the Treasury was engaged in the monotonous chore of reviewing the concierge's records at the Ritz to see whether, by chance, any of the establishment's guests had stored a particular diamond necklace in the hotel vault. It was a tedious, dead-end task, but his supervisor had ordered him not to leave a single stone unturned, and Claude Boulanger was a man who obeyed orders.

His heart began to race when he found an entry made the previous afternoon, checking in a diamond collar valued at fifty thousand francs. Quickly, he confirmed with the front desk that the guest in question was still registered at the hotel. By God, this would make his career! He picked up a telephone, his fingers trembling with excitement, and placed a call to his supervising officer.

"Hello, Captain Bossard? Lieutenant Boulanger here. I have found something very interesting. I suggest you order the immediate arrest of Mr. Janos Bacso, a Hungarian national currently staying at the Ritz in the Place Vendôme."

At five o'clock, a waiter at Angeline's glanced repeatedly at the door, waiting for a particular girl to enter. He would normally have refused the role of courier, but the size of the tip pressed upon him by the desperate-looking, dark-haired gentleman, and the description of the girl to whom he was to deliver the note, made him change his mind. Ah! That must be the one. He waited for the beautiful woman to be seated, then with all the elegance he could muster from his short, stocky frame, he handed the letter to her.

A minute later he regretted it, regretted it with every ounce of his romantic Gallic blood. What bastard would make a woman cry like that? What dirty bastard would do that to such a beautiful woman? Why, the bastard should be taken out and shot!

Late that night, Leo Hoffman left the train station in Marseille, hired a cab to take him to a dock at the bustling port, and boarded a ship bound for Shanghai.

CHAPTER 6

THE GIRLFRIEND

❦

MUNICH, 1925

Martha leaned her head back against the firm, worn leather of her seat, and tried not to think.

The words that he'd written found a rhythm in the cadence of the train's steady movement as it rolled along the tracks. "Please trust me," the steel wheels murmured. Please trust me. Please trust me. Please trust me. Martha lifted her head slightly and shook it, desperate to dislodge the unbidden words from her brain. Still they haunted her. Please trust me. Please trust me. Please trust me.

The Great War had given Martha's entire generation an early introduction to sorrow, and she was no exception. Martha lost her mother during the winter of 1919, at the age of twelve. Although it was influenza and not a soldier's bullet that had killed Ruth Levy, Martha would never shake her conviction that the war had contributed to her Mother's death. By the winter of 1919, the residents of Munich had insufficient coal to warm their houses, insufficient food to warm their bellies, and insufficient faith to warm their spirits. Martha believed that her mother had died from the cold that the war brought to them all.

She had mourned her mother, long and deeply. But nothing had ever prepared her for the pain she felt rip through her as she read Leo's letter. She had anchored her soul in his, only to have the promise of a lifetime of fulfillment jeopardized by a few hastily written words.

Please trust me. Please trust me. Please trust me. The words continued to taunt her. How could she trust him? The whole scenario was so far-fetched. Martha had promised herself not to read the note again until she arrived in Munich. Now she broke that promise, digging the crumpled and tear-stained piece of paper out from the bottom of her purse. Looking at the page served no real purpose, however, for every word was burned into her brain. It carried this message:

My Darling Martha,

I don't expect you to understand this; all I can ask is that you trust me. Please trust me. I cannot meet you. I have already left Paris. I have betrayed some powerful people, who were doing something illegal, and am now in great danger. You would be threatened, too, if you were with me, and I cannot allow that.

I think I know of a place where we can live the life that we tasted last night. It may take me a while to get there, and it may be some time before I can send for you. But I swear that I will. Please trust me. Please wait for me. I cannot live without you.

I know that this note will bring you tremendous pain, and for that I am desperately sorry. I dare not ask your forgiveness. I can only tell you that I adore you. Please hold onto that.

Forever yours,
  Leo

What could have happened? Whom could he have betrayed? Were the police after him? Was he really, this moment, fleeing for his life? Who was this man she had fallen in love with?

She tried to think about all this in a practical, realistic way, the way her sister Bernice would. The way her father would want her to. Obviously, this was an untenable situation. When he contacts her, why, she can decide what to do, after hearing his explanation. If he does not, well, then she would go on with her life. They were together for only one day, after all. Only one night, really.

The self-imposed lecture did not help. She could not think the way Bernice and her father did, with their ability to apply logic to every situation. She could not square, with logic, her abandonment by Leo with the love she had seen in his eyes, and the love she had felt in his arms. She knew the words he'd written must be true, terrifyingly true; otherwise the truth of the words he'd spoken to her during their night together would be in doubt. Her heart would not allow her to harbor any doubts about the depth and sincerity of his love.

One night. A volcano explodes and destroys an entire countryside in one night. A hurricane rushes ashore and destroys an entire island in one night. An earthquake hits and destroys an entire city in one night. For Martha, Leo was a typhoon, a volcano, an earthquake. She could not just go on with her life as if she had not met him. She had to believe that he meant what he said. She had to believe that he would find her. She had to hope that his explanation would be one that she could live with.

She had to trust him. Or her life would not be worth living.

It had been too difficult to stay in Paris once he was gone. On the morning she and Leo parted, Martha had been able to let herself in to her host's apartment without being discovered. This had, at least, spared her the embarrassment of a confrontation that would surely have eventually involved her father. After buzzing through that morning like an intoxicated bee, Martha collapsed for a long nap in the afternoon. When she awoke, she explained to her puzzled hostess, Madame Bernard, that she had been late coming in the previous night because she had run into a college classmate. Martha told the slightly skeptical Parisian matron that she planned to go out with her friend again that night, for dinner, and would probably be out late again; in fact she might even spend the night with her friend and her parents at their hotel in the Latin Quarter. Normally uncomfortable with deception,

Martha found it easier to lie in a foreign tongue. One could blame one's awkwardness on the language.

The friendly old couple was surprised to see their lovely guest return that same evening, a scant two hours after her sunny departure. She shuffled through their front door, face puffy and eyes swollen, complaining that she did not feel well. Madame Bernard, always worried about the flu in December, hustled the drained and weary Martha off to bed, where the exhausted girl stayed the entire next day. Martha then announced that she wanted to go home.

The fretful woman quickly sent a cable to Martha's father, explaining that his daughter did not feel well. "No fever, no vomiting; not very ill, but wants to come home. Will arrive tomorrow mid-morning," she wrote. Fortunately, it was not a difficult trip: one overnight express from Paris, and a change of trains in Stuttgart. She could sleep most of the way.

To herself, the astute little Frenchwoman thought the girl looked heartsick, but she dared not share *that* diagnosis with Martha's father, or with her own husband, who had known Martha's father since they were both in school many years ago. The possibility was both plausible and perplexing. When could she have—? How—? Well, this was Paris, after all. She only hoped that Martha's tender young heart had not been too badly damaged. And, she hoped that Martha would get home before the young man showed up on their doorstep to apologize. The lady of the house did not want to witness any romantic upheavals. She had lost both of her sons in the war, and had faced more than enough trauma in her own life. She did not wish to share anyone else's. She no longer had the energy for it. She would help Martha pack her bags and keep her theories to herself.

Martha's train arrived in Munich only slightly delayed by the copious quantities of snow that poured from the sky during every Bavarian winter. As she descended the stairs to the platform, Martha was touched by the worried look she saw on her father's normally impassive face.

David Levy's heritage was Jewish, but his family had lived for ten generations in Frankfurt, and he was as German as any Prussian. A teaching post at the University brought him to Munich when he was in his early twenties, and he had met and married his wife in the refreshing atmosphere of the Alpine air. Yet he had remained essentially unaffected by the more open Bavarian way of life. David Levy had never felt comfortable operating on an emotional level. The greater the crisis, the calmer his approach. But today, he was obviously relieved to see his youngest daughter, and Martha appreciated the fact that his concern, for once, was transparent.

If anyone had ever been bold enough to ask Professor Levy which of his two daughters was his favorite, he would have said he loved them both equally. In fact, in his heart, he knew that this was not true. Bernice was his eldest. He was often startled by how closely her thoughts tracked his own, and reassured by how easily they understood each other. She lacked the flighty nature of most women, and knew that cool-headed reasoning was the key to handling any problem. She also understood the futility of tears and the discomfort they caused men, so she rarely resorted to them. She would never be a beauty; her plain features too closely resembled his own. David Levy knew in his heart that he loved Bernice more, for she had been the perfect child for him to raise. She had been so easy.

Yet it was Martha to whom he felt the greater responsibility, precisely because she always seemed balanced on the edge of some harrowing danger, from climbing up on tables as a toddler, to escaping from the house to watch the Palm Sunday riots in the spring of 1919, during the short-lived reign of the "Bavarian Soviet Republic." One could never be sure what the child would try next.

These past five years had been particularly challenging, for her mother's death had initiated Martha's adolescence, and David Levy was ill-equipped to deal with the tears and the tirades she seemed unable to control. But somehow, through it all, he knew that Martha loved him, and it was a love that filled him with awe.

His wife's love had always made him feel inadequate, for he had never known how to return it. When Ruth died, David knew the only way he could thank her for all the love she had given him was to take care of her Martha. For Ruth had understood that Martha was born with a more restless spirit than she, or her husband, or their brilliant daughter Bernice possessed. He knew he owed it to Ruth to love and protect Martha.

He knew that to protect her he had to teach his impetuous and unruly daughter to rein in her dangerous emotions; he had to persuade her that only cool heads and clear minds would succeed in these turbulent times. To educate her in this manner was the only way he knew how to express the love he felt. He could only hope that it was enough.

Now he was chiding himself for having let her go alone to Paris. Yet she'd wanted to go so badly! And, she seemed so grown up, so practical, in suggesting that she take the trip as soon as her exams were finished, even though the weather might be bad, so that she could look for a job right after Christmas. She was determined to take off at least one semester and work, to see if that helped her become more motivated to succeed at her studies. Given her admirably rational plan, and the new potential for self-discipline it revealed, Professor Levy thought that a short trip to Paris was not such a bad idea—moreover, he'd trusted his old friend Michel Bernard and his competent wife to look after her. What had gone wrong?

Professor Levy walked up to Martha and put his arm around her shoulder, giving her a light squeeze. He was not prone to displays of affection. A public hug was profound, coming from Professor Levy.

"So, you don't feel well?" he asked. She looked tired. He would get a doctor, just in case.

"No, I'm fine, really. Just too much rich food, I guess, and not enough sleep. I tried to see too many things in too short a period of time. No self-restraint. Isn't that what you always accuse me of?" Her question could have been provoking, but it was not. Delivered with a tired smile, her words seemed to contain an element of resignation that David found both reassuring and slightly disconcerting. A change had come over Martha. He could not quite put his finger on it. She looked at him with eyes that seemed...different.

He hired a cab to take them home, an unusual luxury for the frugal professor, because one could generally walk wherever one needed to go in Munich. As they passed through the snow-covered rooftops of the town, Martha felt comforted by the friendly familiarity of her home. She could see the massive twin towers of the Frauenkirche, climbing boldly to a height of 350 feet, each adorned with a clock. But, where one would expect to find graceful Gothic spires, each tower of the church was topped with a low, round, copper cupola. The townspeople had run out of money to finish the steeples in 1488, so they were capped by the cupolas, with the idea that appropriate spires could be added later. But by the time more funds were available, the people of Munich decided not to make any additions to the church. They liked it just the way it was. For all of their fun-loving ways, Bavarians hated change. For the most part they were as immoveable as the mountains that surrounded them.

Martha and her father lived on the northern outskirts of Munich, near the university, just south of the village of Schwabing. This little hamlet, nestled at the northern edge of town, had grown through the years into a bustling artist's colony. The cultural menagerie of Schwabing attracted an eclectic mix of painters, sculptors, composers, writers, and mere admirers of the arts. Some who came to soak up the creative energies of the place, like Vasili Kandinski, Franz Marc, Thomas Mann, and Bertolt Brecht, exploded like comets into international view. Most remained obscure.

The older townspeople of Munich regarded the Bohemian community to the north as something of a mildly bothersome, occasionally entertaining nuisance. The students and younger residents of the city found Schwabing an essential part of life. To Martha, Schwabing was a haven that made her continued existence in Munich possible. An ironic smile briefly touched her lips as the taxi passed a sign giving motorists directions to the main street that cut through the heart of Schwabing. The street's name: Leopoldstrasse. Leopold Road. If only it could lead to her Leo.

Martha and her father spoke little during the short ride to the house. He wanted to ask her about her trip, what she had seen, and what she thought of Paris, but her uncharacteristic reticence made it clear that she did not feel like talking. Once inside their small but comfortable home, he broke the silence.

"Well, Harry will be happy that you are home! He has been moping around like a lonely puppy. You should call him up. Perhaps he will come over and read the latest avant garde poetry from Berlin for you tonight. Or bring his violin. You can sing, with that lovely voice of yours. Harry loves to hear you sing, and I would not mind a private concert, myself." He pantomimed the playing of a fiddle as he moved around the small room in a rough parody of a waltz, and Martha laughed in spite of herself. She was not used to seeing her intensely reserved father perform such antics.

"Maybe I will call him," she said as her laughter subsided. Funny, she'd not even thought of Harry in three days. Leo had swept him completely from her mind. Dear, sweet Harry.

Henrich Jacobson, known to all of his friends and relatives as "Harry," was originally from Leipzig. He'd come to the University at Munich to study engineering, and everyone agreed that Harry would be a brilliant engineer. Everyone also agreed that it was a shame. It was a shame to be so very talented at something that was so irresistibly practical, when it was obvious that Harry's first love was, and always would be, music. But no one, at least, no true German, could ignore a gift like the kind that God had given Harry – the amazing ability to divine the complexities necessary to hold a bridge together, or simplify the intricacies of raising a sky-scraper, in order to indulge oneself in the tranquility of a sonata for the violin. Music was not a "real" career, unless one was extraordinarily gifted; and, although Harry was good on the violin, *very good,* he could not wield a bow with the same virtuosity with which he could wield his mechanical pencil.

Harry himself realized this. So he resolutely pursued his degree in engineering, winning prize after prize in student competitions, all the while entertaining himself and his closest friends with his musical skills. He kept his fantasy of playing with a symphony orchestra tucked away in a solitary corner of his imagination.

Harry had another fantasy as well. He wanted to marry Martha Levy.

At first he'd worshiped her from afar, the way one would admire a rare object of art. He saw her regularly on the campus. Even before she enrolled as a student, she often came to hear special lectures, or to have lunch with her father. Sometimes it seemed that he could sense her presence before he could actually see her. He would feel a glow in his stomach, and a quickness to his heartbeat, and then there she would be: honey-spun auburn hair dancing around her face, green eyes trapping the sunlight like a pair of emeralds.

Occasionally she would smile at him, a frank, matter-of-fact invitation to friendship, but Harry could only blush and look away. He was too shy and too in love to just start talking.

Then Harry realized that this enchanting princess, whose visage floated through his bittersweet daydreams as he played lovesick tunes on his violin, was none other than Bernice Levy's younger sister. Bernice, unlike Martha, was eminently approachable. She was not an intimidating beauty, and she was a fellow engineering student, although she was a year ahead of him, and her skills leaned toward electrical, rather than mechanical, engineering. He could certainly talk to Bernice. He would just have to work up the courage to talk to Bernice about Martha.

He rehearsed his speech for weeks. On a bright April morning, he caught up with Bernice after a lecture, and asked her if she would like to go with him for a hike in the foothills, now that the weather had warmed up. He would bring a picnic. She could bring—her sister.

It was not the first time that a young man had tried to use Bernice as a means of access to Martha. Bernice was not really offended. It was, after all, a predictable and sensible strategy. Bernice had long ago accepted the fact that Martha was the pretty one, and she was too busy with her engineering studies to devote any serious amount of time to romance. But David Levy was exceedingly protective of his inordinately pretty, high-spirited younger daughter, and Bernice knew better than to acquiesce in Harry's plot without her father's permission.

"Harry Jacobson," said Bernice in a stern voice, "My little sister is only seventeen. If you would like to court her, you'd best ask my father, not connive with me." She had to stifle a laugh as a look of utter mortification filled Harry's soft brown eyes. Harry would make an excellent engineer, but Bernice suspected he would never be very good at wooing women.

"Oh, I couldn't, I mean, I didn't mean—"

"Of course you did. You're not the first. But it's a dead-end, that's all." The wretchedness smothering Harry's usually convivial features made her take pity on him. Harry had to be one of the more harmless men she'd ever met—not that she herself really brought out the beast in anyone. But Bernice didn't think that there was a beast inside Harry. He was so earnest. And decent looking, too – trim but not a weakling. He had nice height, wiry brown hair, and an intelligent, warm look to his eyes. Martha would start dating eventually. They couldn't keep the floodgates closed forever. Harry might be a good choice. She thought it over for a moment, while Harry stammered some more apologies.

"Oh, stop. I'm going to help you. Come to my house for dinner next Thursday night. Afterwards, we can study for our physics test together. It will give my father a chance to look you over—and give you a chance to meet Martha." Dazed with joy, Harry pumped Bernice's hand until her shoulder shook. She tolerated this for a moment, then sent him off with, "Look, get out of here before I change my mind. I'm already late for my next class!"

So began the special friendship of Martha and Harry, under the watchful but eventually trusting eye of Professor Levy. Five months later, in September, Bernice was a graduate student, in Austria, and Harry was beginning his last year at the university. Martha, who was by then eighteen, had enrolled for her first semester in college.

She had always been a reasonably good student, but studies at the university required a more intense focus, and a drive for a particular discipline. To her family's dismay, Martha did not feel driven. She did her best, trying to keep up with her work, but fell behind as soon as she was tempted by any sort of distraction.

And Schwabing provided all sorts of distractions. Luckily, she experienced most of them under the careful protection of her dear friend, Harry, whose unthreatening love she took for granted. He never pressured her; never expected anything more than a hug and a swift good night kiss. Martha felt completely safe with him.

Not having a mother to talk to, and not feeling close enough to Bernice to discuss anything more personal than a grocery list, Martha was left with a vague sense that there must be something more to romance than the shared joy of an evening in a literary cabaret, something more intense than the pleasant contentment she felt when she saw Harry's earnest face light up at the sight of her. But she did not feel compelled to explore the issue too closely. She'd spent too long mourning the loss of her mother's love, and trying to earn her father's, to be concerned about capturing anyone else's.

Near the end of her first semester, Martha tried to confront the nagging restlessness invading her life. She decided that her general sense of dissatisfaction stemmed from boredom with school and boredom with Munich as well. By December she concluded that a vacation and a job were the twin solutions to her ennui. A vacation to Paris, on her own, and a new career! Surely that would cure her. Reinvigorate her.

Then she met Leo. Then she understood what she'd been missing. And now that she'd made that discovery, her whole existence seemed wrong without him. In her mind's eye Martha saw a picture of herself, standing in the center of a stage, surrounded by all the people she knew in Munich. Everyone was prepared for the curtain to rise. Everyone else knew his cues and his lines. But she did not. She was in the wrong play.

No, she would not see Harry today. She did not know what she would do today. Or tomorrow. Or the day after that, or the day after that. Except wait.

❧

Time crept forward. Martha refused to leave the house and refused to see anyone. She said she wanted to take advantage of some time alone to relax and read. After making her see a doctor, who confirmed that there was nothing physically wrong with his normally gregarious daughter, Martha's anxious father had no choice but to chase Harry and the rest of her worried friends away. "It's a female malady," he explained with some consternation, hoping his words were true.

Christmas Eve arrived. The Levys, like many other German Jewish families who, over time, had become fully assimilated into the German way of life, practiced neither Judaism nor Christianity. They retained their faith in God; but, instead of following an established religion, created an informal household liturgy, grounded in a deep respect for the Ten Commandments, and blending some of the traditions of their heritage with secular celebrations of certain Christian holidays. It was, therefore, not unusual to find an old German Jewish family that celebrated Christmas, but not Hanukkah; Passover, but not Easter.

Christmas had been Ruth Levy's favorite time of year, and after her death Martha carried on the tradition. She decorated the house, cajoled Bernice into helping her prepare mulled wine and treats for the carolers who strolled through the neighborhood, and bought small presents for her sister and her father. Bernice and Herr Levy reciprocated, although each one participated only to please Martha. Neither one cared too much about what was, in their opinion, a pagan celebration of the winter solstice co-opted by the Christians to celebrate the birth of their Savior. Neither of them possessed the romantic spirit that allowed for the creation of Christmas magic. Martha, on the other hand, believed.

This year Martha again performed her annual rituals. She decorated the tree, put fir branches and candles in the windows, and cooked a lovely Christmas goose. But she did so with no magic in her heart. Her thoughts focused on one single sentence, one sentence that she repeated to herself, day after day, minute after minute. "Leo is the head concierge at the Bristol hotel in Budapest. He is due back the day after Christmas. The day after Christmas!"

Martha did not really think that Leo would be back at the Bristol on December 26th. If he were really in danger, how could he just go back to his regular job? But the people at the hotel might know something. She could telephone the Bristol, and ask about him. She needed to know where he was.

To make an international call from Munich, one had to go to the post office. That is where Martha went, precisely at 2:00 in the afternoon the day after Christmas. One hour later, the operator put her call through.

A bland, "Go ahead, Miss," signaled that the connection had been made. Martha's heart pounded in her ears so loudly that she could barely hear. She took a deep breath.

"May I speak to the manager?" she queried in German. She already knew from Leo that most businesses in Budapest used German as a second language, because so few outsiders spoke Hungarian. "It's a matter of some urgency," she added.

"One moment, please." The silence stretched across the miles. At last a male voice responded.

"Mr. Orgovany at your service. Whom do I have the honor of addressing?"

"My name is—Maria Schwartz. I am looking for Mr. Leopold Hoffman; I am a distant cousin. I understand he works there?"

"He did. If you will forgive me, this is, frankly, a strange day for a cousin to be calling from out of the blue. What is this all about? The police have already been here asking about him. Is he in trouble?"

Martha could not hide the disappointment in her voice. "You don't know where he is? You haven't heard from him?"

His voice took on a suspicious tone. "No, and frankly, Miss, I would not tell you anything that I have not already told the police. He went on vacation. To Vienna, I think. He was supposed to report to work this morning, and he did not. I checked his rooms, here at the hotel, and he is not there. Do you know what all this is about? Miss, ah, Schwartz?"

"No. That is, I do not know why the police would want to talk to him." A sudden wave of fear hit her, and uttering a hasty, "thank you," she hung up. Her stomach ached with disappointment. But what more had she expected? At least, she knew that Leo had told her the truth. He was from Budapest. He worked at the Bristol. He was in trouble. Confirmation of that much was something. But that was all she had.

Her body felt like lead. She could not go on like this. She would give him six months. Six months. Six months and then what?

"Then who knows?" she said aloud, as she trudged home through the snow, fighting back the tears that threatened to overwhelm her again. "Who knows?"

❦

The knowledge she gained from her telephone call to the Bristol and her self-imposed deadline of six months gave Martha the strength to come out of hiding. The following morning she asked her much-relieved father to tell Harry that she would speak to him the next time he called.

The eager young man was at her door a few hours later.

"Martha, how are you feeling? We've all been so worried about you!"

"Oh, Harry. I'm alright. Just tired from my trip, that's all."

She looked at his apprehensive face, and felt a rush of tenderness for him. *Please*, she prayed. *Please don't let Harry love me the way I love Leo. I don't want to hurt him that much.*

To her father's surprise, after a short search for a job, Martha took a position as a librarian's assistant at the University. He thought that her desire to pursue a career would have led her to sell clothes in a ladies' shop, or to work as a photographer's assistant – something at least mildly glamorous. Instead, Martha threw herself into the world of books, the world that was her father's home, the world from which only a month ago she'd wanted to escape.

But Martha found the library a comfortable place. Her days full of catalogue numbers and retrieval requests, she did not have to engage in a real relationship with the people who inhabited the world to which she no longer felt connected. The cerebral quiet helped her recover some measure of tranquility. She worked. She thought about Leo. And she waited.

The head librarian noticed a distinct increase in the number of young men studying in the library during the hours that Martha was on duty. Martha's supervisor was happy to note that Martha seemed oblivious to this phenomenon, and, rather than encourage any disruption on the part of her admirers, concentrated quite satisfactorily on her duties. Of course, there was invariably someone who offered to help her with the heavy books she had to carry. Martha politely declined each offer with a smile that made her rebuff seem like a rare gift. She was unaffected by both the attention she received and the sensation she created.

Harry Jacobson was ecstatic with this new situation. He spent the better portion of each weekday at a table in the library reading room, where he could catch frequent glimpses of Martha as she made her way around the stacks, reshelving books with a delicate hand. He could barely keep his mind on his studies.

Every day when Martha got off work, Harry would greet her and offer to walk her home. Carefully staking out his claim in full view of the other hopeful admirers, he would help her on with her coat, and take her hand with gallant firmness. Implausible as it seemed to the other young men surrounding her, Martha Levy did not seem interested in spending time with anyone other than Harry Jacobson. The herd of hopefuls vibrated with envy every time Martha left the library under Harry's courteous escort. He was a nice enough guy, they said to each other, but not worthy of *her*. How could a nondescript guy like Harry capture a firebird? Where was the fairness in that?

Always grateful for Harry's company, Martha started to worry that she was, in some way, leading Harry on. He was her shield, and her companion, but she knew, now, that she was not in love with him. At times Martha felt compelled to straighten out any misunderstanding that might be building between them, but she never found a way to broach the subject without sounding presumptuous, and Harry had never formally declared his love to her, although there were times when such a declaration was written plainly on his face. Martha was also afraid that she would lose Harry altogether if she were tell him that she felt differently about their friendship than he did. Until she heard from Leo, she was reluctant to do or say anything that would jeopardize her relationship with her friend, for Harry was, in his kind, mild way, very precious to her. So she let things be for the time being, aware of the selfish undercurrents that kept their little boat rocking along, unwilling to say anything that might capsize it.

Ultimately it was Harry who forced the issue, in a manner that took Martha completely off guard.

"Would you like to go for a picnic tomorrow, now that the weather has finally gotten warmer?" he asked one April evening as he walked her home.

"Why yes," Martha responded warmly. "What a lovely way to spend my day off." She loved hiking through the countryside in April. A sharp crispness still enveloped the earth, yet Mother Nature coquettishly revealed the soft colors of spring. It was an optimistic time of year.

Martha was totally unaware of the fact that Harry had just reissued the exact invitation he had given her sister Bernice one year earlier. He repeated the words as a good luck omen. She had to come with him. His dreams depended on it.

The next afternoon found Martha and Harry seated on a worn woolen blanket, savoring soft bread, sausages and dried fruit, while they admired the formidable peaks of the Alps carving white shadows into a crystal blue spring sky. They'd chatted amiably about everything and nothing as they made their way into the foothills of mountains. Now a comfortable silence descended, as they enjoyed the view and their lunch.

Harry had rehearsed this scene in his head dozens of times over the past few weeks. Yet somehow, all of his eloquent speeches deserted him as he contemplated the beauty of the scenery, and the promise of his future, a future that could, that must, include Martha.

"Martha, this will be my last term at the University—"

"Well I know that. Have you decided where to go for your graduate degree? Is it to be Berlin after all?"

"Yes—I mean, No. That is, I have decided, and it's not Berlin. Listen." He looked into her eyes with ominous intensity.

"Martha, I am going to America."

Martha's eyebrows shot up in two perfect arches, framing her emerald eyes like amber rainbows. Her mouth opened slightly. She wanted to say something congratulatory; all that came out was an echoing question.

"Going to America?"

"Yes, America." Harry's hands now gestured freely, and his words poured out ever faster, as he found the courage to say what he wanted to tell her.

"You see, Martha, my darling, I have been accepted by the graduate program of mechanical engineering at the Massachusetts Institute of Technology. Well, it's not Harvard, but it's better than Harvard if you're an engineer. And Boston is a city alive with music! Oh, Martha. I'm going to the United States of America. I'll be there at least four years for my doctorate, and then, perhaps, I can stay. For if one is building the cities of the future—isn't America the country with the brightest future? The place where there is space and democracy and opportunity? Isn't that where I need to be? Isn't that where *we* should be?"

The import of his last question escaped her, as she contemplated the image of Harry busily building skyscrapers in Manhattan. America! What an ambition!

"When will you leave?" she asked, hoping it would not be too soon. She would miss him. She both enjoyed and depended upon his friendship.

Harry seemed taken aback by her question. "When will *I* leave? When will *I* leave? Martha, I want you to come with me. As my wife. I want to marry you. Oh Martha, my beautiful friend, please, will you marry me? Marry me and come to America!"

Now the surprise on Martha's face turned to alarm. Could he be serious? Of course he was. She'd known, in her heart, for months, that this moment was inevitable, although she'd selfishly refused to admit it to herself. She knew that she loved Harry as a dear friend, and she knew that to him, she meant more. Much more. Her heart ached for him. She did not know how to make her answer any easier for him to hear.

"Harry, I—"

"Don't!" He raised a finger to her lips. Her face told him everything. He could not bear to hear a refusal.

She needs more time, thought Harry wildly. It was a jolt, after all. Not just a proposal, but a request for her to leave her home, her country, her family. He mentally kicked himself. It was too much to expect, a positive answer to all that at once. He must give her time.

"Martha, please, do not say no. Not yet. I know this is all very sudden—that is, my scholarship, and wanting to go to America. Surely my love comes as no surprise to you. Would you at least tell me that you will think about it? Please? Don't just—say no."

Martha knew what her response ought to be, but the words stuck in her throat. How could she hurt Harry like that? *No, my answer is no, I don't love you the way you love me.*

"Oh, Harry, I am so…overwhelmed. I didn't realize that you were so…so serious about me. And leaving Munich…leaving Germany…this is all so sudden. I don't know what to say. I haven't really thought about marriage yet; I just don't know what to say. But I'll think about it. Please give me some time."

A smile transformed Harry's features. "Fine," he said cheerfully. "That would be fine. Wonderful. Take all the time you need." Martha could see the bright tears of relief in his eyes.

Later that night, Martha lay in her bed, on her back, unable to sleep, her slender arms tucked behind her head. She stared at the ceiling and thought about Harry's proposal.

She knew her father would approve. He was so obviously delighted that Martha was keeping company with such a stable, trustworthy fellow. Martha could sense the relief and happiness in her father's smile every time he wished them a pleasant "good night," as she and Harry left for an evening out. Did everyone expect them to wed?

She rolled over, inadvertently twisting herself in her sheets, and angrily kicked her legs in an effort to untangle herself. The source of her irritation was not the offending bed linen. She was angry at herself. Angry at herself for holding on to a fantasy, and angry at herself for being tempted to let go of it.

Harry would leave at the end of May, he said, right after his graduation. Seven weeks. In seven weeks she could be a married woman, on her way to live in a prosperous country with an adoring husband, who would undoubtedly be respected and successful, a husband who would love her, honor her, and cherish her, a husband who would never get in trouble with the police, would never hide things from her—

A husband who would never make her heart sing. A husband who could never make her forget Leo.

Martha put her pillow over her head and let out a muffled cry of frustration. Damn Leo! Why hadn't he gotten in touch with her? Where was he? How long could she go on waiting and hoping, living in limbo, unable to make any decisions about her life? Four months of waiting, tortured by her memories and her desire…. And poor Harry! She rolled over on her back again, pulled her pillow out from under her head, and hugged it to her chest. How long could she make him wait? Could she be honest, and tell him that if she married him, she would enter their marriage in friendship, hoping that love would grow? Would he have her on those terms? Could she live by them? Could she make love to Harry?

Burning tears crept out of the corners of her eyes. She could feel Leo wrapped around her, pushed deep inside her, his fingers lost in her hair, his warm face buried in her neck, nibbling and kissing her flesh. Was that one night all she was to know of intimacy and passion? Oh, where *was* he? Was he safe? Didn't he know how much she needed him?

But the night held no answers. And once again, as on so many nights since Christmas, Martha cried herself to sleep.

Martha's indecision eventually gave Harry the answer he needed, but not the one he wanted to hear. Two weeks before he was to leave, he asked Martha to join him on a walk through the English Garden, the public park in the center of Munich that often served as the scene for romantic rendezvous. He stopped when they reached a peaceful spot in the center of the park, on the edge of the tranquil lake, where an ancient willow tree's arching limbs provided a touch of shade from the glare of the late afternoon sun, and a bit of shelter from curious eyes.

"Martha," he began, as they both settled down in the long grass, "I know that if you had made up your mind about marrying me, you would have told me yes or no before now. And I want you to take more time, as much time as you need, to keep the answer from being no."

She started to say something, but he cut her off, not willing to let her speak until he had finished.

"No, please listen to me. I think it would be best if I were to go to Boston by myself. Then, after a few months, you can come visit me, and see how you like it, and see how you like being with me, in another place. Then, you can decide." He gave her a wry smile. "Who knows? You might even miss me a little."

"Oh, Harry!" Martha threw her arms around his neck and started to cry. Her shoulders shook with prodigious, heart-wrenching sobs. She cried because she *would* miss him. She cried because she felt lucky to be loved by someone so kind and patient. She cried because she was so wretchedly guilty that she could not return his love. She cried because she was in love with the wrong man.

"What's this, what's this, my sweet darling?" Harry murmured. His own heart, far from feeling heavy, was gloriously light. She *would* miss him, then! There was still a chance!

"Please, Martha, don't cry," he continued, stroking her back until he felt her crying subside. He pulled away from her slightly. "Look, I have a present for you. Will that cheer you up?"

Martha could not help but smile. Harry was so thoughtful. Why could she not love him the way he wanted her to? With a loud sniff she accepted his offer of a handkerchief, wiped her eyes and blew her nose. "You should not be giving *me* a present," she protested. "You are the one graduating. I should be giving you a present."

"If you will accept this gift, and agree to think a little while longer about my proposal, that would be a perfect graduation present."

Harry pulled a long, slim case from the pocket of his jacket.

"I wanted to get you an engagement ring, but I did not want you to feel pressured to accept it. So I had this made for you, instead, my beautiful songbird, to remember me by when I am living across the ocean, always thinking of you." As he finished his sentence, he opened the box.

Martha gasped. Inside was a golden medallion on a long chain. Carved into the surface of the gold was the image of a nightingale, sitting in a rose bush, wings spread and breast held high as it exploded into song.

"Oh, Harry," breathed Martha, her voice full of admiration and gratitude. "I can't possibly accept this. It's much too valuable. It's the most beautiful thing I've ever seen."

"You can't possibly not accept it," he responded firmly. "It was made for you, Martha, for you are the most beautiful thing that I have ever seen, and sing with the most beautiful voice I have ever heard. You *have* to keep it. Whatever happens between us, whatever the future holds for us, this is yours. Because you have made this past year the happiest time of my whole life."

Martha felt her eyes fill with tears again. She fought them back, her eyelashes fluttering like butterfly wings. She allowed Harry to put the chain around her neck. She allowed him to kiss her; not the usual, light wisp of a kiss that signaled the end of an evening, but an ardent, if somewhat clumsy, embrace.

"You could do worse than Harry," her father told her.

"You could do worse than Harry," her sister told her.

You could do worse than Harry. Martha whispered to herself as she stared again at the ceiling, faced with yet another restless night.

But her heart would not listen. *Six months. You promised me you would give him six months.*

She would try to ignore her heart. She would try to be practical. She would try to put Leo behind her. She would try to stop hoping. And, maybe, she would go to America.

⚬❧

"Martha," called David Levy, "I have a letter for you."

Martha looked up from the mass of flowers she was arranging. It was now mid-July, and the summer blossoms were at their peak. She tried to keep a fresh arrangement on the dining room table. Fresh flowers always lifted her spirits.

"Again? From Harry? Already?" she responded with a pleasant laugh. During the two months that Harry had been gone, she had received 10 letters, two mailed before he even left Germany.

"I do not believe so," came the somber response as her father entered the room. "I went by my office this afternoon to catch up on a few things, and, of course, to pick up any correspondence. There was one letter in my box that seemed a little strange. No first name, just Herr Professor Levy, care of the University in Munich. No postal code. It must have taken a long time to find me. But when I opened the letter, it contained another sealed envelope, with your name on it."

"For me?" Martha said weakly. Her hands began to tremble. She buried them in the flowers.

Professor Levy's face darkened. "I did not open this letter to you, Martha, out of respect for your privacy, but I find this a very curious situation. Whom do you know in Shanghai?"

"Where?" She could barely get the word out.

"Shanghai. In China. The postmark shows the outside envelope was mailed from Shanghai."

"I—I don't know," she faltered. Her heart beating wildly, she leapt forward with the first outright lie she'd ever told her father.

"Oh, yes! It must be that girl I met in Paris. She was going to Shanghai to do missionary work. I'd forgotten I'd given her my address. I thought it would be fun to get a letter from China, to hear about her adventures as a missionary. I guess she lost my address, but remembered you were with the University here." She busied herself with the flowers, pulling one after another out of the vase, then studiously putting it back in a new position, endeavoring to convey the impression that she was concentrating on achieving perfection with her artistic composition.

Professor Levy gave her a puzzled look. "You never mentioned that you met a girl in Paris."

"Yes, oh, just another student. An American girl. We met in front of a church, and had coffee together." She was amazed at how smoothly the lie grew once it had emerged.

For a moment Professor Levy said nothing. Then he drew the letter out of his pocket. Wordlessly, he offered it to Martha from across the table.

Martha realized that she could not take it from him. She was sure that if she stopped her compulsive motion with the flowers he would notice that her hands were shaking violently. She tried to feign disinterest, but now her voice sounded strained.

"Oh, Papa, could you please just leave it there on the table for me? I haven't time to read it now."

"Very well." Professor Levy tossed the letter on the table and turned to leave the room. He paused at the doorway, and glanced over his shoulder at Martha, still busy with her flowers. "I will be in my study, if you me for need anything," he said, a slight question creeping into his voice. Martha smiled at him. The setting sun shimmered through the window, bathing Martha and her flowers in a golden halo. It was a beautiful sight.

He had no way of knowing that he would never see her again.

Martha kept her hands clenched around the stems of the flowers until she heard the door of her father's office close. Her hands were bleeding from where she had grabbed the thorns on the roses. She did not notice. She lunged for the envelope. There it was: her name neatly printed in block letters. Underneath, in smaller script, she saw the word, "personal."

Holding the envelope to her face, she tried to detect some trace of Leo's presence from the paper that had traveled across the world, Martha scrambled to her room. She closed the door. She sat down on her bed. She tore open the envelope, and began to read:

My Darling,

I'm not a religious man, but if there is a God, I pray that he guides this letter into your hands. I know of no other way to reach you.

I'm in Shanghai. My first few months here were not easy. I didn't contact you sooner because I was afraid that, if I did, someone might use you to try and find me. I could not put you in jeopardy.

I hope you can forgive me for what I put you through. I hope to have the rest of our lives to make it up to you. All I can tell you is that I betrayed some members of the Hungarian fascist party, who would like to see me killed for what I did. If you remember Hitler, and what he stood for when he tried to take over Bavaria in 1921, then you will understand the kind of people that I am dealing with.

It's not safe for me in Hungary, or Germany, or France. Perhaps nowhere in Europe. So I came to Shanghai.

This is an amazing place. I'm doing well now, and want, with all my soul, for you to join me. I have not stopped thinking about you for a moment. I want to keep the promises I made to you the night that we met. The night my life began.

I've enclosed a bank draft to cover your passage to Shanghai. It's a long journey, and will take several weeks. Please cable me at the address below with your decision. I love you so very much.

Please come. Please come right away.

Forever yours,
Leo

Martha thought she would stop breathing. She thought her heart would stop beating. A thousand questions clamored through her head. What would she say to her father? How could she explain this to Harry? How could she leave her home and her country to go to a terrifyingly foreign place like Shanghai?

But even as she listened to the chorus of doubts rising within her, she knew she had to leave. Now that she knew where to find him, she could not take any steps that did not lead to a life with Leo. And she knew that she must leave immediately, without hesitating, so that the qualms taking shape in her mind did not grow into an insurmountable barrier.

How could she face her father? He would talk her out of going. He would look at her with those dark, serious eyes and convince her that she was being ridiculous. She dare not confront him.

Frantically, she sat down at the small desk in her room, picked up a pen, and started to write:

Dear Papa,

I know this will come as a shock to you, but I have fallen in love, and am leaving Bavaria to join the man I will marry, in Shanghai. I'm sorry that I have not been honest with you. I know that this will hurt you, and for that, also, I am truly sorry.

Please don't worry. I know that I'm doing the right thing. I know that you have always tried to teach me to be sensible, but I think that our hearts speak a different language. I must listen to mine. I will keep in touch.

Your loving,
Martha

She reread the note quickly, realizing how inadequate it was, yet unwilling to risk writing anything more. She must go, now.

She packed a small suitcase, retrieved her small savings from under her mattress, pinned Leo's bank draft to the inside of her coat, and, without a word or a backward glance, walked out the door of her father's house.

It was not until she was seated in the train, miles outside Munich, that her brain started to function again, and she realized that she still wore Harry's medallion around her neck.

CHAPTER 7

THE SPECULATOR

꙰

SHANGHAI, 1926

For the fifth time in as many days, Leo Hoffman paced up and down the wide sweep of waterfront boulevard known in Shanghai as the Bund. Although the brutal humidity of August hindered all movement, every limb of Leo's frame radiated impatience as he made his way along the riverfront. Periodically, his anxious body froze, and his eyes swept across the opaque water of the Whangpoo river.

It was not a scenic river, like the Danube, or a romantic one, like the Seine. The Whangpoo was ugly, and slow moving. It stank of mud, and decay, and human abuse. Even now, after living in Shanghai for six months, the overpowering stench of the river sometimes startled Leo when he opened a window, or stepped out onto the street. It lay waiting for him, like a lethargic old beggar, too complacent to try and attract his attention with any ruse more energetic than an assault on his olfactory organ. The Shanghailanders said that one got used to the smell, in time. Leo wondered.

But for all of its natural indolence, the Whangpoo was a frenetic waterway. It had been seized, dredged, and made useful by foreign hands eager to exploit the enormous Chinese market. For the British, the Americans, the French, and the Japanese, the Whangpoo was now the carotid artery of the China trade. Manufactured and imported goods were piled onto barges in Shanghai harbor, then transported twelve miles down the lazy, smelly Whangpoo to the mighty Yangtze. From there, the valuable cargos dispersed into the vast Chinese countryside, via a network of waterways that flowed through the interior for thirty thousand miles. Up the Whangpoo to Shanghai came rice, cotton, silk, tea, and tobacco; peanuts, rosewood, leather, and tung oil. And silver. Vast quantities of silver. Yes, the Whangpoo might smell of refuse, but it also smelled of money. It was, as the Shanghailanders claimed, a stench one could get used to.

Leo stopped his compulsive pacing and scanned the busy river traffic. Boats of every shape and description jostled and dodged each other in the gray-yellow light of early evening, covering the harbor with a floating quilt of tramp steamers, passenger ships, sampans, and junks. This menagerie of vessels brought cargo to and from the massive freighters anchored closer to the Yangtze mouth, as only smaller craft could navigate the silty, shallow port of Shanghai. The squat sampans served as water taxis, and also as houseboats for thousands of Chinese. From the shore Leo saw charcoal cook stoves belching out black smoke, and blue cotton laundry hanging out to dry. Here and there a Chinese toddler played in split pants while attached to a mast by a short leash.

But this evening Leo's eyes swept over the exotic Chinese vessels without interest. The one boat he ached to see was not yet there. No steam launch from the Peninsular & Oriental Steam Navigation Company cut through the foamy yellow water toward the sturdy piers that lined the foreshore of the Bund. It was now seven o'clock. Martha would not arrive tonight.

With a short sigh of frustration Leo turned on his heel and headed towards Nanking Road, back to the cool shelter of the Palace Hotel bar and the ephemeral comfort of a brandy. He cut a path through the mass of humanity crowding the walkway. The last vestiges of daylight would soon disappear, but the Chinese entrepreneurs who worked the Bund with territorial possessiveness were still active. He passed a wizened old coolie selling hot, succulent pork dumplings. A round-faced, smiling matron peddled bamboo trinkets and jade earrings. A tired pregnant woman dressed in pink silk squatted behind a pile of embroidered slippers for sale. They, and dozens like them, filled the air with a steady din of enticements, encouragements, boasts and insults. They cried out in Chinese, in pidgin English, and in broken, bastardized French. Leo ignored them all, as they shouted to be heard above the engines, whistles, and horns of the harbor. The noise one had to get used to or go deaf, or crazy. Incessant noise, like the stench of the river, was part of life in Shanghai.

The collapse of the Manchu Dynasty in 1911, and the weakness of the subsequent republican government, left the Chinese empire at the mercy of competing warlords. These ruthless land pirates divided the once-mighty kingdom into private fiefs, slaughtering those who resisted. But Shanghai remained an island of calm productivity amidst the anarchy. There, under the tender protection of warships flying the flags of five different countries, the invisible hand of capitalism guided the lives of a million Chinese and fifty thousand foreigners with relentless economic discipline.

Since the 1840's, treaties guaranteeing "extraterritoriality" to the foreign residents living within two geographic districts, the French Concession and the International Settlement, rendered the Shanghailanders subject only to the jurisdiction and laws of their respective countries, as interpreted and executed by the local Shanghai Municipal Council. If an American committed murder in Shanghai, he might be punished. For an economic crime, he was virtually untouchable. Greed and vice were mainstays of Shanghai commerce, and Shanghai justice was as shallow and corrupt as the waters of the Whangpoo.

Never had there been such a boisterous blend of East and West; never had there been such clamorous coexistence of the devout and the deviate, the prosperous and the penurious, the opulent and the oppressed. Fortunes were made and lost everyday. Staggering wealth and stunning poverty existed side by side, each a tribute to the unique world that was Shanghai. It was, as Leo had been told seven months earlier by the crude American James Mitchell, a perfect place to begin one's life anew. The best asset a fugitive could bring to Shanghai to aid him in the metamorphosis from hunted and haunted to secure and wealthy was a sizeable bankroll. The second was a good supply of raw luck. Leo had arrived in Shanghai with both.

Six months earlier the Shanghai weather had been in the throes of its opposite but equally uncomfortable extreme. Shanghai's winters brought with them a damp, insidious cold, that bore no relation to the invigorating briskness of a Hungarian winter. Dozens of beggars froze to death every night, their stiff bodies stretched alongside automobiles equipped with sable lap rugs to keep their affluent occupants cozy. The only decent thing about winter in Shanghai was that it did not last long.

Despite the uninviting temperature, on the day of his arrival in Shanghai Leo had abandoned his small cabin just after sunrise. He found a little-used corner of the deck and waited, wanting to catch a glimpse of the land that might mean his salvation.

For the five long weeks of the voyage he had kept to himself, engaging in civil conversation when necessary, but unwilling to risk making the acquaintance of any of his fellow passengers. He did not disembark at any of the ship's ports of call, so that he did not have to show his passport to anyone other than the ship's captain. He wanted to make sure that no one would remember him, or be able to identify him. No one should be able to connect him with a murder in Paris. For the time being, he needed to be left alone.

Given his desire for privacy, Leo was not pleased when he saw another cashmere-clad passenger saunter out into the cold air of early dawn. Before Leo could withdraw the new arrival spotted him, and headed his way, obviously ready for a conversation.

"Good morning! Cosgrove is the name. Lawrence Cosgrove." The trim, middle-aged Englishman offered Leo his gloved hand. Leo shook it without responding to Cosgrove's greeting, barely meeting his eye in acknowledgement.

The Englishman paused, puzzling over the lack of a reaction on Leo's part.

"I say," he said, now a bit hesitant, "You do speak English, don't you?"

Leo reconsidered his cool response. He did not want to insult anyone; he just wanted to be ignored. This man would not forget him if he behaved too rudely. A small smile of resignation skirted Leo's mouth, as he replied politely, but without enthusiasm.

"Yes, I do."

"Ah, good. I thought so." Cosgrove looked relieved. He went on.

"I don't speak anything but my mother tongue. Well, I can manage in a French restaurant, you know, but I am not what you would call conversational. In French, that is. First time to Shanghai?"

"Yes, it is." This man Cosgrove was obviously feeling chatty. Leo would have to let him blather on for a bit before excusing himself.

"Well, you are about to get your first peek at Chinese soil," the garrulous gentleman continued, inclining his head towards the blue-gray waves rocking the ship. "The sea water will change color soon."

This piqued Leo's curiosity. "Really? Does the water become that shallow so far from shore?" He colored his normally perfect English accent with a trace of French, and a touch of German. He did not want to give away his origins.

"No, my lad! It's the mud of the Yangtze delta. Seeps out from the river and stains the ocean a sort of yellowy brown, for miles out. Lets you know what you're up against, in a way. Mud from the river stains the sea, stains the soul. Shanghai is that kind of place."

Leo smiled despite himself. "Are you a missionary, then?"

"Good God, no! Although Shanghai attracts a large number of them, and for good reason. I'm an architectural engineer, actually. I've had several excellent commissions in Shanghai over the past few years, though I haven't been back since '21. Frightfully difficult place to build a proper commercial building. Everything sinks into the mud. This time out I'll be working on the engineering plans for the new Customs House on the Bund—that's the main street lining the harbor. Sort of a financial district, only with cargo ships unloading right out front. But you'd think you were sailing up to the heart of any European capital, with all the stone work and marble columns. Our new building will be the crowning glory of the Bund. Should be about a year before I head back to England." He paused, giving Leo a chance to respond. Then, obviously unbothered by Leo's lack of participation in the conversation, Cosgrove kept talking.

"First time there, did you say? Not such a bad decision, really. It's rather a good time to be getting to Shanghai. The whole city is booming. Again. Things were off a bit right after the Chinese outlawed the importation of opium, but now the Shanghailanders—that's what the white residents call themselves—are making money faster than they can think of ways to spend it. Of course, once the big merchants began making money, that is, *real* money, everything else just followed along—doctors, lawyers, architects, the telegraph, tramways—why, there are suburbs full of Tudor homes and Mediterranean villas; you can even import roses and magnolias for your garden, if you like. Buy anything you want in the department stores. It's downright civilized, Shanghai is. Except, of course, for the fact that one is in China." He finished his soliloquy with a snort of amusement, still entertained by what was obviously a well-used joke.

Leo digested all of this information without comment. He was beginning to reconsider his strategy. Perhaps a chat with this Cosgrove fellow would prove useful, after all. He himself knew so little about Shanghai, except for two, equally important facts; he could enter without a visa, and there was money to be made there. Rather than excuse himself, Leo opted to pursue the conversation.

"You sound like an old China hand," he remarked, smiling and injecting a bit of admiration into his voice, encouraging Cosgrove to go on. The older man seemed flattered.

"Oh, no, not really. Not like some of the chaps out here. Taipans, they're called: the real industrialists. The men in charge. It's an odd society. Classless, in a way. Money is the only calling card you need. The only thing a well-placed silver dollar cannot obtain for you is a seat on the short end of the Long Bar at the Shanghai Club. The Club is the one place that caters to a more, shall we say, *traditional* British crowd. But the rest of the city...." He spread his hands, palms up. "Few rules, no limits."

"So, most of the foreign residents are British?"

"No, actually, though the King's subjects probably control the biggest slice of the pie. My friends there tell me that the problem now is the White Russians, who started pouring in after I left in '21. Poor bastards. They're the only whites actually subject to Chinese law, for they have no government of their own to protect them. Ghastly business. Stateless, helpless, fleeing for their lives from the Soviet Reds. Lots of pretty Russian women, though, if you are interested in paying for that sort of thing. Caused the whole white community to lose a lot of face, but, without changing the city's entire immigration policy, there was no way to keep the poor Russian bastards out. Some of them claim to be royalty, of course, which is hogwash. Anyone with a shilling to their name would have gone to England, or France, or—well—anywhere, other than Shanghai."

Leo tried to ignore the touch of apprehension that brushed against the bottom of his stomach. "Why? If it's a place of such opportunity?"

Cosgrove chuckled. "Well, let me put it like this. I am only a periodic visitor, but from what I have seen, Shanghai is a damn fine place to *get* rich, and not a bad place to *be* rich, but it's a wretched place to be poor."

"In my experience, there is no good place to be poor."

"No, no, I guess not. But there must be better than Shanghai." The Englishman grew pensive, and stared out at the ocean for a moment. Leo, thinking that their discussion had ended, was about to take his leave when Cosgrove snapped out of his somber reverie.

"So, are you heading to Shanghai at the behest of your company?"

"No," Leo shook his head, and looked down at the ship's rail with a small twist of a grin. "I'm on a more—independent venture."

"Ah," said Cosgrove. He did not press further. Dimly Leo remembered Mitchell's words: "If you knew anything about Shanghai, you would not have asked that question, for no one goes to Shanghai if he has anywhere else to go...."

"Look there!" he then heard Cosgrove saying. "See the water? It's gone brown." Leo looked. So it had. They were approaching the land of his future.

The two men continued their conversation for the better part of two hours, as the ship cruised across the few remaining miles of the East China Sea and into the placid mouth of the Yangtze. Like most loquacious people, Cosgrove's favorite topic of conversation was himself, and he developed a naive fondness for anyone who gave him the opportunity to expound upon his life experiences. He therefore took an immediate liking to Leo, who easily elicited from him a wealth of information about life in Shanghai, including a recommendation on where to stay.

"I'll be lodging at Broadway Mansions, in an apartment that our company maintains for part-timers like myself. But I'm sure you will be quite comfortable at the Palace Hotel, until you find your own place to settle into," Cosgrove insisted earnestly. Leo appreciated the advice. It gave him a place to start.

So Cosgrove talked and talked and Leo listened; however, evidently mindful of Shanghai etiquette, the Englishman asked Leo no more questions about himself. Nor did he suggest that they get together once they reached their common destination. It was as if the older man were waiting, politely and without expectation, for Leo to make an overture.

Torn between his desire to cling to the safety of anonymity and his hunch that Cosgrove could prove a useful acquaintance, Leo decided that he could not pass up the opportunity to gain a potential entree into Shanghai's upper crust. By the time the ship lowered its anchor, they had arranged to meet in two day's time, for what Cosgrove called "a rousing Shanghai evening."

"I'll just leave a message for you at the Palace. It's been a pleasure," said Cosgrove as the two parted. Leo felt comfortable with his decision to pursue the man's acquaintance. Information translated into confidence, confidence into security and security into sending for Martha. He was ready to get started.

But started at what? Hours later, settled into a comfortable suite at the Palace Hotel, he tried to come up with a feasible plan. With a small pocket knife he removed the Cartier necklace from its hiding place in the lining of his overcoat, and laid it out on the bed. The stones shimmered, cold and beautiful, unaffected by bloodshed, by heartache, by flight. He lifted the heavy necklace to eye level, dangling it gingerly from the clasp. The diamonds caught a stray sunbeam and fractured it into a hundred tiny rainbows, scattering them around the room.

Now he understood the true reason that Károly had been interested in this particular necklace. He saw the logic of buying a necklace made up of smaller, but perfect, stones. A single large gem would have been easier to trace. While the individual stones would never fetch the same price as the original Cartier necklace, their simplicity rendered them fungible. Marketed discretely, they would never be traced back to the original piece. And there were over forty of them.

Leo was no longer interested in working for a paycheck. For Martha, he needed protection. He needed security. He needed money. He needed a lot of money, the kind of money that could be used to build an unscalable wall between his new life and his past. But to obtain that kind of wealth, he would have to take risks. He must somehow multiply the value of the diamonds several fold.

Leo studied the necklace. It was his ticket to freedom, or his writ of execution. He had to use it correctly.

"Well," he said to the stones in Russian, "Until I discover the best way to use you, my little friends, I had best take care of you." As he expected, a small sewing kit was included with the complementary hotel toiletries. He carefully stitched the necklace into the lining of a wool vest, a vest that he could wear with several different suits. It was very cold. Wearing a vest all the time would not appear unusual.

After bathing and changing, Leo ventured into the hotel lobby. He had long since learned that the best way to attract money was to convey the impression that you did not need it. The pennies he would save by staying at a lesser establishment would not matter, in the long run. If he went broke, they would not matter; if he succeeded in converting the necklace into significant wealth, they would not matter. What mattered was the opportunities he seized upon, *right now.*

Leo could see that the Palace was an establishment worthy of the name. It sat on the corner of the Bund and Nanking Road, where the financial world and the shopping district converged. The proud hotel catered to the well-to-do, itinerant population of Shanghai. Japanese, French, British, American and Chinese businessman lounged at the bar. Busy wives and mistresses flitted through the lobby, where impressive piles of hat boxes, suitcases and steamer trunks testified to the financial success of their mates. High heels clicked on the marble floor. Telephones rang. Ice clinked musically inside the crystal glasses served by slim Chinese waiters, clad in white. To Leo, it was an engagingly familiar scene.

He approached the concierge's desk. According to Cosgrove, the Brits seemed to carry the most clout. He therefore launched into a breezy, upper-class British accent.

"Hello, good man. I'm a new arrival here. Any ideas on where to buy a rather nice piece of jewelry?"

The young Belgian gentleman behind the desk studied Leo for a fraction of a moment. Excellent suit, perfectly fitted. Impressive posture. His stance suggested he was used to service, and casual about money. Lacked the bad teeth and weak chin of a typical British aristocrat. Still, he was probably a Lord, thought the concierge. Better send him to a nice place.

"May I suggest Katiana's? Her shop is about a mile down the way, near the big department stores, on Nanking Road. She has an unusual collection of quality items, including quite a few pieces of Russian and Chinese imperial jewelry. Just give her my card and she will be sure to show you her best." *And she'll be sure to pay me a commission.*

"Wonderful. Actually, come to think of it, I suppose I need to pick up some of the local currency first."

"The cashier will be happy to oblige."

"Very good. Thanks much."

Once outside, Leo turned left to head up Nanking road, and was immediately engulfed by the crowd. He'd lived in Budapest, and had been to Paris, but he had never experienced anything like this. On Nanking Road, there were herds of people, mostly Chinese, crowding the sidewalks, the street, and the storefronts. There were literally people everywhere, along with dozens of different ways of transporting them, their wares, and their purchases. There were rickshaws, wheelbarrows, ox-carts, pony-carts, handcarts, pedicabs, scooters, and bicycles. Human beasts of burden trotted along with bamboo poles slung across their shoulders, bent double by the weight of the baskets full of fish, firewood, or brick that dangled from each end of the pole. The tram clicked and hummed its way up the avenue. A few automobiles chugged arrogantly through the maze of wheels and faces. A turbaned Sikh directed vehicular and pedestrian traffic at each major intersection, making no real distinction between the two.

And then there were the stores. Cosgrove had been right. You could buy anything on Nanking Road. Leo passed the American Book Shop; The Chocolate Shop (advertising its "famous American ice cream sodas"), and the Lao K'ai Fook silk shop, bursting with bolts of shantung, pongee, and iridescent silk. He walked by jewelry shops and optometrists, shoe stores and a store that sold nothing but baby carriages. Exactly one mile from the Bund were the department stores— Sincere, Sun Sun, and Wing-On, where one could buy German cameras, French perfume, English leather goods and Japanese pearls, or play ping pong, billiards, or roller skate, listen to music, or just have a drink and watch the sea of faces roll by. It was chaos. But, at least for the immediate future, it was home.

Later that day he was back in his hotel room, necklace in hand, prying the first of the stones free with a pair of pliers he had picked up at a hardware store. By studying Madame Katiana's inventory and inquiring rather directly about prices, he now knew, roughly, what one of his own stones was worth. Now he would sell one. Selling more than one might be dangerous, for he had no idea what type of information, if any, would be available about the theft. One transaction would test the waters.

He also knew where to go to sell his diamond. He would go straight to the place Madame Katiana had warned him to stay away from: Avenue Joffre, the heart of the "White Russian" district in the French Concession. Leo had no doubt that she found some of her own pieces there, or else she would not have tried so vigorously to steer him away from the "crooks and cheats on Avenue Joffre," when he inquired about other dealers in estate jewelry.

The following morning he hired a rickshaw to take him to Avenue Joffre. Skirting the boundary of the old Chinese walled city, the even trot of the sinewy coolie brought Leo, with surprising speed, to the heart of the French Concession, and the lengthy boulevard that had earned the nickname, "Little Russia." The road was lined with dress shops, fur salons, Russian restaurants, and questionable nightclubs. Here and there a small knot of shabby men clustered around two compatriots playing chess. Banners advertised instruction in mathematics, Russian, French, and tutoring for musical instruments of all kinds. Leo was surrounded by Russian music, Russian writing, Russian voices, and Russian faces. He felt like he had turned a corner and crossed the border.

Leo elected to investigate the neighborhood on foot. Stepping down from the rickshaw, he tossed the coolie puller a tip he did not yet realize was far too generous. Rather than express gratitude, the cunning Chinese leveled several loud mandarin curses at Leo, decrying his stinginess, hoping that the tall foreigner would be embarrassed into giving him more. When he could see that no more coins were forthcoming, the coolie added a few more curses for emphasis before picking up the poles of his rickshaw.

Oblivious to the small drama being staged for his benefit, Leo strolled casually down the street, his frosty breath creating a mist a foot above the heads of most of the other men and women on the street. He walked down alleys and side streets, looking for the Cyrillic characters indicating a jeweler. He needed the right sort of jeweler. He needed a man of talent, and a man who could be trusted.

At last he saw a sign that intrigued him. The Russian word for jeweler decorated a small silk banner, hung over the door to the basement entry of a nondescript two-story building. Leo descended the uneven stairs and knocked on the plain wooden door.

"Da," a voice answered. Leo walked in.

It took a moment for his eyes to adjust to the dark, for the small half-window let in little light. Leo could make out an armchair, a small Franklin stove, and a workbench displaying the tools of the jeweler's trade. For an instant he thought he saw a large, long-haired animal crouched on the stool at the bench. Then the creature turned towards him, and Leo could see the face of an old man, peering out of what appeared to be a fur cape. *Muskrat,* thought Leo.

The man spoke, again in his native Russian.

"May I help you in some way?"

Something in the old man's voice put Leo at ease. He heard sincerity in his words. It was not the voice of a shopkeeper waiting to pounce upon a prospective client, but the welcome of a humble artist, looking to be of service. Leo knew he had come to the right place.

"I hope so," Leo responded, Russian words flowing effortlessly from his lips. "I have something I would like to sell. Something that will, I think, interest you." He removed a silk handkerchief from his breast pocket.

With a patient expression the old man extended a pale, wrinkled hand from underneath the mound of fur engulfing him, and gestured for Leo to approach. Leo did so, and placed the handkerchief on the table. He unfolded it to reveal the diamond.

Wordlessly, the jeweler lit a candle, then put on a bizarre pair of glasses. Two cone-shaped magnifying loupes were positioned where ordinary lenses should have been, giving him the visage of a monstrous insect. Holding the diamond close to the flame, the jeweler inspected it carefully. Still, he did not speak; but a sharp intake and exhale of his breath caused the candle to flicker, which let Leo know that he was impressed.

"If it is what it appears to be...." he murmured. Putting the stone back onto his table, he removed his glasses, and picked up a small brown bottle from which he extracted liquid with a dropper. The acid splashed harmlessly off the diamond, then hissed slightly as it ate into the varnished wood of the workbench.

"A marvelous stone. A beauty. Emerald-cut, five carats, colorless and perfect. I am afraid that I do not have the resources to pay you what it is worth."

Leo had come prepared to bargain. "What could you give me for it?" he inquired, ready to counter any offer.

"What I could give you is irrelevant, unless you are desperate, and you do not strike me as a desperate man. Not yet, at any rate. Believe me, my son, I have given many desperate people the help that they needed. But I cannot help you. I could cheat you, but I cannot help you."

Startled, Leo realized that the man was not adopting a coy bargaining strategy; he was speaking the truth. Leo's frustration quickly crowded out any sense of gratitude. How long would it take to find the right person? He could not live long on the remains of his one thousand francs. He must sell at least one stone, soon.

"Do you think that you may know of someone who would be interested in such a stone, and willing to pay a fair price for it?"

For a moment there was no reply, and Leo was about to repeat the question, when the old man spoke.

"There is a man, a Chinese, who comes here to my shop, for he knows I occasionally acquire worthy pieces. His name is Lee Wusong. He works for an influential man. A rich man. This man, for whom he works, is very difficult to impress. But even Liu Tue-Sheng is impressed by perfection, and he has three wives to satisfy. Do you have three such diamonds?" The old man smiled, revealing teeth that Leo wished had remained unseen. Nonetheless, he smiled in return.

"Perhaps."

"Even better. I will give you Mr. Lee's address. You may tell him that Olanavich sent you. He will speak to you. When he finds the time." The wrinkled hands appeared again, to scribble a Chinese name and an address on the back of a calling card, which the jeweler then courteously extended to Leo.

"Thank you."

"It is of no consequence. Thank you for sharing with me an object of such rare beauty." The old Russian carefully wrapped the diamond back into its temporary home, and handed the handkerchief back to Leo, who thanked him again, and turned to leave. Just before opening the door, he stopped short.

"This gentleman, Liu Tue-Sheng, is he discreet?"

Another brief silence. Then, a non-answer.

"You are new to Shanghai."

Leo stepped back into the center of the tiny room. He had the feeling more details were forthcoming.

"Yes. Is there something that I should know?"

The old man shrugged. "If you do not yet know of Liu Tue-Sheng, you soon will. They say he is the head of the Green Gang, an ancient and secret organized crime society. They say he is responsible for gambling, prostitution, kidnapping, and most of the illegal opium trade. They say that he has compromised the integrity of the entire police force of the French Concession, and the French Ambassador as well. They say that he has a private army. I know that he serves on the board of two banks, a hospital, and several charities; I know that he keeps his word and pays his debts. I would say that you can trust him to be discreet about where he acquires his diamonds."

This time Leo did more than thank Olanavich. He took a handful of silver coins out of his pocket and laid them on the table. Then he went back out into the cold.

Leo decided to delay his call on Mr. Lee until after his meeting with Cosgrove. He wanted to run Liu's name past the Englishman to see if he could confirm any of the information the old Russian had given him. He was not disappointed.

For their night on the town Cosgrove brought them to Mina's, a club that, judging from the crowd, seemed to appeal to affluent British bachelors. The Russian hostesses were eager to please. The food was good, and the drinks were only slightly watered down. A raucous floor show consisting of scantily-clad, long-legged women provided intermittent entertainment. Cosgrove was thoroughly enjoying himself.

After giving his companion a brief, fictional account of his own life, (he admitted to being "in the hotel business," and said he was from Vienna), Leo spent a long evening listening to Cosgrove recount the history of Shanghai, elaborating on his own personal dossier, and discussing in excruciating detail the engineering challenges encountered by the intrepid settlers willing to build a European city on the silty swampland that was Shanghai. Leo congratulated Cosgrove on his brilliant architectural achievements, and then brought up Liu Tue-Sheng.

"Tell me, what do you know about a man by the name of Liu Tue-Sheng?"

Cosgrove raised his eyebrows. The cigar he was savoring tilted up at a forty-five degree angle. He removed it to speak.

"Good Lord! You haven't gotten mixed up with him already, have you?"

Smiling, Leo shook his head. "I've just heard some interesting things about him, and wondered how much of it is true."

"Well, chances are it's all true and then some. What have you heard?"

"That he is obscenely rich, has three wives, and has the French police in his pocket. That he is involved in prostitution and opium smuggling. That he is a kind of a gangster, but seems to have carved out a respectable niche for himself, at least in some circles."

"Well, that is all true enough, except that I don't know if I agree with the 'respectable niche' part. Liu is a character alright, and a damn dangerous one. Why, I heard that he once sent a coffin 'round to someone he thought had cheated him. Had it delivered to the front door, just like a telegram. Chap had the good sense to leave the country, too, chop chop. Liu doesn't make empty threats."

Cosgrove paused for a moment to look at the tip of his cigar. To his dismay, it had gone out. He signaled for one of the hostesses to come over and relight it for him. A tall brunette did so, suggestively striking a match without taking her luminous eyes off Leo. Leo did not respond. Cosgrove did not appear to notice. He took another puff of his cigar, briefly watched the resultant circle of smoke hover over the table, then resumed his speech.

"And as for the French police, why, the frogs on this side of the Pacific don't know the meaning of the word integrity. I have no doubt he has the whole force sewn up. Good thing he hasn't yet wormed his way onto the Municipal Council."

"I hear he owns a bank, and is on the boards of several important charities, including a hospital."

Cosgrove gave Leo a curious look. "Listen here. I don't know what kind of deal you may be cooking up, but Liu is a bad character. Rather than fight corruption, he profits from it. He has covered his evil tracks with a veneer of respectability, but the polish can't hide the dirt underneath. Oh, I've heard he's a man of his word, but I wouldn't put it past him to sell his children if the price were right. They just don't have the same conscience, these Chinese. Even if they seem trustworthy, doesn't mean they won't do you in – just that they won't lie to you about it. Doesn't mean you'll see the knife coming, though."

"I'll keep my eyes open." The reappearance of the dancing girls curtailed their conversation, and gave Leo a moment to think. It sounded like Liu might be just what Olanavich had suggested. Wealthy and wicked, but discreet. Just the man to approach with some black market diamonds. Three of them. One for each wife.

The next day he tracked down the address Olanavich had given him. It lead him to a handsome villa on Bubbling Well Road, in the British residential section. Mr. Lee was not at home. Leo left a message, neatly written on the back of his own freshly printed calling card, displaying his new address at the Palace.

Mr. Lee,

A mutual friend, Mr. Olanavich, suggested that I contact you regarding the purchase of some precious gems. Please feel free to get in touch with me, at your leisure.

Then he waited.

For one week he heard nothing from the mysterious Mr. Lee. To pass the time he tried to busy himself by learning more about life in Shanghai. He knew that the people who worked in his hotel could pass along valuable facts. Cloaked with the invisibility of servitude, they learned things about the wealthy and the powerful that would be useful to know. He engaged the hotel pianist, the flower shop girl, and the bartender in cozy conversation. Reticent at first, they all eventually talked freely. It was impossible not to talk to Leo.

He also hired a real estate agent to show him houses, pretending that he was quite ready to buy one. He picked an agent who was as gossipy as Cosgrove. Leo soaked up details about his new home as quickly and intensely as he had when he was young boy new to Budapest. Then, just as he was about to find another avenue for disposing of the first of his diamonds, he received a telephone call.

"Mr. Hoffman?" The voice sounded raspy but cordial, and definitely Chinese.

"Speaking."

"This is Mr. Lee. Our mutual acquaintance, Mr. Olanavich, tells me that you are new to Shanghai, and suggests you have something of value in which my employer may be interested. He thought you may have three such items."

"He did?"

"Yes. I must confirm such things."

"Of course. I understand."

"Mr. Olanavich indicated that you are Russian. Yet, you speak

English with no accent. Very difficult. My compliments."

"Thank you." Leo offered no explanation. His origins were irrelevant. Mr. Lee continued.

"Could you possibly bring these items to a meeting this evening?"

"This evening? Well, yes, I suppose that would be possible. What did you have in mind?"

"Do you know the Willow Lake Tea House?"

"I have heard of it."

"You will find it most charming, I am sure. Shall we say, five o'clock?"

"That would be convenient."

"Very well. I will arrange for a private room. Ask for me when you enter."

"Of course."

"Then, until this evening."

"Yes."

"Goodbye."

Leo knew exactly how to get to there. The Willow Lake Tea was in the old Chinese section of the city, Nantao. It sat in the center of a small lake. One reached the decorative oriental villa via a zigzagging footbridge, a path designed to confuse evil spirits, which, according to Chinese lore, could only cross water in a straight line.

Leo arrived on time. He was immediately shown to a small, private room. A full English tea had been laid out on the low table. Mr. Lee was waiting.

He was a small, dumpling-shaped man. He wore his black hair greased to one side, and he was dressed in a comfortably cut, crisp wool suit. He gave no indication that theirs was anything other than a purely social visit, making small talk for the better part of an hour, regaling Leo with bits and pieces of historical information about Shanghai. Leo knew better than to push. He knew he was being evaluated.

Just when Leo thought his meeting would prove fruitless, Mr. Lee asked to see the stones.

He looked at them for several minutes, saying nothing. Then he looked up. A sparkle of intrigue glinted deep within his dark brown eyes.

"I will communicate with my employer. If he is interested, I will contact you."

Leo received a note from Mr. Lee two days later. Something about the obsequious air with which the hotel clerk delivered it made Leo curious about the size of the tip that had been passed to ensure that it reached his hands. As he opened the tastefully plain envelope, Leo could not help but notice that the stationary was from Gump's, in San Francisco. He read the letter with interest:

My employer would like to meet with you regarding the transaction you proposed. A driver will be sent to escort you. Please be prepared to leave the Palace at 3:00 P.M. tomorrow.
   Mr. Lee

Leo noted that the invitation did not provide the opportunity to respond negatively. If the time were not convenient, it implied, then you must change your plans. This confirmed one fact regarding Liu Tue-Sheng: he was accustomed to power. Leo knew better than to tempt the man's patience.

The next afternoon, at precisely two fifty-five, Leo took a seat in a comfortable leather chair in the lobby of the Palace. He did not have long to wait. A bear-like Asian man, his barrel chest crammed into a western-style pin-stripe suit, strode into the lobby at a moment before three. His bearing communicated that he was on a mission. Glancing around the crowded lobby, he zeroed in on Leo and marched over to his chair. He spoke to Leo in the hissing, deeply accented speech of a coolie who has just moved beyond Pidgin English.

"Meesta 'Offmann?"

Leo's heart pounded inside his chest, but he did not stand. He had to establish his authority over Liu's subordinates.

"Yes?"

"The cah await."

"And for whom is the car waiting?"

This puzzled the driver. "You not espec a cah, sir?"

"I am not in the habit of climbing into strange limousines. If you have instructions suggesting that I should accompany you, you must first tell me who issued the invitation, and where we are going."

Leo could tell he'd stumped the man. He could see the consternation building across his features as he weighed his alternatives.

"We go to Meesta Liu Tue-Sheng house, sir," he blurted out.

"Very good." Thus informed, Leo stood up. "I will retrieve my coat." Now grateful that Leo had not caused a problem, the driver held the lobby door open for him as the two left the building. He did so with no loss of face. This man was surely not as powerful as his own master, but he was not a servant. A servant would not dare to ask such questions.

Settling into the back seat of Liu's Rolls Royce, Leo unconsciously felt for the three diamonds nestled in his breast pocket. Now, finally, something was happening. This was his first chance to turn disaster into triumph. His first chance to create a future that could include Martha.

With many aggressive maneuvers and much blowing of the horn, Liu's driver pushed through the chaos of Nanking Road. Once clear of the commercial district they sped past the gracious lawn of the municipal racecourse, then turned left onto Mohawk Road, which took them into the residential heart of the French Concession. Within twenty minutes the car stood outside the gates of Liu's estate.

Leo was immediately struck by the fortifications. The compound was surrounded by an eight-foot brick wall, crowned with vicious-looking slabs of broken glass. The guard at the gatehouse peeked into the back seat to confirm Leo's presence, then looked in the trunk as well. Once granted admission, the car meandered up the long, winding driveway. Small guard posts dotted the landscape at regular intervals. Despite the intense security, the grounds were serene and beautifully landscaped, a pleasure for the senses even in the middle of winter.

The vehicle reached the main house and pulled up under the stone porte-cochére. The mansion was built in the manner of an Edwardian villa. Arches, balustrades and Palladian windows endowed the facade with an airy symmetry. The gigantic building looked like it had been imported stone by stone from Europe.

A young Chinese servant dressed in a floor length gown of starched white cotton greeted Leo at the door. Once inside, the resemblance to a European residence diminished. The entrance hall was lined with glass cases, displaying not antiques or bibelots, but an impressive arsenal of rifles. Beyond the entrance hall the decor was unmistakably Chinese. Elaborately carved, high-backed chairs, silk settees, exquisite screens, and numerous plants and porcelain pots filled the rooms. Here and there Leo spotted a costly European piece: a Louis XIV clock, and a Chippendale chair. Either Liu had an excellent eye, or he knew enough to take the advice of someone who had one. Either scenario bode well for Leo.

His guide stopped in front of what appeared to be the entrance to a private study. Before showing him in, the boy executed a delicate but professional frisk of Leo's person. Leo acquiesced without comment, then was shown into the room.

Lustrous rosewood paneling glimmered on the walls. The room's grand Palladian windows offered a view of a small Buddhist temple, tucked under the branches of an ancient willow tree. The study contained two writing tables, with several matching mandarin-style chairs. The carved wood was inlaid with mother-of-pearl. Rolls of parchment, which Leo took to be correspondence, covered the desktops. A few feet from the desk a mahogany dragon rose four feet into the air to form the base of a pedestal. Balanced upon the dragon's curved tail was a five-gallon crystal bowl, containing a large, fan-tailed goldfish.

Leo had only a moment to admire the view before he heard footsteps. As he turned to face the door, Liu Tue-Sheng entered the room.

He was thin, terribly thin, but tall for a Chinese; his gaze met Leo's directly. The long, traditional Chinese robes he wore accentuated his height. Liu's costume was fashioned from heavy, cream-colored silk. The high mandarin collar and wide sleeves were trimmed in a floral pattern, embroidered with red and gold thread. The hem stopped just short of the floor, to reveal pointed, western-style boots.

High, gaunt cheekbones punctuated Liu's long, narrow face. What remained of his hair was gray, and cut short. His nose added no character to his features. There was nothing particularly intimidating about this man, except for the fact that his black eyes conveyed absolutely no emotion, like the eyes of a shark.

"Mister Hoffman. I am Liu...Tue-Sheng. Thank you for accepting my...invitation." He delivered the words in precise, near-flawless

English, but the cadence of his speech was stilted. Leo suspected that his awkwardness resulted from the concentration required to avoid the pitfalls of an oriental accent. It seemed that Liu would rather speak slowly than sound like a coolie. Again, Leo was impressed.

"Thank you for inviting me to your beautiful home. It is an honor."

Liu acknowledged this compliment with a slight motion of his head. Swinging a wide sleeve away from his slim frame, he gestured to one of the chairs.

"Please be seated. I regret that we have not much time today to conduct our business. You have brought the stones with you, I assume?"

"Of course."

Liu took a seat behind one of the desks, and cleared several scrolls out of the way.

"Would you be so kind as to let me examine them?"

"It would be my pleasure." Leo placed the handkerchief containing the diamonds on the desk, then reclaimed his seat.

Liu unrolled the handkerchief carefully, allowing each stone to roll onto the wooden surface. He then picked them up one by one, and held each up to the light for a fraction of a moment before setting it back down on the desk.

"Exquisite."

With this comment, Liu rose, and drifted over to the fish bowl. The crystal orb's graceful resident detected the presence of its master, and greedily explored the surface of the water. Liu removed a pinch of a flaky brown substance from a small porcelain container sitting next to the bowl. With meticulous care, he sprinkled the fish's repast across the water, and then spoke again, the motionless brocade of his silk-covered back still facing Leo.

"I have been assured that the three diamonds you offer are spectacular. I assume that you could, if necessary, locate others of a similar caliber?"

Leo began to panic. Liu knew! Why else would he think there were more diamonds? This was a trap! He was as good as dead! With every ounce of self-control he possessed, Leo remained outwardly calm. He must find out whether he was in any real danger.

"Why? Would you be interested in more?"

"There is that possibility." Now Liu turned, moving with the unhurried air of a man used to setting the pace of a conversation. The expressionless eyes once again focused on Leo.

"If we could reach an appropriate arrangement, I have an acquaintance who might find your diamonds useful. He is involved in—shall we say, a certain project—which requires that he distribute reasonably large amounts of capital to various interested persons—"

"Payoffs?" interjected Leo, wanting to demonstrate that he knew why such arrangements were made. A pause was the only confirmation he received.

"These people, with whom he is dealing, are peasants. They do not trust paper money, and silver *taels* are quite cumbersome to move around the country. Gold, is, of course, an alternative, but it would seem that a quantity of stones, such as these, could also prove to be a convenient way of transferring funds from my friend's hands to the greedy hands he must placate."

"What do you mean by a quantity?"

"As many as you can obtain."

"I see." Leo's mind was racing. Liu's story sounded plausible, but it had been his own gullibility with respect to Károly's scheme that had landed him in this predicament in the first place. On the other hand, what did he have to lose? If Liu intended to see him arrested in order to collect some kind of reward, then he already had enough evidence to connect Leo to the stolen stones. Maybe his best alternative was to dump all of the damn things now and hope Liu did not turn him in.

A lull of awkward proportions was starting to develop when Liu spoke again. "Are you a gambler, Mr. Hoffman?"

The nonsequitur took Leo off guard. He answered with some hesitation, wondering where the question would lead.

"I have been known to play an occasional game of chance."

"Good...I, also, enjoy a game of chance from time to time. All Chinese do. It is in the blood. The desire to take risks. To seek a shorter path. For most Chinese, the long path leads only to suffering. Most of the Europeans who come to Shanghai are also seeking a shorter path. Or running away from something. Or both."

Leo interpreted this as an opportunity for him to explain the reason for his own presence in Shanghai, but Liu did not seem inclined to wait for an answer.

"There are times when one's path crosses another's at a mutually convenient time. Perhaps this is such a time for the two of us. Perhaps we should take a chance, together. What do you think?"

"I'd like to know the terms of the wager."

"Of course." Liu brought the tips of his fingertips together and rested them under his chin for a moment before continuing. "Your diamonds are lovely. And very valuable. But I have found that there is nothing as valuable as information. I will give you a choice; you may receive, for your diamonds, the full value of what one could buy them for from a jeweler on Nanking Road—what do you call it—"

"Retail value," interposed Leo.

"Yes, retail," continued Liu with a small nod, "Or, I will pay half of that amount. In the latter case, I will also give you a piece of advice on how to invest the proceeds. This information could prove much more valuable than the diamonds themselves, but that success is not guaranteed."

Leo's brain churned. The man must at least suspect that the diamonds were stolen. But in that case, why would he bother to offer anything more than street value for them? Where was the catch? Could he get anything else out of Liu that might help him decide what to do?

"I can obtain no more than forty diamonds," stated Leo in a crisp tone. "Does that affect the terms of your offer?"

"No. I had hoped for more, but forty diamonds could prove very useful."

"And what is the nature of this `investment advice,' that you mentioned?"

"One cannot, as you Europeans say, expose too much of one's hand, Mr. Hoffman. I will say only that I genuinely believe the information to be of tremendous value, if handled...properly. Does the possibility of multiplying your investment in your diamonds intrigue you?"

"Did I ever say that they were my diamonds?"

"Ah! My mistake. I did not take you for a broker. Perhaps it is the owner of the diamonds with whom I should speak." Liu issued this suggestion matter-of-factly, and rose from his chair. Startled, Leo raised his hand.

"There is no one with any greater negotiating power than I."

The words had the desired effect. Liu resumed his seat. He shrugged.

"So, now it is time for a decision. Will you take what you and I know the diamonds to be worth, or will you take a chance?"

The eyes did not flicker. Leo detected no trace of a smile. He doubted the man even had a sense of humor. But there was something about him that seemed trustworthy. Not because he seemed morally upright, not at all; it was as if lies were simply not worth his time. He was ruthless, but he was not a liar.

Honor among thieves. "I will take the information, and two-thirds of what the diamonds are worth."

This time Liu did smile, conveying satisfaction at a bargain well made, rather than pleasure. He gave Leo a nod of approval.

"A brave choice, and an intelligent one. I did not misjudge you. Tomorrow, at eight o'clock, my associate, Mr. Lee, will meet you in the lobby of the Palace hotel. He will accompany you to a place where the authenticity of the diamonds can be verified. You will then receive your money, and a letter containing the information of which I spoke. And now, forgive me, but I have other affairs to which I must attend."

Liu rose, extending a hand to Leo. The tough, thin fingers felt like the claw of a bird. He overcame the urge to shudder.

A moment later he was back in Liu's limousine, oblivious of the driver, and ignoring the scenery that had fascinated him only a short time ago. He'd passed some type of initiation. He wondered why Liu agreed so readily to the higher price. He wondered if the diamonds were the real reason that Liu had wanted to meet with him. After all, Liu could have ordered Mr. Lee to handle the entire transaction. He wondered if Mr. Lee were going to lead him straight into the welcoming arms of the French police. What sort of investment opportunity he had bargained for? And when, and how, would he see Martha again?

❧

The next day Leo received another letter on Mr. Lee's stationary. He was to bring his "merchandise" that night to an address located in the old Chinese section of the city.

An hour before their scheduled appointment, Leo emerged from the warmth of the Palace Hotel into a brutally cold, damp night. For this trip he preferred to be responsible for his own transportation. It was difficult to escape from a moving automobile. Wary even of the wretched rickshaw drivers huddled outside the hotel's entrance, Leo made his way on foot into the contorted maze that was the original city of Shanghai.

The neighborhood did not inspire confidence. Unlike the welcoming European face of the Bund, the Old City retained a hostile oriental countenance that made all but the most experienced China hands feel ill at ease. The layers of ancient buildings, crouched along their narrow, winding streets, provided the perfect setting for an ambush. Leo moved cautiously, senses alert, trying to discern whether he was being watched or followed. The bent and shrouded figures shuffling quickly along the twisted windswept streets revealed nothing. The only apprehension he could detect was his own.

The address led him to what appeared to be a money changer's shop. As it was long past regular business hours, the sparsely furnished store looked deserted, but the ever punctual Mr. Lee responded instantly to Leo's light tap on the heavy wooden door.

Once inside, Leo handed the man a small leather case containing forty emerald-cut diamonds from the Cartier necklace. Nodding and smiling politely, Mr. Lee pulled a bell cord, and, within seconds, invisible hands lowered a small wire basket through a circular hole in the low-slung ceiling. Lee then placed the unopened satchel in the basket, which promptly disappeared in the same fashion. During the day, unseen clerks in the upstairs room would normally count currency, convert it, and extract a commission. Tonight, in the tiny room above their heads, an expert was carefully examining each diamond to make sure that Liu Tue-Sheng was not cheated.

Leo managed to make polite responses to Mr. Lee's chatter. His nerves were stretched to the limit. The minutes ticked by, and he waited. It was worse than waiting for a screaming mortar shell to find its point of impact. For now his future mattered more than it had during the war. Martha made it matter.

After what seemed like an eternity the basket came back through the hole in the ceiling. The satchel was still there. Smiling once more, Mr. Lee retrieved it and handed it back to Leo.

"Please examine contents, to note that all is satisfactory."

Leo did as he was asked. The diamonds were gone. In their place was what seemed to be an enormous quantity of cash in pounds sterling, and a small white envelope.

"Everything looks in order." He wondered if he should count the money.

"Please, count," said Mr. Lee, correctly reading his thoughts.

Leo did so, examining each note for signs of genuineness. He did not intend to be paid in counterfeit notes after what he'd been through.

"There does not seem to be a problem with the money."

"And, the envelope? Please?"

Again, Leo followed Mr. Lee's suggestion. The envelope contained a plain, small white card. Printed on it, in English, were the words:

Rubber makes a nice birthday gift.
Buy some today.

Leo's stomach tightened into a small knot. He stared at the flippant message, his anger rising. He was a fool!

"What does this fortune cookie mean?"

Mr. Lee's polite expression did not change. "The information is there."

"Information? What information? I was supposed to receive some information I could use to enhance my profits. This is just—"

"The information is there," Mr. Lee said again, his bland face betraying nothing.

Leo stared at the sparse words. Rubber. Birthday. It clicked. Leo knew what he was supposed to do. He'd gambled. Now he must act on this tip, and see if the gamble would pay off.

❦

On a balmy evening in early June, Leo accepted an invitation from Lawrence Cosgrove to dine at the Shanghai Club. As a non-English person of ambiguous origin, it was doubtful that Leo could ever become a member of the stolid British institution, but the mere invitation to dine with a member demonstrated a certain level of prestige in Shanghai society. Leo accepted with pleasure.

The chef at the club prided himself on providing traditional English dishes for its members, whose palates were unabashedly unadventurous. Leo and Cosgrove enjoyed a hearty meal of roast mutton and Yorkshire pudding. Leo was in the process of warming his brandy over a candle, placed at their table for precisely that purpose, when he decided to bring up the subject that he had been dying to address all evening.

"Lawrence, ever done any trading on the commodities markets?"

"Good Lord, no!" A touch of self-righteousness crept into Cosgrove's voice. Leo knew he was about to receive a lecture.

"Commodities? I don't even venture into the stock market. No better than a trip to the Derby, all that nonsense. Hoping the price of this will go up, so that will come down. Ridiculous, I say. A bank is the only decent place to keep your money. Solid interest. That's the only sensible way to hang on to what you've got."

"What if you want to do more than just hang on?" Leo asked with a grin. By now he knew Cosgrove well enough to goad him a bit. When aggravated, Cosgrove rumbled and sputtered like a tea kettle boiling over. Leo found it an entertaining spectacle.

"Then invest in something you can control! Not a piece of paper worth no more than what someone else is willing to pay for it at the closing bell! Who knows what your money will be worth the next day? Why, look at what's happened with the rubber market. First, the financial pages eat up the news that the Bolsheviks are stirring up trouble on the Malay Peninsula, causing unrest on the plantations, destabilizing production. Next the word's hot that Japanese troop ships have been seen in the area, and in the Philippines. Then it's not the Japanese or the Reds, it's some disease threatening the whole region. It's not as if any of this can be verified or disproved in time to prevent wild market fluctuations. The world's full of greedy bastards who lunge at the rumors like starving hyenas. I say, leave the whole bloody mess alone."

"Wise advice," Leo replied, "but too late."

"Oh, no," Cosgrove responded, not without sympathy. "What did you get into?"

"Rubber futures."

"Good God! How long ago?"

"About five months ago. In late January. Right after I arrived."

"Whatever for?"

"A hunch."

"Hunch? Hogwash. I wished you had talked to me first. How badly have you been hit?"

Leo could not help but smile. "So far, so good."

"Really?" Cosgrove looked skeptical. The "rubber situation" had been one of the major topics of conversation at the club for three months. Like a bucking bronco, the gyrations of the rubber market had tested the nerves of many a seasoned trader. Most of the men bold enough to jump in when rumors of an imminent supply disruption sent prices leaping up sold out the moment the market headed south. The last dive devastated several prominent Shanghai Club members, who dumped their devalued positions only to see the price soar back to an all-time high within ten days.

"So you're not out yet?"

"Not yet."

"Brave cuss, or stupid. How much longer do you plan to give it?"

"I'm not sure." But this response was disingenuous. Leo knew exactly when he was going to sell his holdings. Tomorrow morning. June 10th. For no better reason than the fact that it was Liu Tue-Sheng's birthday.

Leo would never know whether Liu was behind the rumor mill that had played havoc with the rubber market for the past five months. Maybe he was giving the gangster too much credit, but he could not help but think that the tip Liu had given him as partial payment for the diamonds was part of a larger plan. It awed him to think that one man had sufficient power, or courage, to manipulate a commodity vital to world trade. Leo had played his part, making a significant purchase just as the market started to rise. He had held on through the agonizing months of spring, waiting, seeing his hopes raised, and then dashed, as his investment doubled, then quadrupled, then crashed, then soared.

From time to time during those tumultuous months Leo felt a vague sense of guilt. But his own desperation soon silenced his raw conscience. After all, he told himself, he did nothing more than invest and hang on. He had not spread any rumors himself. He took the same risks as any other investor. He had no guarantee that Liu's plan, if it was Liu's plan, would succeed. He had nothing to cling to other than hope and patience.

His patience—and his gambler's instincts—had paid off. Men whose nerves were not as strong had been broken. But Leo was rich. Very, very rich. Tomorrow he would cash in his chips. And send for Martha.

"Yes, my friend, I managed to survive the rubber debacle. And I have another piece of news for you. I think I will be staying in Shanghai for some time."

"Really? Taken a liking to the place, have you?"

"It gets into your blood, doesn't it? All this luxury—" Leo made an expansive gesture, taking in the club, its marble floors, the mahogany bar, the attentive waiters—"available for so little. And the anonymity to enjoy it."

Cosgrove's eyes communicated his curiosity. "Ah, so the anonymity appeals to you, does it?"

Leo paused, aware that he had let down his guard. But surely there was no harm in admitting he had come to Shanghai for the same reason as so many others. He lifted his glass.

"Yes. Here's to Shanghai, Lawrence. The miraculous place where broken lives begin anew."

As Leo offered his toast, Cosgrove gave him an odd look, as if he knew something that Leo did not, but elected to keep it to himself. Yet he raised his glass to Leo's, and, as the crystal goblets rang out their accord, the older man gave Leo his good wishes.

"Very well then, Leo. To a new life. May it be a long and happy one."

"For me and my wife."

"Your wife?"

"I mean, the woman I hope will soon be my wife. If she will still have me."

"My word! All sorts of secrets are pouring out of you tonight, Leo. Is this lucky lady here in Shanghai?"

"Not yet. Soon I hope. I will let you know when she arrives. I don't even know yet if she *will* come."

Six weeks later her telegram arrived. Martha was on her way.

Alone at night, Leo trembled with anticipation at the thought of having Martha in his arms, alongside him in his bed, rising to greet him in the morning. She had not given up! She was coming to Shanghai! And he had the money he needed to take care of her, to protect her. Oh, how he would spoil her! Nothing was too good for Martha. Nothing.

Everyday he toured the Bund, aching to see her. He knew she could not possibly arrive for weeks, yet still he prowled the docks, unable to keep himself away. He could sense her. She was coming to him.

CHAPTER 8

THE TYCOON

❦

Martha stepped onto the dock and felt it lurch beneath her feet. Dazed, she reached out and clutched at a pylon to steady herself. The wood felt moist and solid. She realized that the pier she was standing on had not, in fact, moved. The motion of the sea still tormented her brain, that was all: the unrelenting motion of the loathsome ocean.

During her voyage the attentive captain had assured Martha daily that, as long as she was able to keep down some of what she ate and drank, seasickness would not kill her. More than once during the past five weeks she would have preferred a quick, painless death to the torment she experienced during her journey. The nausea subsided once they reached the China Sea, and she thought the worst was behind her. Until the earth started moving, too.

Another wave of dizziness hit her. She took a deep breath and placed her hand over her mouth. The smell was not helping. Nor the noise. The overwhelming strangeness of Shanghai assaulted her senses: the stench from the river; the sing-song voices of the coolies unloading cargo with their unfamiliar, rhythmic chants; the horns and bells of the ships, bicycles and automobiles; the pleas of the beggars and the hawkers; the sticky heat; the sunburned foreignness of the faces staring at her with inquisitive admiration.

It was too much. She was too weak. She stood still, unable to move any further than the five thousand miles she had traveled to be there.

Then she saw him, and burst into tears.

In two long strides Leo reached her. Sweeping one arm around her shoulders and the other beneath her knees he lifted her off her feet and carried her as one would a small child, holding her close to his chest and murmuring comforting words as the anguish of the past nine months poured out of her in a stream of stuttered sentences and salty tears. He carried her down the dock, towards the shade of one of the trees on the thin stretch of park lawn that separated the river from the hot pavement of the Bund. He sat down on a small public bench, still holding her in his arms, as she sobbed and stammered, heedless of the curious and critical glances of their public audience. He stroked her silken auburn hair and rocked her, until she pulled her head away from his shoulder and looked at him, her eyes begging for reassurance.

"I love you, Martha Levy," he said.

It was enough.

She said nothing for a moment, then started to talk again, more calmly this time, wiping away her tears with the heel of her hand.

"Oh, Leo, I can't believe I fell apart like this. It's just that I've been so sick. The voyage was horrendous. I don't care if I never set foot on another boat as long as I live. Were you seasick?"

He smiled down at her, his heart so full of love he could not speak. Then he enveloped her in another huge hug.

"I promise. No more boats."

"Good," came the muffled reply. She squirmed to get free and, with one last sniffle, looked around.

"Goodness. What a spectacle I'm making. I'm sor—"

Leo touched a finger to her lips to cut her off. "You have nothing to be sorry for, my darling." His face then drew closer to hers, until their lips met. The warmth of her mouth instantly ignited his passion and he pulled away, acutely aware of their surroundings, and his overpowering need for her.

"Come on, my love," he said, standing up and easing her to her feet. "Let's go home."

They collected her one small suitcase from the dock, then returned to the busy traffic of the Bund, where Leo hailed a rickshaw. With Leo's assistance Martha stepped up and sat down in the peculiar little cart, her eyes wide with amazement as she took in the small, grinning coolie who was delighted to have been chosen to take them to their destination.

"He can't possibly carry us both!"

"Of course he can. Especially you, you tiny little thing. The wheels carry most of the weight."

"But it's barbaric! Being toted about by a human being!"

"Not as barbaric as letting him starve to death, which, I assure you, is a common alternative. I'm sure that this man considers himself quite lucky to be able to lease a rickshaw. We do him an honor by getting in it and helping him feed his family—or buy his opium." Leo chanted an address in Chinese. The coolie picked up the handles of his vehicle and trotted off at a brisk pace. Martha was relieved to find the regular, swaying motion of the rickshaw oddly soothing after the unpredictable movement of a ship at sea.

"Did you say opium? Is it true they all smoke opium? Leo, were you speaking Chinese? What is that man selling? My goodness, but it's hot!" Despite her queasiness, the exotic panoply passing by filled her mind with dozens of questions. She gave Leo's arm an excited squeeze.

Leo felt a surge of joy at Martha's touch. He shifted to face her and covered the small hand gripping his arm with his own, never taking his eyes off her face.

"Martha, my darling, I hear you speak and I think I must be dreaming. I've dreamed of you so often. Day and night. I just can't believe you're really here."

He looked at her like she might vanish. With that look he offered himself to her, all he was, and all he would ever be. Martha read his gaze, and understood. She touched the fingers of her free hand to his face. All of her doubts and questions settled like dust in an attic corner, far away from her heart.

"I love you, Leo. I will always love you."

He seized her fingers and kissed them, each tip, one by one. After he had planted a fervent kiss upon her thumb she brought his hand to her lap and gripped it there.

"Don't ever let go," he said quietly.

"I won't. Never again," she answered. "Never, never again."

They sat silent for a while, basking in the sweet pleasure of their reunion. Leo could feel the heat of Martha's body as she pressed his hand against her thigh. He wanted nothing more than to bury his face in the soft curve of her neck. But he would have to wait. Until they were home. Or longer. She might need some time, he chided himself. She had been through so much, on his account. Patience.

At length he spoke, thinking that he should tell her something about her new home.

"Well," he said, "as you can see we are heading into the nicer residential neighborhoods. Shanghai isn't all cargo and beggars and noise. I know this must seem so strange, to find me living on the other side of the world, but—but I hope you will grow to like it here."

"It seems so foreign, but—strangely familiar at the same time. Most of the buildings don't look the least bit oriental."

"Not in this part of town, but wait until you see the old section of the city—or some of the Chinese palaces in the French Concession. By that I mean—"

"Oh," Martha interrupted proudly, "I know all about the Concessions. And extraterritoriality, and the Nationalists and the Communists, and Sun Yat Sen, and war lords, and the White Russians, and hundred-year-old eggs—"

"Wait! Slow down! Where did you pick up all this expertise?"

"From the ship's captain."

"I see." An unmistakable note of jealously crept into his voice. "So you turned the captain into your own private tutor? That must have been very informative."

"Leo, please!" Martha was more amused than insulted by this subtle accusation. "Because I was so seasick I had to spend a lot of time on deck, and the captain would come down and chat with me occasionally. I made clear that I was going to Shanghai to meet my husband—" she tripped over the word, and glanced away with a touch of embarrassment. "There was nothing 'private' about it. He was just passing time. And he was old enough to be my grandfather. And I wanted to find out something about the place where I was going to live." She did not mention that being under the captain's unofficial protection conveniently kept the other men on the ship from making unwanted advances. She intended to put the whole wretched journey behind her.

"Your husband," said Leo playfully, brushing a finger across the tip of Martha's nose. His pout evaporated.

Martha blushed outright this time. "Well, you did ask me to marry you. Or don't you remember?"

Earnestness quickly replaced Leo's lighthearted expression. "Martha, the thought of making you my wife, legally my wife, has never left my mind. That was the whole reason I came to Shanghai."

As he spoke, the rickshaw pulled up in front of a glorious Georgian mansion. Behind the wrought iron fence that surrounded the property, the home presented an image of perfect symmetry. Black shutters accented the cream stucco walls, and the front portico extended from the massive front door in a wide semi-circle, punctuated by four Doric columns. The rickshaw coolie laid down his load in front of the main gate and waited patiently for Leo to hand him his fare. Martha did not move.

"Why are we stopping?" she asked with grave curiosity. "Who lives here?"

"I do. And so will you, at least as of today." replied Leo, playful again. He descended from the cart and extended his hand to help her down. Martha remained motionless.

"What? Here? In this house? This mansion? You're not serious."

"Well, if you don't like it, say so, and I'll buy another. Although I did negotiate a rather good deal on this one. The man who built it was in the shipping business. He lost his fortune a little over a month ago, when a typhoon demolished most of his fleet. Seems there was some scandal involving the maritime insurance. He sold me all the furnishings as well—the interior of the place is quite nice. If you would just come in, and take a peek around. Then you can pass judgment." He spoke in a teasing tone, but he was quite serious. He would sell the place as quickly as he had bought it, lock, stock and barrel, to please Martha.

Martha stared at the house for a moment, then her eyes returned to

Leo. She gave him a look that could convey only one meaning, and he felt a rush of blood to his groin.

"I think the only room I need to see is the bedroom." Her tone was casual, but her cheeks flushed. She stepped down from the rickshaw. Desire flowed like a palpable force between them.

In his haste to get her inside Leo forgot to pay the driver, whose loud howls of betrayal forced him to return and hand over the fare. By this time his head household servant, Duo Win, had opened the gate to greet them. The rest of the staff, inherited directly from the previous owner, waited in a dignified line just inside the front door. Dressed in their best white cotton uniforms, they respectfully bowed, in turn, to their new mistress.

Seven Chinese faces moved before her in a blur. Martha was conscious only of Leo's arm around her waist, his breath so close to her neck, and the hardness of his thigh as it brushed up against her hip. Every delay seemed an eternity.

"Tea ready. Please to come," offered Duo Win politely, after everyone had been introduced. He was the only servant who spoke English.

"No, thank you, Duo Win. Madame would like to rest right now," said Leo, trying to sound serene although his pulse was racing. Damn! This was taking forever.

"Very good. Will turn down bed for Madame."

"No, no—thank you. We'll manage." Leo escorted Martha up the wide marble steps of the double staircase that led to the second floor. Seven pairs of eyes watched with barely concealed amusement. He reached the landing and paused.

"Duo Win, everyone take the rest of the day off."

"Sir?"

"I said, everyone is off duty for the rest of the day. Leave the house. Go shopping. Take a holiday."

"All?"

"Yes, damn it. Everyone."

"Cook too?"

"EVERYONE! RIGHT NOW!"

Leo's roar scattered the group in the foyer. Taking Martha's hand, he led her down the hall to the master bedroom suite. He did not point out that the rosewood four poster bed had been carved in Siam, or that the antique mirror over her marble-topped vanity came from Venice, or that the silk carpet on the floor had once belonged to an Indian Maharajah. He brought her to the center of the room, released her, walked back to the door and shut it, determined to shut out the rest of the world.

Words were no longer necessary. She reached out to him and he came to her, locking her in his arms as their mouths met and opened, hungry to share the deepest part of themselves.

Martha felt his tongue in her mouth and moaned; the sound of her yearning inflamed him even more. Dropping his embrace he seized her face in his hands. He kissed her chin, her cheeks, her temples, her eyes, and then he returned to her lips, seeking and demanding. With trembling fingers Martha stroked the corners of his mouth as his tongue claimed her again. She stroked his ears, his neck, and his back, urging him onward, lost in an abyss of desire.

He could have taken her immediately, tearing off only the pieces of clothing that barred their essential coupling. But he wanted to relish all of her. He tried to reach behind her and unclasp the top of her dress. After one unsuccessful effort his ardor refused to let him waste any more time on buttons. Turning her roughly he ripped them off in a single effort. Martha's crumpled linen chemise fell to the floor, instantly forgotten.

Martha brought his hands to her breasts. Still behind her, he cupped one in each hand and massaged them upwards, fondling her nipples between his thumb and forefinger. The taut buds strained against the silk of her short slip. He pulled the flimsy garment over her head and flung it away. Martha quickly kicked free of her shoes, and turned to face her lover. She stood before him with no thought of modesty or embarrassment, rendered completely comfortable in her nakedness by the force of her need for him.

Leo dropped to his knees and removed her panties, and then her stockings, savoring each inch of flesh as he peeled each item off her body. When she was completely undressed, he began to nibble and kiss her inner thighs, first one, then the other, while stroking the backs of her legs with long, fluttering caresses.

Martha rewarded him with a series of short moans, and buried her hands in his hair. He kissed his way up to the small, pointed bones of her slender hips. She rocked them gently, as if he had already entered her. His face was just inches away from the golden-red tangle of hair covering her pubic bone. He could not wait much longer. He picked her up and laid her across the bed.

"Oh, yes, please, please, yes!" Martha thrust her hips forward in an agony of longing. Leo threw himself on top of her, still fully clothed. He pinned her hands close to her head and pushed himself against her.

"Can you feel how much I want you?

She wanted to answer him but a groan of passion was the only sound she could make. Leo kept talking to her, murmuring close to her ear.

"You are mine, Martha. Mine forever. Can you feel how much I want you? Do you know how much I love you?" He stood up and kicked off his pants. Martha tried to sit up, but he guided her back down onto the bed.

"Don't move. Not yet." Still standing, he leaned over the bed, pulled her body towards him, and entered her with one smooth thrust. Martha cried out again, an exclamation of pure joy. She wrapped her legs around his lower back and tilted her pelvis up, encouraging him to enter her more deeply. Holding onto her hips, he pushed further, until their bodies bonded completely.

Leo stood motionless, possessing her, pulsing inside her. He did not move, because he knew one stroke inside her would trigger his climax, and, as much as he longed for the release, he wanted this moment to last forever.

Martha's hand traveled towards the point where their bodies became one. She stroked her lower abdomen, welcoming his presence there. She then rocked her hips one time.

Leo exploded. His back arched and he pressed even deeper into her as spasm after spasm rocked his body. A low growling moan escaped him as he came, answered by Martha's cries of delight as she shared his pleasure.

It was several minutes before his pounding heart slowed and his spine relaxed. Without withdrawing from her body he took off his jacket, his shirt and his tie, then pressed his naked body to hers. Their kisses overflowed with tenderness now, their passionate demands momentarily sated.

"You are my wife, Martha Levy."

"And you are my husband, Leopold Hoffman."

"I missed you so much."

"I love you so much."

"My Aphrodite."

"My darling."

"My love."

And so their endearments continued, until at last they nestled together in the big four poster bed, her back curled up against his stomach, his arm beneath her head, and drifted into a sleep of cozy contentment.

⊛

He awoke after dark, and saw her standing at the window, his shirt wrapped around her like a nightdress. An apparition of extraordinary loveliness, bathed in moonlight. He remained silent, cherishing the sight of her.

"Consummation," he whispered, not realizing that he'd spoken aloud.

She turned toward him, and smiled.

"What did you say, darling?"

He was slightly embarrassed to have been caught thinking aloud, but decided to answer, anyway.

"I said, 'consummation.'"

Her smile deepened and she blushed, but moved closer.

"Is that an observation or an invitation?"

"Both." He sat up and patted the bed next to him. "I was looking at you, and thinking about how lovely you are, and about making love to you, and it just occurred to me that our lovemaking is the essence of that word—consummation." He did not add that he had a large basis for comparison. There was no reason to hurt Martha with his history. Any part of it.

She sat next to him and tucked her feet under his thighs.

"Would it be possible to consume something of a different nature first? For the first time in weeks, I'm hungry."

"If you insist! Supper shall be ready in a moment." Leo reached over to pull the bell cord that summoned Duo Win, then stopped, his hand in midair, when he realized that no one would be in the kitchen to hear it, for he had turned all of the servants out of the house. Deciphering his movements, Martha laughed.

"I don't suppose we can give the whole staff the day off every time we make love, can we?"

Responding to her teasing, Leo laughed as well. "I guess not. I would have to make every day a holiday."

"What a pleasant thought," she said, abandoning her seated position and curling up next to him.

"House would be a wreck, though," he added absent-mindedly as she began to stroke his chest. Could he persuade her to wait a few minutes before heading to the kitchen? Then again, why not make love there, too?

Leo did not get the opportunity to make this suggestion. Martha bolted upright, eyes full of anxiety. "Leo, this house! What is going on? How could you afford all this? What have you been doing for the past six months? How do you go from being a concierge to—lord and master of a place like this?"

Because I murdered and stole and gambled, Leo answered silently to himself. *Because I had to find a way of staying alive and out of prison, in order to be with you again. Because I had to have money to protect you and make you happy. But how can I ever tell you about all that? Would you, could you, still love me, knowing what I have done?* No, he could not tell her his story, at least, not all of it, for he could not bear to lose her if she could neither understand nor forgive what he had done.

Leo inhaled and exhaled deeply, then pulled Martha back down next to him. He turned to face her, so that they were lying side by side, hands clasped between them, their faces only inches apart. Her eyes were serious now, and so full of love that Leo felt a lump form in his throat. What had he ever done to deserve love like this? That this beautiful woman would wait for him, and cross the world for him, bringing a heart so full and pure? He closed his eyes and inhaled again. Then he began to speak.

"Martha, I was not in Paris on a holiday. I was there to function as an interpreter for a group of businessmen."

"As an interpreter?"

"Yes. You noticed, when we were in Paris, that I speak several languages. We're speaking German now, because that's your first language. But I seem to have a special talent for languages. I pick them up easily.

"Someone I knew in Budapest decided that I was the person he needed to facilitate an international business transaction. It wasn't really legal, for it supposedly involved buying weapons for the Hungarian army in violation of the peace treaty. But this man, and the group he was with, appealed to my sense of national pride, and, I suppose, I have to admit, my vanity. So I agreed to help them. I thought I would be helping myself, and Hungary."

He shifted onto his back and stared at the wall, choosing his words carefully, anxious to get close enough to the truth to be credible without incriminating himself.

"You know I had just arrived in Paris when we met. The morning I left you in front of Notre Dame, I discovered that the men I was helping were not working for the Hungarian government at all. They were secretly members of the Hungarian Fascist Party, attempting to acquire weapons for their organization. Rather than cooperate, I decided to foil their plans."

"What did you do?"

"There was a story in the paper that morning about a Hungarian army officer who had been arrested at the Hague passing counterfeit French francs. That gave me an idea. I contacted the man responsible for selling the weapons, drew his attention to the article, and warned him, in confidence, that he had better make sure the Hungarian group he was dealing with did not intend to pay him with fake francs. I assumed, of course, that the deal would be called off immediately. Or at least delayed. I planned to lay low for the day, meet you at five o'clock, go with you to Munich, and be done with the whole business. But when I returned to my hotel to collect my passport, I found that I had underestimated the people with whom I was dealing. I discovered another man, whom I knew to be a member of the Hungarian Fascists, in my room. Dead."

"Dead? How?"

"If you mean how was he killed, I don't know, exactly. There was too much blood to tell easily, and I didn't want to examine things too closely."

"Oh my God, Leo, how awful!" Martha threw herself across Leo's chest and hugged his shoulders, her eyes filling with tears. She knew that he had abandoned her for a reason, but she never imagined anything so appalling. How could she have ever felt a moment of self-pity?

Leo continued, stroking her hair as he spoke.

"I knew at that moment that I was meant to take the blame for the murder. I suppose the leader of the group I was with thought the dead man was the one that had betrayed them, and that I was expendable. At any rate, I had to leave the country immediately."

"But Leo, couldn't you prove you were innocent? I would have told the police that you were with me all night, and couldn't possibly have killed anyone."

He responded with an ironic little laugh. "Martha, I am Hungarian. You are German. The French hate us. What's more, we're Jewish. I learned after the war that Jews make the most convenient scapegoats. The murder was orchestrated by powerful people with international connections. There was no way the French police were going to let me off the hook—not even with an alibi as beautiful and believable as you."

"But why didn't you go to Germany? Or England? Somewhere closer?"

"I'm a Hungarian citizen. I cannot travel freely in Europe without both entry and transit visas. I didn't know how far they would look for me. I knew I had to get beyond their net as quickly as possible."

"So you came to Shanghai."

"So I came to Shanghai."

"But will you be safe here?"

"I think so. As safe as I could be anywhere in the world. I was a little fish, and people don't tend to ask questions here. No one cares much about the past. It's amazing that way."

"And the house?"

"Something happened that the Fascists had apparently not counted on. The murdered man evidently had some scheme of his own going on the side. When he was killed, he had a lot of money with him, which I felt I had, in some way, earned a right to. So that money brought me here."

He heard Martha gasp. "You went through a dead man's pockets?"

"Not exactly. He must have taken off his coat before being killed. I guess he was waiting for me to return. At any rate, I saw the coat and searched for a billfold, looking for some identification. I found his papers, and his money. That is how I confirmed who the dead man was: the police chief of Budapest, a pig of a man. Knowing the trouble I was in, I removed the cash. I didn't even realize how much was there until I was on board the ship to come here."

"But Leo, didn't it occur to you that they could charge you with theft as well? That taking the money would make you look guilty?"

"So they could put me in jail for theft and then hang me for murder? No, Martha. I knew the dead man by reputation, and I knew there was no way he'd come by the money honestly. I saw my chance to evade their plans for me and I took it. Unfortunately, I could not take you with me, for I did not know how to find you, and every moment I stayed in France placed me—and our future together—in greater peril."

"But why did you take so long to send for me?"

"I didn't want to put you in danger. I needed some time to make certain that I was safe here. I couldn't send for you until I was sure that they were not looking for me. And, I needed to know that I would have a future worthy of sharing with you. Until then, it was pointless. It was better for you to just forget about me."

"As if I could."

Hearing the tenderness in her voice, Leo felt relief flood through every limb of his body. It was going to be alright. Martha was satisfied with his story. She could still love a man falsely accused of murder, who had taken what was not his, out of self-defense.

"When I arrived here, I discovered that I have a talent for investment banking, and, after a rocky start, managed to turn my initial investment into a tidy sum."

"A tidy sum! This must cost a fortune! The house, the servants—"

Leo grinned. "That, my dear, is one of the luxuries of Shanghai. I can keep seven servants for the price of one decent gardener in Europe. The house was not inexpensive, but did not cost nearly what it would have anywhere else. To make money is the main reason people come to Shanghai. The addiction to luxury one develops here is one reason they stay. Will you stay and be the queen of my castle? Could you be happy here?"

"Anywhere, with you, my love. Anywhere."

And they decided to put supper off for a while longer, after all.

⊙†⊙

They were married four days later, at eleven o'clock in the morning, in the office of a Justice of the Peace in the French Concession. Martha wore a simple ankle-length wedding dress, created especially for her by the leading American designer at one of Nanking Road's finest dress shops. He designed the dress in pale green silk embroidered with violets, saved, he claimed, "for the purpose of adorning a truly beautiful redhead." Lawrence Cosgrove and the Justice's elderly secretary served as their witnesses. At the proper moment, Leo held Martha's hands, and uttered the vow he had longed to make since meeting Martha in Paris over seven months ago.

"I, Leopold Gustave Hoffman, take you, Martha Katrina Levy, to be my lawful wedded wife; to have and to hold from this day forward, for better, for worse; for richer, or poorer; in sickness, and in health; to honor and cherish, forsaking all others in steadfast love, 'til death us do part."

"Til death us do part," repeated Martha, in turn. And then, flooded with emotion, she looked at the diamond band encircling her finger and thought, no. Ours is a bond not even death could break.

They celebrated with a festive brunch at the dining room of the Palace. The effervescence of the champagne matched the newlyweds' bubbly mood.

"So this how it feels like to be blissfully happy," sighed Martha, leaning against Leo's shoulder, feeling giddy and more than a little tipsy. She was not used to champagne and felt its effects very quickly.

"I want you to be this happy every day," said a slightly less tipsy Leo, meaning it.

"Oh, Leo, may I see the license?"

"Why? Don't you believe we are married? You signed it, after all."

"Oh, you silly darling! Of course! I just want to read it. I didn't really get a chance to look at it when I signed it. I want to see it again, in print. With my own two little eyes, where it says, `Mr. and Mrs. Leopold Hoffman.' Pleeazzze."

"Alright then." A guarded note had entered Leo's voice, but Martha did not notice. He pulled an official-looking piece of paper out of his breast pocket and handed it to his wife.

"Ah, there it is." She sighed another happy sigh and carefully spread the document out on the table in front of her. A quizzical expression soon wrinkled her forehead.

"Leo, what's this?"

"I thought you spoke French," he responded, his tone deliberately light.

"I do. I understand it. But what I mean is, why does it say here that we're Catholic?"

"Does it? What an embarrassing mistake."

"Well, shouldn't we have it corrected?"

"Why?"

"It's an official document. I mean, it is our *marriage* license. I don't want to start our marriage with a lie."

"A lie! That is a bit harsh, isn't it? Most Hungarians are Catholic. The old girl at the office probably just assumed I was, and that, therefore, you were, too. Doesn't change anything. We're not any less married. French law respects the civil ceremony, not the religious one. It's not worth the trouble to correct it."

"But it's not right! It's not who we are!"

"And just who are we?" replied Leo, serious now. He lowered his voice. "Did you decide to be Jewish?"

"Don't be ridiculous."

"Do you go to synagogue?"

"No."

"Do you follow the laws of Jehovah and Moses?"

"No, I mean, the Commandments, but—"

"Did your parents?"

"No, but Leo—"

"Do you even know a single Hebrew prayer?"

"No, but it doesn't—"

"But what? When I was a boy, growing up in Budapest, I was taught that one's religion was irrelevant. It was the age of science! The age of reason! Hard work and talent are all that matters! God was a matter of conscience. Well, it seems that's only true when there's enough food to go around. When someone goes hungry, the hungry blame the Jews. When there's a war, the losers blame the Jews. When the country collapses, they blame the Jews. I won't have my children blamed. Not for famine, not for financial chaos, not for war. I did not choose to be born Jewish, and I chose for my children not to be born Jews."

Martha stared hard at the piece of paper in front of her, trying to make sense out of Leo's words. Through the diminishing fog of her champagne euphoria, she comprehended that the misinformation on their marriage license was not the secretary's mistake. Leo had given the wrong religion on purpose. This fact troubled Martha in a vague, inexplicable way. She'd never felt as if she'd had a meaningful connection to her Jewish heritage, but it did not feel right to have it snatched away from her with the stroke of a pen. It seemed—blasphemous, somehow. She thought of her father, and Bernice. Living under some false pretense would make her feel even further away from them. How could she make Leo understand?

He interrupted the growing silence, correctly reading her thoughts.

"Do you think God cares? Don't you think that my relationship with God should transcend the label others have given me?" He took his wife's hand. "Martha, I love you, and I know who you are, and being called Jewish has nothing to do with it."

"I don't know, Leo. It doesn't seem right, somehow. It seems like a charade."

"Listen, my darling." His face was close to hers now. He spoke with earnest intensity. "We have come to a place where we can begin our lives—all over again. Without stigma, without fear, without poverty. Why handicap ourselves? Why handicap our children? We have nothing to lose."

Martha pondered all that he said. The idea still disturbed her, but she couldn't find a way to contradict Leo's logic. As a young teenager she had seen, first hand, a man called Adolph Hitler try to take control of the government of Bavaria, mesmerizing his followers with a speech given in a Munich beer hall, preaching hatred of the Jews. Hitler had gone to jail for his attempted coup. But what about the ones who listened so raptly to his hateful words? Were there others like Hitler out there?

Martha looked at her husband, who was toying with the remains of his dessert, similarly lost in thought. He was so handsome, so intelligent, so self-confident, so tender. Why should it matter if he chose to evade a heritage to which he felt no connection? A heritage that had probably caused him only pain. Most everyone in Germany was aware of what had happened in Hungary after the fall of the short-lived communist government: the slaughter of the communist ministers, and the massacres that followed in the countryside. The killing of people whose only crime was their Jewish ancestry. Martha knew Leo's parents were dead, but did not know how or when he had been left on his own. Had his family been caught up in the bloody aftermath of the war?

She started to ask, then relented. She would ask someday, but not today. Not on their wedding day. She did not want him to relive any nightmares today. There was so much about him that she did not know. She would have years to solve Leo's many riddles. For the time being, she must be satisfied that he did what he did because he wanted to protect her. And their children. She doubted that the piece of paper in front of her would provide much protection, but she did not protest again.

Her glass of champagne had gone flat. The violets on her wrist had wilted. Her giddy mood had evaporated, replaced by a sleepy melancholia. She wanted his arms around her, to fall asleep surrounded by his strength. She touched his sleeve.

"Darling, my husband, let's go home."

"Whatever you desire, my love."

"Could we just spend the rest of our wedding day in bed?"

Now he had to smile. "Why of course, Mrs. Hoffman. Of course."

⚛

Later that evening Leo gave Martha a wedding present.

"But Leo! That's not fair! I have nothing for you!" she insisted, making an effort to hand him back the small silver box.

He pressed it back into her hand. "Martha, your presence is the only present I will ever need. And no more struggling, or I will open it for you. It's fragile."

Enticed by her love of surprises, Martha yielded and opened the box. She lifted out a miniature porcelain swan, no more than six inches long, but so lifelike it seemed ready to float from her hands into the air. Two tiny emeralds glittered in its eyes.

"How lovely!" Martha cried, genuinely pleased. She placed it on her dresser. "He will be there to greet me every morning."

Leo laughed. "Perhaps if we ever run out of money, it will lay us a few golden eggs."

"Sorry, sir. I think it was a goose that did the golden-egg-laying. Swans are only useful for decoration."

"Then he will be in good company in this room," replied Leo, taking her in his arms and planting a barrage of kisses on her hair.

"Excuse me," Martha replied, pretending to be insulted. She dodged her head this way and that to avoid his continuing kisses. "Are you implying that I am only good for decoration?"

"Far from it," he responded, his forehead touching hers. "I mean only that you are the most beautiful thing I have ever seen. And I adore you."

"Why thank you, Mr. Hoffman."

"You are most welcome, Mrs. Hoffman. Come to think of it, I know a very good way for you to thank me."

Martha rolled her eyes and giggled, her good humor completely restored.

"Again?" she exclaimed with false exasperation.

He grinned a truly lascivious grin. "And again and again and again and—"

Martha interrupted him, putting a finger to his lips. Her other hand reached out to his waist and untied the loosely knotted sash of his dressing gown. Her eyes glowed.

"With so much to do, I had better get started."

And so, she did.

CHAPTER 9

THE BYSTANDERS

෧෬෨෬෧

SHANGHAI, 1927

During the nineteen twenties the collective consciousness of the civilized world turned its back on the horror of the Great War and concentrated, instead, on the pursuit of pleasure. Fed up with sacrifice and responsibility, the citizens of the victorious countries threw themselves into a celebration that lasted close to a decade. Life became an unending party. And nowhere was the party longer, or louder, or more festive, than in Shanghai.

Flush with wealth and inebriated by love, Leo and Martha cheerfully joined the revelry. They danced away the afternoons at the tea dances hosted by the Astor House Hotel; dressed in white tie and sequins to attend the latest Hollywood movie at the new cinema in the French Quarter; led the charge to investigate the newest, most promising restaurants, and were regularly seen at the clubhouse of the municipal racetrack, where Leo's love of horses grew to include the stubby, native Mongolian ponies that only the smallest jockeys could ride.

Often, they finished their evenings in the company of gossipy friends at the glamorous Club Casanova, or soaked in scandal at the notorious Lido. They entertained frequently at their home, and at their country club, the newly-built Çercle Sportif Francais, which boasted a roof garden for summer dancing, a ballroom for winter parties, and a magnificent indoor swimming pool decorated in vivid art-deco style, as well as badminton and tennis courts.

During the searing heat of summer they fled to the ocean, to Tsingtao, and stayed in the Grand Hotel, an imposing white structure decorated with lacy pediments and carved spires, like a fanciful gingerbread castle. Beauty and laughter floated through their lives with the welcome regularity of a sultry summer breeze.

Martha was rarely homesick. She soon abandoned her native German, speaking only the most popular tongues of French and English. She took great joy in little frivolities, activities that would have caused her father to shake his head in disapproval. She joined a garden club, a music appreciation club, a literary society devoted to the popular novel, and an amateur drama society. Her lifestyle was not atypical, for while the men of Shanghai made money, their wives had to keep busy, and with a house full of servants there was little to do in the way of household chores, other than plan menus and periodically redecorate.

At times Martha felt as if she'd been given a second chance at childhood, untainted by tragedy and war. She knew she was ridiculously lucky, but seldom questioned how or why she deserved her new life. Leo loved her. That was reason enough.

Occasionally, her practical German conscience would rebel against the self-centered nature of her daily routine, and she would throw her boundless energy behind one of the charities attempting to do something about the plight of the poor in Shanghai: the beggars, the abandoned children, the homeless families. But the infinite scope of the poverty and suffering she witnessed overwhelmed her, and she anxiously returned to the security of the celebration that was her life with Leo. Leo, who spoiled and pampered her, who brought her laughter and made endless, enchanting love to her, who never talked down to her or made her feel foolish or unintelligent. Leo, who made her life begin.

Leo loved being responsible for Martha. He took delight in all of her accomplishments, from a beautifully executed dinner party to mastery of a new English phrase. His heart told him that he'd been given custody of a special treasure. He was the devoted trustee of an incomparable work of art. It was his duty to ensure her happiness.

It struck him hardest when he caught sight of her suddenly, hurrying through the front door, back from one of her many meetings, or popping out of the bath, her glorious auburn hair wrapped up in a towel turban. At those impromptu moments the depth and intensity of his love for her seized him with a physical force that could have been agony. But it wasn't, any more than the violent muscular contractions of an orgasm could be called pain. She was part of him.

They were gregarious and generous with their time, but their special closeness to each other excluded all others from any bond deeper than casual friendship. Neither had a need for a special confidante or playmate. Both enjoyed the companionship of their own gender, but never lingered long within it. Lawrence Cosgrove was the closest friend Leo ever made in Shanghai. His return to England six months after Martha and Leo's wedding caused a moment of sorrow and a good justification for a lavish party, but no deep sense of loss. There was no empty place in Leo's life that Martha did not fill. The company of others was a pleasant entertainment, but only Martha was essential. And only Leo was essential to her.

"It's so *unseemly*," complained one wealthy British widow, whose long list of companions included many married young men new to the wicked ways of Shanghai, "for such a handsome young man to be so *blatantly* in love with his wife." And the young men of Shanghai had to agree. It was unfashionable for anyone as enchanting as Martha to be so taken with her husband. Such a shame. Her brilliant smile and charming conversation yielded occasional comfort, but no hope, as she and Leo moved like brilliant particles through the kaleidoscope of concentric circles that shaped Shanghai society.

And so the party continued, until the winter of 1927. Then, for a few brief and bloody days, the music stopped.

❦

Leo woke with a start. He lay rigid in his bed, his heart beating ferociously in his chest. The nightmares came so rarely now. He had forgotten how real it could seem – how real the noise, and smells, and pain of war could feel, captured in the silence of dreams.

In this dream he lay in a ditch, trapped beneath barbed wire, struggling to free himself. The wire cut into his flesh, and the stench of blood and sulphur suffocated him. A muddy hand stretched toward him. "Get out man, get out!" a male voice shouted. Leo closed his eyes, trying to recall the image. Whose face had it been, reaching down to him? The soldier trying to help him had been Lawrence Cosgrove.

Martha stirred beside him. Leo rested a hand along her thigh, seeking comfort in the peacefulness of her dreams. He tried to steady his breathing, to calm his traumatized subconscious.

Lawrence Cosgrove. How odd.

Then he heard it, in the distance, a sound like thunder that was not thunder. The low, booming rumble set his heart hammering again, with renewed vigor.

Mortar fire.

The bedroom window rattled slightly as the echoes of sound reached the panes. Leo slid cautiously out of bed, making sure not to wake his sleeping wife. He crept toward the window, and drew the curtain back.

Nothing.

The glow from a three-quarter moon revealed only the familiar shadows of homes and gardens, tranquil in the crisp chill of a frosty February night. No strange lights on the horizon. No fires. Nothing to suggest war or catastrophe.

But there it was again. Coming from the direction of the river. Another booming rumble.

Leo quickly donned his cashmere dressing gown and headed downstairs. He could not see the river from their house, but someone would be on duty at the desk of the Palace Hotel. Someone there would know what was happening.

He went to the telephone in his office and rang the hotel. The clock on his wall showed four thirty. Two rings. A calm and dignified British voice answered.

"This is the Palace Hotel. How may we be of service?"

"Leo Hoffman here. Who is this speaking?"

"Oh! Mr. Hoffman. Good to hear from you. This is Richard Fletcher. I was the bell captain when you were residing here."

"That's right. Good to speak to you, Richard. So you're working the night desk now?"

"Yes, sir."

"Well, congratulations on the promotion. You'll soon be running the place." Leo had little patience for small talk at the moment, but small talk, especially flattery, was a necessary precursor to the extraction of significant information. Patience.

"Thank you, sir. So kind of you to say so. What can I do for you this evening? Or rather, this morning?"

"I tell you, I've been hearing some thumps and bumps that sound like mortar fire. Is that possible?"

"I am afraid so, sir. It seems that General Chiang Kai-shek is making his presence known."

"What? Is the bastard actually going to attack Shanghai?"

"Well, we all hope not, sir. But he did a nice job of it in Nanking, didn't he?"

"Almighty God. What's being done?"

"Well, I've heard the Americans are moving their warships down the Yangtze to protect the harbor here. I imagine the others will jump in soon. No one would want the Yanks to get all the credit for saving us, eh?" The young Englishman chuckled at his own slim wit, and Leo joined him, feigning amusement. He had to know more.

"So what's the artillery fire about? Who is Chiang fighting?"

"Well, it's not really clear at the moment, sir. Civil war does get confusing, doesn't it? Last report is that he's just shelling a bit as he goes, to ward off potential resistance from Sun Chuan-fang, the reigning warlord at the moment. We can't see anything burning from here."

"Good."

"You should think about coming down, Mr. Hoffman. There is quite a party going on. Loads of reporters. Most of the Municipal Council. They're running between here and the Astor House like it was a relay race. Highly entertaining."

"Thank you Richard, but I think I'll wait for the sun to come up.

There's no serious danger at the moment? No—call for evacuation?"

"No sir. No real trouble yet. Just Chinaman against Chinaman. They all know better than to bother the International Settlement or the French Concession. A few European warships would make pretty short work of the whole Chinese Nationalist army."

"Right you are. Thank you for the information. It has been a pleasure talking to you."

"And you, sir."

They rang off. Leo lowered the receiver back to its hooked cradle. No danger. Was such unruffled bravado justified? He knew this was not the first time that political unrest had threatened Shanghai. China had gone through varying degrees of internal revolt since the collapse of the Manchu dynasty. But for the most part, other than the inconvenience of an occasional influx of Chinese refugees, the Concessions of Shanghai were unaffected by the war raging between Peking and Canton. They stood untouched: a rich, glittering sanctuary from civil war, a tribute to capitalism and the power of gunboat diplomacy. And, the Shanghailanders believed, an invincible one.

Until now. For this new general, Chiang Kai-shek, in his quest to recreate a nation out of the private kingdoms of China's many warlords, seemed willing to take on the foreign powers as well: those countries that had, for close to a hundred years, kept strategic pieces of his homeland as private playgrounds. Worse, he had the backing of Soviet Russia. The General and his troops had already forced Britain to return its concessions further north, at Hankow and Kiukiang. Would Shanghai be next?

The Western powers were not willing to take any chances. Too much money was at stake. They'd moved quickly to protect their investment. In January of 1927, Britain, America, Japan, France, Italy, and Spain rushed troops to Shanghai. They were to serve as a warning to the General, and to the Soviets. Leave Shanghai alone.

Their faith bolstered by this evidence of the world's commitment to their safety, the Shanghailanders turned the threat of invasion into yet another excellent excuse for a party. They arranged entertainments for the arriving troops, ranging from brothel trips to hockey games to billiard tournaments, and waited for the General to arrive.

Now, one month later, he was pounding on Shanghai's door. For the first time in two years, Leo felt fear. He remembered life in an occupied city. He remembered the looting of Budapest, and the terror of feeling defenseless. But he had nowhere to go. No safe place to take Martha. They had to wait and hope the foreign powers were prepared to back up their bravado with action.

When the sun came up the following morning, residents of the French and International Concessions found themselves inhabiting an armed camp. Barbed wire barriers had been erected around the entire settlement. Military guards patrolled the streets.

Within a few days the real show began, and the Shanghailanders discovered they once again had front row seats to the Chinese civil war theater. Smoke clouded the horizon. Gunfire and mortar shells could be heard above the usual panoply of commercial noise. But as the Shanghailanders had hoped, the violence remained strictly confined to the sections of city under Chinese control, and the fighting lasted only a few days. With the help of Communist forces loyal to Soviet Russia, Chiang Kai-shek conquered the Chinese sections of Shanghai.

Then, nothing. For weeks there was no significant military activity. Spring came, and the foreign residents began to relax. It seemed the General would respect the Concessions, after all.

To celebrate the apparent end of the hostilities, Leo and Martha decided to go in search of a Russian tea house Leo had visited once, before Martha's arrival. Leo loved reviving the ritual of late afternoon tea. It reminded him of happy times at home with Miksa and Erzsebet, when life was civilized, and his expectations knew no limits.

"Isn't it lovely to walk outside again, without worrying?" sighed Martha with languid contentment, hugging Leo's arm as they strolled along the Avenue Joffre. The April air was cool and crisp, and the heavy fragrance of cherry blossoms blotted out the smell of the river. Leo could not remember the precise address of the tiny establishment they were seeking, so they explored at their leisure, poking their noses around every corner. Soon they left Avenue Joffre behind, and found themselves on the outskirts of the French Concession, where restaurants and cafés competed with innumerable small shops for space and the attention of the passing public.

Leo found a small street that looked encouragingly familiar and start-ed down it, Martha in tow. He was so intent on rediscovering his café that he scarcely noticed the small group of Chinese men huddled across the street. Chinese men always gathered on the streets in the early evening to gamble, gossip, or to argue about politics; they were part of the scenery.

But Martha noticed something unusual, and slowed her pace. Three men stood in a semi-circle with their backs to the street, clad in the ubiquitous blue cotton suits worn by the working class Chinese. Two more men stood in the center of the circle, and another, a young man, knelt in the center of the small ring. Why was the young man on his knees? Were his hands tied? Martha tugged on Leo's arm.

"Leo, look, there's something strange going on there—"

He did not hear her, having just located the tea house. "Oh, there it is, Martha, just across from the lantern shop—"

"Leo, look!"

This time Martha's voice caused Leo to spin quickly on his heel. As he turned he caught the sound of a shout, full of youthful defiance. He knew enough of the language to understand the words.

"Long live the revolution!"

A burst of gunfire followed. The small group scattered in five dif-ferent directions. The young man lay on the ground, blood pouring from the wound where a portion of his skull had been blown away. Bits of his brain stuck to the pavement. His legs still quivered.

Martha screamed. Her eyes were riveted to the gory sight before her. Leo grabbed her shoulders and spun her around, pressing her head to his shoulder.

"Don't look, Martha. Let's get out of here. Don't look."

Her screams turned to whimpers, and she began to tremble.

Leo heard a whistle blow. He started to panic. Within minutes the sidewalk could be swarming with French police. He had no desire to serve as a witness. He had no useful facts to share, and did not want his own background investigated.

"Come on, Martha! We have to get out of here." He grabbed her hand and pulled her along behind him. They walked quickly away from the scene without encountering anyone. No one at all. When they reached the Avenue Joffre, Leo hailed a cab. They did not leave the house for five days.

All around the city, the massacre continued. Day after day, night after night, the Shanghailanders closed their doors and averted their eyes while mercenary thugs controlled by the Nationalists slaughtered the Communists within their ranks. After all, the foreign residents told themselves, there was no reason for the Europeans to get involved; this was distinctly a Chinese political problem, and the Chinese had a different notion regarding the sanctity of life. Perhaps because there were so many of them.

And so with guns, knives and treachery, Chiang Kai-shek consolidated his power. He was supported this time not by the Russians, but by the wealthy Chinese without whom he could not rule the country. Wealthy men who wanted a unified China, but did not want their property nationalized by the Communists. Men who owned banks, and ships and factories, and the souls of other men. Men like Liu Tue-Sheng.

The remaining Communist members of the liberation army soon fled the city. The General then left Shanghai to establish a Nationalist government at Nanking. On his arm was his new bride, Maylong Soong, sister of Mr. T.V. Soong, the new government's Minister of Finance, and one of the wealthiest men in China.

The Concessions remained inviolate. The wire fences came down. The soldiers came into town to drink and purchase the favors of women, and merchant ships returned to the harbor. Life resumed its normal frenetic pace. A short memory was a handy attribute, if one wanted to live at ease in Shanghai.

Leo was not so sanguine. The sight of the factories burning across the river lingered in his mind. Just as the Derkovits family had linked their fortune to the fate of Hungary, he had linked his fortune to Shanghai's future. He'd invested in several businesses operating in the war-damaged industrial zone. He owned rental property in the Chinese districts, and undeveloped real estate outside the French Concession. Luckily, this time his losses had been minor, but the next time, if there was a next time, he could face a major financial setback.

War was a risky business, and there was no guarantee that the political situation in China would not adversely affect Shanghai's economy in the future. Leo had experienced enough of poverty. Without another country that would take him in, he was not free to leave Shanghai. But his money could travel. Money could not be so easily seized or burned or destroyed by revolution. At least, not money that was invested in the safest, strongest country in the world—the United States of America.

By the end of the summer, Leo sold everything. With the help of a broker he invested his entire fortune in the stocks of American companies. He could not go to America, but his money could. It could grow there. And keep Martha safe.

CHAPTER 10

THE REVELERS

❦

As the sounds of war and revolution quieted down, the music began again. In the interest of continued economic cooperation between the International Settlements and the new government of China, Sir Elly Kadoorie, one of Shanghai's wealthiest men, decided to host a gala honoring Chiang Kai-Shek and his new bride. He invited the elite of Shanghai society, Western and Asian, to a dance at his home, Marble Hall, named for the tons of Italian marble he'd imported to build the mansion's massive stone fireplaces.

On the night of the party, Leo surprised Martha with an early Christmas present.

"My darling, they are so beautiful—I don't know what to say!" said Martha as she lifted an emerald and diamond necklace from the velvet box he'd just handed her.

"Not as beautiful as your eyes."

She batted her lashes at him. "Thank you, kind sir. Could you help me put it on?"

They moved to stand in front of the mirror in the foyer. "Well, now there's a good looking couple," Leo quipped, pointing at their reflection.

The light faded from Martha's eyes. "They should have beautiful children, don't you think? But that doesn't seem to be in the cards, does it?"

Leo fastened her necklace for her, and planted a few kisses on the back of her neck, just below the edge of her bobbed hair. "Darling, the doctor keeps telling us there's no reason why we can't have children. We just have to keep trying. If you like, I'll take you back upstairs and we can try again right now."

A grin replaced Martha's wistful expression. "And miss a chance to dance in Marble Hall? Not likely!"

"Well, I won't allow you to dance with anyone else tonight, that's certain. I couldn't stand it. You're irresistible in that dress." Despite the trend towards heavily beaded, calf-length chemises for evening wear, Martha wore a long gown of emerald green satin. In back, the fabric draped in a long cowl to her waist, exposing the creamy skin of her back and shoulders to maximum advantage.

She turned to face him. "I promise not to test you. Just one dance with old Silas Hardoon."

"The old man's ticker couldn't possibly take it."

"Don't underestimate him. I heard he bought his wife in a Chinese brothel."

"And to think I was lucky enough to find you in a pastry shop. Saved all that money."

Martha laughingly clubbed her husband on the head with her small velvet bag, and they made their way to the Marble Hall.

⚬⚭⚬

It was the party of the decade in a city that appreciated fine parties. Towering champagne fountains poured glass after glass of bubbling wine into crystal glasses. Bejeweled revelers danced under the radiant light of thirty six hundred electric bulbs, clustered on Bohemian crystal chandeliers swaying from the sixty-foot ceiling. Banquet tables offered up delicacies from every nationality represented in Shanghai: Chinese dumplings, shaped like swans and stuffed with shrimp; roasted quail; French cheeses; Italian pasta and bread; blintzes stuffed with caviar; beef tenderloin medallions, and desserts of every kind.

By midnight, the heat of the many electric bulbs caused the crowded ballroom to become uncomfortably warm. When Martha excused herself to go powder her nose, Leo decided to step out onto the balcony on the lower terrace to cool off.

To his dismay, he was not alone. Also on the balcony, enjoying the fresh but frigid night air, were none other than Chiang Kai-shek himself, along with his wife. And Liu Tue-Sheng.

There was no way for Leo to back away and return to the ballroom without being rude, for all three people had turned to look directly at him. Nonetheless, he tried.

"Excuse me. I did not mean to interrupt what must be a private conversation. Good evening."

No luck. Liu was gesturing for him to join them. How could Leo turn down the honor of meeting the General, the man who might one day rule all of China, without insulting everyone present? He stepped forward.

"Mr. Hoffman. How nice to see you." The awkward cadence of Liu's speech rang in Leo's brain like a warning.

"Good Evening Mr. Liu. Yes, it has been some time," he responded with cool civility.

"I trust life in Shanghai has treated you well?"

"I have no complaints, thank you."

"Nor have I. General, please allow me to present Mr. Leopold Hoffman, a successful Shanghai businessman."

"It is an honor, General Chiang." Leo knew better than to shake hands. He acknowledged the General's nod by responding in a similar fashion, making sure that his own head descended a noticeable distance lower, to show his respect.

"And, Madame Chiang, Mr. Hoffman."

Here Leo was free to display his Hungarian courtesy. He bent low over the dimpled hand that the General's wife offered him from beneath her sable wrap, bringing his heels together smartly as he did so, and pressed his lips to the back of her palm for a fraction of an instant.

Then, he committed an unforgivable breach of etiquette. He did not let go of her hand. He held it, staring at it. Staring at the ring she wore: a five-carat, emerald-cut diamond, glittering up at him like an old menace.

An uncomfortable cough from the woman whose hand he clutched brought Leo back to his senses. He released Madame Chiang's hand. His head jerked up with a snap and he met Liu's eyes.

The man was smiling.

Leo tried to retain his composure as three sets of eyes looked at him expectantly. "It is lovely to meet you both, and may I offer my sincere congratulations on your marriage. Now, if you will please excuse me, I must meet my wife before she is lost in this crowd."

"Of course," said Liu. "One must not leave such a beautiful woman alone too long."

Leo did not like the thought that Liu even knew of Martha's existence. Without another word, he turned and left the terrace.

Within a few minutes Martha rejoined him, but Leo's encounter with Liu had taken the pleasure out of the evening. He saw only the diamond on Madame Chiang's hand. Liu had given the Cartier diamonds to the General to help finance his war, of that Leo was certain. Had those stones helped pay for the guns that Chiang used to massacre his communist brethren, once the General decided he'd toss his lot in with the likes of Liu rather than rely on the Russians?

Leo felt like a pawn on a chessboard, the size and scope of which he could not ascertain. He did not like the feeling. He wanted to leave, to get away from Liu and the General and the crowd of people celebrating the survival of a city that had no right to exist, yet continued to do so.

Martha looked up at him. "Leo, do you feel unwell?"

"Fine, just tired. I don't know that I will last much longer."

She acquiesced immediately when he suggested they leave; she could tell he was no longer enjoying the evening. They'd reached the entrance to the ballroom when Martha paused, listening.

"Oh, Leo! A waltz. They're playing a waltz. No one plays waltzes anymore. Could we please dance one more time?"

He could never refuse her. "Of course, my darling."

The waltz, which had been the scandal of their grandparents' generation because it called for such close physical contact between the sexes, was now viewed as hopelessly old-fashioned by the emancipated libertines of the roaring twenties. However, Leo was a child of the land of the waltz, and to the offspring of the Austrian-Hungarian Empire the waltz was a romantic ritual, not a mere dance that could fall out of favor as quickly as yesterday's hemline. Leo could waltz more gracefully than most men could breathe.

He took Martha's small hand in his and led her back to the all but empty dance floor. They paused for an instant to catch the rhythm of the music. Then with one quick step backwards, Leo and Martha floated into the dance. They moved in effortless unison, gliding in swift circles around the room, stepping and turning as though the music emanated from them, as if their dance granted the spectators permission to share, for a moment, the magic of their special union.

Leo could sense every eye upon them, and his heart filled with emotion as he looked at Martha. He was dancing a waltz with his beautiful wife, his most beloved treasure, making love to her through the music, and he knew he was the envy of every man in the room.

"By God, you're worth a revolution," he whispered in the air above her ear. She did not catch his words, but heard the love with which he uttered them, and turning slightly to face him, she smiled.

CHAPTER 11

THE BANKER

❧

SHANGHAI, 1929

"Missus sick again today, Mistah Leo. She no come down."

Leo took a last sip of his coffee and put down the newspaper he'd been reading. "I think it's time to take her to see the doctor, Wei. Yesterday she was too tired to move, and it's not like her to skip breakfast." As modern as Shanghai was, they were nonetheless exposed to a myriad of tropical diseases, from malaria carried by the voracious mosquitoes to cholera spread by vegetables washed with tainted water. Martha was not running a fever, but there was no easy explanation for her illness. She was hardly ever sick. He did not want to take any chances.

They left the house to take Martha to her doctor's appointment just before nine o'clock, on a cold and dreary Tuesday morning. Fog horns boomed loudly across the water as almost invisible boats tried to navigate their way through the thick haze blanketing the river. The whole city seemed subdued.

The doctor's office was located a few blocks off the Bund. The nurse admitted Martha quickly, and Leo waited uneasily in the sitting room. He told himself not to fret, that there was probably nothing seriously wrong with his wife; but where Martha was concerned, he was not a patient man. He tried to occupy his mind by rereading yesterday's edition of the

North China Daily News, but the stale news did nothing to curb his rest-lessness. It occurred to him that he could run up the street to his broker's office, and to ask him about the status of his latest investment: shares in a coal mining company in the American state called Pennsylvania. Running an errand would make him feel more useful. Leo tapped on the glass that separated the waiting area from the nurse's station.

"Excuse me. Do you have any idea how long my wife will be?" he asked the friendly-looking matron seated behind the window.

"I'm sure it will be at least an hour, if not more, sir. With all that nausea the doctor will want to run some tests. Would you like a cup of coffee?"

"No, thanks, but I may run out for a moment. Please tell her I'll leave the car and driver for her, but, well, I'll be right back."

"Of course, sir." The nurse shut her glass barrier with an indulgent smile. Feeling a touch of guilt and a hint of relief, Leo left.

He quickly covered the few short blocks to the Bund, and stopped at the Ewo building, where the offices of Jardine, Matheson & Company, the largest trading company in the Orient, were located. Leo's securities broker leased an office on the third floor.

Leo's investment advisor was a man by the name of Burton Damion. He was American, New York born, Harvard educated, and well-respected for his ability to make money for his clients, and himself. A vague rumor traveled around that an investment scandal in New York was responsible for Burton's relocation to Shanghai, but one never knew the truth behind the story of anyone's decision to come to the city. His references were good, and with his hands-on experience as a trader in New York, Burton's presence allowed some of the wealthy citizens of the city to tap into the New York stock exchange with relative ease. Leo liked him. In the two years since he decided to put his wealth into the American stock market, he'd made a decent amount of money by following Burton's advice. Lately, encouraged by his success, he'd started engaging in margin trades which allowed him to diversify his portfolio even more by using part of it as collateral for loans to buy more shares. So far the strategy had worked quite well.

Leo tapped on the door to Burton's office. He did not want to leave

Martha for long, in case she received some distressing news about her health. If Burton was free, he would be back at the doctor's office in ten minutes, and it would be ten minutes he did not have to spend sitting, worried and restless, in the sterile medical office.

Hearing no answer, he stepped inside. He saw no sign of Burton's secretary, but the door to his private office was closed. Leo thought he heard the sound of someone sobbing. Without thinking he opened the inner door.

The secretary was there. So was a policeman, and so was Burton, or rather, the remains of Burton. The back of his head was plastered all over the window, a red and brown patch of gore, blotting out the gray view of the Bund.

"What in God's name has happened?"

At the sound of Leo's voice, the woman looked up and blinked, as if she'd just come from a dark room into bright sunlight. She opened her mouth, then snapped it shut again. Her eyes were swollen from crying.

"And who might you be?" the policeman asked, blustering with British efficiency.

"Leo Hoffman. I'm a client."

"Well, Mr. Burton won't be keepin' any more appointments, sir. He's checked himself out. The gun's still right there on the floor, right where it ought t'be, so there ain't no doubt about what's happened. This poor lady heard the shot."

Leo stared, dumbfounded. "Burton? Killed himself?"

"I'd say so. Didn't take any chances on missin' did he? Awful business." He made a notation in his notebook, and continued to talk.

"He must have had quite a hot wire to the `States. The word is just now gettin' across the water. 'Black Monday,' they're callin' it. Didn't have much money in the stock market stateside, yourself, did ya sir?"

The bottom fell out of Leo's stomach. He swallowed, then bit his lower lip. "A bit," was all he could manage.

"Well, that bit's probably gone up in smoke, sir. The New York stock market crashed. I heard there's stock brokers poppin' out of windows like champagne corks in Manhattan. Pitiful blokes. It's only money, after all. Well, you better go now, sir. I'll see to this poor lady. What a mess. Poor bastard." Clucking and muttering, the man turned his attention back to the corpse.

Out on the street, Leo noticed a small cluster of men gathering on the steps of the Hong Kong & Shanghai Banking Corporation. The impressive entrance to the city's most prestigious bank was flanked by two enormous bronze lions, whose paws were kept shiny by innumerable Chinese who did not pass by without rubbing them for good luck. Leo felt tempted to go and rub one now. It could not be true. There must be some mistake. He went to join the group on the stairs, under the massive white dome that symbolized the wealth and power of the men who owned Shanghai.

As he approached, he caught bits of conversation. The tones ranged from highly agitated, to curious, to smug. Leo stepped up to listen.

"No, there's no doubt about it. The whole market's been wiped out, and the world financial markets are already following Wall Street's lead. This is a disaster of unprecedented proportion."

"Wonder how many chaps will be put out of business. We surely don't need another bunch of well-to-do beggars. That White Russian business was enough."

"I can't believe it could happen so quickly. How could it all collapse so quickly?"

"Surely it will pick up again."

"You will need a miracle the likes of which has not been seen since Jesus walked the earth to salvage anything out of this mess."

"I wonder who will feel the worst of it. Thank God I wasn't in."

Leo could stand no more. Now he knew it was true. He was ruined. He had put all of his faith in the American stock market, buying small pieces of American companies, sharing a part of the nation he knew he would never be able to see. And now he was left with nothing.

He staggered backwards, and came close to tripping down the stairs. A friendly arm reached out to steady him.

"I say there, are you quite all right?" Leo shrugged off the helpful stranger's assistance.

Martha! How was he going to be able to tell Martha?

He stumbled back to the doctor's office in a daze. Without a word to his driver, Leo wandered in to the office. Martha was standing in the waiting room.

"Oh, Leo! Darling! How troubled you look. You are so pale! But everything is fine, darling! It's better than fine! Everything is wonderful!" Tears filled her eyes; her voice caught in her throat, but she was still smiling.

"Leo, we are going to have a baby! When I had just about given up hope! The doctor says I have to be careful, but if I follow this special diet, and don't tax myself too much, there shouldn't be any serious problems. Oh Leo, darling Leo, we are going to have a baby!" She threw her arms around his neck.

Leo held her tightly. In his lifetime he had comforted many women. He had held Erzsebet, and Martha, and many others whose tears mattered much less, as they cried in sorrow, and in joy. But the tears confronting him now were his own. Tears of jubilation, and tears of anguish.

Once again, within the space of a few short hours, his life had been radically altered. Somehow, he must find a way to start over again. He crushed his beloved Martha to him, and thought about the new life inside her, a life for whom he was responsible. A life so much more important than his own.

He could not tell Martha about his financial losses, for he could not stand to bring her any grief or anxiety, especially now. Nor did he want to have to admit to her how badly he had failed. He would have to keep up appearances, somehow, pretending that nothing had changed. At least, until the baby came.

⊙⊱⊙

Later that night, he sat alone in his library, sorting out his options. According to the financial information he'd been able to scrape together, they were not completely destitute, but close to it. He could mortgage the house to buy time. But he had to produce some income. He'd have to get a job.

He needed a position that would allow them to continue their current lifestyle. He could not bear to ask Martha to abandon the life of luxury that he'd created for her. And he wanted no less for his child.

He evaluated his personal assets. He was fluent in several European languages. By this time he could also speak and understand a good deal of Mandarin, and some Cantonese. He was able to get along well with people from diverse backgrounds. He possessed a modicum of financial knowledge, from his investments over the years. Given the economy of Shanghai, it all pointed in one direction. A bank.

But how to go about getting a position? He couldn't just wander up to the door and drop off a resume. He would not be hired at any of the city's truly prestigious institutions if the word got out that he really needed a job. No one wanted to pay top dollar for a "well-to-do beggar." Not in Shanghai.

He would have to conduct his search by word of mouth, in the most informal settings. After all, Shanghai was a small community. *I'm interested in carving out a place for himself in the business community,* he would say. *Want to put down some roots, now that a baby is on the way. Might be amusing to learn something about the banking business.* He would put the word out casually, at the country club, and the Shanghai Club, on the golf course, and over a glass of brandy at the Astor House. At least, he could start his search that way.

To Leo's delight, his plan worked. Within a few weeks he received a telephone call from Maximillian Berbier, a vice president of the Commerce Bank of China.

"Mr. Hoffman, I am pleased to find you at home," the Frenchman said. His English was heavily accented, but more than acceptable. He seemed enthusiastic.

"Mr. Hoffman, I do not believe that we have actually met before, but I know that we have many mutual acquaintances, especially among the members of Le Çercle Sportif. I know that I have seen you and your lovely wife there on many occasions."

"How kind of you to remember us."

"Well, it is not kindness at all that motivates my call to you today, but good business sense. I understand from some conversations with colleagues at the club that you might be interested in a position with a financial institution."

Leo acted nonchalant, despite his quickening pulse. *A prospect!*

"Why, yes, actually. Funny you should hear about that. What a small little fishbowl we live in."

"Yes, no doubt. Well, we've been looking for some time for someone to help us in the area of business development. Would something of that nature interest you?"

"Perhaps. I would be happy to discuss it."

"Could you come in tomorrow? That is, if you have no other pressing engagements?"

"I think I could find time to slip in during the morning."

"Excellent! Shall we say, ten o'clock?"

"Wait—yes, that should work out nicely."

"Good. And I am sure you know the address—"

"Certainly. On the Bund, next to the *North China Daily News* office."

"*Exactement.* I'm looking forward to meeting with you."

"The pleasure is all mine."

Mr. Berbier turned out to be a small, fidgety man, whose thinning hair and full mustache made him look older than his forty-five years. He'd been in China since 1910, he told Leo. It was a difficult place to leave, once you got used to the small inconveniences of mosquitoes and civil war, *n'est-ce pas?* One could live so well in Shanghai.

Leo listened attentively to Berbier's routine description of the bank's history, its growth and current assets. He finally interrupted.

"And how do you think I may be of service to this prestigious institution?"

"Ah, yes. Well. In fact, I believe that one of the members of our board of directors would like to discuss that with you. He is waiting in the president's office. Shall I show you in?"

Curious, Leo followed the small man up the grand mahogany staircase leading away from the main banking floor to the office suites located on the second story. Why would a board member be interviewing him? Why not the president of the bank? Or another vice-president? Well, he didn't know that much about the banking business. He had a lot to learn.

Berbier crossed the second floor lobby. Leo could not help but notice the presence of several armed guards. Here was a bank that took security seriously.

The Frenchman led Leo through a set of double doors, intricately carved with scenes from Chinese history. The doors opened onto a small outer office, obviously an executive secretary's work station. No one sat at the desk.

Berbier knocked on the door to the president's office. There was a muffled response. Berbier did not open the door. Instead, he walked away from it, saying as he did so, "I will leave you now. You may go in."

Startled that he was expected to make his own introduction, Leo conjured up all of his self-confidence, opened the door of the inner office, and walked in.

There was a tall man, an oriental man, seated at the elaborate *bureau plat* that served as a desk. He had swiveled his chair around so that his back faced the door, and was gazing out of the large picture window that presented a panoramic view of the Bund. The man did not have to turn around for Leo to know who he was.

Liu Tue-Sheng swung his chair around unhurriedly, almost regally. Leo stood in front of his desk, saying nothing, but feeling as if his life in Shanghai had somehow come full circle.

"Mr. Hoffman. Good morning. I do apologize for this subterfuge, but I was not altogether sure that you would accept my invitation for another business meeting. Please, sit down."

Leo debated making a quick departure. He was sure that he did not want to be a part of anything this man would have to offer, but he sensed that he had been lured into a trap, and had to learn the nature of it, before he could plan his escape.

Leo dropped into a chair and crossed an ankle over the opposite knee, wanting to give the impression that he was comfortable and not at all surprised.

"Of course, Mr. Liu, I knew of your affiliation with this bank," Leo lied smoothly, "but I did not think that my presence here would concern you."

"Ah, but it concerns me exclusively, Mr. Hoffman. You see, it has come to my attention that you are seeking employment."

"I thought it might be amusing to learn something about the banking business," responded Leo calmly. Liu did not acknowledge his remark.

"It has also come to my attention that you recently lost a great deal of money, that you have mortgaged your house, and that your lovely wife is expecting a child."

Leo flushed with humiliation. He leapt up, determined to leave and avoid any more embarrassment.

"Please, please. Mr. Hoffman," Liu went on in a cordial tone, "These are simply facts that have come to my attention. I do not mean to insult you."

Defensive anger tugged at the edge of Leo's self-control. "Not much gets by you, I suppose. But why are you so interested in *me?*"

Liu considered this query, apparently unperturbed by Leo's hostile tone of voice. "If you will retake your seat, I can explain," he answered, the stilted cadence of his speech now grating on Leo's nerves like a metallic screech. They stared at each other for a moment. Leo, torn between his pride and his need to know the answer to his question, deliberated silently. Liu waited, still as a spider in its web. Leo sat down. Liu spoke.

"You see, Mr. Hoffman, at the time of our first transaction, I surmised that you were a man of unique talents. I am engaged in a variety of business enterprises, some of which, such as this bank, are quite straightforward. Others are more complicated."

Like running revolutions and smuggling opium, Leo thought to himself. He kept his face blank as Liu continued.

"For these, more complicated enterprises, a man with your particular talents could be very useful. However, four years ago, when we first met, I suspected that, for you, mere financial reward would not produce the—flexibility—required to assist me in those enterprises. So I waited. And I collected information.

"It is true. I have made it my business to know yours. I know many, many things about many people. As I told you at our first meeting, nothing is as valuable as information. Information overlooked by others often proves helpful. When I learned that you were seeking employment, I thought that now would be an opportune moment to discuss your talents. And how we could once again prove useful to each other."

Leo could sense the bait dangled before him. It had been so easy, the first time; one compromise and he had made a fortune. He was embarrassed and irritated, but he was also curious.

"What did you have in mind?" he demanded stiffly.

"You have an unusual ability, Mr. Hoffman, to make a singular impression, while blending into your environment. An old Russian believes you are a Russian aristocrat. A concierge insists you are a British Lord. An American tycoon thinks you are a self-made millionaire, months before you have succeeded in making a fortune. And while Shanghai is not a closed society, after a short period of time, you and your wife—what is the expression? You are 'rubbing elbows' with our town's most elite citizenry, in a manner that is particularly impressive given that your fortune is—was—comfortable, but not grand enough to buy that much influence.

"All this goes beyond your phenomenal skill with languages, Mr. Hoffman. Men trust you, and women find you desirable. Your charm is a key to many doors. Doors I need to go through, and cannot, because I have a certain reputation, and because I am Chinese. Frankly, I need ears behind those doors. You can be those ears."

Leo was flabbergasted. "Are you telling me that you want me to spy for you?"

"An indelicate description of your duties, but not entirely incorrect. Of course, you would be given a regular position, with the title of vice-president, at this bank. You would assist in garnering new business, meeting potential clients, and explaining our services. All quite legitimate. A business conducted over dinner and on the golf course, with the assistance of a generous expense account. And...French passports. In exchange for all this, I will occasionally ask that you execute a special errand. But, for the most part, you will just...keep your ears open."

Leo could not believe what he was hearing. It was all so simple. So easy. And so vile. Any information he gave Liu would surely be used for nefarious purposes. He would never work for this man. He stood up again.

"Thank you for the compliment, Mr. Liu," replied Leo, his sarcasm contradicting the meaning of his words. "I am deeply honored that you think I am worthy of your consideration. But I am afraid that I cannot accept your offer." With this, Leo took three steps towards the door.

He reached for the doorknob, but his hand never touched it. His fingers halted, inches away from the crystal orb, as he heard Liu Tue-Sheng serenely inquire:

"Are you aware, Mr. Hoffman, that under the Napoleonic code there exists no statute of limitations for the crime of murder?"

Leo dropped his arm and turned around. Liu was still looking directly at him. His impassive expression had not changed.

"You may not know that I have a very good relationship with the French prefect of police here in Shanghai."

Leo listened, over the sound of the blood pounding in his ears. He knew what he was about to hear.

"Letters and warrants regarding crimes committed in every French-speaking corner of the world pile up on the poor man's desk, just in case a perpetrator or two sneaks into the French Concession of Shanghai. My friend would drown under these papers, if I did not help him sort through them.

"After our original transaction, I became curious as to the origin of your diamonds. I wondered if perhaps any of my friend's papers pertained to the theft of a quantity of perfect stones. I discovered this document. Of course, I have made photographic copies. Important documents have a way of disappearing. One must protect them."

Leo took the proffered piece of paper. It was a warrant, issued in Paris, for the arrest of an unnamed Hungarian national, on charges of theft, counterfeiting, fraud, and murder. The document contained a precise physical description of Leo. It was dated December 23rd, 1925.

Liu kept talking, never taking his eyes off Leo's face. "My friend has never seen this. He is a busy man. He does not have to see it. He will not. If you will agree to be—flexible."

Leo's brain was churning. He tried to think of a way to out. He must flee. He must take Martha and leave Shanghai.

And go where? Brazil? In her condition she would never survive an ocean crossing; her trip from Europe had nearly killed her. He'd lost his sister, Klari, in childbirth; he would not take any risks with Martha's health. Back to Germany? There was no guarantee he could even get into the country. Hong Kong? Even if he could get in without proper documents, he would not be beyond Liu's grasp. The gangster had connections there as well.

Within a few brief seconds he considered and rejected a dozen alternatives. There was nowhere for him to go. He was trapped. He knew it. And Liu knew it, as he waited for Leo's response.

"My wife must never find out about this. I must have your word on that."

Liu leaned forward and removed the warrant from Leo's hand. "A most excellent decision, Mr. Hoffman. Most men find me a very reasonable employer. As long as I receive their full cooperation."

CHAPTER 12

THE SPY

ฌฆฌ

SHANGHAI, 1937

"Your mother and I have a surprise for you, little love, but you'll
have to come downstairs to see it," Leo sang out as he burst into the
playroom. Without hesitation, the little girl sitting on the floor dropped
the book she was reading and stretched out her arms. She loved to be
picked up by her father. She especially loved it when, with a sudden cry
of, "*Allez*," he lifted her high above his head and then lowered her onto
his shoulders, as he did now.

"And, Mademoiselle, how is the view from the top of the world?" he
asked, knowing what the reply would be.

"*Comme c'est beau*," the little voice answered. "Papa, it's beautiful
here on top of the world."

"Ah," he always responded, "then that is where you shall stay!"

Martha abandoned her own perch on the window seat and followed
them as they bounded into the hall. "Leo, please! A seven year old is too
big for such behavior!" Her smile belied her words.

Madeleine clasped her hands under her father's chin to keep from
falling off his shoulders as they bounced down the stairs. "Is it a big surprise, or a little one?" she asked, her voice full of delight.

"It's bigger than you are, little princess!" Leo trotted across the foyer, then pulled up in front of the closed parlor doors, waiting for Martha to catch up. When she reached them he slipped Madeleine back down to the floor, and gave his daughter a slow, exaggerated wink.

"Go in and see what it is, Maddy."

Giggling with anticipation, Madeleine opened one of the double doors and peeked inside. Her eyes swept the familiar room, searching for something new. There! In the corner, gleaming in the midmorning sun, stood a baby grand piano.

"Oh! Papa! Maman! I can't believe it!" Madeleine rushed in to admire her new possession, her parents close behind.

"Gaston, one of the musicians at the club, said you were very interested in his piano, and that you even tried to play it. Your father and I thought your interest in music should be encouraged, my darling. You'll have lessons now, and play as often as you like." Martha stood beside the piano, and savored the joy on her child's face. A face so much like her own, with the same green eyes and small features, but framed by a thick mane of curly black hair, just like Leo's.

"Oh! It is *so* beautiful!" Madeleine climbed up onto the ebony bench, and brushed her fingertips across the keys without making a sound. "I will have to learn a song to play for Grandpa. Does Grandpa have a piano?"

She looked up to see the light fade from her father's face. Her mother turned away, and said something sharply in German.

German. That other language, the one she did not quite understand. Madeleine used to think of it as the language of happy surprises. German preceded Christmas presents, picnics, and birthday parties. Now it meant something different. German meant bad secrets. German meant something was wrong.

She hung her head. She must have asked the wrong question. Again.

Madeleine heard her mother leave the room. Her father let out a deep sigh. Then he was sitting beside her. They both stared down at the keyboard.

"Maddy, listen to Papa," Leo said at last. "I know that Maman told you that you were going to visit Grandpa in Germany, but I'm afraid that is not going to happen just yet."

"We're not going?"

"Not yet. I don't think that it's safe to travel right now."

"Oh." More silence. She was still half afraid to speak. What if she asked another wrong question? But she had to know.

"We will go to Germany *someday*, won't we, Papa?"

"Someday, I'm sure you will go, my darling. Now, can you play a song for Papa?"

"I don't know any songs yet, Papa. But I'll learn some soon. I listen very well. May I go see Maman now?"

Leo nodded, his thoughts already elsewhere. Maddy slipped off the bench and tiptoed to the door. She hated the thundercloud of tension that could burst into a room, at any time, without warning. She was not capable of predicting it, but she did know how to react to it. Do not ask what is wrong. Just be quiet.

Pausing in the doorway, Maddy peered back over her shoulder. Her father was standing now, staring out the window, hands thrust deeply into his front pockets. He looked worried. Still unnerved by the thought that she was to blame, Maddy dashed out of the room.

Where could Maman have gone? Maybe to their bedroom.

Normally, Maddy relished any opportunity to go into her parents' bedroom. It was a fantastic place, an oasis of interesting and beautiful things. She loved to sit at her mother's dressing table and pretend the beautiful crystal perfume bottles were elegantly dressed courtiers, dancing at an imperial ball. Her favorite was the porcelain swan, who presided over the entire menagerie, an enchanted prince greeting his guests. The swan occupied a position of honor in front of a photograph of Leo and Martha, taken on their wedding day. Martha was looking straight at the camera, her face full of joy. Leo was looking down at Martha, his complete devotion visible even to the camera's detail-blurring eye.

There were other pictures in the room, mostly of her parents at fancy grown-up parties. Maddy loved helping her mother get ready for a party. First, Martha would flood her room with music—she kept both a radio and a Victrola in the bedroom. After Martha bathed, Maddy helped her mother decide what to wear. Together they would carefully evaluate the selection of appropriate garments laid out earlier by the maid, at Martha's request. Somehow Martha always made Maddy feel that her opinion was a critically important factor in making the final choice.

After choosing a dress, there came the cosmetic ceremony. Martha followed the fashion dictates of the time, which called for thinly tweezed eyebrows, heavily lined eyelids, and a carefully defined mouth. Maddy, fascinated by the whole elaborate procedure, handed pencils and pots to her mother on command, like a sous-chef assisting the master.

Once her mother had finished dressing and applying her makeup, she would put on her jewelry. What would it be tonight? The pearls? Or the emeralds that were the same color as Maddy's eyes? Maddy's last duty was to hold a hand mirror behind her mother's reflection at the dressing table, so that Martha could assess the final result. With a satisfied smile, Martha would reward her daughter with a long hug. "How could I get dressed without you? You have the eye of an artist!"

"But this is not a party day," sighed Maddy to herself as she trudged down the hall. Wait—wasn't that the radio playing in her parents' room? Heartened, she closed her eyes and wished that her mother would sing along. Her mother's beautiful voice was one certain antidote to tension.

When she reached the doorway she saw her mother sitting motionless on the bed. She, too, wore a fretful expression.

"Maman," began Maddy as she crept into the room, "I don't mind about not going to Germa—" She stopped in mid-sentence. Her mother was holding a slim, gray velvet box. It was the home of her mother's golden songbird!

From the time Maddy was old enough to sit still, the appearance of the gray box signaled the beginning of her very favorite game. "Shall we see if Mr. Songbird is home? Would you like for him to sing?" her mother would ask, then rap sharply on the top of the box.

"*Salut, Monsieur! Êtes-vous là?* Are you home? It's little Maddy! She would like to hear you sing!" Next Martha would whisper, in a conspiratorial tone, "*Oui*, I think he is home today," and carefully remove a necklace from the box. Out came a nightingale, carved onto a gold medallion, hanging on a thick golden chain. Maddy watched and listened, entranced, as Martha swung the medallion from her fingertips, and sang—and sang, and sang, with a voice every bit as captivating as a real nightingale's.

But she had not seen Mr. Songbird for nearly a year. More than a year—it had been just before her sixth birthday. She and her mother were upstairs, sitting on the floor in the master bedroom, and Mr. Songbird was in the middle of a wonderful concert.

Over her mother's shoulder Maddy saw her father appear in the doorway. She pointed to him and was about to burst out with an excited greeting when his eyes silenced her. At first warm and tender, they shifted with mercurial speed into icy blue pools of wrath. Speaking in rapid German, he stormed into the room, snatched the necklace from Martha's fingers, and flung it savagely at the wall.

Stunned, Maddy burst into tears. Without a word, her mother scooped her up and carried her out of the room, down the stairs, into the living room. She settled into a large chair by the fireplace.

"*Ça va, ça va, ma cherie, mon enfant.* It's alright, he didn't mean to scare you, he didn't mean to scare you," she crooned, rocking the distraught Maddy until she fell asleep, exhausted by her tears.

Nothing was said the next day. No mention was made of the incident, and no apologies given. Maddy dared not broach the subject, so frightened was she of her father's inexplicable rage. But after that day, the game stopped. Martha still sang to Maddy, but the necklace never reappeared.

Once or twice, when Maddy was feeling particularly brave, she asked if Mr. Songbird could come out to play. Her mother would only shake her head sadly. "No, *cherie*, Mr. Songbird is not home today."

Excited, now, at the sight of the box, and hopeful that her mother might remember their game and sing for her, Maddy was about to ask if "Mr. Songbird" was home when her mother used her free hand to cover her eyes.

"Maman! Do you have a headache?"

"No, Maddy. Please, *ma petite*, run to the kitchen and ask Wei Lin to give you some lunch. I think she has a cake for you to taste."

"But I'm not hungry, Maman! Could you—"

"Go now, *cherie*, Wei Lin will want you to taste it while it's still warm."

Her voice sounded so—strange. Like she was about to cry. Panic rose in Maddy's small throat. She sometimes heard voices, raised in anger, in middle of the night. She often felt tension envelop the house like static electricity. But she had never, ever seen her mother in tears. Petrified of doing something to make the situation worse, Maddy turned and fled the room.

Unaware of his daughter's distress, Leo stared out the front window of his home, and tried to empty his mind. He gazed at but did not see the curiously European houses lining the street, each one built in homage to a country on the other side of the world. He saw but did not notice the elegant gardens, all carefully tended by Chinese servants. He saw but did not see the family's new Cadillac, basking on the driveway in the blistering August heat like a huge black beetle. He saw nothing.

He paged through the dictionary in his mind. Six languages. "*Nem*," in Hungarian. Then French: "*Non*." German: "*Nien*." English: "*No*." Russian: "*Nyet*." In Mandarin: "*Bu*." He often found that the simplest words worked best to clear his mind, as he leafed through the catalogue of nouns, verbs, conjugations and cognates he'd committed to memory. *Hideg*, he continued in silence. *Cold. Froid. Kalt. Lerng.*

But today the technique did not work. He repeatedly lost his place in his drill. Words eluded him. He thought only of the journey his wife wanted to undertake. The journey back to Germany, to see her father.

The completeness, the violence of the changes he had experienced in his own life left no room for nostalgia. He did not need to go back to his home. He had no intention of going back. Ever.

Silently he cursed Bernice, the sister-in-law he had never met. He did not know her, but Martha's description made him feel as if he did. The telegram she sent last week was just what he would have expected. No excess sentimentality. Just the facts.

Situation intolerable. Have opted for France over Shanghai. Will leave when father improves or dies. Good luck to you. B.

Leo winced as he recalled the argument that had followed Martha's receipt of the telegram.

"Leo, I want to go and see them before they leave. Before he dies. To let him meet Maddy. He's my father. I owe him that much."

"It's too dangerous. Don't you listen to what people are saying? People of Jewish decent aren't wanted in Germany. It's insane for you to go back now. We've invited them to visit time after time. I've offered to pay for their passage. Now they have refused, again, to come join us. Why should you have to go all that way to apologize for falling in love?"

"He's my father. He is *dying*. My sister and her husband are leaving their home to start over, just as we did. Who knows what will happen? This may be my last chance."

"Last year your father was removed from the university faculty because Hitler made it illegal for Jews to teach. Do you think the Nazis will have a 'Welcome Home' banner waiting for you? Even if you could get a visa, which is doubtful, how could you even consider going back to Germany with those lunatics in charge?"

"The danger is exaggerated. You make it seem like our lives would be in jeopardy. The Nazis are throwing Jews out, not locking them up."

"They may lock me up."

Martha let out an exasperated gust of air. "It's been so long! Over twelve years! They couldn't still be looking for you now."

Leo could not tell her that Liu Tue-Sheng would make sure he never even made it out of the city. He snapped back with a credible rejoinder.

"And what if my name is on some list somewhere when I apply for a visa? Is this trip worth that much to you?"

Her aggravation deepened. "It may be just as unsafe to stay here! The Japanese are going to invade any day now. How do we know that this time the settlements won't be involved?"

"Because the Japanese have picked a fight with Chiang Kai-shek, not the rest of the world. Chiang lost a lot of face by letting them take Manchuria. Then he sat back and let the Japanese have Shanghai's industrial zone; he can't afford to let them get the rest of Shanghai as well. There's no reason to think the Japanese will not respect the treaty rights of the European countries, even if they do grab the other Chinese sectors of the city away from Chiang. Troops are already in place to protect the foreign settlements, just like last time. We'll be safe. Nothing has changed."

"I'm going, Leo, with you or without you. I am *going* to Germany."

"I forbid it. I won't pay for your passage."

"I'll find a way to go without your help!"

"You stubborn fool! How can you even consider doing this? Traveling alone, just you and Maddy? To a country run by Nazis? I won't permit it!"

"I must! I have to go! I have to!"

In a burst of clarity, Leo understood the source of his fear. Maybe she was not just going to her father. Maybe she was leaving him.

He dared not give the thought form; he dared not express it aloud. Perhaps Martha did not yet realize, herself, that part of her burning desire to go back to Germany stemmed from her desire to escape from their marriage. Perhaps there was still time to convince her to change her mind.

The next day he locked their passports in a safe at the bank. He knew that if she discovered what he had done it would lead to another, even more bitter confrontation. But he had to take the chance. He could not let her go.

❦

Moving away from the window, Leo collapsed onto a chair, head in his hands. For several years it had been bearable. With a working knowledge of all the major languages spoken in the Concessions, Leo became a fly on the wall of the Babylon that was Shanghai.

His meetings with Liu were rare. At times he received a note containing a name, and he would undertake to find out all he could about that person. Or about a pending business transaction. Or a government raid. He didn't like it. It was not difficult work. Just distasteful.

And Liu kept his word. He paid Leo handsomely to lead his double life. Established at the bank, Leo continued to live the life of a well-to-do businessman during a time of worldwide recession. No one in Leo's social circle knew that he was on Liu's generous payroll. No one knew that confidences whispered at the bar made it to Liu's ears. No one knew that a boast about a business coup could soon be used to help a competitor. No one knew that Leo Hoffman could not be trusted, because everyone did. Trust him.

At first Leo's conscience did not bother him too badly. He was sure he could find a way out, for himself and Martha and their child. He would do this distasteful work for just a short period of time, he told himself, until he could find a way out of Shanghai.

He tried not to link, in his mind, the information he'd passed to Liu with the arrest of one man; he closed his eyes to the financial ruin of another. Those men were not innocent. They'd made their choices. Leo was paying the price for his own mistakes; now they paid for theirs.

Then, Liu raised the price.

Four years ago, Liu ordered him to "befriend" a certain young woman. A young woman named Amelia. A young woman who was married to a much older man. A man whose business interests made him an…inconvenience.

And she was just the first of many. Leo had access to women who were unable to keep their desires, or their husbands' secrets, to themselves. Another valuable source of information.

He told himself he was not really being unfaithful. He told himself he was just an actor paid to play a love scene. He was no different than Douglas Fairbanks or Errol Flynn. Except, he had no choice but to follow Liu's direction. He was not allowed to walk off the set.

The smell and taste of other women haunted him. His guilt ate at him, a sour leprosy of shame.

Over time Leo became violently, irrationally jealous of Martha, as if she were the one betraying him, as if she were the one keeping secrets. He wanted to know where she was at all times. He checked up on her constantly. He seethed if she laughed too enthusiastically at another man's joke, or held another man's gaze for too long. She had not danced with another man for years, not daring to risk Leo's rage.

Sometimes he made love to her with a fervor bordering on desperation; at other times he could not bring himself to touch her, thinking that his caresses would corrupt her. He knew his behavior was ridiculous; he knew he was hurting her. But he could not help himself. His self-loathing lit a monstrous fire within him, and the flames scorched them both.

It had taken this, her threat to leave, to make him realize how close he was to disaster. How close he was to losing her. And he did not know what to do. Except to tell her everything. And that, he was sure, would drive her away completely.

CHAPTER 13

THE WIFE

ༀ᠘ༀ

Martha had trouble explaining, even to herself, why she felt compelled to go to Germany without Leo, or why she discounted the risk involved. Bernice's telegram had given her a reason to leave Shanghai. She did not yet connect her desire to leave with the gradual changes in her husband: the jealousy, the over-protectiveness bordering on lunacy, the outrageous accusations.

Initially, when his behavior started to change, Martha thought Leo must be hiding some financial problem. Like most married women of her generation, Martha left all of the family finances in her husband's hands. She did not have a clear idea of where their money was, or how much they had. Of course, they'd stopped spending money as lavishly as they had before the Depression. Even though Shanghai's economy had been hurt less than most other port cities, the mood had changed. It was impolite to flaunt one's wealth when so many people had lost so much.

But her cautious inquiries among their acquaintances confirmed what Leo claimed; he was doing quite well at the bank. Money did not seem to be the cause of the turbulence in their lives.

And it was difficult to stay angry, for Leo always took the blame for their arguments. Apologies followed every outburst; self-recrimination countered every groundless accusation. Sometimes, he seemed better, less volatile, and she thought she had her old husband back again. For a while. Then the arguments started again.

Yet, as bad as the situation was at times, she could not imagine life without him. At least, not in Shanghai.

The city was also changing. Every day it became a more dangerous place. At the moment it seemed certain that the Shanghailanders would be treated to another violent spectacle. The Japanese were intent on expanding their holdings in China. Chiang Kai-shek had to stop them.

For weeks the Chinese residents of Chapei, Nantao, and Hongkew—all the Chinese sections of the city— had been flooding into the International Settlement and the French Concession. Those who could afford it rented rooms at inflated prices from landlords always ready to profit from the misery of their human brethren. Others squatted in the blistering hot streets of the city, surrounded by their meager possessions and their screaming children. When the complaints from the Shanghailanders grew vociferous, the Municipal Council started herding the peasants into temporary refugee centers.

Everyone knew why they were coming. They were clearing the battleground.

All summer Japan had been moving against Chinese positions to the north. Chiang did not respond. He realized that his army could not withstand a long campaign, stretched across the country from Nanking to Peking. So he challenged the invaders in the place the Western powers cared about most, in the arena he knew best. Shanghai.

Martha was afraid. Despite Leo's confidence, the idea of living through another war scared her. In the past Leo's love and reassurance had been sufficient to calm her fears. But this time his explanation did not seem to help.

Her sister's telegram had given her a legitimate reason to leave. She wanted to return to Germany to make amends. Her father had never been cruel, just emotionally incapable. She wanted to make her peace with him before he died. She could see her sister, and meet her brother-in-law. She could reconnect with her family, and have some time to think. To think about why her marriage was crumbling, about why loving Leo had become so painful.

Martha sat on her bed, holding tightly to the golden necklace. The first time she wore it in front of Leo, she'd told him about Harry, and he never seemed to mind that she kept the necklace as a keepsake, a gift given to her by an old friend. Until the last time he saw it, when he'd terrified poor Maddy with one of his sudden rages.

Dear Harry. She heard from her sister, in one of her early letters, that he'd been devastated by the news of Martha's hasty marriage. Martha truly regretted having hurt Harry, and her family, so badly. She tried to reassure Bernice and her father that she was happy by sending regular updates about her new life. A life that had started out so wonderfully.

How had things worked out for Harry in America? Had he married an American girl? Her own life would have turned out so differently had she joined him there. Now, she felt trapped by the life she'd wanted so desperately wanted all those years ago....

Unless.

They kept her good jewelry locked in a vault at the bank, and she could not get to it without Leo's knowledge. But Harry's necklace was made of gold. She could sell the medallion to pay for her passage to Germany.

Tomorrow, she would take the necklace to a jewelry store and find out how much it was worth. Perhaps she could rely on her dear friend Harry to help her again, after all.

※

An overnight rain did little to dissipate the sticky heat. Leo was already gone when Martha awoke. She donned a light cotton dress and went downstairs. Maddy was having breakfast in the morning room, under the strict scrutiny of the cook, Wei Lin.

"No egg, no grow. Too skinny to get husband," admonished the diminutive Chinese lady, herself a grandmother several times over.

"But the yolk is runny! Maman, it makes me sick to look at all that oozy stuff. Please tell Wei Lin I don't have to eat it."

Martha inspected the offending egg. "Wei, it is a little underdone. You know how picky she is. But you must eat your toast, Maddy."

Vindicated, Maddy spread a dollop of strawberry jam on her toast. Martha reached for a croissant. She never had more than bread and coffee for breakfast.

"Wei, where is Mr. Hoffman?"

Wei snorted before answering, obviously offended at having her egg rejected.

"He say, good breakfast, Wei. He like egg. He say, tell Miss Martha be home soon." With another injured sniff she scooped up Maddy's plate and stalked off to the kitchen.

At that moment Leo walked through the front door. The sound of his footsteps made Maddy leap up from the table.

"Papa! Good morning Papa," she greeted him, her arms outstretched.

Leo kneeled down and gave his daughter a hug and an absent-minded kiss. He looked at Martha, an unspoken question in his eyes.

"Good morning, Leo," she asked quietly. "Where have you been this morning?"

"To check on the hostilities. Shots were fired yesterday to the north, at Yokohama Bridge. Chinese soldiers have taken up positions along the northern edge of the city. There are warships moving up the Whangpoo. The Settlements seem well protected."

"So we get to watch another war," Martha commented dryly, helping herself to milk and sugar.

"It seems that way."

Martha thought furiously while she stirred her coffee. Leo did not seem too apprehensive, but she did not want to go on her secret errand if it was truly dangerous to do so. Nor did she want to cause Leo any unnecessary distress. Normally he played tennis on Saturday afternoons, just before tea. She quickly thought of a legitimate reason to leave the house around that time.

"Leo, I was to stop by the dressmaker today, and thought I might bring Maddy along. We could have tea at the Cathay Hotel after my fitting. Do you think it would be safe?"

Leo considered her question. "I suppose so," he answered after some deliberation. "You should be safe on the Bund. Take the car. I'll have one of the regulars fetch me for my tennis game at the club."

Martha gave him an appreciative smile. She had not lied. She had told him two-thirds of the truth. Later she and Maddy would visit Madame Olinov, Shanghai's most exclusive dressmaker, whose shop was in the ground floor of the Cathay Hotel, the newest architectural showpiece on the Bund. They would have tea in the hotel lobby lounge. Then they would slip up Nanking Road and pop in a jewelry store or two. She wanted to go back to Germany, and she was not going to give up easily.

Their car turned left off Foochow Road and onto the Bund at just after four o'clock that afternoon. The normally busy street was packed with people: refugees and relatives; school children and mothers; rickshaw pullers and beggars; coolies, shoppers and tourists; call girls, bankers, merchants and businessmen. They covered the street, the lawn, the docks, and the sidewalks. Even the rooftops of the Bund's stately towers were being used as observation platforms. Everyone was watching some activity across the river.

"What on earth is going on?" asked Martha with apprehension as Maddy pressed her face to the car window.

"Look, Maman, look! The planes!" Across the water, less than a mile away, ten Chinese warplanes buzzed and spun like wrathful insects over a Japanese battleship anchored near the Hongkew wharf. Over the din of the carnival atmosphere Martha could hear the rattle of anti-aircraft artillery.

Their driver rolled down his window for a brief conversation with a Russian compatriot, who was watching the action through a pair of binoculars. He then turned to Martha.

"Well, Mrs. Hoffman, this man says the Chinese bombers have been at it for some time. First they attacked the Japanese factories over in Hongkew, now they're trying to blow up their flagship, the *Idzumo*. Says they haven't hit a thing yet."

Martha surveyed the scene with foreboding. By now they were packed in on all sides; the car could neither move forward, nor turn back. This was insanity. It wasn't safe. If they couldn't leave, she thought, at least they could get out of the road.

"Listen, Maddy dear, we may as well get out and walk. The Cathay is only a few blocks away, and the car will never make it through all this."

A loud boom brought a loud cheer from the crowds. Maddy pointed out the window, her eyes wide.

"Look! Look! Maman! They've blown up the Hongkew dock!"

"That's quite enough sightseeing for one day," said Martha firmly. "Pick us up at the Cathay at six o'clock," she instructed, opening her own door. Ahead she could see the stately pyramid-shaped roof of the Cathay Hotel. Soaring twenty stories high, the luxurious structure sat on the Bund across Nanking Road from the Palace Hotel, completely overwhelming its older rival.

As they approached the hotel Martha sensed the crowd dispersing. Glancing back up to the sky she saw the Chinese planes breaking formation, and felt a rush of relief. It was ridiculous, standing around to gawk at a bombing raid as if it were a target shoot. Even though they were landing several hundred yards away, those bombs were real. But the spectators acted like the air raid was nothing more than an interesting show: a comedy, given the inexperienced pilots' lack of skill in hitting their target.

Martha and Maddy walked into the air-conditioned lobby of the Cathay, stopping to give the doorman a friendly greeting. She would skip Madame Olinov's. They would have tea, and stay at the Cathay until things calmed down outside. The rest of her plans would have to wait.

Martha requested her favorite table, near the rear of the lobby, with a nice view of the Bund. It was the best place for people-watching in all of Shanghai.

She had just taken her seat across from Maddy when a thunderous roar caused everyone to look out at the Bund. Martha jerked her head up just in time to see a huge wall of water rise up from the Whangpoo, like a hideous brown monster emerging from a swamp. It towered over the Bund for a fraction of an instant, and then crashed onto the street, drenching everything and everyone for a block and a half.

There was no time to react before the second bomb fell. A crater opened in the pavement in front of the Cathay doors. Somehow, her reflexes responded, and Martha threw herself over her daughter's body, tipping over the child's chair and sending them both to the floor as hot air and glass blasted into the room.

Every window along the front of the building shattered from the force of the explosion. The doorman who had greeted them a minute earlier was blown backwards through the door and into the lobby. His body skimmed like a penguin on ice across the smooth marble, until it stopped, lifeless, in front of the reception desk.

For a moment there was silence, punctuated by the sound of people thrashing through broken glass. Then the screaming began.

Martha pulled Maddy under the table. They crouched there, petrified.

"Maddy, oh my God, Maddy, are you hurt? Are you alright?" Martha tried to hug her daughter and inspect her for wounds at the same time. Tiny shards of broken glass clung to their clothes.

"I think so," replied Maddy, her voice low and quivering.

"Are you bleeding? Does it hurt anywhere?"

"No. Except my ears feel funny."

Martha realized that her own ears were also numb from the sound of the explosion. Not knowing what else to do she frantically tried to brush the fragments of glass off Maddy's clothes. As she did so, tiny splinters of glass pierced her gloves. Small red stains appeared on her white linen fingertips.

Madeleine's eyes grew wide at the sight of the blood on her mother's gloves. She emitted a whimper that grew into a howl.

"What is it, Maman?! What happened?! What happened?!" the terrified girl shrieked, thrashing in her mother's arms. Martha held fast to Maddy's shoulders, afraid to move for fear another bomb was already on its way.

"It was a bomb, Maddy. One of the planes dropped a bomb. But we are alright, darling. We are alright." To her own muffled hearing her voice sounded far away and unnaturally calm. Maddy continued to cry but ceased struggling. They would wait, for the moment, huddled under the table. Until someone came to tell them what to do.

⊙✿⊙

Two miles away a group of four men dressed in pristine tennis whites were engaged in a competitive game of doubles at the Çercle Sportif Francais. Leo tossed the ball to serve. He watched as it reached the perfect spot in the air, two feet above and slightly forward of his head, but he did not swing his racquet, and the ball fell back down to the ground. Something had distracted him. A noise. A noise like thunder. Thunder on a sticky hot, sunny day. Thunder from the direction of the Whangpoo.

"Did you hear that?" he asked, not really needing confirmation, but soliciting it nonetheless.

The other men looked at each other. One of them shrugged. "The Chinese have been trying to bomb Japanese positions in Hongkew all afternoon. Maybe they finally hit something."

"If that was a bomb, it was closer than Hongkew," said Leo's partner soberly.

Leo dropped his racquet and headed off the court at a trot. A knot was forming in the base of his stomach, a sickening, gut-wrenching knot. As he mounted the steps of the club he heard another distant boom. Chills ran up his spine and he started to run, not stopping to give a word of explanation to the puzzled friends he left behind, or the bemused club members he passed, as he sped through the clubhouse and out the front door, shouting at the taxi driver who habitually parked in front of the club at this hour for the convenience of members who drank too much whiskey with their tea.

He wrenched open the cab door and jumped into the car. Cold sweat mingled with warm perspiration on his skin.

"The Bund," he barked in Russian to the startled driver. "To the Cathay Hotel. Go. As fast as the devil or I'll drive this Goddamn thing myself."

They got as far as the intersection of Avenue Edward VII and Szechuen Road, one block behind the Bund, before the pandemonium in the street completely blocked traffic. Leo bolted from the car. The driver did not even try to ask for his fare.

A crazed mass of people fled in every direction. Leo grabbed the arm of the first white person he saw. The man's face was ashen. Bloodstains covered his trousers.

"What's happened?" Leo bellowed, panic coursing through every vein.

"They've bombed the Settlement," the bewildered man replied in a vague manner. "They've blown away the Palace and the Cathay Hotel. There are so many people dead. So much blood. So many people...."

Leo jerked back as if he'd been struck in the face. The knot in his stomach became a burning abyss. The man turned and wandered away, still mumbling to himself.

"It's not true!" Leo shouted hoarsely at the retreating figure, unwilling to believe what his senses were telling him. Then Leo began to run again, as fast as he had ever run in his life. He shoved or side-stepped the motionless and the hysterical, thrust aside anyone who got in his way. He was at Nanking Road. He turned the corner. He stopped short.

Nothing during his experience as a soldier during the Great War had prepared him for the carnage that assaulted his eyes. The Chinese planes had dropped three bombs on the Bund. One bomb landed in the Whangpoo, another in front of the Cathay, and a third dropped straight through the roof of the Palace, exploding inside the building and blasting away one whole side of the hotel. Mutilated bodies dangled from the wreckage of the Palace like pieces of twisted laundry. Clouds of acrid dust hung low in the air, hovering over loose piles of glass and steel and mortar, now mingled with severed bone, and flesh, and blood. A chorus of terror and pain rose from the throats of five hundred wounded. Seven hundred lay dead. European and Asian, young and old, rich and poor, innocent and evil; all were united in a sudden, grisly execution.

Tears burned Leo's eyes. A wave of nausea swept over him. *Martha. Maddy.* He ran once more, tripping over bits of rubble and slipping in the blood that ran in the street like rainwater. He repeated their names aloud, over and over, until the mantra became a frenzied cry of horror and hope.

He saw the Cathay, and the crater in front of it. Something caught at his foot, causing him to stumble and fall. It was a small Chinese boy. The bone of his left shin had broken completely through his skin. He howled piteously for help. Leo pushed himself up off the ground and dashed forward. His hands and knees were now drenched in blood.

He climbed through what had been the grand entrance to the Cathay Hotel, shouting the names of his wife and child. There were so many people hurt. Others were there helping, clearing away glass and debris so that the injured could be freed from the wreckage.

And then he heard it, the shrill shout of a little girl, calling to him through the chaos.

"Papa! Papa!" Maddy screeched. She raced to him and wrapped her quaking arms around him. Martha was right behind her, tears streaming down her cheeks.

Leo hugged Martha to him, wrapping Maddy between their two grateful bodies. He closed his eyes.

"Oh thank you, dear God," he sobbed, the first real prayer he had uttered since childhood. "Thank God, thank God. Thank God." Wiping his eyes, he took one step back to inspect them.

"You aren't hurt?" It was a plea, not a question.

"No, we're—alright," replied Martha with a touch of incredulity.

"Then let's get out of here," ordered Leo. He wiped his hands off on his tennis shorts, then whipped off his shirt and tore off a long strip of fabric, trying to use a piece that was not sullied with blood.

He squatted down next to Maddy, gave her a kiss, and another big hug. Then he looked her straight in the eyes.

"My brave little princess, I'm going to cover your eyes with this and carry you away from here. You put your face in my shoulder and don't even think about looking up until I tell you to. Alright?"

Maddy nodded, her little chin still trembling. Leo turned the strip of fabric into a blindfold and tied it firmly around Maddy's closed eyes. Before picking her up he said to Martha, "Keep your eyes on the ground, Martha. Don't look around you. Hold on to my arm. You've already seen enough."

"I'll try." She managed a weak smile.

"That's my girl." Picking a careful path through the rubble and the gore, Leo led his family home.

❦

He waited until they had each taken a warm bath, changed into comfortable silk pajamas, and sipped some hot broth, provided by a pinch-faced Wei Lin. He waited until Maddy fell asleep on the big bed in her parent's room, nestled between her parents, one small hand holding that of her father, the other tucked into her mother's. He waited until he and Martha were settled together on the overstuffed leather couch in the parlor, a decanter of brandy on the table in front of them. Then he began.

"Martha, we have to leave Shanghai."

"I know."

He picked up a lock of her hair and let it ripple through his fingers. What would he have done if he had lost them today? What reason would he have to go on living? They must leave. He must find somewhere safe for them. He did not care what price he had to pay, as long as they were safe.

"It may not be so easy for me to get out. There are…well, there are some things about me that you don't know."

He stood up, and took a step away from her, running his hand over his head and down the back of his neck. When he turned around to face her he saw the question in her eyes.

"You see, Martha, I was not entirely truthful with you about why I came to Shanghai. There was more to my story. But I was afraid that you'd leave me if you knew the truth. I was afraid I would lose you. And I knew I couldn't bear it."

Her eyes welled up with tears, yet she did not interrupt. She looked at him and waited. He had no idea how long she had been waiting.

Leo paused again, not sure where to start. Then the truth poured out.

"I killed a man. When I was in Paris. Imre Károly, Chief of Police of Budapest, was found dead in my hotel room because I killed him. I killed him in self-defense, but there were no witnesses. And I—probably could have gotten away without killing him, but I wanted him dead. He'd murdered my foster mother and uncle. And then I stole a diamond necklace from him, a necklace I knew had been paid for with counterfeit francs. I stole it because I knew it was the only way I could ever hope to be with you."

Martha listened, immobile on the couch.

"When I came to Shanghai I sold the diamonds to one of the most powerful men in China. You know of him. Liu Tue-Sheng. He's powerful because he's rich, and ruthless, and behind almost everything illegal that happens in this part of China. But I sold him the diamonds, anyway, because I was desperate. And then I made even more money in a commodities market manipulation that Liu somehow pulled off. So I was rich. Then you came to Shanghai. I had everything.

"But the stock market crash wiped me out. I didn't have the heart to tell you then. You were so excited about the baby, and I so badly wanted to give you both a beautiful life. Liu found out about my predicament and he—well, he made me go to work for him.

"I really am wanted for murder, Martha, and Liu is holding onto a valid warrant for my arrest. It may be, with all the time that has passed, that I'd be safe, that no one is still looking for me. But they'd start looking the minute that Liu turned me in. He'd make sure of it. Not only because I'm a valuable commodity for him, but because to do otherwise would show he was merciful—a weakness that a person in his business can't afford to reveal. So I'm stuck here. But you are not. So you and Maddy must leave."

He sat down in a chair across from her, afraid to go any closer. A long, fluid silence flowed between them, ebbing and dividing into different emotions: remorse and anger, contrition and indignation, sympathy and sorrow, as the weight of his story settled over them both.

At last Martha spoke, fighting back her tears. "What do you mean, you work for Liu Tue-Sheng? You work at the bank. How can Liu keep you in Shanghai?"

"I spy on people, Martha." Leo said flatly, his self-deprecation obvious. "I eavesdrop, and uncover secrets, and collect dirty laundry. I'm an informant. And in exchange for the information I provide, Liu Tue-Sheng, member of the board of the Commerce Bank of China, puts money into my account every month. I chalk it all up to commissions on new business."

Martha looked down at her hands, then up at the ceiling, then to the door. When she faced Leo again, her features were twisted with pain.

"I could forgive you almost anything, Leo," she said, her voice breaking. "I know that—that if you killed that man in Paris—you had a reason. And I know that if you took—something or did—something to survive, that you did what you truly believed you had to do. I'm not as naive as you think I am. And these times we live in—people do things that they would not otherwise do, to survive. But it's so—hard for me to accept that you didn't trust me. That from the very beginning, you did not trust me. That you couldn't trust me to forgive you for what you did—out of love for me, thinking an easy life was more important to me than the truth. And I don't know—if I can—forgive you for what your guilt has—done to you. And done to us." She buried her face in her hands and cried anguished sobs.

The sight of Martha in tears sent a fresh torrent of guilt raging through him. He pressed his fists together, fighting the urge to reach for her, searching for words to explain why he'd taken so long to confess.

"At first I thought I was protecting you Martha, first you, and then Maddy. I wanted you to be happy. To be with me, and to be happy. I didn't know what love was, until I met you. I thought that true love was fragile and precious, and I was afraid to test its limits. I'd already put you through so much. I thought that by not telling you the truth I was keeping you safe. And as things got worse, it seemed impossible to risk losing you, for every day I had more to lose. But I finally had to admit that I was only protecting myself. Not just my life, but what I wanted our life together to be."

Leo's voice caught in his throat, and he did not know how much longer he could go on talking. "All I can say is, I am sorry, my darling. I never—wanted things to be this way. I just—wanted you to be with me, and be happy. But now you and Maddy are better off without me. You must go to a place where you can be safe, and I can't keep you safe here. I want you to join your sister and her family when they get to France."

Martha did not answer. She continued to cry as Leo took a seat beside her. He stroked her shoulder tentatively, still afraid to touch her, afraid he would upset her even more.

"Whatever I've done, Martha," he said, his voice breaking, "Whatever I've done, I've done loving you, my darling. And I am so sorry that I got it all wrong."

He closed his eyes and kissed her hair; tenderly, reverently, trying to convey in that single act how precious she was to him.

Still crying, Martha jerked her head away. As she moved she felt him cringe. Then, like a disciplined rider pulling hard on the reins of a runaway horse, she pulled herself away from her anger. *There is no time for this. There is no time for anger. Not now.* If it was within her to forgive him, then she must forgive him now. Their circumstances could not tolerate indecision. She took a deep breath and turned her head towards his. As their lips touched, Leo detected the change in her emotions. Engulfed by grateful passion, he kissed her face, her throat, and her neck. He swept her silk pajamas off her shoulders, and he worshiped her.

Lost in his ardent caresses, she smiled. She had her husband back. The man she loved. The man with whom she shared her life, a life that could not be beautiful or complete without him. Yet something that had been perfect was no longer so, and would never be again.

"I won't go to France without you," she whispered later, as they drifted into a healing sleep.

"We'll see," Leo said, his heart glowing with renewed strength. Martha loved him. She would always love him. He felt invincible.

CHAPTER 14

THE VICTIM

❧❦❧

The next day the Chinese government issued its official apology.
An accident. The bombing of the Bund by the Chinese pilots had been
an accident. An accident! And fifteen minutes after the first three
bombs had devastated the Bund, two more fell at the intersection of
Avenue Edward VII and Tibet Road. One struck the Great World
Amusement Center. On Thursday it had been a six-story fun house,
entertaining visitors with tight rope walkers, acrobats, gambling tables,
slot machines, professional letter-writers, fortune tellers, shooting gal-
leries, ice cream shops and dumpling stands, prayer temples and women
of ill repute. On Friday it had been converted into a refugee center. On
Saturday it became a pyramid of death for a thousand people, most of
them Chinese, who had come to the Settlement to escape the war. Flesh
and shrapnel from the explosion rained down on the Englishmen playing cricket at a nearby park. Also an accident.

The significance of what had happened was not lost on the
Shanghailanders. Intentionally or not, Chiang had broken the rules. If the
Taipans and their families, their homes and their silver, their port and their
ponies, if all that could not be safe, then Shanghai would cease to exist.
Already, the evacuations had started. The British wives and their children

boarded the *Rajputana*, bound for Hong Kong. American families sailed away on the *President Taft*, Germans on the *Oldenburg*. Shanghai was now a war zone, the myth of its sanctity exposed. It was time to leave.

But for the outcasts, for all those no longer welcome in their native land, and the few who refused to believe that Shanghai was dying, leaving the city was not so easy. To leave, you needed permission to enter another country. And permission was not easy to obtain.

The grim reality of the situation soon became clear to Leo and Martha. The Nazi government would not allow Martha to return to Germany, for she was of Jewish heritage. The French government would not allow her to enter France until she could prove she had relatives established there. The United States was similarly out of the question. Even visas for Hong Kong were restricted to British nationals until the immediate refugee crisis had abated. For the time being, there was no decent place for Martha and Maddy to go, even if they were willing to leave without Leo. They would have to wait.

After a few uneventful days the remaining foreign residents of the city emerged from hiding. Perhaps the boundaries of the French Concession and the International Settlement would be respected after all; there did not seem to be any compelling reason to stay inside. If not, well then, an errant bomb could land on one's house as easily as it could land on the country club. May as well go have a drink, mused the Shanghailanders as they studied the night sky, painted a macabre red by the incendiary blaze of Japanese bombs pulverizing Hongkew and Nantao. Life was too short to stay thirsty.

Martha and Leo felt safer at home. Their house was in the heart of the residential district of the French Concession, and they hoped that its distance from any likely targets would keep them safe. Still, Leo ventured out from time to time for news, and Martha went in search of groceries and other staples, for their Chinese servants refused point-blank to leave the property for fear of being shot or captured by the Japanese.

Nine days after the bombing of the Bund, Maddy bounded into the breakfast room where her parents were finishing their coffee and poring over the morning edition of the *North China Daily News*. She jiggled her mother's knee.

"Maman, I have to show you something!" she exclaimed in an urgent stage whisper.

"Oh yes?" replied Martha in a similar tone. She put down her section of the paper. "Shall I go see it now?"

"Yes! And you too, Papa."

"I will be along in just a minute, little love. Just let me finish my coffee."

Maddy made a face. "Finish your *paper*, you mean. Well, then, Maman will be the lucky one, and you will have to be second." With this admonishment, she dragged her bemused mother from the table.

In a moment they were in the parlor. Martha saw her daughter's entire collection of dolls and stuffed animals arranged on the sofa, creating an attentive audience. She pointed her mother to a vacant chair.

"Madame," she said solemnly. "The concert is about to begin."

"Oh, why thank you," responded Martha with gracious decorum. She took a seat.

Maddy skipped over to the piano bench and executed an elaborate curtsy. Martha applauded. After giving her mother an appreciative smile Maddy plopped down onto the piano bench, her small feet dangling four inches from the ground. For an instant she posed her ten little fingers over the keys. Then she began to play.

Within seconds Martha's mouth fell wide open. She listened, astonished, as Maddy played, from beginning to end, an energetic rendition of Scott Joplin's "Peanut Butter Rag."

"Maddy! That was fantastic!" She flew to where her daughter sat beaming with delight, and wrapped her in a hug.

"How long did it take you to learn that? Who's been teaching you? Is this a secret between you and Papa?"

Radiant, Maddy shook her head. "No, Maman. There's no secret. Gaston, who plays the piano at the club, showed me how to play it. Then I came home and figured out how to do it by myself. I told you, I listen very well."

Puzzled, Martha pondered Maddy's explanation. "You mean—you taught *yourself* how to play that piece?" she stammered. Maddy nodded proudly.

"How long did it take, for you to teach yourself, I mean?" Martha faltered, thunderstruck by what her daughter was telling her.

"Well," said Maddy, swinging her feet as she thought about her answer, "Gaston played it for me at the club when we were there for dinner with Janine and her parents, so however long that was, you know, since you bought the piano for me, I guess. A few days. But I can do it faster now, because I know where all the sounds are in the keys. But I can't reach the pedals. It would sound better if I could reach the pedals," she finished matter-of-factly.

"Leo!" called Martha, moving toward the door. "Leo, come here! You have to hear this!"

They bumped into each other at the doorway. Leo caught sight of the pile of stuffed animals and dolls on the couch.

"Oh, how marvelous! A concert. May I listen to the encore?"

"By all means," answered Martha, her eyes still wide. She motioned to Maddy. "Go ahead, darling, play your song for Papa."

Maddy gave Leo a sly sideways smile, then turned her attention back to the keyboard. She played the piece again, flawlessly.

Leo clapped enthusiastically. "Brava, Brava!" he called as Maddy stood up to take a bow. Then Leo turned to Martha.

"Well, I guess the joke's on me. How long has she been taking lessons?"

"Leo," exclaimed Martha, "She has not had any lessons. She taught herself. In just two weeks. Isn't that right, Maddy?"

"Hmm hmm," Maddy answered, turning a fidgety pirouette. She was starting to get nervous. Her father had a funny look on his face. Maybe it was time to stop talking.

Leo motioned for Maddy to sit back down on the piano bench, and then sat beside her. Martha started to speak, but Leo held up his hand to silence her.

"Maddy, did you really teach yourself how to play that song?" He sounded affectionate but solemn. Maddy nodded.

"How did you do it?"

Maddy hesitated. She so wanted him to be happy with her. She hoped her explanation would please him.

"Well, Papa, you see, each of these keys makes a sound. Gaston told me it is a special musical sound, called a "note." Here is "C," then "D." It goes up to "G," but that's all, and then it just repeats itself, so it's really easier than the alphabet. The black keys are "sharp" for up, and "flat," for down. If you fall, you fall down flat, so that's easy to remember.

"Gaston played this song for me, a few times, and I listened very well, and then I came home and learned where each note lives on my piano, to play it. So that's all. It wasn't too hard." She flashed him an uncertain little smile.

Martha could not restrain herself. "Leo, is that possible? Could she really be so talented? Just naturally gifted? She's only seven!"

"I suppose so," Leo answered. He thought about his own gift. Words were, after all, sounds. They crept into his memory and stayed there. They made sense to him in a way he knew made him different from other people. Musical notes could live in Maddy's little head just as easily as six languages now inhabited his.

Then he noticed the look on his daughter's face.

"Oh, Madeleine, my magnificent Madeleine! Don't be afraid. We think it's wonderful! You're wonderful! How lucky we are to have such a talented daughter!" He picked her up and spun her through the air before setting her down in front of the crowded couch. Her concern alleviated, Maddy giggled, basking in her father's praise.

"Now Maddy," Leo said in a mock-serious tone, wagging his finger at the population on the sofa, "if we are to have concerts here fit for royalty, don't you think a new doll is in order? A new queen for your collection? Someone worthy of your performances?"

"Oh, Papa! Really? But my birthday is past already, and Christmas is so far away!"

"Nonsense! A pianist with your talent deserves a regal audience. You shall have lessons, starting tomorrow. And we—I—will ride my stallion to court and invite her highness, the queen of fairyland, to come and pay you tribute."

Maddy glanced at her mother, expecting her to intervene. But Martha's face showed no disapproval; she was smiling at Maddy, her eyes glowing. She looked back at her father. He, too, was gazing at her with unabashed adoration.

Normally, Maddy was not a greedy child. But there was one thing she wanted with all of her girlish heart. Now she saw her opportunity, and took it.

"Papa, there is a doll; oh, she is so beautiful! We saw her last month at the department store. Do you remember, Mama? The ballerina? She's a queen, I guess. She's wearing a tiara. Oh, Mama, would it be alright?"

Martha smiled, "I think if we are to have such fabulous concerts in the house, a new doll would be perfectly fine."

"Then you shall have it," Leo exclaimed, tapping his blissful little prodigy on the forehead. "And you shall have it in time for a concert at tea!"

"Can we all go?" Madeleine cried, her face full of joyful expectation.

Again, Martha looked at Leo. He considered Maddy's question carefully before answering. "It should be safe. The department stores are as far from the harbor as our house, and even farther away from the French Concession border. I suppose we can all go. It will do us good to get out. We can even see if there is anywhere open for lunch."

Madeleine clapped her hands. Martha smiled. Leo beamed at his family, his heart glowing with love.

The cheerful group set out on its expedition just before noon. Refugees were still flooding into the Settlement from the Chinese Municipality of Greater Shanghai, as well as the surrounding countryside. Their street-clogging presence made driving difficult. It took a good thirty minutes to make what should have been a ten minute trip.

When the car reached the point where the two huge stores, Wing On and Sincere's, flanked Nanking Road, they discovered that parking was impossible. Leo tapped their driver on the shoulder.

"Just leave it running right here. I'll dash in. You can't cause any bigger traffic jam than what's already here. Shouldn't take five minutes."

"But you don't know which doll it is, Daddy," Maddy pointed out logically. "I have to come, too."

At that moment, a uniformed traffic policeman tapped on the windshield. "Please keep it moving, sir. With all these extra bodies in the road, we can't be blocking traffic. Move along, please."

"Look, Leo," Martha broke in quickly, "I know just which doll it is.

You stay here with Maddy in the car, and drive around the block. I'll be back here in five minutes, and we'll just go home for lunch." She leaned over and gave her husband a quick kiss, then hopped out before he could protest.

"Five minutes," he called after her, savoring the taste of her kiss. The policeman tapped on the window again.

Maddy opened the window and smiled up at him. "My mommy went to get me a doll."

"Very nice," he responded cheerfully. "Now tell your Daddy to move along, or I will have to give him a ticket."

"As you wish," Leo replied, playfully saluting the officer. "Go around the block, Peter. In this traffic that alone will take us more than ten minutes." The driver complied, edging the car through the morass of automobiles and other wheeled contraptions.

Martha quickly maneuvered her way into the busy department store. She went directly to where a display of porcelain dolls from Austria were arranged in a large glass case, and spotted Maddy's choice immediately. Sixteen inches tall, with fair pink skin and blushing cheeks, the doll's chestnut hair was braided around her head and adorned with a tiara of Bavarian crystal. She was dressed in a ballet gown of red silk taffeta and white tulle, with red velvet slippers to match.

Martha flagged down a saleswoman, who unlocked the case and retrieved the coveted dancer.

"A pretty doll for a pretty girl?"

Martha beamed. "The best, the most beautiful little girl." *Now if only they could find a way to get out of Shanghai.*

"I would like it gift-wrapped, please."

"Certainly, Madame." Martha followed the saleswoman to her register. She opened her purse and dug around for her wallet. As she did so she heard a noise. An odd noise, above the din of the crowd.

She looked around. What was that strange sound? It was high and thin, like a shrill voice stretched taut, melting into a scream. No, a whine. A metallic, whistling whine. The sound of a bomb hurtling through the air.

Within seconds the laws of physics ruthlessly eviscerated the expectations of humanity. The first floor of Sincere's was obliterated. One side of Wing On collapsed. A thousand people died instantly, or bled quickly to death. The hysterical survivors, insane with fear, screamed and stampeded through the forest of broken glass and dismembered bodies. Outside the corpse of the traffic policeman dangled from the electric wires overhead, like a gruesome marionette, directing the dance of death beneath him. A broken water main sent a bloody waterfall cascading into the street.

Martha had no time to react, no time for fear, and no time for regrets. She had no time to remember the sensation of Leo's caress, or the sweet touch of Madeleine's slender arms around her neck. She had no time to remember the smell of Bavarian wild flowers in early spring, the sound of her mother's voice, or to picture her husband and daughter together at the breakfast table. She heard a wall of noise, and felt a rippling sheet of pain. And then, darkness.

CHAPTER 15

THE ADVENTURESS

૭౿⌒⌒౿૭

Amelia Simmons stood on the Hoffmans' doorstep, waiting for someone to respond to the doorbell. She did not fidget, nor exhibit any visible sign of irritation, as the seconds became minutes, and still no one answered her summons. She waited. Then she rang again, and she waited again. She did not tap her slim crocodile-clad foot, check her lipstick in the brass reflection of the decorative doorknocker, or readjust the hat that covered the smooth chignon into which she had twisted her straight blond hair. Her demeanor was neither patient, nor benign. Hers was the menacing forbearance of the scavenger.

As she studied the cracks in the door, the sticky Shanghai heat sent a bead of sweat rolling down the back of her long white neck. *God, I detest this place.* She hated the heat and the noise and the stench of it. But like many of the human scavengers and parasites found in Shanghai, she stayed because the city's decadent prosperity provided a better home for their kind than anywhere else in the world.

Now Shanghai was dying, giving her the perfect reason to leave: self-preservation.

From birth Amelia had focused on one goal: her own satisfaction. She ran away from home at the age of fifteen, hoping to circumvent the drudgery of her family's working class existence in a small town outside Detroit, Michigan. And going to San Francisco would have been a good start, except that the man with whom she left neglected to mention that he was already married. He handed her over to a friend in the entertainment business, who took one look at Amelia's legs and decided that she ought to be a dancer.

Amelia's troupe came through Shanghai in 1922. She hated the weather, and despised the Chinese, but could smell the opportunities the city offered. By that time she'd learned that the quickest way to a man's bank vault was through his bedroom door. Tempted by the knowledge that many wealthy Shanghailanders desired female company and asked few questions, she located a nightclub owner who agreed that her long legs, firm white breasts and throaty voice would fill up more than a few seats in his cabaret, and then rented a tiny apartment in the International Settlement.

Amelia soon enjoyed a steady stream of generous sponsors. Two years later she startled a middle-aged patron with an affirmative response to his spontaneous marriage proposal.

In Shanghai, a tarnished past was no more than an inconvenience, and an impressive marriage could whitewash a background more sordid than Amelia's. But to her disappointment, she soon realized that her husband's position as a vice president of a tobacco export company did not produce what she considered sufficient income. After warming Reginald Simmons's bed, Amelia proceeded to chisel away at his conscience. She eventually convinced him that honesty was an admirable trait only in children, priests, and idiots. He started to embezzle, and she began to live the life she felt she deserved.

Amelia could have left Shanghai when Reggie died. She had her own hefty little nest egg, expertly skimmed from Reggie's ill-gotten gains. But something—or rather someone—made her decide to stay.

What would it be like to see him again, face to face, alone? Her heart began to pound at the thought. The very possibility of seeing Leo brought back a flood of erotic memories. She remembered the feel of his hands, the taste of his kiss. That smell that was most distinctly *him*. Most of all she remembered the distant look in his eyes, a distance she had thought, for one slim moment, she could breach.

Their affair did not last long: a mere fifteen days. He ended it diplomatically. It had been a pleasant interlude, with no expectation of an encore. No one with an ounce of pride could have objected to how Leo had handled himself, and Amelia had plenty of pride.

At first she did not connect Leo with the scandal that resulted in her husband's suicide. The people did not confront Reggie at his firm until a year after Leo broke off their liaison. She did not really miss her dearly departed. His money and her independence were more than sufficient consolation for the loss of his stodgy company. But it was inconvenient for his life to have ended the way it did.

Then, one sultry evening six months after Reggie's death, Amelia saw Martha and Leo dancing together at the popular nightclub on top of the new Cathay Hotel. Her heart leapt at the sight of him, but she wisely kept her distance, and studied the two of them.

The expression on Leo's face as he looked at his wife was what gave her the first clue. Amelia was a woman of considerable experience. She knew that his gaze was not the look of a man who searched elsewhere for entertainment.

Ever since that moment, she could not shake the notion that Leo played some role in Reggie's demise. In her clever brain she replayed every conversation she'd had with Leo during their two-week affair. It seemed to her that she never really told Leo that Reggie was stealing; however, looking back, she probably said enough for an insightful, suspicious mind to put two and two together.

It wasn't until afterwards that she'd learned her dear Reggie had jumped from embezzling to smuggling opium, using his tobacco shipments as a convenient cover. While a lucrative move financially, cutting into the opium market made Reggie an inconvenience for Liu Tue-Sheng. And Leo worked at the bank that many whispered was a cover for Liu's other, more profitable businesses.

A wry smile played upon her lips as she thought again about how coolly Leo had used her. Of course, she'd exploited many people in her life, but she never expected for anyone to give her a taste of her own with such finesse.

For a while she was tempted to plan some revenge. But Amelia never acted rashly. After critically examining her situation, she perceived that vengeance was not her true goal. What she wanted was Leo.

She'd felt something different when she was with him, something more than pleasant physical passion. In his arms she'd remembered the few things she actually liked about herself, and was even able, for a few tantalizing moments, to abandon all of her disciplined self-control. She'd felt...free.

Yes, Amelia wanted Leo. She wanted him back in her bed. And she wanted him to look at her the way he'd looked at Martha.

With her usual pragmatism, Amelia discerned that destroying Leo's marriage would be counter-productive. That would only make him hate her. And she had to hope that Leo didn't know *that* much about her past. Unlike Reggie, Leo did not seem like the type of man to take home used merchandise, no matter how alluring the packaging.

No, given her colorful track record, she could not hope to break up his marriage. She would have to wait, and capitalize on someone else's mistake. Someone else would expose Leo for mixing sex and business (for she had no doubt he had done so before and would do it again) and then she, Amelia, would swoop down and snatch Leo away from Martha's wounded little paws.

For three years she waited. She learned everything she could about Leo and his family. And now, an errant bomb, and not Leo's infidelity, eliminated Martha from the equation. No matter. Once again, Amelia's perseverance had paid off. This was her moment. She intended to seize it.

He can't love a dead woman forever, she thought, as the manservant, Duo Win, answered the door in response to her persistent ringing. The fact that Martha had been dead less than forty-eight hours did not give Amelia a moment's hesitation. She did not see herself as callous; she was merely practical. She wanted to leave Shanghai. In light of the dangers posed by the Japanese invasion, it made good sense to leave immediately. She wanted Leo to go with her. To accomplish this, she had something to offer him. Something she thought Leo would be unable to refuse: an American passport.

Duo Win looked at her in annoyance. He did not recognize the woman on the step, and he did not wait for an introduction before dismissing her.

"No come in, missy, Masta no see! No talk! Missy Martha die! No come in!"

Amelia came prepared for such a rebuff. As Duo Win closed the door, she swiftly pushed a twenty-dollar American bill into the crack between the door and its frame, just above the door knob. When the door slammed shut, it trapped the bill so that a few inches stuck out on either side.

It was a staggering amount of money, probably more than the poor servant had ever seen so close to his own nose. Amelia clutched her end tightly. After a moment she felt a tug. She tightened her grip.

"No, my dear. No open door, no money."

There was silence, then another tug. Amelia waited. The door creaked open. Duo Win's guilty face peeked out.

Amelia pressed into the room, skillfully tucking the twenty into Duo Win's hand as she slipped by him.

"Let's say I pushed my way in, why don't we? Go ahead and make a fuss." She moved quickly to the center of the foyer.

Duo Win, grateful to have an alibi, started to yell, "I say no come in! Bad lady! Mista Leo too sad! No see no one!"

After a moment of this ranting Leo appeared on the first floor landing. Maddy was right behind him.

Amelia looked up at them. She scarcely noticed Maddy, whose pinched and tear-stained face peered over the railing with a pathetic stare that would have melted anyone's heart—anyone's but Amelia's.

Leo looked wretched. His face was gray, his skin unshaven, and two deep lines had appeared on his forehead. Amelia was not deterred. She was relying on the fact that, in time, his grief would pass. He would recover, and be deeply grateful that she had saved them.

"Leo, I came as soon as I heard. I can't tell you how badly I feel for you…for both of you. I know how you loved her."

Leo looked at her with consternation, not conveying any indication that he understood what she'd said. He made no move to come downstairs. After a moment he cleared his throat. Ragged words emerged.

"Amelia, I appreciate your coming, but we are not up to receiving visitors. I'll have to ask you to leave."

Amelia knew that additional pleasantries would serve no purpose. She came directly to the point. "Leo, I need to speak to you. Immediately. About your future...and Madeleine's," she added, baiting her hook. Leo did not respond. She walked to the bottom of the stairs, looking up at him with all the sweetness she could muster.

"Amelia, this is really not the time—"

"Leo," she implored, "how much time do any of us have left here? I know you'll want to hear what I have to say."

Leo sighed, conveying the impression that he would agree to listen because he did not have the energy to argue. He gestured to Duo Win, who was still hovering furtively near the front door.

"Duo, please take Miss Maddy down to the kitchen, and see if Wei Lin can tempt her into eating something."

Duo Win scampered up to collect his small charge. Maddy hesitantly allowed herself to be led away. She cast one panicked look at her father before exiting the foyer.

Leo showed Amelia into the front parlor. He waited for her to take a seat on the sofa, then positioned himself on a chair near the fireplace, politely communicating that he intended to remain as far away from her as possible. Amelia decided not to be insulted.

Amelia realized that she was nervous. It was an unfamiliar sensation. She thought about lighting a cigarette, and decided not to. Better to plunge ahead.

"Leo," she began, "please believe that I am here only as a concerned friend. Have you thought about what you and Maddy are going to do?"

Do? What was there left to do? What did it matter now that Martha was gone? He'd thought about nothing but the explosion for the last forty-eight hours, replayed again and again in his head. He saw the buildings collapse and heard Maddy's screams. His life had stopped at that moment.

"Look," he said, after a significant pause. "This is pointless. Whatever you have to tell me—"

"Marry me and come to America."

He stared at her, shocked beyond words. She rushed into the void, explaining and cajoling.

"Leo, I know this is ridiculous, coming to you this way. You and Maddy are safe, here, for the moment, but for how long? No one knows if the Japanese will respect the International Concessions, and the Chinese army is going to abandon Shanghai any day now. The rest of the world has given up on us—no one is willing to rescue Shanghai this time, because this time the war between Japan and China will destroy the city's ability to keep making money. And where can you go? Back to Vienna? If you'd been comfortable there, you wouldn't have come to Shanghai."

She paused, allowing the obvious truth in her words to sink in. "Maybe you don't care about what happens to you, but I do. And Madeleine deserves a chance at happiness, in a place where the death of her mother will not haunt her. I know it may seem cruel, even—obscene for me to come here, today, with an offer like this, but we've no time for proper etiquette. I've booked a first class cabin on the *President Jefferson*. It leaves in five days. Once its berths are full, no more American ships will be leaving Shanghai until—until God knows when. Everyone who could get out already has."

She paused again. Leo still stared at her. She looked down at her own slim ankles, neatly crossed in front of her, and finished her speech.

"I know you don't love me, and I know our marriage will exist only on paper. We can get a divorce as soon as you like, or as soon as the law will allow, without jeopardizing your American residency. But at least you can get out. I don't want to leave you and your beautiful daughter living here, not knowing if the next bomb will fall on you, and Madeleine as well. Or to find out one day that you were killed, and Madeleine left alone in one of those ghastly orphanages...." She stopped short as real tears filled her eyes. The idea of Leo's dying really did upset her.

Leo closed his eyes. He sat back heavily in his chair, as the pain of his loss overwhelmed him. A question hissed out of his lungs, like stale air from a balloon.

"Why are you doing this?"

But he knew why, even as he asked. Women like Amelia always found a way into his life. They were like cockroaches, who crawled in

and out of the cracks of human weakness and managed to survive anything. Women like his first lover, the Countess Julia.

In his life there were only two women he'd loved and wanted to protect: Erzsebet and Martha. And he'd failed them both. He thrust his face
into his hands.

Suddenly he was aware of Amelia's presence next to him. She put her
hand lightly on his shoulder as she spoke.

"I won't lie and say that I grieved over Reggie the way you're griev-
ing over Martha. But I do know what it's like to be alone. Maybe this
isn't the right time, but I've never had the chance to tell you—the time
we—spent together—really meant something to me. More than you
ever knew. And I know that I'll never replace Martha. I'm not trying to.
But I do care about you, Leo, and I want to be able to help you and
Madeleine. At the very least I can help you escape from this hell hole.
And maybe, at some point, you and I...can help each other overcome
our...loneliness."

Leo's self-hatred responded instantly to her touch, raging inside him
like a caged animal in search of a violent release. His entire body flexed
with tension as he fought his urge to hurt the woman next to him, to
violate her. Instinctively he clutched the arms of his chair, to keep himself from striking her.

Amelia could see the outline of his erection through the linen of his
trousers. Encouraged, she did not guess it was inspired by fury and not
desire. She took off her hat and knelt on the floor, next to his chair,
ready to service him then and there.

As she started to bring her head to his lap Leo grabbed Amelia by
the hair. She looked up at him, her light brown eyes wide with lust and
anticipation, excited by what she mistook for passion.

Leo returned her stare with cold malice. For the second time in his
life he felt overcome by a thirst for revenge—but this time, there was no
one to blame for his pain but himself. He had killed Martha, by keeping her in Shanghai. Why should he bother to go on living?

For Maddy.

If he threw away this chance to elude Liu's grasp, he might not get
another. And to go to America—under different circumstances, it

would be a dream come true. Leo forced himself to relax his grip. He had no reason to be angry at this woman. On the contrary—he had used her. As far as he knew, Amelia's sins were no worse than his own.

Now Amelia was trying to help him, just as Julia had tried to help him so long ago, when she'd warned him not to go back to the villa the night Károly murdered József and Erzsebet. His anger ebbed away. When he spoke his voice was dull with resignation.

"I will take you up on your generous offer. But we can't celebrate prematurely. Are you sure I can get into the country?"

Amelia stood up and straightened her skirt, subduing the exhilaration she felt.

"We can be married in two days. Spouses of American citizens are being given immediate permission to enter the States in light of the crisis here. All we need to do is show up with your passport and our marriage license. I thought we could go to New York, at least initially." She wanted to stroke his face, but decided against it. Instead she stood before him, meekly waiting for him to tell her what to do.

Leo rubbed his hands across his unshaven face. There was nothing left for him to do but go forward. He must salvage a life for Madeleine.

"No one must know I am leaving—I have my reasons. Can we get married just before we board the ship?"

"Of course."

For a while neither of them spoke. Then Leo stood up. He looked drained. "Amelia, I do not want Madeleine to know about our marriage until the absolute last minute. As you can readily understand, she...may not take it well. Please be patient. And...thank you."

Amelia managed to keep her smile small and humble.

CHAPTER 16

THE GAMBLER

☙⟳⟲❧

Leo did not tell Madeleine that they were leaving. He placed a call to Tokyo, and contacted a wealthy Japanese client of the Commerce Bank, who had once mentioned to Leo how much he wanted to relocate to Shanghai. Life in Japan, under the new military regime, was becoming too Spartan: too restricted. Even jazz music had been outlawed. Shanghai still glittered across the East China Sea like a pulsating, decadent oasis. Now Leo offered to sell the man his own glorious Georgian manor, with all its furnishings, at a very reasonable price. Gloating over his good luck, the client agreed to wire the funds directly to a specific bank in New York, and made plans to move to Shanghai the moment the Chinese retreated from the city.

Leo knew that by selling his house he was taking a chance, for it gave Liu Tue-Sheng the opportunity to discover that he planned to leave. But Leo did not want to rely on Amelia for money, and his home was his most significant asset. He was counting on the fact that Liu would be preoccupied by the war, and that hostilities between Japan and China would necessarily limit Liu's contacts with the Japanese. Things were not going well for Liu's friend, General Chiang. Under the circumstances Leo hoped the gangster would not find out that one of his minions was planning to escape.

Leo waited until the morning of their scheduled departure to go to the bank and wire the remainder of his savings to his new bank account in New York. He executed the transaction himself, then went upstairs to his private office, to empty the small vault containing Martha's jewelry and their passports.

Once in his office, Leo locked the door, then squatted on the floor behind his desk and tossed back the Oriental rug that covered the safe. With a few deliberate manipulations of the dial the tumblers clicked. He opened the steel door and started to transfer the boxes containing Martha's jewelry to a briefcase. Here was the string of pearls he'd bought her for her thirtieth birthday. The next box contained the emerald set he had given her one Christmas. Then came the art deco bracelet, studded with onyx and tiny diamonds. Each jewel glinted with painful memories. He tried not to think about the childlike joy with which Martha had received each present, or how each piece had looked against the soft marvel of her skin. His hands began to shake.

The safe was now empty. Still overcome by his grief, it took him a moment to realize what was wrong. The passports. The passports were not there.

Leo groaned. He slammed the door of the small safe shut. There, along the outside edges of the lock, he could see shiny scratches on the metal surface, testifying to where the lock had been forced open.

"Damn!" he shouted, slamming the side of his fist down onto the hard metal. His hand vibrated with pain from the harsh contact, but his brain paid no attention. His mind was bent by grief, guilt, and desperation.

"You filthy son of a bitch!" Leo growled, standing up and shaking his bruised fist at the nonexistent Liu. "You have no power over me now, you bastard—I've lost everything! Do you hear me? Everything! You can't thwart a man with nothing left to lose, you bastard! You'll give me back those passports or you'll have to kill me! And if you kill me, you'll be doing me a favor! You understand? A favor! If you'd killed me years ago Martha would be alive now! She'd be alive! She'd be alive!"

A knock on the door brought him to his senses.

"What is it?" he barked.

"Is everything alright, sir?" a female voice inquired. A secretary. She must have heard him shouting.

"Yes. I'm fine. My wife died. Now go away," he replied hoarsely. He heard the sound of her heels clicking down the hall as she retreated. He thought again of Martha.

He could not give up. There may not be any hope for him, but the one thing he could do for Martha was to try and save their daughter: to get her away from the dangers of war, and the threat that Liu might ultimately use Maddy as leverage over her father.

By now it was almost noon. Their ship was due to sail at six. He was to meet Amelia at the Justice of the Peace at two o'clock. Two hours. Two hours to find Liu Tue-Sheng and win his life back. No—Maddy's life. His life was over. He picked up his briefcase and walked out, back down to the Bund where his car and driver were waiting.

He stopped at his own home for a moment, then proceeded to Liu's compound. The guard waved his car in, as if he had been expected. Leo was not surprised. Liu knew him well enough to know that he would come.

This time he was not escorted to Liu's study. After the anticipated body search, the houseboy took him outside, to an enormous greenhouse. At the far end of the structure Liu sat in one of two high-backed, wicker chairs, surrounded by rare orchids. *Like the snake in the garden of Eden*, thought Leo. In front of Liu a small bamboo table was set for lunch. Two bodyguards kept watch at either end of the glass-enclosed building. They appeared to be unarmed.

Leo knew he must stay calm. Rude demands would be futile. For all of his western attributes, Liu still had the soul of a Chinese. Leo could not succeed unless he allowed Liu to lose gracefully. To save face. He had to stick to his plan.

"Good...afternoon," Liu greeted Leo with his stilted speech. "Please sit...down."

Leo forced himself to sit.

"Mr. Liu," he said cordially, "I believe that you have some property of mine. Some property that I need to retrieve."

"And what would that be, Mr. Hoffman?"

"My passport. And my wife's."

"Ah, your wife. I am so sorry to hear about your wife. A beautiful woman, with a good heart."

A muscle twiched in Leo's lower jaw as he fought to control himself.

"Thank you. She, of course, will no longer need a passport, but my child is listed on hers."

Liu raised a thin black eyebrow. "You are planning to leave Shanghai?"

"I think you knew that."

"Yes. However, from my point of view, Mr. Hoffman, your departure would cost me money. If General Chiang retreats, as I am afraid he soon will, I shall have to move my operations to Hong Kong. I have already reserved a suite at the Peninsula Hotel there. I could use a man of your talent here, in Shanghai, to help me stay informed. In fact, it would be…essential to many of my business arrangements."

Leo shook his head. "You don't need me, Mr. Liu. Shanghai is dying. There's no more money to be made here. You and the General must concentrate on winning this war. I'm afraid I'm no longer able to offer you my services. I am resigning my position at the bank."

"And if I refuse to accept your resignation?"

"Then I will kill you."

The faintest hint of surprise flickered across Liu's features.

"But of course, you will also die," he replied calmly.

Leo leaned forward. "You cannot kill a man who is already dead, Liu Tue-Sheng. I died when my wife died."

"But you are unarmed," Liu pointed out. He remained unruffled. He could have been discussing strategy during a friendly game of chess.

Leo held out his hands, never taking his eyes off Liu's face. "There are many ways to kill a man, Mr. Liu. Neither of your bodyguards speaks English, and I speak Chinese. If you call to them you will be dead before they can reach you."

"And your daughter?"

Leo twisted his lips into a barren smile. His hands dropped to his knees. "Ah, for my daughter I am willing to gamble." He paused. He must choose his words carefully.

"You said once that you were a gambling man, Mr. Liu. This time, I will make you a proposition. We will play a game of cards."

"And what do I stand to gain?"

Leo reached into his breast pocket. As he made this motion the two body guards approached, poised for action. With a subtle waive of his hand Liu sent them back to their stations.

From his pocket Leo removed the swan he had given Martha as a wedding gift. He placed it on the table.

Liu looked at it impassively. "The swan is pretty, but not much of an incentive, Mr. Hoffman."

Leo raised his fist over the fragile porcelain trinket. "Appearances can be deceiving," he said softy. With one swift motion, he brought his fist down on the swan's back, crushing it. From the shards of porcelain he removed the last four of the Cartier diamonds. One by one he laid them on the table in front of the gangster.

"I propose that we cut a deck of cards, and each draw one. The higher card wins. If I win, you will give me the passports, I will leave Shanghai, and you will keep these diamonds. If you win, I will stay in Shanghai, and continue to work for you. But you will, with your usual methods, use the diamonds to arrange for my new American wife to get immediate custody of my daughter, so that she can leave Shanghai on the *President Jefferson*, this evening."

"And if I refuse to play?"

"Then I will kill you. By the time the order to kill me has sprung from your throat, you will be dead."

"And your daughter will be dead soon afterward."

Leo flinched. The only way he could protect Maddy was to get her out of Shanghai— away from the bombs, away from the Japanese, away from the clutches of this monster. And the only asset he could use to buy her freedom was himself.

"Another reason for both of us to take this wager, Liu. If you play, you keep something of value: your life. And no matter who pulls the higher card, you win, for you will retain either the diamonds, or my services. And either way I win, for my daughter will get out of Shanghai. But if we do not play, we both die."

There was a brief moment of silence. In the distance a bird sang out three shrill notes, and was quiet.

"And I suppose, Mr. Hoffman, you brought a deck of cards with you?"

From his pocket Leo removed a new deck of cards. The seal was unbroken.

A tiny smile touched Liu's face. "Mr. Hoffman, you never disappoint me. But tell me, what makes you think that I will let you leave this room alive, after threatening me, no matter what the outcome of our little game of chance?"

Leo looked Liu in the eye. "Because you are a man of your word. As am I."

Liu acknowledged the statement with a slight incline of his chin. "You may shuffle the cards, Mr. Hoffman."

⊗✝⊗

Forty-five minutes later Leo was in the attic of his house, retrieving two large suitcases. He brought one with him into Maddy's room, where he found her staring out the window, while Wei Lin read a story. He could not tell if Maddy was listening.

Leo excused Wei Lin, then sat down on Maddy's bed. He held out his arms and she came to him, sitting on his knees and wrapping her fragile arms around his neck. She looked so much like Martha, lying there sweetly against his chest, that for a moment Leo thought he would break down again. He waited until he could speak.

"Madeleine, we're leaving Shanghai."

Maddy looked up at him, struggling to make sense of his words. She had difficulty understanding anything said to her since the explosion. Words floated into her ears and rested there, waiting for her to go back and listen, later. Later she would hear their echoes, and force herself to understand.

Having grown up in Shanghai, where men picked dead beggars up off the street every morning and women left unwanted infants out to die every night, Maddy understood death. She understood that death meant gone forever, that dead things did not wake up, and did not come back. But death was something she associated with stray animals, and poverty, and Chinese people. Maddy did not understand why it had happened to her mother. All Madeleine knew was that her mother's presence in the store had been her fault.

She tried again to listen to what her father was saying.

"I want you to help me pack, *ma princesse*. You can fill up one big suitcase with your favorites—clothes and toys. Whatever you like."

Maddy made no response. Leo hugged her, then slid her off his lap. When Maddy saw the suitcase, she understood.

"Are we coming back?"

He shook his head, "No, my dear. We're going to America to live."

Maddy made no comment. She looked around her room. "Can I bring whatever I want?"

"Yes Maddy. Anything you want to bring, as long as it fits in this suitcase."

Maddy walked out of room. Leo followed her down the hall to the master bedroom. He watched as she strode purposefully to Martha's dressing table and carefully picked up the wedding picture. A puzzled look crossed her face as she glanced over the dresser, searching for something she did not see. She turned to face Leo, bewilderment crinkling her small features.

"The swan, Papa. Where has the swan gone?"

Again Leo's voice caught in his throat. "It flew away, *cherie*. It flew away when Mama died."

Leo could see Maddy trying to comprehend his words. In a moment she went over to Martha's lingerie dresser and rummaged through the top drawer, eventually withdrawing a gray velvet box. With the picture and the box in hand, she walked back over to Leo.

"This is what I want to bring, Papa. It doesn't matter about the rest."

Hot tears burned the back of Leo's eyes as he gazed at his daughter, looking up at him so matter-of-factly. He knew that at that moment he should feel love, but all he felt was grief.

After convincing Maddy to put some clothes and a couple of toys in her suitcase, he called all the servants into the foyer. He told them he was leaving, gave each one a small bundle of cash, and assured them that the new owner had agreed to keep them on. He did not know if they would stay to work for a Japanese, but he felt he had done his duty. He then instructed Duo Win to pack his own suitcase, and left to meet Amelia.

The ceremony at the Justice of the Peace was brief and sterile. They did not exchange rings, and did not kiss. Amelia knew better than to push her luck.

At six o'clock, Leo and Maddy met Amelia on the Bund, at the edge of the wharf where the *President Jefferson* was anchored. A brass band played cheerful American tunes. People surged around the dock, shrieking out last minute instructions and receiving farewell hugs, deliberately ignoring the nearby wreckage of the Cathay and Palace Hotels. A long low whistle from the ship's throat signaled the final call to board.

Madeleine held tightly to her father's hand. As the threesome boarded the ship, she did not ask Leo who Amelia was, or why she was there.

The bursar approached them as they stepped on deck. "Passports, please. Tickets. Thank you."

Amelia handed over the ticket for a first-class cabin, and her passport. Leo handed the officer a passport and an official-looking document. The man inspected each document in turn, then handed back everything but the tickets.

"I'm sorry sir, but you will have to say goodbye to your wife and daughter here; we can't let anyone below deck today."

Amelia corrected him. "No, he's coming with me."

"No, Amelia, I'm afraid that I'm not."

The look on Amelia's face instantly convinced the bursar that he wanted no part of this conversation. "I'm sorry ma'am," he said, edging towards the next two passengers. "You'll have to step aside and sort this out. I can give you five minutes."

Leo took a few steps away from the crowd, pulling his hand away from Madeleine's as he did so. After a moment's hesitation Amelia followed. Her eyes narrowed in anger as she faced her new husband. "What the hell do you think you're doing?" she spat out. "I didn't agree to bring her without you. What on earth are you up to?"

"I can't come with you. Not yet. Because we're married, I'm able to give you custody of Madeleine. Please take her to New York, and take care of her. I'll join you as soon as I can."

"As soon as you can? Leo, this is ridiculous—"

Her protests were cut off by Leo's lips against her own. His arms surrounded her. His kiss was urgent, passionate. It left her breathless.

"I will join you as soon as I can," he said again.

Amelia's head spun. She could capitalize on this turn of events, she thought as she caught her breath. She looked down at her new ward, aware of the little girl's anxious eyes upon her.

Leo knelt down and spoke to his daughter.

"Madeleine, this is Amelia. She is going with you to America."

Maddy smiled with dutiful politeness, her stance edged with wariness. Amelia smiled back. She wondered what the child thought about that kiss.

Leo grasped Maddy gently by the shoulders. "Maddy, Amelia is going to take you to New York." He waited for her to say something. A light of comprehension dawned on Maddy's face.

"Is she going to be my new nanny?" she asked innocently. Amelia quickly stifled an incredulous snort.

Leo glared up at Amelia, then quickly turned his attention back to his daughter.

"Not exactly, Maddy. You see, for us to be able to go to America, I need to be married to an American citizen. Amelia is American, and she agreed to marry me, so that we could leave Shanghai, and be safe. There will not be any bombs in America. But I can't leave quite yet. I'll come for you soon. In the meantime, you must be a good girl, and mind Amelia. I promise I will come for you, just as soon as I can."

Again, it seemed to take awhile for Maddy to absorb this. Then her eyes grew wide. She looked at Leo in horror.

"You mean, she is your *wife?*" she shrieked, her little voice rising to a pitch that easily pierced the roar of the crowded deck. "Your *new wife?*"

"Maddy, Maddy, calm down, please. It's alright. She's really just a friend." Leo tried to hold Maddy still, but she would not be comforted. She hit her father, flailing away at him like a crazy thing.

"I hate you! I hate you! How could you! How dare you!" She screamed over and over again, writhing and pummeling Leo with all her might. In desperation Leo twisted her around and pinned her arms behind her back. She ended up facing Amelia, and the sight of her new stepmother caused her to fall instantly and eerily silent. But the enmity reflected in Maddy's green eyes was unmistakable.

"I apologize, Amelia. I should have expected this." Leo said gravely, looking at Amelia over Maddy's shoulder.

Amelia did her best to arrange her features into what she hoped was an expression of maternal concern.

"That's alright, Leo. Of course it's upsetting. Madeleine and I will soon be friends, you'll see." *And if not, I'm sure we can find a lovely Catholic boarding school near Manhattan. Let the nuns beat some manners into the little bitch.*

CHAPTER 17

THE BOARDER

୧ᏄᏄᠪᡑ୭

NEW YORK, 1939

"Again, Madeleine. And please, this time, *try* to concentrate on the rhythm," Sister Edwina admonished her pupil, not bothering to temper her exasperation. She punctuated her sentence with a frustrated sigh. The small wooden piano bench upon which both she and Madeleine sat creaked nervously as the heavyset woman shifted her weight.

Madeleine took a deep breath and began to play again, striking each note on the shabby old upright piano with stiff, awkward movements. Unforgiving echoes bounced off the barren plaster walls. An hour locked in a dark closet in the Mother Superior's office had finally convinced her to obey the nun's request that she take piano lessons. Several sharp raps with a ruler persuaded Maddy to hit the right notes, as she learned how to read music. But nothing could make her play well.

Six iron bars secured the room's one window. The scant sunlight that slipped through this barricade cast long, striped shadows across the scarred wooden floor. To the side were stacked several milk crates full of rhythm instruments: bells, blocks of wood, maracas, and tired tambourines. An amateurish oil portrait of the Virgin Mary provided the only decoration on the withered gray walls. The Holy Mother's eyes were upturned, as if she, too, were begging for some heavenly miracle to assist the unwilling student who now sat in the room.

Sister Edwina closed her eyes and winced as Madeleine once again assaulted Bach. She'd never seen a pupil put forth so much effort, only to attain such mediocre results. The girl had been taking lessons for two years. Edwina thought that Mr. Hoffman must be delusional, to insist that his child had any sort of musical talent. But his letters to Sister Gabriella, the convent school's headmistress, always contained generous bank drafts "to cover the cost of Madeleine's musical instruction." Unfortunately for Sister Edwina, Sister Gabriella knew a gold mine when she saw one. Leo's wish that his child learn how to play the piano would be granted, whether Madeleine liked it or not.

Sister Gabriella administered Madeleine's punishments with a clear conscience. She doubted the child would communicate with her father about the type of persuasion used; Sister Gabriella had encountered students like Madeleine before. There was a great deal of anger, and far too much pride, packed into her stubborn little body. The girl would not complain. Nor did it occur to the headmistress that Mr. Hoffman might object to her methods, even if he were informed. In her experience, absentee parents seldom interfered. She sincerely felt that it was her duty to teach Madeleine obedience, and humility. If that was all she learned from her music lessons, then the money Mr. Hoffman invested was, in Sister Gabriella's view, money well spent, despite the child's lack of musical success. Madeleine's lack of ability was Sister Edwina's cross to bear.

"Enough!" snapped the music teacher as Madeleine finished her less-than-soulful rendition. Sister Edwina hefted her considerable bulk off the bench. The doughy flesh of her double chin quivered with discontent as she spoke.

"You may be excused, Madeleine. But you must go to the library tomorrow and ask Sister Constance to allow you to listen to a recording of that piece. Try to capture some of the *essence* of the music. I have told you a hundred times, Madeleine. There is more to playing the piano than just hitting the right notes."

Maddy sprang from the bench, eager to escape her ordeal.

"Yes, Sister Edwina. Thank you, sister Edwina," she said politely, without a trace of the resentment she felt. In an instant, she collected her books and her sweater, and sped out the door.

The majority of the one hundred girls enrolled at St. Mary's Elementary School were day students, dismissed at three o'clock into the waiting arms of nannies, drivers, and mothers. The school could accept only half a dozen live-in students, for it had not been designed as a boarding school. The six small bunks and six chest-of drawers that lined the walls of the attic room where the boarders stayed were put there as a temporary concession to a few particularly wealthy parents whose travel schedules made it hard to deal with the special challenges posed by children deemed "difficult." When it became clear to Sister Gabriella that the school could charge a significant premium for the extra attention given to such students, the arrangements became available on a permanent basis.

For the past two years, Madeleine had been one of the six. It was a convenient arrangement for Amelia, who was not sure that Leo would approve of sending his daughter away to a boarding school, but did not relish the thought of having a child around the house every evening. This way, Madeleine was out from underfoot, but only a moment away, should Leo make a sudden appearance. As one month drifted into another, and the first year into a second, Amelia could almost forget that she had a stepdaughter conveniently tucked away in Manhattan's most exclusive convent school. Oh, Leo knew that Madeleine was at a Catholic school; Amelia had obtained his consent to that much. Amelia felt safe in her decision. Why would he object to a boarding school? After all, he'd abandoned his daughter. Madeleine was a well-tended little piece of bait, sitting in a convent in New York, luring her father to come for her. To come for her and back to Amelia.

Her one assurance that her plan was still working were the letters that Leo sent every month, containing a simple note and a bank draft. Every letter made the same promise. He would come within six months. As long as Leo covered Madeleine's expenses and the nuns took care of her, Amelia tolerated the wait.

She enjoyed her life in New York. She picked her escorts from a pool of rich, bored young men, whose trust funds and Ivy League educations enabled them to ignore the unpleasant consequences of the current economic depression. These young dilettantes were easy prey for a woman like Amelia. She could wait for Leo, she decided, as long as she stayed adequately amused.

Still, she did not take any chances that her plan might go awry. Amelia screened every piece of mail that traveled from Shanghai to New York and back, including all the letters sent to and from the sour old headmistress at St. Mary's. Madeleine had not once written to her father. Amelia did not encourage her to do so.

The other boarding students were never there very long. Most of the girls who boarded did so only for a short time: a month, a weekend, or a two-week holiday. During the first summer, after Madeleine had been there about a year, three other girls stayed with the Sisters. Madeleine became friendly with one of them: a plain, shy little creature named Jennifer, who cried out at night with nightmares that seemed as terrifying as Madeleine's own. But when the fall term came, Jennifer's parents divorced, and she was sent to Vermont to live with her father's family. Madeleine did not write to her. By now she accepted the fact that people simply disappeared.

Madeleine was pleasant to the rest of the day students, yet did not have one real friend among them. There were so many things that set her apart. She knew nothing about American life; she even spoke English with a British accent. She knew songs and games in French, not English, and could not recite the Lord's Prayer properly for weeks, having learned it in French, from the French sisters who ran the day school she attended in Shanghai. She accepted what was given to her, and never asked for anything, not so much as a glass of milk. She could not forgive herself for making the request that had killed her mother.

The defiance she felt played itself out in subtle ways. She said the rosary backwards, or tucked unwanted bits of Friday's fish into the pockets of her school uniform, until she could excuse herself to the bathroom and flush them down the toilet. For the most part her rebellions went unnoticed. But the piano lessons were another matter.

She could not find a voice for the terror that rose in her when sister Gabriella first told her to sit down and play. There was no way for Madeleine to explain to the unsympathetic headmistress that she had killed her mother and lost her father by playing the piano. When the Sisters convinced the distraught child that she must play or suffer unrelenting punishments, she capitulated. But she deliberately played badly, using her skill to turn the music into noise. The look of suffering on Sister Edwina's face was Madeleine's only comfort.

She took her lesson at four o'clock on Thursday afternoons, and it was supposed to last for one hour. Luckily for Madeleine, half an hour was generally all that Sister Edwina could bear. The fat woman's laziness enabled Madeleine to enjoy a small taste of freedom. Rather than escort her to the library, where the other borders remained confined until time for evening prayers, Sister Edwina instructed her student to report to study hall. Knowing that she was not expected until past five, Madeleine dawdled in the hallway for the better part of an hour.

To her amazement, no one asked her any questions when she slipped into the dreary room where the other boarders sat reading and working. She realized that as long as she showed up before vespers at six o'clock, the nun in charge of study hall did not know that Madeleine was not at her piano lesson, and no one else knew she was not in the library. For almost one hour, once a week, she was free.

At first she spent her stolen time in the small powder room underneath the stairs, hiding and reading a *Bobbsey Twins* novel left behind by a former boarder. When she finished the book, she became bolder. She would creep from room to room in the convent, not touching or disturbing anything, just exploring and relishing her solitude.

She could move more quietly than a mouse. At the slightest sound she would freeze, and duck behind a curtain, or under a piece of furniture. But the sisters were governed by a strict routine. Between four and six every afternoon they stayed in their individual rooms, praying or reading. Madeleine had the convent to herself, as long as she kept away from the library, and the Sisters' sleeping quarters.

Today she was already plotting a new path as she skipped out of her lesson and down the hall. Today she would take her most ambitious step—to the kitchen! Maybe she would even sneak a cookie from the big brown jar where the ginger snaps were kept, doled out, two to a person, after each Sunday dinner by the dour cook, Sister Margaret. Wouldn't the stingy old thing be mad if she ran one cookie short this week!

It took Madeleine just under ten minutes to reach her goal. She took a full thirty seconds to open the door, moving the iron handle in minuscule increments, making sure it didn't squeak. Once inside, she walked around the room with practiced, silent steps, savoring the delight of being where she shouldn't.

She saw the cookie jar on a high shelf, and decided it was well out of reach. After having explored the kitchen, she tiptoed into the small room beside it. It was no more than a closet, lined with shelves where the sisters kept their clean table linens. Stacked on the floor were white cloth bags, half as big as Madeleine. She cautiously peeked inside one. Laundry. Madeleine knew that the convent's laundry was sent out somewhere; her own blue plaid uniforms, white blouses, panties and socks disappeared from the bin in the attic at the end of each week, then reappeared in a stack on her bed, neatly folded and ready to be tucked back into her drawer. It never occurred to her that the Sisters did the laundry. Having grown up in the privileged, segregated society of Shanghai, she assumed there were Chinese people in New York to take care of onerous chores like laundry.

At one end of the linen room was a heavy wooden door, gray with age. A sliding bolt across the center kept it firmly shut. Madeleine stared at it in fascination. What was behind that door?

Madeleine looked at the clock on the wall. She had a good twenty minutes before she had to be in the dining hall. Heart pounding, she reached up and tugged at the bolt. Once released, it slid easily to the side. She turned the handle. The door swung open.

She found herself looking out into the service alley that ran between the convent and the brownstone next door. The door led outside. It was a door to the world.

Madeleine stood completely still, overwhelmed by her discovery. She could feel the cool September air brushing her face, tempting her to step out. Dare she? Dare she?

She moved through the doorway. As soon as she was outside, the scents and sounds of New York lured her toward the street. She could hear the murmur of a thousand voices mingling with the sounds of mechanical movement. She could smell car exhaust, fish, and bread baking. From the moment she'd arrived in the city Madeleine had not been allowed to go anywhere alone, nor been able to choose a destination. She marched in line with the other students on their outings to the park, to museums, and to the library. She was a yo-yo, tossed out into the city by the sisters and then yanked quickly back in, always attached to her string. Now she had a chance to break free, at least for a moment.

Madeleine took a few timid steps towards the street, then remembered to turn back and shut the door to the laundry room, checking first that she would still be able to open it from the outside. This accomplished, she took a deep breath, and ran.

She stopped when she reached the edge of the alley. The bustle of activity on the street reminded her of Shanghai, except that there were no Chinese. She smiled at a well-dressed woman walking a dog. The woman smiled back. She heard the hoarse shouts of the taxi drivers, and the bleat of their aggravated horns. She knew that six blocks away, straight down Eighty-Sixth Street, was Central Park. And she would go there. But not today. She did not want to risk discovery, and she did not have much time.

Ten minutes later she was in the library. The thoughts in her head had nothing to do with the history book in front of her. The boldness of her plan made her shiver with anticipation. But she could wait. One of the things Madeleine had learned during the past two years was patience.

It was three weeks before she was able to antagonize Sister Edwina into cutting her piano lesson to a mere twenty minutes. She made it to the kitchen in less than five. By four-thirty she was on the street, skipping happily toward Central Park, with forty-five precious minutes to spend any way she wished.

The sight of a large crowd gathered on the lawn just inside the park's entrance intrigued her. Several people were waving signs, and one person seemed to be getting attention by shouting some sort of slogan, which was greeted with roars of approval.

Madeleine edged closer, curious but cautious. She read two of the placards. One read, NO AMERICAN BLOOD in big red letters. Another said, KEEP OUR BOYS HOME.

On the outskirts of the crowd she saw a girl with thick, flaming red hair, who looked to be about her own age. The girl also wore a parochial school uniform, though hers consisted of a green plaid skirt, white blouse, and green sweater. She sat on a large rock, scribbling furiously on a page of a spiral notebook. Every few seconds she paused, watched the crowd, then started writing again. When she stopped to listen she would stick the end of her pencil between her teeth. Having had her wrist slapped with a ruler by the nuns for absentmindedly engaging in the identical habit, Madeleine was immediately envious.

The girl was taller than Madeleine, and had the typical complexion of a red-head: ivory skin brushed with dozens of tiny freckles. When writing, her small, straight nose would wrinkle in concentration, like a bunny's. Madeleine's curiosity got the best of her.

"Hello," she said, when she got within talking distance.

The girl's eyes opened wide. She spun her head around to look at Madeleine, her shoulders pulling up towards her neck in a defensive reaction. When she realized that Madeleine was not someone she knew, she blew out a quick gust of air, signaling her relief.

"Hi. Isn't this just the keenest thing you ever saw?"

Madeleine glanced over again at the crowd, which now numbered close to fifty people. A woman was speaking, talking about the death of her sons in Europe. She was standing on a wooden crate, so that she could be seen and heard. Around her chest she wore a silk banner, emblazoned with the message, "America First!"

"What's this all about?" Madeleine inquired politely, turning back to the girl, who was writing again.

"Just a sec," she answered, still writing. When she finished the sentence, she looked up.

"It's the war. A war protest. You know, people who don't think we should get involved in another European war. People who don't think Hitler is our problem."

"A war?" repeated Madeleine. "Where?" Her words came out as, "*A waw? Whehah?*"

"Hey," the girl responded, eyes alight with interest. "Where are you from, anyway? You talk like Vivien Leigh."

"Do I?" responded Madeleine, pleased with the comparison. She'd never seen a movie featuring Vivien Leigh, but she'd seen her picture in a movie magazine left behind by one of the day students. Madeleine studied it for hours before dropping it out the attic window, to keep the Sisters from discovering that some of their students exposed themselves to such decadence. She'd loved the glamorous photograph of Miss Leigh, who'd been chosen to play Scarlett O'Hara in the movie version of *Gone with the Wind,* a book Madeleine hadn't yet read, but intended to, once she could find a way to get her hands on a copy.

"Oh, sure. Are you English? Wow! Then you're fighting Hitler! I should interview you! What's your name?"

"Wait!" exclaimed Madeleine, both embarrassed and pleased at the attention she was receiving from this outgoing American. "I'm not English. I'm from Shanghai. And I don't know anything about a war in Europe, although there was a war going on when I left Shanghai...."

Her words trailed off into silence as she thought about what the war in Shanghai had cost her. The events she herself had caused. She had long since concluded that her father sent her to New York with Amelia because he blamed her for Martha's death. And why shouldn't he? It *was* her fault. If she had not asked for that doll, her mother would not be dead.

Madeleine regretted having started this conversation. Her engaging companion gave her no chance to retreat.

"Shanghai? You mean, Shanghai, *China* Shanghai? You must be kidding. You don't look Chinese."

At this, Madeleine had to laugh. "Of course not. There are loads of people in Shanghai who aren't Chinese." In Shanghai it didn't seem to matter where you were from. Either you were Chinese, or you weren't. She assumed it must be the same here in America; one was American, or one wasn't. She knew she wasn't, or rather, did not want to be, if for no other reason than Amelia was an American. Then what was she? French was the language most often spoken at her home in Shanghai, and she'd attended a French school, where French nuns taught her French history and began the day with *The Marseillais.* Maddy quickly decided that French would do as a nationality of choice.

"I'm French."

The girl seemed doubly impressed. "No kidding? French? Do you speak French?

"*Bien sur, je parle le francais.*"

"Whoa! What did you just say?"

"I said, 'of course I speak French.'"

"Wow! I really should interview you! I'm from Ireland. Well, no. My parents were. We were all born here—"

A cheer from the crowd interrupted the delivery of her autobiography. The redhead pointed. "There must be twice as many people here now. Look! The cops are here to break it up! We better scram! I'm probably related to one of them, and if Ma hears I came to the park alone again, I'm gonna be blistered for sure!"

The girl grabbed Madeleine's hand, and together they ran across the lawn and through the park gate, onto the crowded sidewalk of Central Park West. Behind them police whistles blared, as men in blue demanded to see a permit for such a gathering, and, shown none, quickly dispersed the crowd.

"Well! That was close. I don't wanna get in another jam."

By this point the young American's slang had Madeleine completely lost. "Jam? What do you mean? And why were we running because you don't want a blister?" she asked, wary and puzzled, but still too curious to flee.

"Hey, you really are a foreigner, aren't you? Look. A jam is a scrape, you know, to get in trouble. Blistered is what my Ma will do to my rear end if she catches me in the park alone again. Haven't you ever caught a good whipping for something?"

"Oh. Yes. I see. Yes, I have, in fact. Sister Gabriella is very good at 'blistering,' as you say."

"*As you say*," repeated the girl with a smile, mimicking Madeleine. The look on Madeleine's face made clear to her new acquaintance that she did not appreciate being teased about her accent.

"Hey, listen. I didn't mean nothing. I just like the way you talk. It's really classy. My name is Katherine. Mary Katherine Anne O'Connor, actually, but I go by Katherine. Just don't call me Kate. Or Mary. And especially not Mary Kate. I *hate* that."

Madeleine tried to take in this avalanche of information while she smiled and politely held out her hand. "How do you do, Katherine. My name is Madeleine. Madeleine Hoffman. But you—" she stammered, trying to summon enough courage to finish her own introduction — "You may call me Maddy. Please."

Katherine shook her hand. "Madeleine, huh? Wearing a uniform, too. So you're Catholic. Well, we got that much in common. Where do you go to school? Listen, let's walk this way while we talk. I found a dime in the curb last week, and I've been saving it for a special occasion. I'll treat you to a soda at The Parkside Grill, over on Columbus. I mean, it's not every day I make a new friend from China, who happens to be French."

Madeleine paused. She'd used up half of her forty-five minutes. She imagined the "blistering" she'd receive if she were late to study hall. If she were back by six, in time for chapel, she could say that she'd been sick in the bathroom. She would probably get a beating, but no one would suspect she'd escaped. Swallowing hard, she decided to take the chance. She wanted Katherine to like her.

"That would be lovely. Thank you."

Katherine smiled, and tucked her pencil behind her ear. This reminded Madeline of the question she was about to ask before their sudden exit from the park.

"What were you writing? And what did you mean by an interview?"

"Well!" said Katherine, heading towards the soda shop, "I'm a reporter. At least, I will be, someday. A journalist. A foreign correspondent. I'll travel all over the world, and write about wars, and people like Amelia Earhart. Now I only write stories for school. Sister Anne keeps telling me to make 'em up, but I think the real world is much more interesting. Like the newsreels at the movies. That's where I found out about Hitler."

"Hitler?" asked Madeleine, more lost than ever. The word had a vague ring to it, like the name of someone she'd met a long time ago, but could not place.

"You know, the guy in Germany who started the war in Europe. The one that crowd was protesting about. See, a bunch of people in America don't want us to go over and fight again. So they're trying to get the message out to President Roosevelt and the people running the country, that just because England and France and Germany are at it again, doesn't mean American boys have to go get killed."

"Oh, that's what you meant by the war in Europe."

"Didn't you even know there's a war on? I mean, it's been a month already," Katherine chided her, genuinely astounded.

Madeleine sheepishly shook her head. "No. The Sisters don't let us listen to the radio. Except for the services on Sunday."

"Wait—you mean, you're at school on the weekends? You mean, you live there?"

Madeleine only nodded, afraid that this fact, and her ignorance of world events, would mean she was no longer acceptable as a friend to a future foreign correspondent.

"Gosh. What did you do to get put in boarding school? Or are you just rich? I've heard of some kids who have to go to boarding school because they're rich. But mostly just the troublemakers have to go, from what *I've* heard. Are you a trouble maker?" Katherine's eyes shone with admiration.

"I suppose...so," replied Madeleine slowly, thinking again of the trouble she'd caused. She was responsible for her mother's death. That must be the worst kind of trouble someone could get in to.

But she decided not to talk about that, nor confess that she had, in the past, been rich. Living well was something she took for granted in Shanghai. All the whites she knew there were rich, except for the Russians and the French nuns. Even some Asians were rich, in Shanghai. How odd, that Katherine seemed to think being rich was awkward, but that being a troublemaker was admirable. Despite her bewilderment Madeleine was even more determined to make friends with this strange new girl.

Katherine continued talking. "Well, I go to St. Agnes, up on Ninety-First. It's just a day school. Sometimes I go on reporting investigations, and tell Ma I had to serve detention, which she never doubts, on account of I really do have to, pretty often. So today I was lucky enough to get wind of this America First rally, and there I was, ready to scoop the story. And meeting you was gravy! What a great day."

By this time they'd reached the soda shop. Katherine strolled in, completely at home, and hoisted herself up on one of the round stools at the counter, gesturing for Madeleine to join her.

"Hiya, Tim. A float for me and for my new friend here, Maddy. She's from China. What kinda float do ya want, Maddy?"

Madeleine pursed her lips. It had been so long since she'd tasted ice cream, she could hardly remember what flavors she liked.

"Same as yours."

"But you don't even know what that is!"

"Don't worry, miss. I'll give you the house special," interjected the soda jerk. His apron showed the colorful remains of a day's work scooping ice cream.

"Good idea," agreed Katherine. "Tim here will take care of you. The best floats in Manhattan, right Tim?"

"You betcha!" The grin Tim flashed revealed a tooth outlined in silver. Madeleine was fascinated, but lowered her eyes when she caught herself staring.

"So you're with Miss Pulitzer here, eh? From China? That's a ways to come for a soda, even the house special," Tim chattered cheerfully, dipping into the ice cream bin with professional ease.

Madeleine did not know what to say. She looked at Katherine for help. Misunderstanding her confusion, Katherine grinned.

"Oh, that's just what Tim calls me. Miss Pulitzer, on account of I'm gonna win the Pulitzer Prize some day. He probably doesn't even believe you're from China; he's always accusing me of making things up. But, I tell him, a reporter deals in facts, facts, facts, facts. Right, Tim?"

"Ab-sa-lootly," cracked Tim, placing two tall Coca-Cola ice cream floats in front of the girls with a flourish. "Betcha never had a float so good in China, eh Maddy?"

Maddy smiled. She took a small sip of the drink. The carbonated liquid tickled her throat, and the sweetness of the melted ice cream filled her mouth.

"*Sheh-sheh*," she said. "That's Chinese for thank you."

Katherine grinned with satisfaction and looked back at Tim.

"See? What did I tell you?"

"You're one of a kind, kid," he smiled back at her, before turning to his next customer.

"So, where do you go to school?" Katherine quizzed Maddy, taking a big swig of her own float.

"St. Mary's."

Katherine winced. "Oh. That's the worst. So you're one of Gabby's girls."

"What?" Maddy was dumbfounded and delighted at the disrespect that Katherine's nickname for the Mother Superior conveyed.

"Sister Gabriella. One of her boarders. You know, word gets around. How did you get out today?"

"I snuck out."

"No kidding! You really are amazing. What grade are you in?"

"Sixth."

"Me too. Are you ten?"

"No, nine."

"Oh. Well, I'm ten. But I won't hold your age against you. So where are your parents? How come you're one of Gabby's girls?"

Maddy paused. She thought of all the lies she'd told the girls at St. Mary's. No. Something about Katherine made her want to tell the truth.

"My mother died two years ago. She got killed in the war. A bomb. My father sent me to New York to live with my step—his new wife. She put me in St. Mary's."

Katherine's eyes grew wide. "Holy Cow. That's lousy. Can't you get your dad to come get you?"

"He doesn't want me."

Katherine looked astounded. She came from a big Irish family. Her own father died when she was only two years old, but surrounded by older siblings, cousins, aunts and uncles, she never much noticed the loss. Her mother was the matriarch of the family, keeper of a boarding house that sheltered as many family and near-family members as it could hold, as they made their way in from the old country and up the economic ladder in the new. The idea that someone in your own family could exile you to a strange country with a stranger was the most appalling thing she had ever heard. Her heart went out to her new friend.

"Well, my dad died. So we are both half-orphans. Anyway, how did you manage to get out from under old Gabby's nose today?"

The girls sipped and spoke, as Madeleine told the story of her escape from the convent, punctuated by frequent questions from Katherine.

"So how're you gonna get back in?" asked Katherine, finishing her soda and her question with a loud slurp.

Madeleine, who had never in her life been able to make such a noise without being reprimanded, decided to slurp the last of her drink before answering.

"Well, I left the door unlocked, so I could sneak back in. I think I'll just tell them that I was in the bathroom. But I'd better be getting back, or there will be no telling what will happen."

"Are you late?"

"I guess so."

"Me too. We better go." Bending over, she fished a dime out of her sock and laid it on the counter.

"That should cover it, Tim. Until next time," she called out, like a regular bar fly.

"Anytime, Miss P!" Tim hollered back over the noise of the milk-shake blender.

"Hey," Katherine added, "can you spare a couple of extra napkins?"

"Anything for you, doll!"

"Thanks!" Grabbing a small stack of paper, she hopped off the stool, and the two girls headed back out into the street.

"C'mon," said Katherine as they headed towards the park. "I'll walk ya back."

As Katherine walked, she kept an eye on the curb, hoping, Madeleine assumed, to find another wayward coin. When they were about a block away from the convent, Katherine paused.

"Phew! That oughta do."

To Madeleine's astonishment, Katherine squatted down, and carefully, with the assistance of Tim's napkins, picked up a largish piece of dog excrement.

"What are you starin' at?" she asked Madeleine with a trace of pique. "I'm doing this to help you out, you know."

Madeleine could not take her eyes off Katherine's meticulously wrapped bundle. "You must be joking."

"Geez, you act like you never saw a turd before. Look, this turd is your friend. When you go back in the convent, sneak into the bathroom, smear a little of this on the inside of the toilet, where the water doesn't really reach, then stick the whole little bundle behind the commode so you can't see it, but you can sure smell it. Phew! This is fresh, so it'll stink up the place great in a minute or two. Then sit on the pot and howl. Be sure to flush it before anyone comes in. No one will doubt you been in there, sick as a dog—ha ha—for an hour."

"I can't carry that," Madeleine protested. "I'll be sick."

"So much the better. If you puke, too, you'll definitely be in the clear. Maddy, if they catch you now, you'll never get out again, and I'll never see you again. The bathroom plan you were hatching was a good one, but take it from me, what you need is some evidence to back you up. This works! It even fooled Ma one time. It's not my idea, you know. It's been handed down, kid to kid, in my family, like a special family recipe. Remember," she offered Madeleine the small bundle, "facts, facts, facts. Nobody can argue with the facts."

Madeleine gingerly accepted the gift. "Well, if I do make it out next week, how will I find you?"

"I'm usually home after school, at least for a while. I'll make sure to be home next Thursday." She gave Maddy the address. "It's not far—just hop on over!"

"Okay!"

"Great! Good luck."

"Thanks! And thank you again for the soda!"

"Ah, don't mention it. Well, good luck!"

Madeleine watched for a moment as her new friend scampered off down the street. She looked at the napkin in her hand. Then she crept back in the convent, and followed Katherine's instructions to the letter. The plan worked perfectly, just as an old family recipe should.

CHAPTER 18

THE RECRUIT

ome

SHANGHAI, 1940

"The Chinese are an inherently dishonorable race, Mr. Hoffman," said the General, just before lifting another piece of delicately fried tempura from its lacquer box. He dropped the shrimp from the tips of his chopsticks into his wide mouth. When he chewed his eyes closed slightly, displaying the sensual pleasure he received from each morsel of food.

Leo watched in silence. He had seen the General slice off a man's head with ruthless fury. Yet the man ate his meal with the grace of a ballet dancer. The officers of the Japanese military presented a study in contradictions. The same man who would unthinkingly disembowel a Chinese peasant could quite easily, in the next breath, discuss the merits of French Impressionism, or quote Shakespeare. All of the Japanese officers he had encountered were both fascinated and repulsed by all things Western; many had been educated in Europe or the United States. But they were uniform in their contempt for the Chinese.

Leo let another moment go by. He knew he must agree with the General's bigoted observation, lest he give offense, but he also knew that he would seem more credible if it appeared that he'd given the matter some thought.

"It is certainly true, that, in my experience, the Chinese live by a different moral code than the one I am used to," he said, before taking a small sip of the sweet, hot sake set before him. "But one likes to think that there is a bit of good in at least some members of the Chinese nation."

The General laughed, not a pleasant sound. "You sound like a Catholic priest, Mr. Hoffman. But I disagree. The Chinese lack the physical, intellectual, and moral qualities required for greatness. They are corrupt, spineless mongrels."

"Their weakness before the Japanese has certainly been demonstrated," Leo nodded in agreement. "Since abandoning Shanghai and Nanking two years ago, the Chinese have not achieved any significant victories."

The General took a swallow of sake. His hand dwarfed the fragile porcelain cup, yet he held it as delicately as a flower.

"If the Japanese had suffered such a defeat—which would, of course, have been impossible—but had their efforts to protect their home failed, as did those of the pathetic Chinese army in their defense of the Shanghai territory, then all of the officers would have killed themselves. Such dishonor would never have been tolerated."

"Now that is an interesting point," Leo commented, his brow darkening. "In my culture, suicide is considered an act of cowardice. It is seen as a way of escape. A selfish act, if you will, rather than one of atonement."

"Ridiculous," replied the General, accenting his comment with a dismissive gesture of his hand. "If one has failed to live up to one's duties, there is no honorable alternative."

"Perhaps. I suppose it depends on whether one considers it more difficult to die, or more difficult to go on living. Perhaps one who has betrayed one's honor must continue to live. He does not deserve to die, for only by living can he be assured of the punishment he deserves. Death may be a release."

"Not a very Christian perspective, Mr. Hoffman. For surely your Christian God would ensure the suffering necessary for atonement after one's death? Continued existence in this world offers the possibility for personal redemption. So is it more selfish to live, and get a second chance, or to die, and take the punishment that God avails? I find the Christian perspective on suicide distressingly contradictory."

"I suppose it is." Leo said no more. His private struggles would remain private.

The General was not ready to cease his criticism of the Chinese, and returned to the previous subject.

"Take, for example, the stupidity of the Great Wall. It stretches for thousands of miles, unassailable. And do the Mongols breach it? Yes. Not by force, but by exploiting flaws in the Chinese character—they merely bribe the guards to open the gates. This would never have happened in Japan."

"Surely not."

"And then this business of Chiang Kai-shek's relationship with this gangster, Liu Tue-Sheng. No Japanese officer would stoop so low. Our loyalty is to the Emperor, not some rich maggot. He strips the wealth of the peasants by selling them opium, prostitutes their daughters, then shares the proceeds with the incompetent General Chiang. Disgusting."

Leo was startled to hear the General discuss Liu with such candor, although he was careful not to show it.

"A most unfortunate situation," he agreed diplomatically. "I'm sure there are many who would be pleased to see Liu eliminated from the equation. He has been a thorn in the side of the Japanese for too long."

"And now he hides behind the English throne in Hong Kong, sitting in the Peninsula Hotel like a pet dog," hissed the General. "We must soon eliminate that problem. And we shall."

Although Leo would've loved to know what plans, if any, the Japanese had to assassinate the man, he changed the subject, lest he seem too interested in the fate of Liu Tue-sheng.

"The British do make some mistakes, but they have done a decent job of standing up to Hitler. The rest of Europe capitulated quite quickly. France surrendered in a matter of weeks."

"Hitler is a genius," stated the General vehemently. "A snake, but a genius. He understands the value of the lightning attack. And his armies are loyal. Like the Japanese. He understands that this type of loyalty is achieved only through racial purity, and rigid indoctrination. Honor comes through breeding, and heritage. That is why mongrel races like the Chinese are doomed."

"And the Americans?"

"The Americans will also fail. But they are not at war."

"No, not yet at any rate. But this war in Europe is only ten months old. It was three years before the Americans jumped in last time. If the British do not turn Hitler back by Christmas, the Americans will come to their aid again."

"You are German, are you not, Mr. Hoffman? Why do you not return and assist the Fuhrer in his conquest? Surely a man of your talents would be useful."

"You are too kind, sir. My business interests have long rested in Shanghai. Given that the Japanese Emperor has generously allowed the international community here to continue its normal activities, there is no place I would rather be."

Leo grimaced inwardly at the irony of his words. There was no where else he *could* be.

He was alive but dead inside, living in a dying city that pretended to be alive. For there was no question that Shanghai was dying. Although it managed to recover from the near-lethal blow inflicted when the Japanese won the city, it now seemed inevitable that Shanghai would die as the result of a protracted illness. The people of Shanghai woke in the morning and saw death in the mirror. Yet they got dressed, and went to work, and held dances, and played until the wee hours of the morning, just as if they had not seen the evil apparition. Silt began to fill the harbor, and trade with the interior gradually dried up, but the trickle of commerce that remained allowed those Shanghailanders who were unwilling, or unable, to leave, to pretend that death would come tomorrow, not today.

And in this dying city Leo had an even bigger role to play. Liu's flight to Hong Kong gave Leo more leeway to make the special arrangements necessary to collect information. He paid off a gambling debt there, arranged a mortgage here, then tore up the note, later, after he and his debtor reached a convenient arrangement. By putting his debtors comfortably at ease and getting them out of embarrassing situations, he made many new friends.

It was particularly helpful that he'd welcomed the Japanese officers stationed in Shanghai. Unlike the remaining French and British, whose natural snobbery and bitter resentment of Japan's new prominence caused them to turn a cold shoulder to the conquerors, Leo had no such inhibitions. He did what he thought was necessary. As he was an adventurous eater, he gladly sampled the disarming Japanese cuisine, including the bits of raw fish that turned over the beef-and-Yorkshire-pudding-stomachs of Shanghai's British residents. He did not have to learn much Japanese to engage Shanghai's new ruling class, since most of the officers spoke moderate to excellent English. The General with whom he now dined was particularly fluent, although Leo found his mix of British and American idioms oddly entertaining.

As usual, tonight their conversation shifted from politics to philosophy to a critique of the current cinema. The arrival of the sing-song girls steered the evening toward more sensual pursuits. Leo was not sure yet whether the General trusted him, but he knew that the cultured man enjoyed his company. And that was a good start.

At the end of the long evening he walked back to his apartment. It was in a new building across the street from the Çercle Sportif Francais. The accommodations suited Leo's status as a loner. He met and mingled at restaurants and the homes of others, using dinner at the French Club as his means of reciprocating their hospitality. Then he retired to his small suite at night, to lose himself in dreams of blackness.

Wading through the silence of the early morning, Leo pondered the General's comments regarding Liu Tue-Sheng. Would the Japanese try to eliminate his nemesis? What would that mean for him? Would he actually be able to join Maddy in America? Would he have the courage to do so?

He sent money, and wrote, and received reports back from the Sisters, and from Amelia, telling him that Madeleine was doing well. He understood that her refusal to answer his letters was the sign of a deep, unrelenting anger, and he could not blame her. His only comfort was the fact that she was alive. Maddy was alive. He had no doubt that he would be better off dead. Yet death always seemed to escape him.

When he'd promised to stay and work for Liu, he had no clear notion of how long that would be, for he had no idea how much longer he would live. After no bombs blew him apart and he refused himself the luxury of suicide, he focused on retrieving ever-more sensitive information, sure that he would be shot in the back by someone who'd realized that Leo had betrayed him. But no one seemed to catch on. Martha was gone, and it was his fault. Yet punishment continued to elude him.

What if Liu was assassinated? Would he dare go to New York? How could he face his daughter? He had killed her mother, then sent her away with a stranger. What if Maddy looked even more like Martha now, now that she was three years older? How could he stand the pain of looking at that familiar face?

But how could he bear to stay away?

◎❦◎

Several blocks away, in the plush home of the American Ambassador, three men were finishing up a totally different sort of evening. Charts and papers, magnifying glasses and black-and-white pictures covered two tables in the library. The air was heavy with cigarette smoke, and the unemptied ashtrays testified to the lateness of the hour.

"There's just no getting around it," said the first man, a naval officer with leathery skin and a tobacco-and-whiskey voice. "If we let England go under now, the Nazis will have the whole of Europe. The Japanese will rule the Pacific, and Hitler will rule the continent. I don't like the looks of that picture."

"But the President's hands are tied. How can we go to war when we've got nothing at stake?" responded the youngest of the group, a blondish gentleman in his early thirties, whose horn-rimmed glasses leant a touch of sophistication to his youthful, Midwestern face.

"Nothing at stake?" barked the naval officer who'd made the first remark, "What kind of rot do they feed you at the State Department, Paul? What about freedom? What about the freedom of all of our trading partners?"

The Ambassador's calm voice interjected.

"We all know how you military men view the issue. The problem is, Gerry, that no one has proven that Nazis are bad businessmen. With the anti-war sentiment as strong as it is back home, we're just not at liberty to step in. No, for the time being, we have to find other ways to assist our European allies."

"And I suppose you are ready with a suggestion?" responded Commodore Gerald Ballard, reaching for another whiskey, not bothering to keep the sarcasm out of his voice.

"Just look at what Paul has brought to us tonight," answered the Ambassador, gesturing to the document-laden tables. "Look at how the Nazis attacked. Their strategy involves a tremendous amount of preparation, on-the-field communications, and, by some reports, a fifth column network of great magnitude. We may not be able to get weapons to the British in the near future, but we can start giving them something vital. Information."

The Commodore snorted. He did not see the look of disdain the young representative from the State Department gave him in return.

"I see. We're to find and loan them another Mata Hari. Only this time instead of working for the Germans, she'll fight to save the free world, is that it?"

Still the Ambassador took no offense. He'd not been in Shanghai long, but he knew that behind Ballard's bluster lay a sharp mind. He would catch on quickly, and his help could prove very valuable. The Ambassador continued.

"Paul has dispatched his responsibility quite well. He's carried the details of the Nazi invasion to every major diplomatic post in Asia. But the fact that he is here proves one thing—the United States has no systematic way of gathering and disseminating strategic information. The reports upon which his facts are based come from a myriad of sources, mostly foreign. And the State Department does not necessarily know what the Office of Naval Intelligence knows, or what the Army's Military Intelligence Division knows. You, Gerry, were asked to this briefing because you are the highest-ranking military officer posted to Shanghai at the moment. But I asked you here for more than just the opportunity to enlighten you. I need your help."

A raised eyebrow was the only response he received, but it was all he needed. The Ambassador knew the Commodore well enough to know that if the man stopped talking, he was intrigued.

Now the Ambassador reached for the whiskey. He poured himself two fingers, looked at the glass for a moment, then set it down without tasting it.

"You've both heard of Colonel William Donovan, of course."

"Of course, sir! Wild Bill Donovan—the most decorated soldier of the Great War—except for MacArthur, that is," exclaimed the attaché. Ballard merely shot the Ambassador a look of annoyance.

"You probably remember, then, that Donovan and President Roosevelt were in law school together at Columbia. Their connection goes back a long way. I am proud to say I've known Bill Donovan since we were boys together in New York. At this moment Bill is in England, ostensibly as a special correspondent for the Chicago Daily News—which is conveniently owned by Frank Knox, our new Secretary of the Navy. Bill is investigating the real story on how well England is prepared to defend herself. That part of his mission is an open secret. But what many don't know is that he has already been putting a bug in the President's ear about creating a centralized agency for the coordination and use of secret intelligence. An organization that could assist us in the kind of covert operations and propaganda that will enable us to help Britain—and the rest of Europe—beat back the Nazis.

"It's precisely because we are *not* at war that Americans have more mobility, not only in Europe, but around the globe. That's helpful. Especially for recruitment purposes. We have to get able men—and women—in place. For if, and when, the President does give a green light to Bill's idea of a coordinated intelligence agency, the start-up time will be crucial."

"You mean, you're asking us to recruit spies?" asked the younger man, delighted at the prospect of getting involved in some cloak-and-dagger activity.

"Not recruitment, really. More just the identification of possible recruits. And we aren't necessarily looking just for Americans. We want to take advantage of our current neutrality to get into enemy territory and lay the groundwork. We need German nationals who understand the evil that Hitler stands for; we need French nationals willing to risk their lives to regain their freedom. And, if the Japanese keep cozying up to the Nazis the way they seem to be doing, we'll need Asians as well. We need to identify people who can be our eyes and ears now, who can then engage in more concrete activities later, should America actually enter the war."

"You're serious!"

"Dead serious, Paul. You and Commodore Ballard here both have a good deal of freedom of movement around the Far East. You are to identify potential—and I emphasize potential—candidates, and advise me. I'll do the rest. You'll never get any confirmation of the outcome of any interviews, for obvious reasons. We are still at the blue-print stage, gentlemen, but the need for secrecy is absolute. We'll be looking at people in all walks of life, but for the moment our priority is to find people who may have a legitimate business reason to go back to Germany, or France, or Holland. Preferably people who move well in the upper circles of society. We must be careful whom we approach. The worst thing that could happen would be to unwittingly get a double agent in our midst. But we must act now, before the Germans suspect that we are involved."

The Commodore no longer wore a sarcastic expression. He spoke thoughtfully, as if he'd already sorted through a thousand different possibilities in his mind and discarded all but one.

"I think I know someone you might like to meet."

◈

On another continent, thousands of miles away, it was late in the afternoon, and Mrs. Margaret O'Connor was in the process of making bread for the evening meal. She peeled one swollen, yeasty mound of dough from the tin bowl where it had rested and risen for a second time, then plopped it down on the floured board set out on her kitchen table every day, at this same time, for the same purpose. Firmly and methodically, she pressed the air out of the dough with the heels of her matronly hands, stretching and pressing, stretching and pressing, until the dough was smooth and soft, ready to be shaped into two long loaves.

"Ma?"

Margaret O'Connor did not pause, not even for an instant. One could not raise a family of seven children, make food for the family and boarders, see to the chores and manage the house if one stopped what one was doing every time one was spoken to.

"Mary Kate, if you've come to help with the linens, we'll be usin' the rose set today. The gravy Mr. O'Leary sloshed off his plate yesterday stained the floral, so I had to change it. Not that I need more washin' this week. But people payin' good money fer room 'n board are entitled to a clean table."

Katherine edged closer. "Ma?" she said again, ignoring her mother's instructions. She focused her eyes on her mother's hands.

"Mary Kate—"

"Ma, I have a problem."

"Well, we'll discuss it after dinner. At the moment I've too many—"

"Ma," insisted Katherine, her voice growing softer, not louder, "Ma, I have a real problem, and I think we'd better talk about it now."

Margaret O'Connor finished forming the loaf, and laid it in a pan to rise again. Without a word she emptied the second tin bowl and began the process a second time. A soft hiss of air escaped the dough as she started to knead the bread.

"So tell me. But dry the dishes while yer talkin.'"

Katherine reached for the dishtowel. She picked up a white ceramic plate, and began to rub it, over and over again. She had no idea what her hands were doing as she talked.

"Ma, you know my friend Maddy, Maddy Hoffman."

"Aye, the little one with such nice manners, who comes over on Thursdays. She's a lovely girl. Did she come today?"

"Well, she has a problem."

"I thought it t'was you with the problem?"

"Well, Maddy is my problem. You see, her mother was killed by a bomb in China, and her father sent her away to live with Amelia, this woman he married, who Maddy didn't even know. And Amelia sent her to—"

"Mary Katherine O'Connor!" Margaret exploded, her plump fist hitting the bread dough in exasperation, "I will not have these stories. I don't care what kind've imagination yer teacher says you've got—"

"No, really Ma! It's true!" Katherine pleaded, rubbing the dish cloth on the now bone-dry plate in faster and faster circles, "I swear by almighty God—"

"AND DO NOT BLASPHEME IN THIS HOUSE!" her mother roared, picking up the bread dough and slapping it back down on the table for emphasis.

Katherine winced, but did not back down. She shoved the plate and towel in the sink and ran to her mother, flinging her arms around the short, stout woman's waist, tears ready to pour from her eyes.

This took her mother by surprise. Mary Katherine was not a crier. She was the youngest, and the smartest, of Margaret's seven children. She had the sort of self-reliant strength that made her a blessing to a busy woman who was mother, father and landlord to a household of hot-headed Irish. Wise as she was to her daughter's tricks and stories, Margaret was not immune to the seldom-seen sight of tears on her youngest's face. She relented, the anger gone from her voice.

"Sit down, Mary Kate, while I finish the bread. Then we can talk while we shell the peas."

Sniffing up her tears, Katherine sat silent in one of the big wooden chairs next to the worktable while her mother rounded up two more loaves, washed her hands, cleaned the flour board and retrieved a bag of English peas and two bowls from the pantry. She handed one bowl to Katherine, who placed it in her lap. She began to split the pods and dump the fresh, sweet peas into the bowl while she talked.

"It's true, Ma. Maddy was living in Shanghai with her parents, and then there was a war, and her mother was killed by a bomb. But then her father didn't want her anymore, after that, so he sent her here, to New York, with this woman, Amelia, who didn't want her either, and she sent her to live with Gabby's girls—ah, I mean, made her live at the convent school at St. Mary's. And she's never had any friends until me, Ma, and I think she's the best friend I ever had—she's so smart, and friendly, and she knows so many interesting things—she can speak England English, and French, and she has seen so much—I mean, she really lived in China! But you see, she sort of—well, she was never allowed to go outside, and then she found a way to get out on Thursdays, and that's how we met. But now the door's locked, and she can't get back into the convent, and she's afraid that Sister Gabriel will make sure that she never gets out again, or that her stepmother will send her somewhere else, and we'll never see each other again. So I thought—I thought, maybe you could talk to the Sisters—or to Amelia—because I know Maddy will get a beating, which she and I both deserve, but I just don't want them to send her away—and I'm her only friend in the whole world," she finished breathlessly, then fell silent, waiting for her mother to respond.

"Where is she now?"

Katherine leapt up, nearly dumping over her bowl of peas. She righted the bowl as it slid off her lap, and set it on the table.

"Oh, Ma—she's right outside, on the steps. Please come talk to her. Oh, I knew you would!"

"Now just hold yer horses, Mary Katherine. I'm not makin' any promises, and this is none of me business. But Maddy seems a sweet girl, and if she's really been through all you say, then, well, maybe a word on her behalf—but I'm ashamed of ya, for letting her come over here every week without the Sisters knowin' about it. That's the cause of the trouble. Dishonesty always is, Mary Kate. I'll deal with *you* later."

"Yes, Ma," Katherine answered, all meekness, willing to accept any punishment meted out. As long as there was some hope for Maddy!

They found her sitting on the front steps, looking as forlorn as a lost puppy. Margaret could not help but be moved by the look of desolation on Maddy's small, heart-shaped face. *This is a child who has seen too much. And not had nearly enough love to make up for it.*

She settled her stout frame on the step beside Maddy, and pushed a strand of her silvery-red hair back up into the bun she always wore during the steamy months of summer.

"I don't approve of how the two of ya have been carryin' on, Maddy. You'd never have been welcome in this house if I had known ya were sneakin' out of the convent."

Maddy's chin dipped even closer to her chest. She studied her fingers through half-closed eyes, unable to speak.

"Is it true what Mary Kate tells me, that ya lost yer mother and yer father sent ya here with yer stepmother?"

Maddy nodded in silent reply.

"You probably won't believe me, Maddy, but yer father was just tryin' to protect ya. Not that anyone could make you understand that, at yer age. So you're afraid you'll be sent away again, is that it?"

Another barely perceptible nod.

"Would ya like for me to go speak to yer stepmother with you? I'm not sayin' I'll have much to tell, but at least she'll know the truth about where ya been."

"Okay," Maddy whispered.

"Well, we best call the Sisters first. They'll be panickin'—and we'll have to make it quick. I have a full house to feed tonight. Mary Kate, go, now, run around the corner and see if yer cousin Michael's cab is still there. He could give us a lift before he starts his shift. Then you and Maureen will have to see to dinner. No—don't even open yer mouth. You're *not* coming. Now scoot."

Forty minutes later Margaret and Maddy were at the entrance to Amelia's Fifth Avenue apartment. The doorman did not recognize Maddy, so infrequent were her visits, and he certainly was not about to let the plainly dressed Irishwoman up unannounced. He rang Amelia.

"Sorry to disturb you, Mrs. Hoffman. There is a woman here with a little girl who claims to be your stepdaughter. Yes? Very well." He hung up the phone, pointing to the elevator in a patronizing manner. "You can go up."

Maddy's nervousness was palpable. Margaret O'Connor's heart went out to the girl as they rode in silence up to the penthouse. Such a small and dainty thing. And so lost.

Margaret O'Connor was not very sentimental. She'd come from Ireland at the age of fourteen, with two older female cousins, and had worked as a housemaid for six years in several homes on New York's affluent Upper East Side, before settling down with her Patrick, a plumber, to raise children. Then she lost him when Mary Kate was barely two. Luckily for the family, her Patrick had always been a soft-hearted soul, and when his second cousin asked him to buy some life insurance, he'd done so, just to help the poor boy along.

Margaret, who at the time had berated her husband for wasting his money on such nonsense, took the proceeds of the policy and put it towards the mortgage, so when the depression hit they were one of the few families in the neighborhood to keep their home. She packed the children and herself into two rooms and took in boarders. Some were relatives, some were not, but all had to pay their way in cash or services to stay. Her two eldest boys were now in the merchant marine, sending home money and letters from around the world. Her third son was a policeman, and still lived at home. Her eldest daughter had married a butcher. At a time when many families did not have enough to eat, Margaret O'Connor kept her brood clothed, educated, and fed. She did so by using her God-given intelligence and common sense, and putting her own family's well-being ahead of everything else.

But Maddy—here was a child who needed help. Margaret could see in her eyes the suffering she'd seen in the faces of young brothers and sisters left behind, in Ireland, before the war. It had been hunger in the stomach that had caused their pain. Maddy's starvation was of a different kind, but she was starving, just the same. Margaret could feel herself wavering in her resolve not to get involved.

When Amelia opened the door to her apartment Margaret looked beyond her, and took in everything. She noticed the fashionable, coldly sophisticated decor, the quality of the silk hanging from the windows, the satin perfection with which Amelia dressed herself. She saw the face of a beautiful, well-kept woman, with no maternal warmth whatsoever. There were no pictures in the room of Madeleine; no hint that the apartment was the home, even the temporary home, of a young girl. She made her decision.

"Will you please tell me who you are, and what you're doing with Madeleine?" Amelia demanded upon opening her door, without inviting them in.

"I imagine we have quite a few things to discuss, Mrs. Hoffman. If ya would be so kind as to have us in," responded Margaret stiffly.

Amelia gave Margaret a look of blunt appraisal. She took in the stout figure, the blue cotton dress, the graying hair tucked into its simple bun. She decided twenty dollars would reward the woman nicely, both for bringing Madeleine home, and for minding her own business. Now if only she could get the nuns to take the brat back. From the tone of Sister Gabriella's voice over the phone, that might be difficult. Running away was not a small offense. Amelia was livid. The whole business was so damn inconvenient. She was about ready to put Madeleine on the first ship back to Shanghai.

"By all means, come in." Amelia stepped away from the door and into the living room. She did not ask them to sit down.

Margaret, who after years in household service was completely undaunted by the capricious moods of the rich and selfish, walked in and sat on the sofa. She held out her hand to Maddy, who moved, zombie-like, to her side.

The older woman's composure made Amelia rethink her own approach. Intimidation might not be the best tactic. Smiling at Maddy, Amelia took a seat across from the two of them.

"You must forgive my rudeness, Miss—"

"O'Connor. *Mrs.* Margaret O'Connor."

"Mrs. O'Connor. But you can imagine how worried I've been during the past two hours, ever since Sister Gabriella called to say that Madeleine was missing from the convent. Why, we had no earthly idea—"

"Oh, I can well imagine." During their whole exchange Amelia had scarcely looked at Maddy, much less inquired after her well-being. Margaret tried to keep the scorn out of her voice as she spoke.

"Mrs. Hoffman, Maddy has been comin' to me house almost every Thursday for the better part of a year. She and me own Mary Katherine, who's just a wee bit older, have become great friends. They met at the park. Seein' her every week, I thought Maddy lived near us. Mind ya, I would have put a stop to it right away if I had known she was sneakin' out of the convent, but she must'a been pretty clever about it all to go along this far without getting' caught.

"I think it's fair to say that Maddy has not been happy with the Sisters, God bless them and keep them, for they do great work, but St. Mary's isn't a proper boarding school, we both know that. And I think yer honest enough to admit that you'd prefer Maddy not be underfoot.

I'm sure you have yer reasons, but I don't think they've anything to do with her, for she's a lovely child.

"I'm sure the good Sisters are quite upset about what's happened, but if she's found the guts to get out once, she'll find a way to get out no matter where you send her, as long as she's unhappy. I've had seven kids of me own, four still at home, so I know a bit about children. I run a boarding house. It's a healthy, clean place. No drinking, no night visitors. The boarders are all fine, upright people, for I've me own family to think of. Maddy would be welcome. I'll charge ya less than the good Sisters do, of that I'm sure, and Maddy will be happy with us. She won't leave. She'll be safe."

Amelia reached for the silver cigarette case that lay on the glass coffee table in front of her. "I don't think," she said as she lit her cigarette, "that an Irish boarding house is exactly what her father had in mind for her."

"From what Maddy told me in the cab on the way over, her father hasn't laid eyes on the child for nearly three years. If it's her happiness he cares about, he'll not object. She can go to school with me Mary Kate—she's a bright one, and got herself a scholarship to St. Agnes. You'll have no complaints about her education."

Amelia blew out a cloud of smoke as she considered the proposal.

"I suppose you have some references?"

"Yes ma'am. I worked for some of the finest families in Manhattan before I married. I can give ya names and numbers, and yer welcome to talk to the Sisters at St. Agnes as well."

"That won't be necessary," decided Amelia aloud. "I'll ring up the convent and give my permission for you to pick up Maddy's belongings. But I want one thing clear—she's to come back here if and when her father shows up. And all mail goes through me. Am I understood?"

"As you wish." Margaret stood up, took Maddy's hand, and headed towards the door. "Well, we'll be goin' then. Good evening, Mrs. Hoffman. We'll be in touch."

"Don't make it too often," snapped Amelia, and slammed the door behind them.

Maddy did not say a word until they were back in the elevator. Then she looked up at Mrs. O'Connor, and, in a trembling voice, asked,

"Is it true? Am I going to live with you and Katherine?"

"Aye, little lass. It's true," said Mrs. Margaret O'Connor, reaching out a calloused hand to stroke Maddy's silken black curls. "You'll have a home with us."

The happiness on Maddy's face was all the thanks she needed.

⊙✦⊙

Two weeks later, across the world, Leo was staring out at the view from the top of the renovated Cathay Hotel. The floor-to-ceiling glass windows afforded a clear picture of what had once been the Chinese district of Hongkew. Now the whole district was called "Little Vienna," having been rebuilt by the 200,000 Jewish refugees who'd settled there since 1938. Most had traveled first to Japan, admitted to the country for reasons that remained a mystery to all but the Japanese. Then they were shipped out of Japan *en masse* and dumped into the burned-out rubble of Hongkew.

Worried that Shanghai would soon be inundated with poor Jews fleeing the Nazi regime, the Municipal Council, for the first time in Shanghai's history, instituted entry requirements. One must have $500 cash or proof of employment before the magic portals of Shanghai would open. The change marked the end of an era.

In the middle of the harbor sat an American destroyer making a stop on its way back to Hawaii. Under the ship's lights Leo could see signs of the busy activity that meant the ship would sail out with the morning tide. It was the only military ship in port at the moment, but there seemed to be many there these days. Mostly Japanese.

"Always a striking view, isn't it?

Leo turned to find the American Ambassador standing beside him. He offered Leo his hand. "Nice to see you again, Mr. Hoffman. I believe we met at Victor Sassoon's event last fall."

As they shook hands Leo thought it unlikely that the Ambassador actually remembered him. The event he referred to had been thrown in the Ambassador's honor nine months ago, shortly after he took up his post, by the richest man in Shanghai. There'd been hundreds of people there, and Leo said no more than a few obligatory pleasantries to the new

Ambassador while going through the receiving line. Something was up.

"How gracious of you to remember me, sir."

"Well, to be honest, you've come to my attention since then. Allow me to refresh your drink." The Ambassador signaled to a waiter, who whisked away Leo's half-empty gin and tonic.

"Do you have a moment? Very good. Let's take this table." In an instant the two men were seated next to the plate glass window, and Leo possessed a fresh drink.

"Cheers," said the Ambassador, then sampled his drink. Leo followed suit.

"Tell me, Mr. Hoffman, did you fight in the last war, or were you too young?"

"Both," answered Leo.

The Ambassador smiled. "Clever enough. Which side?"

"The losing side."

"And you chose not to stay in Germany. What brought you to Shanghai?"

"What brings anyone here? Money. Opportunity. Fate."

"Yet you've stayed here, when many in your position would have left. Why?"

"I had nothing to go back to."

"In Germany, you mean?"

"Anywhere in Europe."

"I see."

"No, you probably don't. For one thing, I'm not German. I'm Hungarian. After the communist revolution in 1919, it was impossible to get a visa to go anywhere. The whole world saw Hungary as a sort of virus-laden body politic, capable of spreading Bolshevism across the world. Those of us who did get out were not always welcome back, especially once the economy sank in '30. I got lucky here, so I stayed."

"Ah, so you're a closet communist."

"Hardly," Leo snapped, more bitterly than he had intended, "though I knew some people who were, and things ended badly for them. No, I'm an apolitical beast. I came to Shanghai to make a large fortune out of a small one. I did, and I stayed."

"It's that simple?"

"It's that simple."

The Ambassador paused, took another sip of his drink, then leaned back in his chair.

"I know several people who think very highly of you, Mr. Hoffman."

"I'm flattered."

"They say you are a man of unusual talent, and very trustworthy. I'm looking for those kind of men."

"I'm not interested."

"You haven't even heard what I am about to say."

"Sir, if you will forgive my bluntness, there is a war in Europe, and a war in Asia. War will soon engulf the world. The United States will not stay neutral much longer. I know many people, and I speak several languages. There is only one type of work I could do for you, and I'm not interested in doing it. But thank you for asking."

"Good. I would have been suspicious if you'd been too keen on the idea. Now please listen to my proposal. There are times in a man's life when he is asked to do something for reasons that go beyond his own happiness—"

"Someone made me a similar offer many years ago. It did not turn out well."

"You mean, you worked for the Hungarian government?"

"No. I was a pawn in the hands of men who wanted to overthrow it. At any rate, the final answer is, politics do not interest me, covert or overt or any other form."

"What do you do?"

"I stay alive."

"Why?"

"Inertia."

"I've heard many good things about you, Mr. Hoffman, but no one told me that that you were a cynic. We're all going to die. The question is why go on living. For money? For your country? For democracy? For your daughter?"

Leo's expression did not change. "What about my daughter?"

"I know your daughter is in America. I know you entered into a paper marriage with an American citizen days after your wife was killed, to get your child out of Shanghai. And I know you did not go with her, even though legally you could have. Why not?"

"I have my reasons."

"I'm sure. And I suspect they have something to do with honor, and loyalty. To whom or to what I'm not sure."

"Don't be too sure of anything."

"Good advice. Mr. Hoffman, you've lived for years without a country. I am prepared to offer you one. Last September, President Roosevelt signed a special executive order making any foreign national of good moral character who joined the American military eligible for U.S. citizenship. The United States Navy could use you—specifically, the Office of Naval Intelligence."

"Did Commodore Ballard have anything to do with this?"

"A little. He mentioned that that he'd had some personal dealings with you. Said you're the kind of person people confide in, that a Father Confessor would come to you to clear his own conscience, and he thinks you speak at least five languages. He was impressed."

"Too easily."

"I think not."

"What makes you think that I wouldn't just become a double agent? Sell secrets to the highest bidder?"

"For one, we know your first wife was Jewish. At least, she would be according to Hitler, with a maiden name like 'Levy,' even if she were Catholic when you married her, as it indicates on your marriage certificate. No one who knew you then doubts how much you loved her. I'd count on that to keep you from helping the Germans this time."

"And the Soviets?"

The Ambassador smiled. "We have to fight one war at a time, Mr. Hoffman."

"No. You do. I don't. I've fought all the battles I'm going to fight."

The Ambassador tipped his glass towards Leo in a silent salute. "Very well. It's seems you really aren't interested. That's a disappointment."

"Thanks for the drink," said Leo, shoving back his chair. Outside he could see the lights blinking on the American ship. *America. Maddy.*

Why was he walking away from this? If Liu found out and sabotaged this plan, then Leo would only suffer the fate he'd long deserved. He leaned back towards the Ambassador.

"I'll need a passport. Mine was lost in '37, during the bombings."

The Ambassador lifted an eyebrow. "I believe that can be arranged."

"And I want to leave tomorrow. On that ship. If I take my time getting ready to go, questions will be asked. People disappear in Shanghai all the time. Just let everyone assume the worst."

"Ah, there, you're in luck. I know the Captain. I'm sure we can make arrangements for you to travel as my private guest. And if he thinks I've made a mistake, he'll just drop you off somewhere in the middle of the Pacific."

"That's alright. I know how to swim."

ଇ❖୭

Leo's interviews, or "debriefings" as Captain Herbert Lewis called them, started soon after the ship reached the China Sea. He told the truth about himself, editing out only the two facts he thought worked against him—that he had taken the Cartier necklace with him to Shanghai, and that he was on Liu-Tue-Sheng's payroll. But he told his interrogators everything else: that he came from a peasant family in Hungary, and had been adopted by a wealthy Jewish family in Budapest. He told them that his family had been killed in the Great War, in which he had fought for just over a year, that his foster mother had been assassinated during the terror following the communist coup, but that he had no connection to the communist party. He told them that he had worked as a concierge at the Bristol, until being recruited by a Hungarian nationalist group, and that he had killed one of their members in Paris, in self defense, after discovering he'd unwittingly played a part in their counterfeiting scheme. And, he explained, it was that murder that had caused him to flee to Shanghai.

Leo thought that staying as close as possible to the truth would be his safest bet. He gambled that the Americans would not be seriously upset about the murder of a criminal fascist; he was right. And he knew the fact that France was now controlled by the Nazis would make corroboration of the details of his story difficult.

"What happened to the necklace?" asked the lieutenant in charge of his interrogation.

"I don't know. I left it in the hotel room with Károly's body. I imagine Janos Bacso retrieved it, or the maid stole it. I'd left the country by nightfall."

"How did you get to Shanghai?"

"I took the money Károly had in his wallet. It was a considerable sum, in English pounds. Probably received in exchange for counterfeit francs, but at the time I did not give the matter much thought. I had to get out of Paris, and I couldn't go home."

"And in Shanghai?"

"I was lucky. I invested what little capital I had, and made a mint in the rubber boom of '26. So I sent for—Martha. All went well until '29. Then I had to start over—so I got a job at the bank."

"And then you lost your wife in '37?"

Lost my wife.

"A rather stupid euphemism. Yes. My wife was killed."

"Is there anyone in Shanghai, or England, who might be able to corroborate any of your story?"

"In Shanghai, no. It's a very private place, and most of the people who were there in '26 left in '37. I suppose you might try to get hold of a man by the name of Laurence Cosgrove, if he's still around, in London. He worked for an architectural firm: Leeds & Gates, I believe."

"And your second wife?"

"A casual acquaintance. She did me a tremendous favor, getting Madeleine out. No one knew how bad it would get, you see…and Martha.…"

"I'm sorry Mr. Hoffman. I know this is painful for you, but we need complete information."

"Of course."

"And why haven't you not tried to get to the U.S. before now? After all, you are technically the spouse of a citizen, and your child is there."

"I was afraid that if I applied for a visa, something about my past might surface—the possibility of being sent back to France for murder does something to chill one's mobility."

"I see. Is there anyone in Budapest we could contact who could verify any of this information?"

"I have no idea. Well. I suppose there may be someone left at the Bristol who remembers me. There was a family friend. A Countess. Julia Podmaniczky. If she's still alive."

Later, in the Captain's quarters, the lieutenant presented his findings.

"Well, he's either perfect, or a perfect fake," he said when he'd finished. "We'll know more once we've located these people he's mentioned. But Captain, what if he's not telling the whole truth about the counterfeiting mess? What if he were in on the whole scheme from the beginning, and just bailed out to Shanghai?"

"What if he was, Lieutenant? We're not looking for boy scouts. We're looking for spies. I'm sure we can trace newspaper stories about that counterfeiting incident. And that was a long time ago—he was 25 then. He's forty now. The fact he came clean with it says a lot."

"I hope so, sir. There's one more detail. He'd like to go to New York and visit his daughter before going into training."

"Sounds fair. Did he say how long?"

"A week."

"You mean he hasn't seen his child in three years, and he only wants a week?"

"Yes."

"Did he say why?"

"He said if he were you, he'd have him followed during that time to make sure that he wasn't making any enemy contacts, and he didn't want to put you to more than a week's worth of trouble."

The Captain roared with laughter. "Lieutenant, I think you're right—he's either perfect, or a perfect fake. In fact, I'll wire ahead to have his sources checked before we reach San Francisco. I have a good feeling about this Mr. Leopold Hoffman. I think he's O.K."

"I hope you're right."

CHAPTER 19

THE FATHER

❦

NEW YORK, 1940

On an unseasonably warm day in early November, Katherine and Maddy emerged from St. Agnes' Catholic School, in the company of fifty other girls equally impatient to make their escape. Above the gaggle of voices and the busy sounds of a New York afternoon, the two heard a familiar voice call:

"Mary Kate! Maddy! Yoo-hoo! Over here, girls!"

Katherine stood still, squinting with suspicion. "Ma's come for us. I wonder what for? She never comes to get us at school."

"We'll soon find out," Maddy replied, with more trepidation. "Come on, Katherine. She's waiting."

A few quick steps brought them together. Katherine immediately noticed that her mother was dressed up—as well dressed as she had ever seen her, short of a wedding.

"Ma, what are you doing with your Sunday coat on? And a hat? And gloves? And those shoes! Has someone died?"

"Hold yer tongue, ya rascal," was Mrs. O'Connor's sharp reply. "Ya have to see yerself home today, Mary Kate. Maddy and I have somewhere to go."

A pit full of dread opened in the bottom of Maddy's stomach. "Me?

Where? What's happened?"

"Here, dear, take me brush and run it through yer hair. That's it. Lucky yer not one to get dirty, like my little Maureen was. 'Til she was thirteen she could find a way to get her face dirty in church, the Lord knows how. You look fine," she commented as she finished her inspection. "Now let's be off."

Katherine refused to be ignored. "WHERE ARE YOU TAKING MADELEINE?"

"I'll thank ya not to be speakin' to yer mother in that tone of voice, Mary Katherine O'Connor," Margaret answered firmly. She grabbed Maddy's hand. "We're goin' over to Mrs. Hoffman's. Her father's sent for her."

"My father?" squeaked Maddy.

"Her father?" Katherine blurted out at the same time.

"Aye, her father. She has one, ya know. And he's here, in New York, and wants to see her. And don't go asking me any more questions, for that's all I know. So we're off. I'll be home for dinner, Mary Kate. Help with dinner when ya get home or they'll be no dinner for you 'til Sunday."

"IS SHE COMING BACK?" Katherine shouted as Maddy and her mother crossed the street.

"I SHOULD THINK SO!" Margaret shouted back, with a good deal more conviction than she felt.

Margaret walked to the corner and started to hail a cab. "Yer stepmother sent a boy 'round with cab fare, said I was to get ya to her place lickety-split. Said yer father is in town and wants to see ya. That's all I know, little one, but don't ya be scared, now. Maggie O'Connor won't let anything bad happen to ya."

Mrs. O'Connor kept up a steady stream of conversation, commenting on anything she saw out the window: hats, dogs, cars. Maddy listened to her reassuring babble in silence. All she really heard was the pounding of her own heart.

As they rode the elevator up to Amelia's suite, Mrs. O'Connor gave her another critical look, followed by a reassuring squeeze to her shoulder. "He'll be proud of ya, Maddy. Don't worry," she said one last time. Then they were knocking on the door.

It flew open.

"Maddy, darling!" cried Amelia, dropping to her knees to hug the dazed child. "Oh thank you, Mrs. O'Connor, for bringing her so promptly. Leo, this is Mrs. Margaret O'Connor. She helps me with Maddy from time to time. In fact, she has a daughter who goes to school with Maddy. A scholarship student. And Mrs. O'Connor is a treasure. A sweeter woman there never was. Isn't that right, Maddy?" she finished, searching for confirmation. Maddy stayed silent, her gaze fixed on the man behind Amelia.

"*Salut, ma princesse,*" said Leo.

"*Bonjour, Papa,*" answered Maddy. She did not move away from the door.

Amelia pulled Maddy into the room. "Thank you, Mrs. O'Connor. We won't be needing you until next week. My husband will be staying for seven whole days. Isn't it marvelous?"

"Yes ma'am." Margaret paused, not knowing what to do. She did not want to cross Amelia, and then have the wretched woman take it out on Maddy. She knelt down to kiss Maddy goodbye.

"Don't ya fret none, lass. I'll see you on Monday, sure as there's a sun and a moon in the sky."

Maddy looked up at her, eyes wide with fear.

"Well then. Ta Ta," Amelia chirped, practically shoving Margaret out the door.

Leo had not taken his eyes off his daughter. She was so beautiful. So perfect. And the spitting image of Martha, with his own black hair. At that moment he understood that he'd found the courage to come see her only because he had a commitment that would make it impossible for him to stay. He was afraid of this child. Afraid of what she might make him feel. Afraid of what it would do to him to lose her, too. It was easier to pretend that she was already lost. It was easier to disappoint her before she could make her expectations known.

"Well," said Amelia, her voice dripping with feigned enthusiasm. "Here we are. All back together. What do you say we go out and celebrate? Come, Maddy, let's change your clothes." She grabbed Maddy's arm and headed down the hall into one of the bedrooms.

To Maddy's astonishment, the room actually looked like it might belong to a young girl. There was a soft pink duvet on the bed, and a collection of teddy bears sitting on a small white vanity. She could also see several new-looking dresses hanging in the open closet.

"Okay kid, here's the deal," said Amelia brusquely as she pulled Maddy's uniform roughly over the top of her head. "You make believe you live here, and we'll get along just fine. You pull any tricks, and when your dad leaves, I'll send you to a convent in Wyoming. Clear?"

Maddy gulped. She wasn't even sure where Wyoming was. She was still hypnotized by the sight of her father. He was so handsome. He looked—the same. Except nothing was the same. He no longer loved her.

"Okay," Amelia was still talking. "So this is your room. Don't offer to show it to Leo—but if he peeks in, it's acceptable. Thank God he called me from the Port Authority, so I had a chance to pick up a few things—enough to get us through a week. But a lot of decisions about your future may well be made in the next few days, depending on how things go for me. Do you understand me?"

Maddy nodded. She understood nothing, except that she desperately wanted her father to hold her in his arms, and at the same time wanted to be somewhere, anywhere, other than where she was right now.

"Alright then. Now, remember, good children do not speak until they are spoken to, and then they give simple answers. You live here, and you go to school at St. Agnes. That's enough."

"Don't you look lovely." Leo smiled at them as Maddy and Amelia reentered the room. "Where's a nice place to go, Amelia?"

"Why, the Rainbow Room. Top of Rockefeller Center. You'll love it, Leo. And Maddy will, too. We've talked about going there when your father got here, haven't we, Maddy dear?"

"Yes, Amelia."

"Well then. To the Rainbow Room it is." His genial tone sounded forced, even to his own ears. "Tell me, Maddy, have you ever tasted a Shirley Temple cocktail?"

Hours later, after cocktails and dinner and a long carriage ride in Central Park, Amelia and Leo tucked Maddy into bed, as if she really lived there, as if the two adults with her were really mother and father to her.

Amelia could not wait to be alone with Leo. She, unlike Maddy, knew her role in the farce they were playing, and had memorized her lines.

"Oh, Leo, it's so good to see you again, to know you're safe." She said once they were back in the living room. "We've both worried so much about you."

"I can't tell you how much I appreciate what you've done for Maddy. I know you never expected things to go on this long—neither did I. But it proved more difficult to get out of Shanghai than I had imagined."

Amelia drew closer to him. "You don't owe me any explanation. Maddy is a delightful child, and I would do it all again in a second. For you."

"Amelia, I'm sorry. I've had our marriage annulled."

"What?"

"It was a simple enough procedure. We were only married a few hours before you sailed. Non-consummation and desertion."

The tenderness evaporated from her voice. "But that's a lie! You deserted *me!*"

"You have every reason to hate me, I know. I took advantage of your generous offer, and it took me much longer to get here than I thought it would."

"Hate you—why, no, Leo," she hastened, recovering her composure. "I only suggested a paper marriage to help get you—and Maddy—out of Shanghai alive. Of course, I had no right to expect—anything more. It's just that Maddy and I have grown so close over the past three years. I really feel as if she's my daughter. I know she'll be so disappointed, if she thinks—of course, I would never want to separate you from your daughter, Leo, but, if you *are* going away again, well, can't we just leave things as they are for now? You said you only have a week in New York before your business with the bank takes you to Europe. Can't we just—" she moved closer to him, putting her hands on his shoulders—"Can't we just stay married for a few…more…days?"

She pressed her body into his, and captured his mouth with her own. Elation mingled with her desire as she felt Leo begin to respond to her kiss.

"NO!" Maddy screamed from the doorway. "NO! It's all lies! She hates me! She never even let me live here! Not that I would want to! But she shut me up with the nuns, and I could never go outside, and they put me in a closet—and it wasn't until I ran away, and Mrs. O'Connor let me come live with them that I was happy, Papa—I was happy there! Please let me go back! Please let me go back! Please let me go back!" The rest of her words were swallowed by tears, as she collapsed onto the floor, sobbing.

Leo pushed Amelia away from him and whipped his head around to look at Maddy. He turned, took one step towards her, then glanced back at Amelia.

Amelia averted her eyes, but it was already too late. Leo had seen all he needed to see. Her hatred for Maddy had surfaced long enough for him to know that his daughter was telling the truth.

"Leo," Amelia implored, as he bent to pick up Maddy, "Leo, darling, she's jealous. That's all. It's been three years, and now she doesn't want to share you—"

"She won't have to." Then they were gone.

Amelia stood alone in the room, stunned into silence. Three years of waiting. Three years of planning, fretting, and longing—all for nothing. All because of that little bitch. She'd had him—she'd felt it—and then—the little bitch couldn't leave well enough alone.

With shaking hands she lit a cigarette and walked into what had briefly been Maddy's room. She yanked one docile white bear off the vanity and threw it savagely against the wall. She hammered her fist into the face of another, hitting it until both china eyes were crushed and the seams had split. Then she took her cigarette and buried it in the bear's nose, laughing bitterly as she heard the fake fur hiss and singe.

After she cried, smashed several glasses, and was well on her way to becoming quite drunk, she propped the burned and broken bear up in front of her and made herself a promise. That little bitch would pay. Somehow, someday. The little bitch would pay.

☙

Mrs. O'Connor was startled by the knock on her front door. The boarders came and went as they pleased until ten o'clock. Surely it wasn't that late—no. She glanced at the old clock on the kitchen wall. It was just past nine. A shiver ran through her. Her son was a policeman; any unexpected nighttime visitor sent an instant alert throughout her maternal nervous system. She wrapped her shawl around her housecoat and said a silent prayer as she hustled to the door.

To her bewilderment, she found Leo standing there in his shirtsleeves. He was carrying Maddy, asleep in his arms, wrapped in the jacket of his suit. For a moment they stood there looking at each other, uncertain of what to say. Leo spoke first.

"May I please come in?"

Mrs. O'Connor recovered from the split-second paralysis caused by her twin reactions of surprise and relief. "Of course, of course sir. Come lay the little lass in bed—'tis this way."

Leo followed the rumpled, sturdy figure down a narrow hallway to the left, and then to the rear of the house. The girls' bedroom was off the kitchen, having once been the dining room. There was little space in which to move, for the room contained two double beds and a cot. Four sleeping faces peeked out from underneath the covers on the beds.

"Put Maddy here," Mrs. O'Connor whispered, pulling down the covers of the cot. Leo did as he was told, bending low to lay his daughter down carefully, then covering her with the warn blanket. She mumbled something but did not wake. Brushing his child's tangled hair away from her face, Leo planted a delicate kiss on her forehead, and stood up.

"This way," whispered his hostess. She was impressed by his way with Maddy. And, she had to admit, by how uncommonly good-looking the man was. With all that black hair and those eyes—why, she didn't think she'd ever seen such a handsome man in all her life, not in this country, or in Ireland, either. He didn't seem like the cold, uncaring parent she'd imagined him to be. There was a story here, and she was determined to hear it.

She led him to what had once been the library, but now served as the parlor, after the enormous boarding-house dining table took over the largest room in the house.

"Now, please, sir," Margaret said, no longer whispering but still speaking softly, "tell me why Maddy's back here, and not at Mrs. Hoffman's—I mean, yer apartment."

Leo sat down in what he hoped was a sturdy chair. He looked as Mrs. O'Connor's face, and realized he could do nothing but tell her the truth.

"To begin with, Amelia is not my wife."

"Not yer wife? But Maddy said –"

"Oh, she *was* my wife, but only on paper. It was the only way I could get Maddy out of Shanghai. The marriage has since been annulled. We never—lived together as man and wife."

"The Good Lord spared ya something there, sir, if ya don't mind my sayin' so."

Leo gave her a sardonic smile, then continued. "You see, three years ago, Shanghai was in the middle of the war between China and Japan. There were bombs dropped on the city—my wife, Maddy's mother, was killed."

"So that much is true."

"Yes. And I couldn't get a visa to get out of China—so Amelia offered to take Maddy. To keep her safe. I kept thinking there would be a way I could join them, but nothing worked out. Until now."

Margaret nodded. As a member of a large immigrant Irish clan, she was no stranger to the obstacles posed by visas and travel restrictions. That part of his story, also, made sense.

"I've written to Maddy often, but I've never received any letters from her."

"Since she's been with us, she hasn't got one of those letters sir, I can swear to it."

"After what I heard tonight, that doesn't surprise me. You see, I only received word about Maddy from Amelia and the Sisters—and they told me that she was doing well. But tonight—tonight Maddy told me the truth. All of it. And I want to thank you for saving my daughter. For giving her a home."

Margaret acknowledged his thanks with a wave of her hand. "Sir, Maddy is an easy child to love. She has a good heart, once she lets it out of the box. I know she's not really one of us—she's not from the workin' class people, that's obvious. But she tries hard to fit right in, and we all love her for it. I've done her no favors, Mr. Hoffman. She's paid her way, and worked besides. We've been glad to have her."

"I know—I know how lucky she is to have you." The irony of the situation did not escape him. As a child, he had been introduced to a new life by a foster family. Now his daughter was having the same experience, only traveling in the other direction: down the social ladder. But maybe Maddy was getting what she needed. This woman obviously loved her.

"I suppose, then, that you'll be takin' her away from us?"

Leo stood up, and walked over to study a faded botanical print hanging on the wall. His discomfort was apparent.

"That had been my original thought. I was going to send Maddy away—perhaps to Switzerland. To a really fine boarding school. You see, I'm only here in the States temporarily. My—business—will take me in many different directions over the next few months. It may be years before I can actually settle down. And that can't be helped. There are—certain circumstances beyond my control."

Rubbish, thought Mrs. O'Connor. But she said nothing. Leo was not finished.

"The one thing that became clear to me, listening to Maddy tonight, was that she wants very much to stay here. I think I'll probably be in Europe. With the Americans. So it will be difficult, perhaps impossible, for me to visit. But I think—that—she would be better off here, with you, than in a boarding school closer to me."

He turned to face the plump Irishwoman. She saw the pain in his eyes.

"You see, Mrs. O'Connor, I loved my wife. And when she died…there didn't seem to be enough of me left over for Maddy. I'm not sure I have anything left to give her—except money, and I can do that from a distance. I think—perhaps—she should stay with you."

Margaret stared hard at him, a mixture of reproach and sympathy coloring her scowl. "Yer nothin' but a coward if ya leave that poor girl. I lost my Patrick nine years ago. I know what I'm talkin' about. Ya can't run away from yer pain, Mr. Leo Hoffman. So just stop running."

It was a moment before Leo responded. "I could give you some excuse. Something close to the truth—that before I can come back, I have to fulfill another commitment. But the real truth is that you and I are made differently, Mrs. O'Connor. I'm no good, take my word for it. And, take care of Maddy for me." He started for the door.

"But wait!" she cried, following him down the hall. "Ya can't just leave! Ya have to say goodbye to the child! Good Lord! How will we find ya?"

"I'll be in touch." He closed the door behind him.

"Holy Mother of God," whispered Margaret O'Connor, her eyes still on the door. "The man has the devil in him, worse than I've ever seen it. If that's what lovin' a woman does to a man, I want no part of it for me boys. Saints preserve them."

CHAPTER 20

THE FAMILY

❧❧❧

"Where's my father?"

Margaret looked up from the mass of eggs she was scrambling to see Maddy in the doorway. The child wore the dress she'd slept in, its elegance now diminished by many wrinkles and multiple splashes of mud.

Margaret thought about all the ruses she could use to put off answering Maddy's question. Breakfast. Laundry. The butcher had to be paid before noon today or she'd lose her good credit.

Maddy did not move. She didn't even blink. Margaret turned off the gas. The eggs could be reheated. Small hearts broke quickly.

"Come and sit down, Maddy. Do ya fancy some tea?"

Maddy shook her head. She padded over to the table in stocking feet and sat down, with all the dignity of a princess royal. Then she asked her question again.

"Where's my father?"

"And is Katherine still sleeping then?"

"Yes."

"Ah, that one could sleep through an earthquake, wouldn't ya say, Maddy? And she may do it someday, if ya listen to her. She'll be travelin' to far-off lands." She fixed herself a cup of tea as she spoke, and threw in an extra lump of sugar. Damn the budget. Today she needed it.

Maddy sat, hands folded in front of her, as patient as a stone.

Margaret took a place across from her, adult-like. The truth would hurt, but it best be out. Let her get used to it while she had other things to do. Tears were best saved for the pillow.

"Well, Maddy, I'm afraid he's left." She saw Maddy's nostrils quiver, but other than that, she showed no reaction. *How quiet this one can be. How much suffering can such a small soul take?*

"It's not that he doesn't love ya, Maddy. He does. These things are hard to explain. And even harder to understand. I know I've told ya this before, but ya have to believe it. He sent ya here to try and save ya from being killed, same as yer mum. He didn't know what a wicked thing that Amelia was. And ya know, people can't just jump from country to country when they want to. It's not like catchin' the bus uptown, darlin.' A person has to have special permissions to come in and out of another country. If you sneak in, and they catch you, why, they ship ya out and never let you back in. Or send you to jail. Or worse. Believe me, we know about these things, we Irish. Yer Dad couldn't just come along." *So he says.*

Maddy still stared at her, immobile. *Please, Lord, help me make sense of the thing to this child. Help me find the words,* Margaret prayed. She'd spent the better part of the night awake, thinking about everything Leo Hoffman had said to her, trying to come up with some explanation to offer his daughter as to why he'd abandoned her again. A reason other than the fact that her father was a broken-hearted coward himself, too caught up in his own suffering to face his pain for the sake of his daughter.

"We had a good talk last night, yer Dad and me. He told me all about how he had to send ya off to America to keep you safe, expecting to be able to join you any day. And ya know dear, he did write to ya. Lots and lots. T'was that awful woman kept yer father's letters away from ya."

That made an impression. A mixture of confusion and incredulity spread across Maddy's face. "He wrote to me? He said that?"

"Aye, and it broke his heart that ya never wrote back. 'Not that I could blame her, Mrs. O'Connor,' he told me. 'Maddy had every reason to be angry at me. But every day away from her was an eternity.'"

Maddy leaned forward. "He said that?"

God forgive me. "That he did. And more. He said he'd thought he would take ya to Switzerland, in Europe, but he could tell from talkin' to ya last night that you wanted to be here with us. So that's what's going to happen. While he's away."

"But where is he, Mrs. O'Connor?" Now the tears appeared, quickly filling her eyes and then slowly escaping down her face. "Where did he go? Why did he leave?"

Margaret steeled herself. She hated lies and the people who told them. But from what she could piece together, after sifting through every word Leo had said, the story she was about to tell Maddy could be something like the truth.

"Ah, well. It's a complicated business, Maddy. You see, America is a marvelous place. And all over the world, people dream about comin' here to live. But if they let everyone in who wanted to be here, why, soon we'd be living like chickens in a hen house, one on top of the other, scratchin' around for food and water and nobody happy about it.

"But knowin' that so many people do want to come to America, sometimes, when the American government needs somethin' done that American people are not too keen on doin' themselves, why, the men runnin' this country will put out a sort of 'help wanted' sign. That's what happened back in the 1860's, when America was fightin' the Civil War. You've studied about that, haven't ya? In school?"

Transfixed, Maddy nodded.

"Okay then. Well, back then, an able-bodied Irishman could come to America, and become a *citizen* Maddy, meaning he could vote and bring in family and really make a life here, if he just agreed to fight for a couple of years in the Union Army, to beat the Confederates. And he'd get paid doing it. So, many did." *And they mostly died. She'll figure that part out soon enough.*

"But we aren't at war now. There's no Civil War. We're not even fighting Hitler. Why would the government want my father to do that? Anything like that?"

Margaret could hear the panic in the child's voice. She reached across the table and patted her hand. "Well, we're not fighting Hitler yet. But in sneaky ways, we're trying to help our friends in Europe. Sending them weapons and such. Remember, yer father isn't yet an American. He can go help. Go to Europe with the Americans who are already there trying to help. Same thing happened last time, you know. Americans joined up with Canadian troops—lot of Irish people in Canada, too, you know—and jumped in to fight the Kaiser early."

Maddy appeared to be sorting all of this information out in her mind. "And that's the only way he'll be allowed to stay here with us? If he goes to fight in the war first?"

"Aye, lass. That's the situation. Now, there, Maddy, don't be cryin.' Yer father is a brave man. To think, he's willin' to be a soldier if it means he can come home to you."

She got up and moved around to where Maddy now lay, arms crossed, head on the table, shoulders shaking with sobs. "But what if he dies?" she managed to wail. "What good will it have done then, Mrs. O'Connor?"

Margaret stroked her back. "He won't die, lass. He might not even be in the real fightin,' a man as smart as yer Dad. He'll likely have one of them desk jobs, helping soldiers keep track of their shoe laces and such."

"What about soldiers and shoe laces?" Katherine stormed into the kitchen. "What happened last night? Maddy, why are you crying? What's going on?"

For once Margaret O'Connor was glad her daughter acted like a bulldog with a bone when it came to getting an answer to a question. "Maddy will tell you all about it, Mary Kate. Now, go wash yer face, dear. That's a love. I have a house full of people who'll be wakin' up and expectin' a morning meal in less time than I care to think about. And the two of ya need to be gettin' ready for school."

❧

When he woke, Leo thought for one disorienting moment that he was back in Julia's bedroom. He stared up at the gilt and paneled ceiling, his head supported by the generous volume of several goose-down pillows, and tried to remember where he was. Oh yes. The suite at the Waldorf.

New York. Amelia.

Maddy.

He sat up. The gin he'd consumed the night before began to extract its punishment. What time was it? He squinted through bloodshot eyes, trying to focus on the clock sitting on the mantelpiece across the room. Only eleven. He still had a few hours.

First he had to make a phone call.

⚶

The girls of St. Agnes piled out the double oak doors of the school's main entrance at precisely 3:00, cascading like a blue-and-white plaid waterfall down the stone steps and out into the street. Maddy and Katherine walked down the stairs together, both lost in thought, both sure they were thinking about the same thing. Neither looked up until a slightly older girl stopped in her tracks near the bottom of the stairs, forcing Maddy and Katherine to pull up short.

The girl pointed at a man waiting on the sidewalk a few feet from where the parade of girls began to fan out in different directions.

"Who's that?" she said loudly, to no one in particular. "He looks like Gary Cooper!"

"Oh, Maddy, it's him!" Katherine hissed, not taking her eyes off Leo.

The older girl turned and faced them. "It's who?"

"That's my father," Maddy replied, scarcely above a whisper.

"It is?" The older girl looked skeptical. "I didn't think you even *had* a father. Everyone says —"

"JUST SHUT UP!" Katherine shoved her red head up into the taller girl's startled face. "Don't go repeating stupid stories when you don't even know the FACTS."

"Okay! Okay! Calm down, ya little heathen."

Maddy ignored them. She just stared at her father. He looked back at her. They both seemed afraid to move.

"Go on!" Katherine bumped Maddy with a shoulder. "He's not here to see *me*. Here. I'll take your books."

Leo watched as Maddy handed her books to her friend, paused, then walked towards him, every step laden with uncertainty. She looked so much like Martha. The resemblance was killing him.

She stopped when she was still a few feet away, eyes wary, and Leo had the sense that if he moved too suddenly she might flee. Not that he would blame her if she did.

"*Salut, ma princesse.*"

He thought he saw something like joy flicker through her eyes before they filled again with suspicion.

"*Salut, papa.*"

Now what? He swallowed hard. "Would you like to go for a walk?"

Maddy glanced back at Katherine, who gave her a look clearly communicating, *What are you waiting for?* She turned back to Leo. "I have a lot of homework"

"We'll make sure you have time to do it all."

"I usually help Mrs. O'Connor with dinner on Tuesdays."

"I asked her permission to take you out this afternoon."

"You did?"

He knelt down, as close as he dared get to her. "Yes, Maddy, I did. And I would like to spend time with you every day, if you like, for the next two weeks. We can go to Coney Island, or to the zoo, or shopping at one of the department stores—"

She cringed. "No. No shopping."

Good God, how *could* he have been so stupid? Martha died the last time they went shopping. "Of course not. No shopping. I can help you and Mrs. O'Connor make dinner."

To his relief, Maddy laughed. "You can't cook!"

He stood up. "Oh yes, I can. I can make Chinese chicken and rice. And roast beef."

"Biscuits?"

"Hmm…. maybe you'll have to show me how to make biscuits."

She gave him another look of amused skepticism, then popped out with, "Can we go to the movies?"

"Sure. Do you go to the movies a lot?"

"No. Only sometimes. But I do love to go."

"Then let's go. We can go to a movie now, if you want."

"Can Katherine come?"

"Today?"

Maddy hesitated. "Well...maybe tomorrow. Maybe...we could be together, just the two of us, today."

Leo smiled down at his daughter. He held out his hand. She looked at it for a fraction of a moment. It was the longest moment of Leo's entire life.

Then she put her hand in his.

He began to walk, shortening his stride to keep pace with hers. "What movie would you like to see?"

"Not a war movie." She looked up at him. "Mrs. O'Connor said that you left last night because you have to go and fight in the war. She said that even though the Americans aren't in the war, that they're trying to help the British people, so that some soldiers are going over to Europe, and that the only way that you would be allowed to stay here in America with us is if you first go help out in the war. She said it was just like when some of the people in her family first came to this country in the American Civil War. When they first came, she said, right off their boats, they had to leave to go fight in the Union army if they wanted to come back and live in New York. Is that true? Do you have to go fight?"

Thank you, Mrs. O'Connor! "Yes, Maddy. That's all true. I do have to go help out in the war before I can come back to live in New York with you."

Her voice dropped to a whisper. "But what if you die?"

Leo knelt down again, and this time cupped her small face in his hands. His love for his child surged within him, like a lion roaring a challenge to the sun.

"Maddy, my little love, I'm not going to die. I'm going to help the British and the French beat the Nazis. And in two years, I *will* come home, and we will live together. And I will always take care of you, Maddy. I will always love you. And I'll make sure that you are never, never alone again."

Her frightened eyes searched his, looking for the reassurance she so desperately needed. She must have seen something there that helped, for at last she whispered, "Okay."

"Okay." He wrapped his arms around her. "I love you, Maddy."
He heard her sniffle. "And I love you, Papa."

He closed his eyes and held her close. He would get through the next two years alive. He would get back to his daughter. And then love would give them a second chance.

To Be Continued...

9/06